FAMILY BETRAYAL

Kitty Neale was raised in South London and this working class area became the inspiration for her novels. In the 1980s she moved to Surrey with her husband and two children, but in 1998 there was a catalyst in her life when her son died, aged just 27. After joining other bereaved parents in a support group, Kitty was inspired to take up writing, and *Nobody's Girl* was recently a *Sunday Times* bestseller. Kitty now lives in Spain with her husband and is working on her new novel for Avon, due to be published in early 09. To find out more about Kitty go to www.kittyneale.co.uk or visit www.AuthorTracker.co.uk for exclusive updates.

By the same author:

Nobody's Girl
Sins of the Father

KITTY NEALE

Family Betrayal

AVON

This novel is entirely a work of fiction.
The names, characters and incidents portrayed in it are
the work of the author's imagination. Any resemblance to
actual persons, living or dead, events or localities is
entirely coincidental.

AVON

A division of HarperCollins*Publishers*
77–85 Fulham Palace Road,
London W6 8JB

www.harpercollins.co.uk

A Paperback Original 2008

1

First published in Great Britain by
HarperCollins*Publishers* 2008

Copyright © Kitty Neale 2008

Kitty Neale asserts the moral right to
be identified as the author of this work

A catalogue record for this book is
available from the British Library

ISBN-13: 978-1-84756-022-3

Typeset in Minion by Palimpsest Book Production Limited,
Grangemouth, Stirlingshire

Printed and bound in Great Britain by
Clays Ltd, St Ives Plc

Mixed Sources
Product group from well-managed
forests and other controlled sources
www.fsc.org Cert no. SW-COC-1806
© 1996 Forest Stewardship Council

FSC is a non-profit international organisation established to promote the
responsible management of the world's forests. Products carrying the FSC
label are independently certified to assure consumers that they come
from forests that are managed to meet the social, economic and
ecological needs of present and future generations.

Find out more about HarperCollins and the environment at
www.harpercollins.co.uk/green

My thanks to my editor Maxine Hitchcock and her team at Avon/HarperCollins. It has been a difficult year for me, but they were always there to offer their kind support. Thanks also to my wonderful husband Jim and daughter Samantha, two precious people who keep me smiling.

This book is dedicated to my dear cousin, Roberta Carter, a woman whose courage in the face of illness has been an inspiration.

Prologue

Nervously, the young woman approached Drapers Alley. She had been told all but one of the houses were empty, yet still her heart thudded with fear.

Had her informant lied? It was possible. There was still venom – spite aimed at her family – locals who wanted to see her, and them, brought low. For a moment she froze, wanting to turn and flee, but she had to risk it – had to tell her mother the awful truth.

Taking a deep breath to calm her nerves, she entered the narrow passageway, skirting the iron bollard that barred all traffic but that on two wheels. The sign was still on the wall, the alley's name, but now her eyes widened. Her father had ruled here – followed by her brothers after his death – and no one had dared enter their domain without permission. She'd been gone for only just over six months but already the D in 'Drapers' had been crudely painted out so that it read 'Rapers Alley'.

Yes, rape may have been one of their sins, it was certainly possible, yet worse had been done – much worse.

The fact that the name had been defaced was all the proof she needed that her brothers had gone, and the tension at last left her body. To one side of the alley a towering, dirty factory wall cut out light, the atmosphere it created grim with foreboding. Above the high wall the upper floors of the factory were visible, lined with a myriad mean, grimy windows. Though it had closed many years ago, it was a building that had dominated her life from childhood, and visible as soon as she stepped outside the front door. She hated it, had longed to see grass and trees, but unlike her nephews, she hadn't been allowed the pleasure of playing in the local park.

Her eyes avoided the factory building and the horror of what would be found inside. Instead she looked to the left and for a moment paused to take in the small row of six flat-fronted workers' houses. They appeared smaller, shabby with neglect, yet the first in the row, number one, stood out as different. This was her parents' home – a home she'd been forced to flee in fear of her life.

As she crossed the narrow cobbled alley, her gaze fixed on the house, a ray of spring sunlight pierced the gloom. Like her, it had dared to penetrate the alley and it momentarily illuminated her mother's window. Was it a good omen? Did it mean she'd be safe? God, she hoped so.

The brass door knocker and letter box gleamed, but instead of smiling, her lips thinned. Now that her mother was alone, she'd expected her to change – to give up her obsession with housework. Her mother had dusted, polished, swept and scrubbed every hour of the day, excluding any opportunity to show her children an ounce of affection.

For a moment she hesitated outside the street door. What if she'd been lied to? What if her mother wasn't alone? Come on, she told herself, show a bit of spunk. You've come this far and nobody would have dared to call it Rapers Alley if they were still around.

Her hand lifted slowly to the small lion's-head knocker and, after rapping three times, she involuntarily stepped back a pace.

The door slowly opened. 'Is it really you?'

'Yes, Mum,' she said, and seeing the smile of welcome on her mother's face, her eyes filled with tears as she stepped inside. What she had to tell her mother would break her heart.

Chapter One

Dan Draper was fond of relating the tale of how he'd found the alley, and on Saturday morning he was repeating it again as he sat facing his youngest son. Dan's pug-nosed face was animated, his huge tattooed arms resting on the table.

At twenty-four years old, Chris Draper was a replica of his father. He shared his light brown hair and grey eyes, along with his tall, beefy build, both of them standing at six foot. But so far his nose remained unbroken and his good looks were intact.

'Yes, you've told me, Dad,' Chris said wearily as he cut vigorously into his rasher of crispy bacon.

Dan carried on as though he hadn't noticed the interruption. 'I'd had a few beers too many and my bladder was bursting. It was sheer chance that I cut into this alley for a slash. You could have knocked me down with a feather when I saw the name. Blimey, it was like fate. Not only that, I saw the potential straight away. With narrow entrances at both ends, cut in half by the bollards, the only thing that can get through is a bike.'

'Yeah, I know.'

'This alley is as good as a fortress.'

Chris nodded, hardly listening as his father rambled on. He looked at his mother, Joan, her hands busy as always polishing the brass ornaments. She appeared distant, unreachable, but Chris was used to this. In his childhood it had upset him, but he was a man now, and he didn't need displays of motherly affection, or so he told himself. She was a tiny woman, two inches less than five foot tall and as usual, she aroused his protective instincts.

'Are you all right, Mum?' he asked.

It was his father who answered. 'Of course she's all right. Why shouldn't she be? Now then, where was I? Oh, yes, there was only one house empty in the alley at the time and I had to tip up a back-hander to the council to get it. Gawd, despite homes being in short supply, you should have seen your mother's face when she saw it. We'd been living in a flat with a shared bog so I thought she'd be excited, but instead she nearly had a fit. All right, this place is small and it was a bit of a squash to fit us all in, but at least we had it to ourselves.'

'Yeah, I was only a kid, but I can remember when

we moved from that dump of a place around the corner.'

'A year later your mother dropped a girl, making it a tighter squeeze. After giving me five sons it was a bit of a shock.'

Chris heard his mother's tut of displeasure but she said nothing, having given up remarking on her husband's coarseness years ago. He looked around the immaculate room, knowing that the outside of the house bore no relation to the interior. In their line of business it would give the game away to flaunt their wealth, yet even so, inside there was every comfort that the business books could account for. Against one wall sat a deep red velvet sofa, the gold tassels along the bottom hanging just short of the Wilton rug. To one side of the small Victorian fireplace there was a matching chair, but Chris's eyes were drawn to the radiogram, which, thanks to his mother's overzealous cleaning, looked as shiny and new as the day his father had bought it. With a small table and four chairs in the centre, the room was crammed to the rafters, yet from the brass fender to the ornaments, everything was sparkling. When they had first moved in there hadn't been a bathroom, just an outside loo, but his father had solved that problem by building an extension, one that took up half the yard. Chris smiled. He hero-worshipped his father and admired how clever he had been when installing the bathroom – one with a secret that only the male members of the family were aware of.

'Oi! Are you listening to me or am I talking to myself?'

'I'm listening, Dad.'

'Right, well, we ain't done bad by Drapers Alley. Over the years, when your brothers got hitched, I saw off the neighbours and a few more bungs to the council made sure the boys got their empty houses.' Dan leaned back in his chair, smiling with satisfaction. 'It's all Drapers living here now, other than your cousin Ivy, but she *was* a Draper before she married that short-arsed git.'

Chris had to grin. It was true. Ivy had married Steve Rawlings, a bloke whose head came up only to her shoulders. Mind, with her looks she was lucky to get anyone to take her on. Ivy was the odd one out and could only be described as ugly. She was tall, big built, with a round flat face, piggy little eyes and thin, mousy hair. The trouble was, Ivy had an ugly personality to match and Chris would never understand why his father had secured a house for her in the alley.

There was a clatter of footsteps as Petula ran downstairs before bursting into the room.

'Dad, can I have some money? Elvis Presley's latest record is in the charts and I want to buy it.'

'I gave you a quid yesterday!'

'Please, Dad,' she wheedled.

Chris knew that Pet would get her own way. She'd been born when he was ten, and had quickly become his father's pride and joy. At first he'd resented this, but gradually, like all his brothers, he had fallen under his baby sister's spell. She had been a beautiful child, and even though she was now a gangly fourteen-year-old, it was plain to see that she'd be stunning as an adult. Pet's hair was almost black, sitting on her shoulders and flicked into an outward curl at the ends. With vivid, blue eyes, a cute turned-up nose, full lips, and slightly pointed chin, her features were in perfect symmetry. Luckily, so far Pet seemed to have no idea how pretty she was.

Petula continued to beg and as usual, she won, Dan putting his hand in his back pocket to draw out a ten-shilling note. 'All right, but this is coming out of your pocket money.'

'Thanks, Dad,' she cried. 'I'll be back soon.'

'Hold on! Eat your breakfast first. I don't want you roaming around Clapham Junction on your own. Chris can go with you.'

'Dad,' she whined, 'I'm fourteen years old and I'll be fifteen in December. I can look after myself now.'

'You'll do as I say.'

Petula pouted, but her father's tone had hardened and she knew better than to argue further. She went into the kitchen, returning with a box of cornflakes. The pout was still there as she poured herself a bowl of the cereal, but she had a naturally light-hearted personality, and soon brightened when Chris winked at her.

'I want to buy a record too so I might as well come with you,' he said, his tone placatory.

Pet smiled, then turned to her father, saying, 'Dad, there's a dance at the youth club tonight. Can I go?'

'What time does it finish?'

'Ten o'clock.'

'Yeah, you can go, but one of your brothers will meet you afterwards to walk you home.'

'Oh, Dad, there's no need for that. It's less than fifteen minutes away. I'll be fine on my own.'

'You'll be met,' he insisted.

'None of my friends will be escorted home. I'll be a laughing stock.'

'It ain't safe for you to be wandering the streets at that time of night, so either you're met by one of your brothers, or you don't go.'

Pet scowled, saying no more as she quickly ate her breakfast. Chris finished his, and they got up from the table simultaneously.

'Right, we're off,' he said. 'See you later.'

'Yeah, and keep an eye out,' Dan warned. 'Don't forget we've got a meeting at the yard later. I want you there by eleven.'

'I'll be there. Bye, Mum.'

Joan obviously hadn't heard them, locked as usual in her own world, but nevertheless Chris still offered a small wave.

The weather was mild as they stepped out into the alley but, dwarfed by the factory wall, they felt the sun on their faces only as they turned into Aspen Street. Chris swiftly looked both ways, but other than a few kids playing there was no one in sight. Nowadays he knew it was unlikely that there'd be any trouble, but even so he was cautious. With the enemies they'd made it was sensible to be vigilant, but Petula's desire for more freedom was becoming a problem. They were supposed to be running a legitimate business so did their best to keep her in ignorance of why she needed protection, but he worried that it couldn't last much longer. Pet was growing up and they'd need to come up with some sort of explanation for her. He'd have a quiet word with his dad later, but in the meantime Chris continued to keep a lookout, more so when they traversed a few more streets and reached Lavender Hill.

Halfway along the hill, past the town hall, the police station loomed, and Chris gave a wry smile as he glanced at it. The Drapers were notorious in South London and had once been thieves, but careful planning had ensured they'd never been caught. It had been a long time since they'd done a job, but the last one they'd carried out had been close. Tipped off about a large consignment, they had cracked a jeweller's safe, and only just managed to get away. Of course, it helped that the entrance to the alley wasn't wide enough to accommodate a police car, but they'd been raided on foot, the rozzers pouring through the gaps at both ends of the alley. He grinned. Of course the police had found nothing then, and never had – the Draper family outfoxed them every time.

Pet broke into his thoughts. 'Look, there's Mrs Fuller.'

Chris saw the woman walking towards them, her mouth tightening as she drew closer. Nearly everyone knew their reputation and feared them, knowing better than to enter Drapers Alley without invitation. Some locals would come to them if they had a problem, and if Dan thought their complaint fair, he'd step in. His reputation was usually enough to put the shit up the troublemaker.

Betty Fuller was one of the exceptions. She had known Chris and Petula's father since they were both youngsters and felt it her right to enter the alley, although she did so rarely.

There was no fear on her face as she approached them. 'Watcha, Chris – Petula,' she said.

Chris merely nodded, but Petula said, 'Hello, Mrs Fuller.'

'How's your dad? Er . . . and your mum?' she added as an afterthought.

'They're fine, thanks.'

Chris knew that Betty Fuller was a gossip and he was anxious to get away, scowling when she said,

'Did you hear that someone done over the off-licence last night?'

'No,' Chris said shortly.

'Oh, so it was nothing to do with you lot then?'

Chris stiffened, annoyed at the woman's nerve *and* the innuendo. 'You must be joking. We run a legit business, and even if we didn't, we wouldn't be interested in a poxy off-licence. If I was you, Mrs Fuller, I'd nip that bit of gossip in the bud.'

The woman didn't pale at his implied threat. Instead she bristled, 'It didn't come from me – I'm only passing on what I heard.'

'Yeah, well, perhaps next time you hear any rubbish, you'll pass on that bit of info, *and* the fact that we won't be happy if we hear any more bad-mouthing.'

'I suppose I could do that.'

'Good. Come on, Pet,' Chris urged, taking his sister's arm and pulling her forward.

Pet was quiet for a few moments as they walked along, but then she said sadly, 'When are people going to stop talking about us?'

'Take no notice. The business is doing well and people are jealous because we've got a few bob. If anyone gets funny with you, let me know.'

'I'm a big girl now and can stick up for myself, but I don't understand why everyone still thinks that our family are criminals.'

'It's just gossip,' Chris said dismissively. 'Now come

on, let's get a move on. There's a business meeting at the yard today, and you heard Dad: he wants me there by eleven.'

As they picked up their pace, Chris hid a smile. Yes, they had become so-called legit, but it hadn't stopped CID from having a go at the yard. They'd wasted their time because all that was on show were building materials and perfectly kept account books. Drapers Builders' Merchants, the family business, was a good front and a cover that served them well. Chris hoped it would continue to do so, especially as nowadays they had a more lucrative sideline, one that was out of the borough and more likely to attract the attention of the Vice Squad. So far they'd been lucky, and had kept the business well concealed, but they were ruffling a few feathers so were always at risk from their rivals.

'What record are you buying?' Pet asked as they reached Clapham Junction. Chris's thoughts had been wandering, and he had just grunted in response to his sister's chatter so now he floundered for a reply. 'Er . . . "The Young Ones".'

'Not Cliff Richard and the Shadows?'

'Yeah, that's it.'

'Cliff Richard isn't bad-looking, but he isn't a patch on Elvis.'

'I'm not buying it for his looks. I rate his backing group, especially Hank Marvin on guitar.'

They turned into the entrance of Arding and

Hobbs, heading for the small record department at the back of the store. At nine thirty in the morning it was almost empty. Chris eyed the assistant, liking what he saw, and smiled as he and Pet approached the counter. It wasn't much fun being Pet's minder, but if this girl was available she'd be the ideal cover. She was young, pretty, and the sort of girlfriend his family would expect him to have on his arm.

Dan Draper eyed his wife as she bustled around. Joan was showing her age, but when he'd married her she'd been a stunner, a bundle of dynamite. Now, though, her hair was greying, her face lined, and the firm body he'd once gone mad for resembled a little round ball. Still, she'd been a good wife, keeping her mouth shut and not asking questions. As if aware of his scrutiny she met his eyes, her hand involuntarily patting her tightly permed hair.

'You spoil that girl,' she said.

'Leave it out, Queen. I only gave her ten bob.'

'Petula should earn it instead of having it dished out every time she bats her eyelashes at you.'

'Don't be daft, woman. She's only fourteen so how's she supposed to earn it?'

'For a start she could give me a hand around the house. It's about time she learned how to cook and clean.'

'The boys didn't have to earn their pocket money, so it shouldn't be any different for Petula.'

'They didn't get the amount of money you throw at her.'

Dan's lips tightened. He wasn't going to stand for this. Joan did all right; she had a large housekeeping allowance, giving her little to complain about. He treated her right, saw that the kids showed her respect, but he was the boss, the man of the house and she'd better remember that. 'If I want to treat my daughter now and again I will. Now for fuck's sake, shut up about it.'

Joan paled, but did as she was told, whilst Dan picked up the daily paper. He turned to the racing page, studying form before picking out a couple of bets. Nowadays he could afford to lay on a good few bob, and a satisfied expression crossed his features. Since they'd got into this new game, things had looked up big time. The money was still rolling in, and though at first he'd had reservations about getting into this line of work, he was glad that his sons had talked him round.

Yes, his dream was closer, but as he glanced at Joan he wondered how she'd fit into his planned new lifestyle. In the near future he was determined to retire – to hand the reins over to Danny junior, his eldest son. A nice house in Surrey beckoned, one with stables for the horses he intended to buy. Instead of a punter, he'd be an owner, mixing with the élite, looked up to and respected. Petula would love it and instead of hiding his wealth he would be able to dress her like a princess. She'd be away from this area and the riffraff, mixing instead with the upper echelons of the racing fraternity.

Joan went through to the kitchen and Dan heard the tap running, the clatter of plates as she washed up the breakfast dishes. Housework. All his wife thought about was housework. How the hell was she going to adapt to living in a big house, with cleaners paid to take over her role? Huh, Joan would probably insist on doing it herself, making a fool of them when they entertained. The trouble was, she had no class. Joan was a born-and-bred Battersea girl, and, unlike him, she had no interest in rising socially. He heaved a sigh. At least Petula would fit in. He'd made sure his daughter spoke well, paying for her to take elocution lessons from an old biddy in Chelsea. Yes, Petula could mix with the best so he'd just have to keep Joan and her working-class attitude in the background.

Dan rose to his feet, passing his wife to go through to the bathroom where he locked the door behind him. Involuntarily, as always, his eyes went straight to the hiding place. Joan cleaned in here every day, but had never discovered its secret. If she didn't twig it, then the police never would. Only the boys knew and he trusted them to keep their mouths shut, his married sons knowing better than to blab to their wives.

He washed and shaved before taking the money

he needed from the secret cache, returning to the living room with it tucked into his back pocket. 'Right, Queen, I'm off. I'm going down to the yard.'

Joan was busy as usual, and just nodded an acknowledgement when he left. As Dan stepped outside, he paused to look up and down Drapers Alley. It felt like his – his kingdom, and in some ways he'd regret leaving it. He patted the money in his back pocket and did a mental calculation. The cash was for stock, more bricks and cement, enough to keep the yard ticking over, but there'd be enough left to place a few bets. The other business was thriving and maybe they'd have to increase productivity to keep up with the demand. It was lucrative, but with five sons and Ivy's husband wanting their share, they needed to push harder.

Dan passed through the narrow entrance, deciding to buy some cigarettes before going to the lockup where he kept his car. He walked the length of Aspen Street, and as he went into the corner shop, two customers moved swiftly to one side. He smiled tightly, taking their obvious fear and respect as his right.

'Morning, Bill. Twenty Senior Service, please.'

Bill Tweedy was showing his age nowadays, his hairline receding whilst his waistline widened. 'Morning, Dan, coming up,' he said, taking the cigarettes from a shelf behind him and laying them on the counter. 'I suppose you've heard that the off-licence was done over last night? I hope I'm not next.'

'No, it's news to me,' Dan said, frowning with annoyance. The off-licence was just round the corner, in his territory. If he found out who the toerags were he'd have their guts for garters. 'Any word on who did it?'

'Nah, but if I get wind of anything I'll let you know.'

'Yeah, do that, and don't worry, I'll sort them out,' he said, paying for the cigarettes.

Dan was still seething as he walked out of the shop. Over the years he had made sure that the area surrounding Drapers Alley was out of bounds to petty criminals. Local businesses, along with the residents, feared him, but were glad of his protection, and if the police asked questions they knew it was wise to keep their mouths shut. Now it seemed that someone was trying it on and would need sorting out. He'd put his boys on to it, but for now, as Dan climbed into his Daimler, he dismissed it from his mind.

There was a powwow today as his eldest son, Danny, had come up with a way to increase the coffers. Dan grimaced, thinking about the rough plan his son had outlined. He felt it too risky, but would wait to gauge his other sons' reactions before vetoing the idea.

For a moment Dan smiled, knowing that if he

voted against Danny's plans, his other sons would follow suit, all bending to his will. If Joan knew what they were up to she'd have a fit, but there was no chance of her finding out. How the daft cow thought the builders' merchants made enough money to support them all was beyond him, but as long as she carried on living in a world of illusions, that was fine by him.

Chapter Two

Next door, in number two Drapers Alley, the eldest son, Danny junior, emerged from the bedroom. His dark hair was tousled and his mouth open in a wide yawn, but even this couldn't detract from his looks. Danny was handsome, a six-foot-two charmer with large, sultry dark eyes and full lips. A long, thin scar on his cheek, the relic of a knife fight, didn't scare off women. If anything the scar added a hint of danger that complemented his rakish charms.

'Why didn't you wake me?' he moaned as he walked into the kitchen.

His wife, Yvonne, pouring him a cup of tea, said shortly, 'I didn't know you had to get up for work today.'

His eyes darkened with anger – he was certain he'd told her there was going to be a business meeting that morning. 'Shit, I'm sure I mentioned it. If I don't get a move on the old man will arrive before me.'

Yvonne pushed the cup of tea towards him, her hazel eyes avoiding his. She was tall, her height emphasised by the pencil skirt she was wearing with a crisp, white blouse tucked in at the waist. Her shoulder-length brown hair was immaculate as usual, and her make-up freshly applied. When Danny first met Yvonne she had reminded him of Wallis Simpson, with the same elegant manner and style of dress. However, unlike the sophisticated woman who had captured a king, Yvonne showed her true class as soon as she opened her mouth. Like his mother, she was Battersea born and bred, her diction letting her down and sometimes grating on his nerves. Even so, he'd been instantly smitten. But as the years passed she'd grown so thin that the woman he'd once been attracted to now resembled a stick insect. Yvonne's jumpiness was generally put down to her suffering with her nerves, but he knew the real problem. The skinny cow wanted a kid, but even though they'd been trying for seven years, it seemed she was barren. Not that it bothered him. As far as he was concerned his life was fine without brats cramping his style. Of course, Yvonne didn't know that; the daft mare thought he was as keen on the idea of a family as she was.

Danny gulped the tea before hurrying through to the bathroom. He had to get a move on or his father might talk to the others before he arrived, putting the kibosh on his ideas. After running water into the sink he cupped some in his hands to splash on his face, decided to forgo a shave, but still smacked some Brut aftershave onto his cheeks. It was a big day today. He hoped his brothers would back his plans but maybe he should have approached them individually first. Danny cursed his lack of fore-thought. Yet surely his brothers would see the sense of it, and if the old man wasn't keen, maybe they'd go against him for once. Yes, there'd be risks, big ones, but the rewards could be vast – a way out of Drapers Alley for all of them.

He returned to the kitchen, drank a ready-poured second cup of tea, and held a slice of toast between his teeth as he tucked his shirt into his trousers.

'See you later,' he called as he left the room without a backward glance.

Yvonne's eyes followed Danny. There was no kiss goodbye, no quick hug of affection, and as the street door slammed behind him, desolately she went upstairs.

In the bedroom she picked up the shirt that Danny had discarded when he rolled home after midnight, and lifted it to her nose. It reeked of cheap perfume, confirming her suspicions that Danny was playing away again. Tears stung her eyes. How many affairs had she put up with? Yvonne had lost count, but each time he'd assured her it would be the last. She was a fool, a mug, an idiot for believing him, but she loved Danny so deeply and couldn't bear to leave him.

Oh, if only they'd had children. She knew Danny resented it, knew that he envied his married brothers with small families, whilst they remained childless. He blamed her, of course, said she was barren and he was right. Maybe that was why he kept having affairs. Maybe if he got another woman pregnant, he'd leave her! Yvonne slumped onto the side of the bed, tears rolling down her cheeks.

Ten minutes passed before Yvonne was able to pull herself together. She then rose to her feet, throwing the shirt into the laundry basket. She had to get a move on – had to make sure everything was clean and tidy in case her mother-in-law popped round. Joan had high standards, ones that Yvonne, always looking for her mother-in-law's approval, fought to match.

She made the bed, and though it was unlikely that Joan would see it, Yvonne ensured the sheets were tucked in with tight hospital corners, plumped the pillows and shook out the pale blue quilt. She then dusted the furniture and aligned the brush set on her dressing table in perfect symmetry.

A glance in the mirror showed her red, puffy eyes. Fearful that Joan would see them, Yvonne ran downstairs to the bathroom to splash her face with cold water. Danny had left a mess, which she quickly tidied up, folding the discarded towel before placing it neatly on the rail. Like Joan's, this bathroom was an extension, added shortly after she married Danny, and Yvonne was proud of it. After her parents' outside toilet and tin bath in front of the fire every Friday night, having a proper bathroom was sheer luxury. Her eyes saddened. She still missed her mother, mourned her death after a long fight with cancer, and couldn't remember the last time she'd seen her father. He had disapproved of Danny, and had forced her to choose between them. It had nearly broken her heart but she couldn't give Danny up – yet as an only child, she had found losing her father hard to bear.

Half an hour later, the kitchen and living room were looking immaculate when there was a rap on the letter box. The door opened and Joan poked her head inside to call, 'It's only me.'

'Come in, Mum. I'm in the kitchen,' Yvonne called back as she arranged her best porcelain cups and saucers. No thick cheap pot for Joan. Carefully pouring the boiling water into the matching teapot, Yvonne plastered a smile on her face as her mother-in-law walked in.

But there was no fooling Joan Draper. 'Have you been crying?'

'No, of course not,' Yvonne quickly protested, knowing that Danny would go mad if she complained to his mother. Quickly finding an excuse she stammered, 'I . . . I've got a bit of a cold, that's all.'

'You want to look after it or it could turn into bronchitis.'

Why anyone would want to look after a cold was beyond Yvonne, but then a lot of the things that Joan came out with sounded daft to her. They weren't religious, but Joan insisted on eating fish on Fridays, and the routine of housework was the same: washing on Monday, rain or shine; ironing on Tuesday; in fact every day had its own designated task. The woman was like a little beaver, always busy doing something, so it was a wonder she took time out every day to come round for a cup of tea. Yvonne found her mother-in-law a bit of a Jekyll and Hyde character: meek when her husband was around, but made of sterner stuff when he wasn't.

'Do you fancy digestive or Garibaldi biscuits?' she asked.

'Digestive, please,' Joan said, but then her lips tightened. 'Chris has taken Pet to Clapham Junction. Dan gave her the money to buy a record, but I wish he'd stop spoiling the girl.'

Yvonne knew that her mother-in-law was wishing for the moon. Dan Draper was a hard man, and despite the fact that his sons were adults, he still ruled them all. Only Petula saw his soft side, and it was true, the girl *was* spoiled. Thankfully, it hadn't ruined her character so far, but she'd be ill prepared if she ever had to face the real world. Petula had been cosseted and sheltered since the day she was born, wanting for nothing. Mind, it wasn't only her father who treated her like a little princess. Her brothers were just as bad, all of them over-protective when it came to their little sister.

Joan's eyes flicked around the small kitchen but it didn't worry Yvonne. Every surface was shiny and clean, everything in its rightful place, and her mother-in-law would be unable to find fault. Yvonne picked up the prettily laid tray, carrying it through to the sitting room where they sat at the table.

Joan hated tea leaves in her drink, so Yvonne poured carefully, holding a strainer over the cups. She then added milk from a matching jug, a spoonful of sugar from a matching bowl, and handed it to her mother-in-law.

'Thanks,' Joan said, then added abruptly, 'Linda's pregnant.'

Yvonne stiffened. Linda had married Danny's brother, George, less than a year ago and they now lived in number five. He was her least favourite brother-in-law, quick to violence, but she couldn't help a surge of envy. They'd been married for such a short time but already had a baby on the way. Oh God, it just wasn't fair. She struggled to pull herself together, forcing a smile. 'That's nice, but is it definite? She hasn't said anything to me.'

There was a pause as Joan lifted the cup to drink

her tea. She then said, 'Linda knows it's a sensitive subject so maybe she doesn't want to hurt your feelings.'

'Once she starts showing, she can hardly hide it.'

'Yeah, that's true. Oh, well, I suppose I'll have to get my knitting needles out again. This will be my fourth grandchild, but it's been a while since I've had to make any matinée jackets.'

Yvonne felt a wave of desolation. It was as though her mother-in-law enjoyed rubbing salt into the wound – but why? She tried to be a good wife, kept the house spotless, and though she and Danny remained childless, Joan had other grandchildren to love. Huh, love – that was a joke. When did Joan ever show any of her grandchildren an ounce of affection?

Yvonne shook her head, unable to help herself from saying sadly, 'I envy Linda. I want a baby more than anything in the world.'

Joan leaned forward to pat the back of Yvonne's hand, saying softly, 'I know you do, love. Don't worry, it might still happen.'

Yvonne blinked wildly to stave off the tears welling in her eyes, but Joan rose to her feet, saying hurriedly, 'I'd best be off. Thanks for the tea.'

Before Yvonne could respond, Joan had gone, and she was left sitting at the table, amazed that her usually cold, undemonstrative mother-in-law had actually shown her a little sympathy.

* * *

Joan almost ran into her front door, closing it quickly behind her. Gawd, she had almost brought Yvonne to tears and that was the last thing she wanted. Of all her daughters-in-law, Yvonne was the only one she had any time for, and she could guess the sort of life Danny led the poor girl.

Joan wasn't a fool, she knew Danny's faults and it was a wonder he'd managed to hold on to Yvonne for seven years. He was a womaniser, but if his father found out he'd go mad. Joan also knew that Yvonne longed for children, but was tempted to tell her what a thankless task motherhood was. She had hoped that after five sons, things would be different with Petula, but like the boys, she favoured her father. Maybe things would have been different if she could have shown them affection, but Joan found it impossible. Her own mother had been a cold, unloving woman, bitter at being a single parent with the stigma it carried.

With a sigh, Joan picked up a duster, absent-mindedly flicking it over furniture she'd already polished. Her mother had been a dirty woman, their home a tip, and they'd been looked down on by their neighbours. During her infrequent attendance at school, Joan had been called a smelly cow and at first she hadn't understood why. It was only as she grew older that she learned about hygiene – learned that her mother's method of rubbing a damp flannel across her face every day, leaving her body untouched, wasn't enough. Her first bath had been a revelation – the water almost black – but from then on she had gone to the public baths once a week, relishing the feel of being clean from top to toe.

She'd known that Dan was a bit of a rogue when she met him but, as he always had a few bob in his pocket, she chose to ignore the gossip. He would buy her presents, make her laugh and she found herself falling in love. When he proposed she had quickly said yes, eager to get away from the dour life she had lived with her mother.

When they moved into their first tiny flat, Joan had been determined to be different, to make sure that her home was always immaculate. At first it had been easy, but as the babies came along it took every minute of her day to keep up. Then, just when she thought her child-bearing days were over, Petula had been born. Though she hated to admit it, Joan had been filled with resentment. She'd had enough of babies, dirty nappies, broken sleep – but she'd hidden her feelings and left most of Petula's welfare to her father and older brothers. That had been a mistake. Petula was fawned on, indulged, but it was too late to change things now. If Joan so much as opened her mouth in criticism, Danny shot her down in flames. His precious daughter was able to do no wrong.

'We're back,' Chris said, flinging open the door. 'I can't stop. Dad wants me down the yard.'

'I thought it was your Saturday off,' Joan said.

Chris looked surprised at her interest. 'Yeah, but there's some sort of business meeting and Dad wants me there.'

'It's the first I've heard of it.'

'He mentioned it earlier. You obviously weren't listening.'

'What's this meeting about?'

Chris's eyes became veiled and Joan knew she was wasting her time. She was always kept in the dark when it came to the business. In truth, she preferred it that way, and berated herself now for asking questions.

'I'm not sure what it's about, Mum, but no doubt Dad will put you in the picture.'

'Yeah, and pigs might fly,' Joan told him.

He grinned, turning to leave. 'See you later, Mum. Bye, Petula.'

'Don't call me Petula. You know I hate it.'

'It was Mum who named you after Petula Clark, who was a child star before you were born, so don't blame me.' On that note, Chris closed the street door behind him.

'It's a daft name,' Petula complained.

Joan ignored her daughter and went through to the kitchen to boil a kettle of water. She would scrub the doorstep before getting the Brasso out to polish the letter box and door knocker. With any luck it might inspire her daughters-in-law to follow suit. Yvonne was the only one who had good standards. The rest were slovenly, and it was about time they pulled their socks up.

She heard Petula thumping up the stairs, followed by the sound of her new record filling the house. Her youngest was growing up, and no doubt she was already interested in boys. Not that she'd have much luck meeting any, especially with her father and brothers keeping her under close guard. The day would come when Petula would rebel, and for the first time Joan felt a twinge of pity for her daughter. The girl would be fighting a losing battle. Any man who came near her would soon be chased off.

By the time the kettle came to the boil, Petula was playing the song again, and Joan closed her eyes against the sound. Every time the girl got a new record it was played repeatedly until Joan felt like screaming. All right, Elvis Presley had a good voice, but by now she knew all his songs off by heart. Her ears pricked. What was this one? 'Good Luck Charm'. Well, it wasn't bad, but Joan decided to get away from the racket. She took a bucket of hot water and soda outside to tackle her doorstep.

'All right, Mum?' a voice called, and Joan's eyes flicked sideways.

Sue was standing on her doorstep, the third house in the row, and Joan hid a scowl. This was her least favourite daughter-in-law. Like her, Sue was diminutive, but the resemblance ended there. With peroxide-blonde hair and a huge bust, the girl looked a bit like the up-and-coming actress Barbara Windsor. Sue was aware of this and had taken to emulating the starlet's gyrating walk and style of dress. Joan shook her head against the sight of Sue's tight sheath dress, her bust thrust out in front as she wandered closer. Unlike Yvonne, she didn't look decent. She looked like a floozie and Joan had no idea what her son saw in her.

'Bob left early for the yard,' Sue said. 'He said something about a meeting. Do you know what it's about?'

'You know better than to ask me that,' Joan snapped as she dipped her scrubbing brush into the water. 'I'm cleaning my step and it's about time you had a go at yours.'

'Why bother? The kids are in and out every five minutes and will only muck it up again.'

Joan's eyes flicked along the alley. 'Where are they?'

'I gave them their pocket money so they've gone straight to the sweet shop to spend it.'

No sooner had Sue spoken than the two lads came careering into the alley, skinny legs pumping, six-year-old Robby in pursuit of his younger brother.

'Mum! Mum!' Paul yelled. 'Robby's trying to nick my sweets.'

'No I'm not,' Robby protested, skidding to a halt beside Joan.

'He is, Gran,' four-year-old Paul insisted, making

sure that, though she was kneeling, his grandmother was between them. 'He's got his own sweets, but he's after my gobstopper.'

'Look, it's up to your mother to sort this out, not me,' Joan protested. 'Go away and leave me in peace. I've got work to do.'

'Yes, come here, boys. After all, you can't come between your grandmother and her housework,' Sue said sarcastically.

Joan looked daggers at her daughter-in-law, but she ignored her, dragging the boys inside and slamming the door. Joan shrugged, unconcerned. When the boys had been born her daughter-in-law had expected her to baby-sit, but she'd soon nipped that in the bud. She'd told Sue that she had no intention of looking after her kids whilst she went out gallivanting – she'd done her stint, had six kids, and wasn't prepared to start all over again.

Joan wrung out the cloth, her mouth grim. Sue resented it, didn't like her, but Joan didn't care. The feeling was reciprocated, but the two women held their animosity in check for Bob's sake. On the surface the marriage appeared fine, but Joan doubted her son was happy. With Sue for a wife and his house a tip, how could he be?

Chapter Three

Back at number three, Sue was grim-faced. Who the bloody hell did her mother-in-law think she was? All right, Sue's own step might be dirty, but there was more to life than flaming housework. When she had met Bob, she had loved the kudos of courting a local villain. She fancied being married to a bloke who had a few bob rather than having to work in a rotten factory, but once they'd tied the knot, things hadn't turned out quite as she'd expected. She had dreamed of being an actress, even a film star, stupidly hoping that being married to a Draper would open doors.

So much for that dream. The Drapers didn't have any links to showbusiness. Bob had been so keen to have her on his arm that he'd lied, and now she was stuck in the alley, surrounded by his family. She hated it, especially being close to her sanctimonious mother-in-law, *and* that uppity cow next door. Yvonne was another one who was housework mad, and not only that, she was a crawler, always up Joan's arse. Not that she envied Yvonne her husband. Danny might be a good-looking bloke, but she wouldn't trust him as far as she could throw him.

Sue thought about her own husband, and though Bob wasn't as handsome as Danny, she'd choose him any day. He was placid, amiable, and despite her disappointment, theirs was a happy marriage, with infrequent rows.

'Mum! Mum, tell Robby,' Paul cried.

'For Gawd's sake, leave your brother alone,' Sue yelled, glaring at her elder son. Robby was a handful and though he'd been at school for only a year, he was already in trouble for being a bully. As was tradition, she'd called her firstborn Robert after his father but although they were similar in looks, their natures were the exact opposite.

'I only want a suck on his gobstopper,' Robby wheedled.

Sue sighed in exasperation. 'Go on, Paul. Give him a suck.'

'No, he won't give it back.'

'Yes, he will – won't you, Robby?'

'Yeah.'

With reluctance, Paul handed the sticky, wet sweet over to his brother, watching in horror as Robby shoved it in his mouth, one cheek bulging like a hamster as he headed for the stairs.

'Mum!' Paul protested.

'Robby, you little sod! Come back here!'

'See, Mum, I told you,' whined Paul, his grey eyes filling with tears.

Paul was a gentle, quiet child, and secretly he was Sue's favourite. When it came to Robby she felt helpless, unable to control her wilful elder son, and usually left any discipline to his father.

'Look, don't cry, Paul,' she placated. 'It ain't the end of the world. I'll buy you another one.'

'Now.'

'No, not now, but we'll pop to the shop later.'

Paul hung his head, his fair, coarse hair sticking up like a brush. Sue swept him into her arms, then, sitting down, she plonked him on her lap. 'Who's my good boy then? I just wish your brother was more like you.'

They sat like that for a while, Sue ignoring the state of the room as she cuddled her son. Her brown sofa was piled with the ironing she'd intended to tackle last night, but then hadn't bothered. The lino on the floor was dirty, the rug by the hearth grimy, yet none of it concerned Sue.

There were footsteps on the stairs, and then Robby appeared, grinning cheekily as he held out the tiny remnants of the gobstopper. 'Here you are, Paul. You can have it back now.'

Paul jumped down, but as he approached his brother, Robby ran round him to take his place on Sue's lap. 'Nah, nah,' he mocked, shoving the sweet back in his mouth.

Sue pushed Robby off, and as he landed with a thump on the lino she reared to her feet. 'You little bugger! Wait till I tell your father. He'll give you a bloody good hiding.'

'Don't care,' said Robby, his chin tilted upwards, eyes defiant.

Paul was crying now and Sue could feel the start of a headache coming on. 'Don't cry, darling,' she placated. 'Look, I tell you what, how about we go next door? You can play with your cousin.'

Paul nodded, mollified at the thought of seeing Oliver, who, though much older than he at nine, was his favourite playmate. 'I don't want Robby to come.'

'I can't leave him on his own, love,' she said.

Robby scrambled to his feet and Sue's voice was hard as she threatened, 'You'd better behave yourself, Robby, and don't upset Oliver. You know Auntie Norma won't put up with any of your shenanigans.'

'He's a sissy.'

'No he isn't, he's just quiet, that's all. In fact, it wouldn't hurt you to take a leaf out of his book.'

Robby scowled, but followed them next door, dragging his feet as they left the house. Sue glanced to her right, saw that her mother-in-law had returned inside, and hoped she'd stay there. She wouldn't put it past the woman to come round later to check up on her and as she hadn't done a scrap of housework, that was the last thing she wanted.

Sue grimaced, but then shrugged. So what? If her mother-in-law didn't like the state of the place, she could just bugger off again.

Sue's husband, Bob, was at the yard, resentful of the fact that he didn't have a car. He could have cadged a lift from his father, or eldest brother, Danny, but it was his job to open up today and he'd had to leave well before them.

There was no denying that they were making good money, but by the time it was shared out between six families, it wasn't a fortune. It was all right for Danny. With no children, he could afford a car, and with a thrifty wife like Yvonne, he had a good few bob to spare.

If only Sue was more like Danny's wife. Instead she was a spendthrift, buying stupid fripperies that he was sure they could do without. The mantelshelf was lined with animal ornaments, usually covered in dust. Every windowsill was the same. Dog ornaments, cat ornaments, some so garish and cheap they looked like prizes from a fairground.

After his mother's obsession with housework he had at first found Sue's attitude refreshing. He'd enjoyed being able to relax in his own home without worrying if he so much as moved a cushion. Now, though, it was wearing thin, especially when it was hard to find a chair to sit on that wasn't piled high with rubbish.

Bob shook his head. No, he was being stupid. He didn't want Sue to be like his mother, or Yvonne, who looked like a cold fish to him. Sue was a cracker, a real goer who liked nothing better than a bit of slap and tickle. He worried sometimes when he saw her looking at Danny, and now he ran a hand through his wispy, brown hair. He hated it, wishing it was thick and dark like Danny's. He envied his brother his height too. Though he had a similar, beefy build, he was a good four inches shorter. He was sure that Sue fancied Danny, and no wonder, but he made sure he kept her happy in bed, well satisfied, something that took a bit of doing at times. Yes, she was a goer all right, but if Danny so much as looked at her the wrong way . . .

An early customer broke Bob out of his reveries, and then a couple more turned up before he saw his father's car pulling into the yard. As Dan Draper climbed out, Bob frowned, noticing that his father was showing his age. His large build still looked intimidating, but there was a slight stoop to his shoulders and a beer belly hung over his trousers. Blimey, when did he get old? He knew his father wanted to retire and was salting cash away by taking the biggest cut, but unless they drew in more money, his retirement would be a long way off.

'Morning, Robert. Are the others here?'

'No, you're the first to show,' Bob replied, wishing

his father wouldn't call him by his full name, but knowing better than to complain.

'Shit. This meeting was Danny's idea so he'd better show his face soon. There's racing at Sandown and I want to be away by one o'clock.'

Bob hid a smile. So, the number-one son was in his father's bad books. Good. 'What has Danny got in mind?'

A black Jaguar screeched into the yard, cutting off his father's answer. Danny climbed out of the car, his face dark with annoyance as he walked towards them. 'I told Yvonne I had to get up this morning, but the silly cow forgot to wake me.'

'Another late night, was it?' Bob asked, hoping to stir trouble.

Danny ignored him, saying only, 'I'm sorry I'm late, Dad.'

Dan wrapped an arm around his son's shoulder. 'Never mind. You're here now, and I'd like to go over the finer details of this plan before the others arrive.'

They moved away and Bob followed, but he was halted in his tracks when his father said, 'Look after the business for now. We'll shut up shop as soon as the other boys arrive.'

Bob stayed behind, inwardly seething. It was always the same. Danny and his father were thick as thieves, whilst the rest of them were left out of the loop until they were good and ready to allow

41

them in. Bob chewed on his lower lip, wondering why his father was blind to Danny's faults. All right, they were all villains, but Danny was more than that. He was a nasty piece of work and a womaniser, but so far had been clever enough to keep his antics from their father.

As Bob walked behind the counter he was wondering if he should put his father in the picture, but then shivered. No, if Danny found out he'd opened his mouth, he'd go ballistic. And you didn't upset Danny, even if he was your brother, not if you wanted to stay in one piece.

Dan sat behind an old desk that was littered with paperwork, receipts, and an ashtray overflowing with dog-ends. 'Your mother would have a fit if she saw the state of this office. Mind you, it's just as well that she stays out of the way or we'd never find a thing. Make the tea, son, and then tell me more about this plan of yours.'

Danny junior switched on the kettle, then eagerly launched straight into his plan. 'There's more money to be made if we diversify into hard porn, a lot more.'

'Yeah, you told me, but have you thought about the risks? If we muscle in on that side of the business we'd be treading on Garston territory, for one thing.'

'We can deal with Jack Garston.'

'I ain't so sure. If the money's as big as you say, he ain't gonna take a competitor lightly. He's got a fair bit of muscle behind him too. So far we only peddle soft porn and we can deal with the small fry in the same game, but Garston's mob . . . well . . .'

'You said it, Dad, small fry. That's all we are too. Yeah, we're making money, but it's peanuts compared to what we could rake in.' The kettle began to whistle and Danny turned to make two mugs of tea, handing one to his father.

Dan pursed his lips. He didn't like being called small fry and had to admit he wanted to be up amongst the big boys. He had a reputation as a decent safe breaker and had pulled off a few big jobs in the past, but this porn game was new to him. They had started it up a couple of years ago, still using the yard as a front, and as it was doing well he couldn't see the sense of rocking the boat.

'I'm not sure, son. For a start, what about distribution?'

'I've already put out feelers and there's a demand – a big one.'

'I'm not sure the girls we use now would be willing to take it up a notch, let alone the blokes. Just what sort of photographs and films have you got in mind?'

'All sorts. They want everything. Bondage, three-somes, queers. A couple of outlets asked for kids and they're willing to pay big money too.'

Unable to believe his ears, Dan's voice rose in anger. 'Do what? Kids! I ain't getting into that.'

'It pays the most.'

'I don't give a fuck what it pays! Christ, son, we're talking about children here! Ain't you got any morals?'

'Dad, we deal in porn so it's a bit late to talk about morals. If the demand's there, we should capitalise on it.'

'No!' Dan yelled, slamming his mug down, regardless that tea slopped onto the desk. 'Our girls and their partners are willing participants, and that's fine with me. They do their act, get paid, but you won't be able to say the same about children. They'd have to be forced! Have you even thought about that?'

The office door opened and Bob poked his head inside. 'What's going on? What's all the shouting about?'

'Get out!' Dan bellowed.

Bob swiftly disappeared, and Danny turned to his father. 'Calm down, Dad.'

Dan sprung to his feet, leaning over his desk and so angry that spittle flew out of his mouth as he yelled, 'Calm down! We're talking about child pornography and you expect me to calm down!'

Danny's manner became placatory. 'Look, Garston provides what the punters want, and that includes kids. It was just a suggestion, that's all, and I must admit I hadn't thought it through. If you don't like the idea we can just forget it.'

'Of course I don't like the fucking idea! In fact, the meeting's off.'

'Hold on, Dad. Don't cut off your nose to spite your face. There's still a lot of money to be made from the other stuff.'

Dan fought his anger as he sat down again, but failed. All right, he was no angel, but he had standards, a code that he lived by. When the boys had suggested getting into this game, he'd been against it, but they had talked him round. He had to admit that the thought of easy money had been a big factor in his decision – that and the fact that he was getting too old for safe breaking, his hands and ears not as good as they used to be. He glared at his son. Christ, using children! Danny said he hadn't given it a lot of thought, but that was no excuse. The boy was his firstborn, he'd been proud of him, yet now it was as if he was seeing his son for the first time – and he didn't like what he saw. Maybe Danny had seen too much – maybe that was it, Dan thought, searching for excuses. Danny had a talent for photography and was involved in the technical side of making the films, but surely that wasn't responsible for turning him into a sick bastard who could suggest using innocent kids? He had to get out of there, to breathe fresh air. Pushing himself up, he growled, 'Wait for the boys. I'll be back later.'

'But, Dad . . .'

Dan didn't stay to hear the rest of Danny's words.

He stormed out of the office, brushing past Bob as he headed for his car. He needed to think, to clear his head. He started the engine and drove off, not caring where he was heading.

'What's up with Dad?' Bob asked as he went into the office.

Danny was behind the desk now, lounging back on the chair, feet up and hands linked behind his head. 'He didn't like one of my suggestions.'

'What suggestion was that?'

'He vetoed it, so there's no point in talking about it.'

'I'd still like to know.'

'Tough. Now bugger off. I need to think.'

Just because Danny was the eldest, he thought he could give out orders, but Bob wasn't ready to give up yet. It gave him some satisfaction to know that Danny had fallen out with their father – a rare occurrence – yet he was still curious to know why. 'Was it to do with this new idea of yours?'

'I don't want to talk about it. Ain't that a customer?'

Bob's lips tightened. He was only fifteen months younger than Danny and was sick of being treated like an underling. All right, he didn't have his brother's brains or looks but he wasn't an idiot. The trade counter bell rang again but he ignored it.

'Is Dad coming back for the meeting?'

'Yeah, I expect so.'

'Why don't you run your idea by me? If I like it, maybe between the two of us we can talk him round.'

'He'll do his nut if I suggest it again.'

'Maybe, but this is a family business and we're all entitled to a vote.' Bob watched as Danny's eyes narrowed speculatively, and hid a smirk. He would never go against his father, but Danny didn't know that. This might turn out to be the ideal opportunity to score a few brownie points with the old man.

'All right,' Danny said, 'see to that customer and then I'll fill you in.'

Chapter Four

Norma Draper tutted with impatience when there was a knock on the door of number four, where she lived with her husband, Maurice. Norma fixed a smile on her face as Sue walked in with her two sons.

'Hello, Sue, I'm surprised to see you so early. Maurice hasn't left for the yard yet,' she added, hoping that her sister-in-law would take the hint and come back later.

'Yeah, but the meeting starts at eleven so no doubt he'll be off soon. Do you know what it's about?'

'I've no idea.'

'Old face-ache said the same, *and* she had the cheek to pick me up about my doorstep.'

Norma smiled, knowing that 'face-ache' referred to their mother-in-law. She had to agree with Sue. Since the day she'd met Maurice, Joan Draper had made it obvious she disapproved of their relationship. All right, she was eight years older than

Maurice, but she hadn't meant to get pregnant, despite what the woman thought. In fact, Norma was deeply ashamed and had hated giving birth to Oliver six months after their marriage. Not only that, she had lost contact with her parents in the process. They had been appalled by her pregnancy and also disapproved of the Drapers – a family they'd decided were as common as muck.

She looked at Sue and said sympathetically, 'Don't let Joan upset you.'

'Where's Oliver, Auntie Norma?'

'He's in the back yard feeding his rabbit,' she told Paul.

'I'm going out there to see him,' Robby said.

Norma liked Sue's youngest lad, Paul, but couldn't feel the same about Robby and tensed nervously as the two boys made for the yard. She was worried that Robby would upset Oliver and wanted to follow them, but as Maurice came downstairs she looked at him worriedly. His eyes were still thick with conjunctivitis, his face wan. Maurice wasn't robust, unlike his brothers, and she worried constantly about his health. If anyone had a cold, Maurice would catch it, then nine times out of ten it went to his chest. If stressed, he suffered with bouts of asthma, the attacks leaving him weak and exhausted. Over time she had learned how to deal with them, and thankfully how to calm him down.

'Are you off to this meeting now?' she asked.

'Yes, I'd better get a move on.'

Sue plonked herself on the sofa, her tight dress riding up to reveal shapely legs. Maurice grinned as he said, 'Hello, Sue.'

'Watcha, Maurice. Do you know what this meeting's about?'

'No, sorry, I don't.'

His smile was warm and Norma felt a surge of jealousy. Unlike her, Sue was pretty, vivacious, big-busted and feminine. Norma glanced at her own reflection in the mirror over the fireplace, disliking what she saw. She was plain, her features too large, with only her long, wavy, auburn hair saving her face from masculinity. She hated her body too, and wished that she had Sue's curves, but when Maurice came to her side, she dragged her eyes away from her reflection.

He dropped a kiss on her cheek, asking, 'Where's Oliver?'

'In the yard with Paul and Robby.'

'I'll pop out there to say goodbye.'

'He dotes on that boy,' Sue said as soon as Maurice was out of sight.

'Yes, I know. He's a marvellous father.'

Maurice soon appeared again. 'I'd best get a move on. See you later, ladies.'

Sue giggled. '"Ladies". Well, ain't that nice?' she said as the door closed behind Maurice. 'Mind you, he must know what the meeting's about.'

'Probably, but you should know better than to ask.'

'Yeah, that's what old face-ache said. I don't know why they have to be so secretive. We ain't stupid. We know they do jobs and we'd hardly go shouting our mouths off. It's been a long time since the last one, though – do you think they're planning another robbery?'

'I don't know,' Norma replied. She didn't want to get into this conversation, hating any mention of the family's less respectable sideline. Her parents thought the Drapers were common, but that was the least of it. If they'd known she was marrying into a family of thieves they'd have had heart attacks. Oh, why wouldn't Maurice listen to her? He was clever, mathematically astute and handled the business accounts. If they left the alley, and his awful family, he could get a decent job. She wanted a better life for her son, a respectable life where she could hold her head up high. Instead she was stuck here amongst this den of thieves. Maybe it wouldn't have been as bad if she could have made friends outside of the alley, but as soon as it became known that she was a Draper, she was avoided like the plague. Norma had dreaded Oliver going off to school, and her fears had been well founded when the other mothers made sure that their children gave him a wide berth. At first Oliver had seemed unaware of it, but had started to ask questions when he found it hard to make friends, ones she found difficult to fob off. It had helped when Ivy's elder boy started at the same school a couple of years later. Oliver had taken Ernie under his wing, but it still angered Norma that she and her son were tarred with the same brush as the rest of the Drapers.

'Any chance of a cuppa?' Sue asked. 'I'm spitting feathers.'

'Yes, of course,' Norma replied, but as she went through to the kitchen her son came stumbling through the back door.

'Mum! Oh, Mum,' he sobbed. 'He . . . he killed my rabbit.'

Norma pulled her son into her arms, holding him tightly. She didn't have to ask who the culprit was, only saying, 'What did he do, love?'

'He said Shaker could fly and launched him like an aeroplane. Shaker hit the wall and now he . . . he's dead.'

Norma's voice rose. 'Sue! Sue, get in here!'

'Gawd blimey, what's the matter?' Sue asked, wide-eyed as she tottered on high heels into the room.

Teeth grinding with anger, Norma spat, 'Your son has killed Oliver's rabbit.'

'No, Robby wouldn't do that.'

'Huh, I didn't say which son, but I see you've jumped straight to Robby's defence.'

Paul came running in the back door, face alight

with excitement. 'He's woken up, Oliver! Shaker's woken up.'

Oliver pulled himself from his mother's grasp and ran outside. Norma followed to see Robby hunkered down beside the rabbit, his eyes wide and innocent as he looked at them.

'He's all right, Ollie,' Robby said.

'Oliver!' Norma automatically corrected as she too crouched down. She hated the diminutive use of her son's name and refused to let anyone use it. Shaker was indeed alive, but lay on his side, trembling as she stroked him.

'You shouldn't have thrown him like that,' Oliver accused as he pushed Robby aside.

'I didn't mean to hurt him. I thought he could fly.'

'Don't tell lies, you nasty little boy,' Norma snapped.

'Hold on, Norma, there's no need to talk to Robby like that. He's only six,' Sue protested.

'I told him, Mummy,' cried Paul. 'I told him that rabbits can't fly.'

Norma looked up at Sue. 'See, out of the mouth of babes – and your Paul's only four.'

Shaker became alert, up on all fours now, his nose twitching. 'Look at that,' said Sue. 'He's all right now so I don't know what all the fuss is about.'

Norma struggled to hold her temper. Robby looked like butter wouldn't melt in his mouth, but she knew what he was capable of and wasn't fooled. The boy might be only six years old, but he had a nasty, malicious streak, and Sue must be blind if she couldn't see it.

'Put Shaker in his pen, Oliver,' she said, 'and you, Robby, I would prefer it if you come inside where we can keep an eye on you.'

'Can I stay out here, Auntie Norma?' Paul asked.

'Of course you can.'

'I want to stay in the yard too,' Robby whined.

'He didn't mean any harm, Norma. It won't be fair to drag him inside.'

Norma's lips tightened. She hated Sue's weakness, the way she pandered to the boy. 'Every time you bring Robby to see us there's a problem. Until he learns to behave himself, he must remain where I can see him. In fact, I would rather you kept him away from my son.'

'Sod you then,' Sue snapped. 'Come on, Robby, you too, Paul. We're going home and we won't bother to come round here again.'

'But, Mummy,' cried Paul, 'I want to play with Oliver.'

'Tough! Now come on,' Sue demanded, grabbing their hands before marching off.

Norma walked inside just in time to hear her front door slam. She was used to Sue's volatile temper. They had fallen out over Robby before, but her sister-in-law had a short memory. No doubt she'd be around again in no time, but Norma just wished that she'd leave Robby behind. If the Drapers weren't so feared, Oliver could find friends outside of the alley, but as it was there was only Sue or Ivy's boys to play with. She wasn't keen on Bob's cousin, Ivy, the woman always trying to cause trouble, but she preferred her older son, Ernie, as a playmate for Oliver.

It was only a few minutes later when Oliver came in, his bony knees grubby, and a piece of hay from the rabbit's hutch stuck in his floppy fringe. Norma's eyes softened as she gently removed it. Like his father, Oliver was thin, with light brown hair, but thankfully he was a robust child. At nine years old he was Dan and Joan's first grandchild, but Joan had little time for the boy. Dan had tried to prevent her from naming him Oliver, saying it was no name for a Draper, but she had stood her ground. After all, she wasn't common like her in-laws. She came from a better family, her father an electrical store manager and their home in Wandsworth far superior to this.

Norma hung her head, thinking back to when she had met Maurice. She'd been lonely, had craved love, but she was so plain that she expected to remain a spinster. When Maurice came along he was the first man to show her any attention, but, afraid of losing him, she had stupidly let him go too far. The question arose again, one that plagued her. If she hadn't been pregnant, would she have married Maurice?

'Can I have a glass of orange juice, please, Mummy?'

'Of course you can, darling.'

As she poured Oliver's drink, Norma knew it was stupid to keep questioning her decision, especially when, in truth, she knew the answer. Yes, she would still have married Maurice, preferring marriage to the life of a spinster. Her two brothers had both married well, and she was the last one left at home, destined to a life of caring for her parents as they aged.

As Norma handed Oliver the juice, she smiled at her son, loving him dearly. He had become her one consolation, and though she couldn't love her husband, she liked him, liked him a lot. But, oh, if only he wasn't a Draper!

When Maurice reached the yard, he rubbed his eyes, then picked at the corners, his finger coming away covered in yellow pus. He'd have to get another prescription from the doc, but hated going to his surgery. He wasn't strong but drew comfort from knowing that his role in the family business was an important one. He kept the books, making sure that no fault could be found in the accounts, the taxes paid on time and in full. The other books, the ones that covered their sideline, were kept well away from prying eyes, but he had them on hand just in case they were needed at the meeting.

'Morning, Bob,' Maurice greeted. 'I've just said goodbye to your lovely wife.'

'What's that supposed to mean?'

'Sue called round to see Norma and was still there when I left.'

'Oh, right,' Bob said, then gestured with his thumb towards the office. 'Danny's been here a while and Chris turned up ten minutes ago.'

'What about Dad? I can't see his car.'

'He went off with the hump.'

'Really, and who ruffled his feathers?'

'He had a bit of a falling-out with Danny.'

'Did he now? What about?'

'Search me,' Bob said, looking pleased as he added, 'but they were having a right old ding-dong.'

Maurice could sense that Bob was being evasive, sure that he knew more than he was letting on. Bob was always a bit funny when it came to Danny – the rivalry plain to see – but he was wasting his time if he wanted to take Danny's place. Next to their father, Danny was the top man, the position unlikely to change. There was only one person their father favoured above Danny, and that was Petula.

'Hello, Maurice,' said Chris as he came out of the office. 'The meeting might be off.'

'Yeah, Bob told me that Dad went off with the hump. Is it worth hanging around?'

'Search me. Danny ain't saying much, only that they had a difference of opinion.'

Maurice studied his youngest brother. Chris was looking snazzy. He had run the gauntlet of fashion, changing from a teddy boy to a mod, and lately had taken to wearing Italian suits. He was a good-looking bloke, a sort of soft replica of their father, and though he didn't have an aggressive personality, he could look after himself. Chris was his favourite of all the brothers, and before he had married Sue they had knocked about together, either going down the pub, or to the local snooker hall.

'How's your love life? Are you still seeing that girl from Chelsea?'

'No, she was getting a bit too keen and hinting about engagement rings.'

'So, you're footloose and fancy-free again. Do you fancy a game of snooker tonight?'

'No can do. I've got a date tonight. I took Pet to buy a record this morning and a nice-looking bird behind the counter caught my eye.'

Maurice raised his brows, but then he shouldn't be surprised. Chris was good at pulling birds, one following another in quick succession. 'What's she like?'

'Tasty, but she's blonde and I prefer them dark.'

'What's the matter with blondes?' Bob protested. 'My Sue's a cracker.'

'Yeah, she is,' Chris agreed, 'but I still like brunettes, and ain't your Sue's hair out of a bottle?'

Bob was saved from answering when their father drove into the yard. He climbed out of his car and, judging by the look on his face, he was still in a foul mood.

'Is everyone here?' he snapped.

'We're still waiting for George,' Bob told him.

'Shit! Well, we'll have to start without him. Lock up, Bob, and then join us in the office.'

Maurice frowned. With their father in this mood he couldn't see it being a very productive meeting. Curious to know what Danny had come up with, he silently followed his father through to the office, Bob and Chris behind him.

Danny hastily took his feet off the table and stood up. 'The meeting still on then, Dad?'

'Yeah, it's on, but you're skating on thin ice.'

Maurice frowned again. It was obvious that Danny had already discussed his plans with their father, but, judging by his tone, the old man didn't approve of them.

They all grabbed chairs and, once seated, Dan said, 'Maurice, did you bring the books?'

'Yes, Dad.'

'How are we doing?'

Maurice opened to the current page, pushing the book across to his father. 'As you can see we've made the same amount this quarter as we did the last. Profits are still good, but I think we've reached saturation point and they're unlikely to increase.'

'Oh yeah,' Dan snapped, 'very convenient. Have you spoken to Danny ahead of this meeting?'

'No. What makes you ask that?'

'It's a bit funny that just when we need to increase profits, your brother has come up with an idea.'

'Well, he didn't discuss it with me,' Maurice said, 'but he's certainly timed it right. What have you got in mind, Danny?'

Danny rose to his feet. 'If we want to make money, big money, we need to diversify. I've discussed this with Dad, but there's one aspect of it that he doesn't like and I expected to drop. However, I had a word with Bob and he's as keen on the idea as me.'

'He's what?' Dan exploded. 'Is this true, Bob?'

'Nah, no way,' Bob protested. 'Danny told me what he's got in mind, but I think he's off his head. I'm with you, Dad. I've got kids and the thought of it turns my stomach. What he's got in mind is disgusting, sick, and I can't believe he even suggested it.'

'Why, you . . .' Danny growled, advancing towards Bob, '. . . you two-faced bastard. I'll fucking kill you!'

'That's enough!'

Their father's order was enough to halt Danny in his tracks, but his fists were clenched as he yelled, 'He said he was for it!'

Bob was pale, his voice wheedling, 'No, Danny. I'm sorry, but when you told me what you've got in mind I was a bit stunned. I can't remember what I said, but maybe you got hold of the wrong end of the stick.'

'Leave it out. I didn't come over on a fucking

banana boat so don't take me for a mug. I don't know what your game is, but you agreed all right.'

'Look, what's this all about?' Maurice asked, his eyes flicking between his brothers.

It was Danny who answered. 'When I discussed my idea with Bob, he said we should have a vote on it.'

'That's right, I did,' said Bob, 'but it doesn't mean I like the idea. I just said it's only fair that everyone gets a chance to hear it.'

'Shut up, the pair of you,' Dan yelled. 'Bob, I'm glad to hear that, unlike Danny, you seem to have decent morals, but there'll be no vote on the shit that your brother has come up with.'

When Maurice saw Bob's smug smile, he was sure that his brother had somehow manoeuvred this to discredit Danny, enabling him to get into their father's good books. He also saw Danny step forward, about to round on Bob again, his face livid. To defuse the situation Maurice quickly asked, 'Just what is this idea?'

It was their father who answered. 'Danny wants us to go into hard porn, but I'll leave him to tell you about the bit that I can't stomach and will never allow.'

'All right, Danny, let's hear it,' Maurice said.

Chapter Five

In number five, George Draper was growing impatient. He'd overslept, not getting up until after ten that morning, and if Linda didn't pull herself together soon he'd have to leave without any grub. Bloody hell, this pregnancy was a nightmare. Linda threw up continuously and looked awful, her face the colour of dough. Morning sickness. Huh! Hers sometimes lasted all day, and if this was what it was like to have a pregnant wife, he'd make sure it was the last time.

He glanced at the clock and his expression turned grim when he saw it was after half-past ten. If he didn't get a move on he'd be late for the meeting and the old man would do his nut.

Linda staggered in through the back door, wiping her hand across her mouth. 'I hate using that outside toilet. When are we going to get a bathroom?'

'For Christ's sake, stop whinging,' George snapped, fists clenched as he fought the urge to smack her in the mouth. Realising that he should have put more value on his freedom, he was already disillusioned with marriage. It had been the thought of having nooky on hand whenever he wanted it that had decided him to propose, and not only that, Linda had been a tasty piece, one he'd been proud to have on his arm.

Marriage had been great at first, sex on demand, but the novelty soon wore off, especially when the stupid mare told him she was pregnant. She was letting herself go too, her face always bare of make-up. Her long, ash-blonde hair still cascaded down her back, but these days it looked like rats' tails.

'I'm gonna be late,' he snapped. 'For fuck's sake, pull yourself together and make me a bacon sandwich. I'll eat it on the way to the yard.'

'Yes, all right, and I'm sorry, George. I won't complain again,' Linda wheedled, but then she raised a hand to her mouth. 'Oh God, I'm going to be sick again.'

George held his temper, just, and as she staggered outside again he yelled, 'You useless cow. Forget my breakfast – I'm off.'

With that, George left the house. His stomach rumbled as he hurried down the alley, his expression dark with fury. When he turned into Aspen Street a bloke was coming out of his house, and though he looked quickly away, George was ready for a fight.

'Who do you think you're looking at? Got a problem, have yer?'

'Nah, mate,' the man said, holding his hands up as though in surrender.

The bloke's obvious fear mollified George, and anyway, with his father waiting he didn't have time to hang about. With a last scowl at the bloke he hurried past, intent now on reaching the yard.

Linda leaned over the toilet, retching, but only bringing up bile now. Oh, she hated this morning sickness. She had hoped that her pregnancy would soften George, but so far all it had done was arouse his anger, making her more afraid of him than ever.

When they'd first met, his dark brown hair, gorgeous blue eyes and a smile to die for had bowled her over, and she had willingly gone out with him. Of course she had heard of George's family, their reputation, but in truth she'd been bored with life and excited at the hint of danger. Her previous boyfriends had been ordinary, staid and, compared to George, as dull as dishwater. She'd been blinded by him, fell madly in love, and at first there'd been no sign of the violence that lay beneath his charming persona.

Linda wiped a hand across her mouth, recalling how during their courtship the other side of George had come to light. He would get into numerous fights, usually a result of another bloke showing interest. God, what a fool she'd been. Instead of seeing what was under her nose, she'd been flattered by his jealousy – proud of his prowess – proud too to be part of a family that was both feared and respected in the area. When they had married, everything had been wonderful at first, but after only two months, George had changed. His violence turned on her, but it was her own fault, she knew that, finding out the hard way not to question him when he came home late without explanation.

Linda heaved again, her head swimming. She felt awful, and longed for her mother's arms. Tears threatened and she gulped, deciding that as soon as she felt better, she'd go to see her parents. George wouldn't like it. If he found out, she'd probably get another smack, but it had been weeks since she had last seen her mum and she missed her so much.

At last, feeling marginally better, Linda made her way inside. She still felt nauseous, unsure if she could make it to her mother's house, but maybe she could pop next door to have a word with Ivy. She'd had two children, so might know something that could settle this dreadful morning sickness.

Of course Sue and Norma had children too, but Linda knew that Ivy would be the most sympathetic. When she had first moved into Drapers Alley, it was Ivy who made her welcome, and nowadays they often had a gossip over a cup of tea. So far she hadn't told Ivy how violent George was becoming, but with only thin walls between them, she felt sure that the woman already knew. Maybe she should bring the subject up, confide in her. Ivy was vitriolic in her dislike of most of the brothers, with the exception of Chris, but so far they had never discussed George.

Linda went upstairs where she took off her night-clothes before stepping into a skirt. With nothing else clean, she pulled a creased blouse out of the ironing basket, but the garments had piled up, several spilling over the side and onto the floor. Her stomach flipped again, and ignoring the mess, she fled down-stairs, one hand over her mouth as she headed again for the outside toilet.

When George reached the yard he was surprised to find it locked. All right, he was a bit late, but surely the old man could have waited. With a tut of im-patience he pulled out his keys.

There was the sound of raised voices as George went inside, but as he stepped into the office, all went quiet for a moment before his father's voice rang out.

'Where the bloody hell have you been?'

'Sorry, Dad. Linda's got morning sickness and I couldn't leave her.'

'Morning sickness? That's no excuse. Your mother had that and it's nothing to worry about.'

George wasn't going to admit that he'd overslept,

so creasing his face into an expression of worry he said, 'Linda was really rough, Dad.'

'Yeah, well, there's no need to get upset. It'll soon pass and she'll be fine.'

George nodded. 'Have I missed much?'

'You've just missed your brother telling the others that he wants to peddle child porn.'

'Oh, right. Is there a lot of money in it, Danny?'

'Yeah, a mint, but it's been vetoed.'

'Why's that?'

A chair went back, crashing onto the floor as Dan reared to his feet. 'Why's that?' he screeched, face red and eyes bulging. 'For fuck's sake, ain't it obvious?'

Despite this display of temper, George scratched his head, unable to understand what was upsetting his father. His eyes swept over Bob, Maurice and Chris, noticing for the first time that they looked none too happy. 'Can someone tell me what's going on?'

It was Chris who answered. 'Danny wants us to go into hard porn. We're fine with that. Adult movies are acceptable, but not ones using kids.'

Out of the corner of his eye, George saw his father sit down again and finally cottoned on that he had better tread carefully. Danny might be for the idea, but it seemed the others were against. 'Yeah, well, I suppose I can see why. It'll be bad enough if the Vice Squad catches us making hardcore films with adults, but if they find kids we could be in the shit – big time.' George's eyes shot to his father, seeking approval, but instead saw him shaking his head with disgust.

'You're as bad as Danny,' he growled. 'We've agreed to the other stuff, but now I ain't so sure.'

Confused, George looked to Danny, and it was he who spoke.

'Dad, listen, as I said there's a mint to be made if we up the ante. Maurice has pointed out that we've reached saturation point with the soft stuff so an increase in profits is unlikely. Yes, we're doing all right, but if you want your early retirement we need to give the other stuff a try.'

'Oh, so it's for my benefit, is it?' asked Dan, his voice dripping with sarcasm.

'We'll all benefit, Dad. We could make a fortune.'

Dan's eyes swept over the others before settling on Maurice. 'Well, you're the brains of the family so what do you think?'

'I've got a few more questions to ask before I make a decision.'

Dan nodded. 'What about you, Bob?'

'Well, as long as we keep away from child porn, I'm for it.'

There was a low growl from Danny, but then Chris said, 'If everything we do is consensual, then I think we should give it a go.'

Dan's lips pursed. 'And you're willing to risk treading on Garston's toes?'

Again there was silence as each brother pondered, but then Danny said, 'If the worst comes to the worst we can always hire a bit more muscle. Do you want me to have a word with some of the boys at the gym, Dad?'

'No, leave it for now. We won't need it until Garston gets wind of what we're up to, and that's likely to be when we start distribution.'

'So it's on then?'

Dan exhaled loudly. 'Maurice still has questions, but yeah, if he's happy with your answers, I suppose so.' He then stood up. 'I'll leave you to go over the finer points. I'm off to the races.'

He didn't say goodbye and, still confused, George looked to Danny, his brother hissing, 'We'll talk later.'

George nodded, and as Danny sat in the chair vacated by their father, he too took a seat, listening to the questions that Maurice raised.

'Have you spoken to the girls and their partners, Danny?'

'No, not yet, but if they don't fancy upping the stakes, we can still use them for soft porn, finding others to take on the hard stuff.'

'They won't be cheap.'

'I've factored that in.'

'And the filming? We use Eddy Woodman now, but he might not fancy the added risks.'

'It's not a problem. I've learned all I need from Eddy, and I've decided to keep this strictly in the family by handling the filming myself. With this kind of operation, the fewer people who know about it *and* where we're based, the better. Bob has proved himself good at editing, so he can take that on. Chris is great with sales so we can continue getting orders and sorting out distribution. George can make up the sets and Maurice can handle the lighting.'

'Will Ivy's old man still do the deliveries?'

'Yeah, but I'll send George out with him just in case there's any trouble.'

'Dad's right,' Maurice mused. 'Garston ain't gonna take this lightly, and he ain't the only one.'

'Fuck them,' Danny snapped. 'There's a market out there, a good one, with room for another crew. All right, we might come across a bit of trouble, but with the money we'll make it's worth the risk. Anyway, as I told Dad, there's plenty of muscle for hire if we want it.'

'That's gonna cost a pretty penny,' Maurice complained.

'Only until we sort Garston out. In fact, if it becomes necessary, I know someone who'll take the bastard out permanently.'

'It may come to that. He's a nasty piece of work and has been known to use shooters.'

Danny shrugged. 'So what? Garston doesn't frighten me and he shouldn't put the shits up you either. Bloody hell, Maurice, we're the Drapers. We're feared – maybe not as much as Garston, but we can soon put that right.'

'Yeah, Danny,' said George. 'In fact, if Garston tries anything I'll take the fucker out myself.'

'That's more like it,' Danny said, smiling with approval. 'There speaks a Draper.'

George was gratified by Danny's remark. He knew he wasn't the brightest of the bunch, but other than Danny, he was the toughest. Maurice was a weakling, and though Bob and Chris could handle themselves in a fight, they didn't have the killer instinct. He'd been around them during punch-ups, and it was usually left to him to put the final boot in, something he had no qualms about doing. His neck stretched, pride in his stance. If anyone wanted to mess with the Drapers they'd have to take the consequences, and that included Jack fucking Garston.

'All right, Danny,' Maurice said. 'I'm in. Does that still go for the rest of you?'

George grinned as one by one his brothers nodded. It had been too quiet lately. The business had been chugging along nicely so it had been a while since he'd had a chance to use his fists. Now, though, things were looking up.

One by one they left, until just he and Danny remained in the office.

There was still something puzzling George. 'I still don't get it, Danny. Why did they veto child porn?

Was I right about the Vice Squad? Is that why they turned you down?'

'No, you silly sod. They don't like the idea of using kids.'

'But you said there's a lot of money in it.'

'Yeah, there is. Never mind. I'll bide my time. Dad's going soft, getting past it, and the sooner he retires the better.' Danny's smile was assured. 'When he does, who do you think will be running the show?'

George scratched his head, but then the answer dawned on him. 'You, Danny, you'll be the boss.'

'Yeah, that's right – with you as my right-hand man.'

'What about Bob? Surely he's next in line to you.'

'No, I don't trust the two-faced bastard. When I run the show there'll be changes – big ones – and I'll need you to back me up.'

'What sort of changes, Danny?'

'For one, what I say goes. There'll be no more bloody votes, and if anyone doesn't like it, they'll be out.'

'You won't be able to do that. The others won't stand for it.'

'Can you really see Bob, Maurice or Chris going up against me?'

'Well, I dunno. Chris might.'

'Not if I've got you on my side, George. He wouldn't fucking dare – none of them would. Now are you with me or not?'

George floundered. There was too much to process and his brain couldn't take it in. Yeah, Dad was sure to retire soon with Danny next in line, but surely it would still be a family business? 'I don't see how you'll be able to make these changes, Danny.'

'I'll make them, you can be sure of that. Be warned, though. If you ain't for me, you're against me.' His eyes narrowed menacingly. 'Do you really fancy taking me on?'

'No, Danny, I'm with you,' George said. He might not be the brainbox of the family, but he knew better than to go up against Danny.

'Good, now come on, let's get out of here. One more thing, George, keep this conversation to yourself. As I said, we've got to bide our time until Dad retires, but when he does . . .' Danny tailed off.

'Don't worry, I know when to keep my mouth shut,' said George as he followed Danny outside. 'I'm off to have a pint. What about you?'

'No, I've got things to do.'

'Oh, right, do you want me to come with you?'

'Sorry, mate, but what I've got in mind only takes two.'

Confused, George said, 'But if I come with you, there'd only be the pair of us.'

Danny chuckled. 'You daft bugger. Yeah, what I've got in mind takes two, but one of them is female.'

'Oh . . . oh, right, I get it.' But as Danny locked the gates, George added, 'What about Yvonne?'

With a wink, Danny said, 'What the eye doesn't see, as the saying goes.'

'You jammy bastard,' George grinned.

He watched as his brother walked away, struck by a thought. If Danny could have a bit on the side, then so could he. Yeah, why not? The next time Linda was too ill, or when her belly was too swollen for a bit of nooky, he'd go on the pull.

Chapter Six

Ivy Rawlings, formerly Draper, scowled as she looked around her living room. This was number six, the last house in the row, and she hated the interior. Money was tight and her battered furniture was second-hand, the surface of her sideboard badly scratched. Unlike her Uncle Dan and Aunt Joan, Ivy had few luxuries and resented it. She *did* have a bathroom, so felt superior to George and Linda, who lived next door in number five, but Ivy had waited over three years to get it. No doubt George, being a precious son who'd been married less than a year, would get preferential treatment, with an extension built soon.

Her lip curled and she took her anger out on Steve, her husband. 'I hear they're having a meeting at the yard. Why aren't you there?'

'I wasn't invited. Anyway, it's my day off.'

'Day off! Leave it out. The yard closes at one o'clock so it's only half a day. You're a mug to put up with it,' Ivy said, shaking her head at her husband's stupidity. 'Do you know what the meeting's about?'

'No.'

Ivy bristled. Getting anything out of Steve was like trying to get blood out of a stone, but she wasn't ready to give up yet. 'Are they planning a job?'

'Leave it out. Your uncle hasn't touched a safe in years.'

'They're up to something. I can feel it in me water. Come on, you must know what's going on.'

'I don't, and even if I did, I know when to keep my mouth shut.'

'Don't give me that. You don't like my relatives, so why the loyalty?'

'It ain't loyalty, you silly cow. It's more like self-preservation.'

'Bloody hell, Steve, you can tell me. I ain't about to blab.'

'Blab about what? For Gawd's sake, Ivy, I've been working for your uncle for less than a year so I'm as much in the dark as you are. I prefer it that way too. I'm happy just working in the yard and doing deliveries.'

'Yeah, but compared to the boys you get paid peanuts. It ain't right, Steve. You do twice as many shifts as them. In fact, they hardly show their faces at the yard, so what do they get up to?'

'I dunno, but I ain't complaining.'

Ivy saw the shifty look in her husband's eyes and wasn't fooled. He knew something, she was sure of it. He'd been a totter when she met him and it had taken her years to persuade Uncle Dan to give him a job in the family firm. Steve should thank her, but instead of telling her what they were up to he'd become as secretive as the rest of the male members of the family. She knew that at only five feet tall Steve was the butt of their jokes and, like her, he was no oil painting. He was thickset, and his lack of neck made his head appear to sit on his wide shoulders. On top of that, his legs were slightly bowed, due to malnutrition as a child. He had nice eyes, though, deep green and fringed by long, dark lashes.

The sound of a ball banging repeatedly against the wall made Ivy's chin jut. She rushed to the back door, throwing it open. The culprit was Ernie, her elder son, seven years old and football mad.

'Pack it in!' she yelled. 'If you want to play with that ball, go to the park.'

'Can I go too, Mummy?' five-year-old Harry pleaded.

'Yeah, bugger off, the pair of you. And you, Ernie, make sure you hold your brother's hand when you cross the road.'

They scuttled off and Ivy heaved a sigh of relief, glad of the peace. But no sooner had the boys disappeared than there was a knock on the door. 'Christ, what now?' she complained.

Steve opened it. 'Watcha, Linda, come on in.'

'Hello, love, you look a bit rough,' Ivy observed.

'I'm sorry to bother you, Ivy, but do you know of anything that can ease this morning sickness?'

Before Ivy could answer Steve said, 'I'm just popping down to your Aunt Joan's.'

'What for?'

'Dan wants me to fix a catch on one of their windows.'

'Oh, so now you're his handyman too. Huh, so much for your day off. I wanted you down at the allotment. You ain't touched it for ages and it's running wild with weeds.'

'Don't start. Fixing the catch won't take a minute.'

'Oh, just bugger off,' Ivy said, glad to see the back of him. No sooner had the door closed than she turned to Linda, her bad mood lifting at the thought of a good old gossip with the only person who seemed to like her in the alley. 'Sit down, love. I'll make us a nice cup of tea.'

'Thanks, Ivy, but I doubt I'll be able to keep it down.'

'You poor cow. I was the same with my first pregnancy. There ain't much you can do about it, but don't worry, it usually only lasts for the first three months. How about a couple of dry biscuits? That usually helps a bit.'

'I'll try anything. I was hoping to pop round to my mum's, but if this sickness doesn't pass I won't get to the end of the alley before throwing up again.'

Ivy bustled into the kitchen and found a few cream crackers, which she put on a plate. With a pot of tea made she poured two cups, placing the lot on a plastic tray to carry back into the small living room.

'Here, get that down you,' she urged. 'How is it going with George? Is he still unhappy about the baby?'

Linda sighed as she picked up a cracker, taking a tentative nibble before laying it down again. 'Things are no better and this morning sickness doesn't help. I was so bad this morning that he had to leave without any breakfast.'

'Oh dear, poor George,' Ivy drawled, her voice dripping with sarcasm. 'He ain't a cripple and could have made himself a couple of bits of toast.'

'George never does anything in the kitchen. He says cooking and cleaning are woman's work.'

'Most men are the same, but if I'm feeling rough, Steve will muck in. He'll even have a go at cooking something simple. Anyway, changing the subject, do you know what this meeting at the yard's about?'

'No, in fact I didn't know there was a meeting. George never discusses the business with me.'

'If you ask me, there's something in the wind. I reckon they're planning a job. It's been ages since they've done one.'

Linda blanched. 'A job! What do you mean?'

'Surely you're not *that* naïve. You must know what sort of family you've married into.'

'Well, I heard rumours, but George told me that nowadays they're just builders' merchants.'

'Really? So you think the business makes enough to pay the wages for six households, do you?'

Linda's brow creased. 'I . . . I hadn't given it a lot of thought, but it's a big yard, so yes.'

'It might be big, but you can't tell me it takes seven men to run it. My Steve does most of the shifts and I'd give my right arm to know where the others disappear to every day. I've tried asking Steve, but he won't tell me anything. Why don't you see what you can get out of George?'

'Oh, no, I couldn't do that! George would go mad if I start asking questions.'

Ivy didn't envy Linda her husband. She'd heard the rows next door, and suspected that George wasn't slow in giving Linda a slap or two. 'Yeah, I've heard him doing his nut.'

'George was lovely when we first got married, but lately, he . . . he's given me a few clouts. I'm scared for my baby, Ivy, and I don't know what to do.'

'Sort him out. Nip it in the bud.'

'I wish I could, but I don't know how.'

'It's simple. If George tries to hit you again, pick up the nearest heavy object, such as a frying pan, and bash him over the head with it.'

'Oh, no, Ivy, I couldn't do that. I'm not strong like you.'

'You don't need strength to bash him with a frying

pan. Men who hit women are bullies. The only way to deal with George is to give him a dose of his own medicine. Once he knows you'll fight back, he'll soon back off.'

'Do you really think so?'

'Take my word for it, love. Now come on, cheer up. Things will look up once you've sorted George out, and you'll soon be over this morning sickness.'

For the first time Linda smiled. She picked up the cracker again, and finished it in no time, washing it down with a gulp of tea. 'My goodness, I've managed to keep it down,' she said.

'That's the ticket. You should be able to pay your mum a visit now.'

With a little colour in her cheeks at last, Linda rose to her feet. 'Thanks, Ivy. I think I'll go and tidy myself up and then I'll do just that. It feels like ages since I've seen my mum and I really miss her. My dad too.'

Linda wasn't the only one, Ivy thought, as she showed the girl out. She missed her parents too. Her father had been Uncle Dan's younger brother, but he'd been killed during the war. She and her mother had been grief-stricken, but Uncle Dan had taken them under his wing, continuing to support them until her mother died. Oh, yes, nice Uncle Dan, kind Uncle Dan – or so everyone thought. Ivy knew better.

At twenty-three years old she had married Steve,

pretending to be grateful when Uncle Dan had secured them the tenancy of this house. Her eyes darkened with hate. She wasn't grateful, why should she be? Not when she suspected the truth. Of course she couldn't prove it, but her resentment had festered until it became an obsession. Oh, she'd make him pay – somehow – someday, she'd find a way. Until then she had to be content with stirring things up, causing mischief for the family at every opportunity.

With a thin smile Ivy consoled herself with the thought that she had a bit of information now. George had been hitting Linda, something that would upset her aunt and put the cat amongst the pigeons. She hated the way her aunt wanted for nothing – the way Uncle Dan called her 'Queen'. Her own mother should have been equally well off, but instead had suffered the humiliation of Uncle Dan's so-called largesse.

Ivy made for number one, looking forward to wiping the smile off her aunt's face.

With a Woodbine between his lips, one eye shut as the smoke curled upwards, Steve Rawlings endeavoured to ease paint-encrusted screws out of the window frame. Joan was bustling about as usual – the woman never stood still. He could hear the thump, thump of Petula's record player, but at least the music was a bit muted since Joan had told the girl to close her bedroom door.

He'd been glad to get away from Ivy's questions, worried that one day she'd wear him down and he'd blurt out the truth. Like Ivy, he didn't have a lot of time for the Draper boys – well, except Chris, who was always friendly – and he was shit scared of Danny and George.

Ivy had talked him into joining the family business, wearing him down with her nagging. They might be better off, but in truth he hated working for Dan Draper. He'd started at the yard and it hadn't been a bad job, until after only a few months he'd been roped into the other stuff.

He'd been happier as a totter, his own man, riding the streets with his horse and cart, picking up scrap from households all over the borough. He may not have made a lot of money, but he'd never been frightened – not the gut-wrenching churning in his stomach he now felt every time he took out a delivery of the shit that the Drapers turned out. He dreaded getting stopped by the police, dreaded a vehicle search, knowing that if and when it happened, he'd have to take the fall. There was no way he'd dare implicate the Drapers – not if he wanted to stay alive.

His lips tightened. Of course, Ivy had no idea that the Drapers produced porn. The daft cow still thought they made their money from the yard, with a bit of thieving thrown in. Ivy still had her suspicions, of course, but there was no way he could tell her the truth, not when Dan had made it clear what would happen if he did. With a sigh he continued working on the catch, but then scowled when Ivy knocked on the door before sticking her head inside.

'Hello, Auntie Joan. Can I come in?' she called.

'I suppose so, but I'm up to my eyes at the moment,' Joan replied from the kitchen, her tone making it obvious she resented the interruption.

Ivy ignored the rebuff and Joan came fully into the room, wiping her hands on her apron as she said, 'I'm cleaning out my cupboards. Everything's upside down.'

'I won't stay long. I just popped down to see how Steve's getting on.'

'I'm nearly finished,' Steve said, annoyed to think that Ivy was checking on him, but when she spoke again he realised the truth of her visit.

'I hear there's a meeting at the yard, Auntie Joan,' Ivy said. 'Do you know what it's about?'

'No,' Joan said shortly, adding as an afterthought, 'why don't you ask your husband?'

'He doesn't know either, do you, Steve?'

'No, I don't,' he said, wishing his wife would leave. His muscles tensed with nerves, hoping she wasn't up to mischief as usual. His hopes died when she spoke again.

'I've just had Linda round to see me, Auntie Joan. The poor girl looks dreadful. She's got morning sickness, but worse, your George has taken to giving her a clout or two.'

Joan paled. 'Did she tell you that?'

'Yes. I think the girl needed someone to confide in, but even if she hadn't, I ain't deaf and can hear a lot through the walls.'

Steve twisted the last replacement screw into place, wanting only to be away from this conversation. Ivy was stirring again – something she took great pleasure in doing – yet he was at a loss to know why. Like him, she had no love for the Drapers, so why the bloody hell had she accepted a house in the alley?

'Right, the job's done and I'm off,' he said loudly.

Neither woman acknowledged him as he scurried out. One of these days Ivy would go too far and he dreaded the consequences. Dan Draper would never take it out on his niece and instead would get Danny or George to take it out on him. He had seen some of their handiwork and the thought made his guts churn.

Joan hardly heard the door as it closed behind Steve. She kept her gaze fixed on Ivy and fought to hide her dislike of Dan's niece, but knew she was failing as usual. There was no family resemblance, and Joan wondered how Dan's brother had produced such an ugly offspring – one with an ugly personality to match. The young woman seemed to enjoy causing her discomfort, taking every opportunity to make trouble.

Even as a child, Ivy had been sly. She could understand Dan helping both mother and child out when his brother had been killed during the war, but was at a loss to understand why he continued to help Ivy when she became an adult. The last house in the row should have been earmarked for Chris, a home for him when he decided to marry, but instead Dan had tipped up money to someone at the council for Ivy to move in with her husband. Not only that, he had gone on to give Ivy's husband a job in the firm.

'I reckon you should give George a talking-to, Auntie Joan. It ain't right that he's hitting that poor girl.'

Joan, doubting the truth of Ivy's story, ground her teeth together. 'I think you must have got the wrong end of the stick. George wouldn't hit his wife.'

'Ask Linda herself if you don't believe me.'

'Oh, I will, you can be sure of that,' Joan snapped. 'Now if you don't mind, I've got work to do.'

'All right, I'm off,' Ivy said, a false look of concern on her face before she turned to leave. 'I hope I haven't upset you, Auntie Joan, but I thought you should know what George has been up to.'

Joan made no comment, but as the door closed behind Ivy, she raised a shaky hand to rub it across her forehead, still unable to believe that George was hitting his wife. She knew that Dan had once been a criminal, and that as they grew up he had roped the boys in, yet he was also a gentleman, bringing the boys up to respect women. Dan might rule her, but he had never laid a finger on her and certainly wouldn't stand for the lads laying into their wives.

Dan had protected them all, yet in the past her nerves had been shattered by the police raids. Dan had laughed at her worrying, telling her they were too clever to get caught, but the only way she had been able to cope was to bury her fears behind a barrier of indifference, all her energies focused on her home. Of course, nowadays they were respectable, running a family business, and thank goodness she no longer had anything to worry about. At least she hoped so, but still she sensed that something was going on, and fear fluttered like a tiny bird against her ribcage.

Joan scuttled to the kitchen. Was Ivy telling the truth? Was George really hitting his wife? With gritted teeth she tackled the cupboards again, trying to force her worries to one side as she vigorously attacked a stain that had dared to appear on one of the doors.

At last, with her emotional barriers in place again, Joan calmed down. She would do what she always did when there were signs of trouble within the family. She'd leave it for Dan to sort out.

*   *   *

Petula switched off her gramophone, returning the record to its sleeve. She moved to the mirror, gazing with displeasure at her reflection. Unlike lots of girls in her class at school, she had hardly any bust, her figure still gangly and boyish. She had hoped that when her periods started a figure would follow, but no such luck.

With a swift look over her shoulder, Petula picked up her satchel, groping under her school books until she found the hidden tube of lipstick. If her dad knew she had it, he'd go mad, but with him out, and Mum busy as usual, she risked smearing some on her lips.

Petula's head cocked to one side. Yes, she looked marginally better, but longed to be glamorous, with a bust like Bob's wife, Sue. Her expression saddened. In truth, her figure and build was more like Yvonne's, a woman that she didn't want to emulate. Yvonne was too skinny, and though she dressed well, her clothes were plain. Sue, on the other hand, wore full skirts and close-fitting jumpers, or tight dresses that clung to her waist and ended just below her knees. Her make-up was bold, skilfully applied, and with this thought Petula wiped off the lipstick before lightly running downstairs.

'Mum, I'm just popping along to see Sue.'

There was only a grunt in reply, but Pet was used to this – used to her mother's distant manner and lack of affection. She also knew that her mother disapproved of Sue and thought she was a tart, but Pet liked her.

In no time she was outside, giving Sue's letter box a rap before poking her head inside. 'Hello, can I come in?'

'Of course you can,' Sue said, but unusually there wasn't a smile on her face.

'Is something wrong?'

'Nah, not really, it's just that I've had a falling-out with Norma. Honestly, I don't know who she thinks she is, but she's getting as uppity as Yvonne.'

'What did you fall out about?'

'She was really nasty to my Robby. The poor kid thought rabbits could fly and launched Shaker. All right, it was a daft thing to do, but he didn't mean to hurt the bloody thing.'

Petula hid her thoughts. Robby was her least favourite nephew, the boy already a bully who picked on his brother and cousins mercilessly. There had been many occasions when she had seen the kids playing outside, and it was always Robby who was the troublemaker, with one of the others usually running home crying. Ivy's boys had taken to staying out of Robby's way, and she didn't blame them, but now, acting the role of peacemaker, Pet said, 'Never mind. You know how protective Norma is of Oliver. I'm sure she'll come round.'

'I don't bloody care if she doesn't. Oh, sod it, forget Norma. How are you doing, love?'

'I'm fine, but I wanted to ask if you'd show me how to put make-up on.'

'Leave it out, Pet. Your dad would go mad.'

'He doesn't need to know.'

'You'll never be allowed to wear it.'

'Not now, maybe, but I'll be fifteen in December and leaving school. It would be nice to know how to apply make-up for when I start looking for a job.' Pet held her breath, hoping that Sue would agree. There were girls at school who already wore powder and lipstick when they went out, and she'd been invited to join three of them at the local youth club that evening. She wanted to go, but couldn't face the embarrassment of being met by one of her brothers. Oh, why couldn't her dad see that she was old enough to walk herself home?

'With the way you speak, I expect you'll be going for an office job, but even when you leave school, I can't see your dad letting you wear make-up.'

'I didn't try hard enough to pass my eleven plus, so I doubt I'll get an office job. I hated it when Dad sent me for elocution lessons too, but now realise they might help. I'm thinking of applying for a job in an upmarket shop, you see, perhaps in Knights-bridge.'

'Good idea, but you'll have to look the part too and a bit of slap would make all the difference. Mind you, I still think your dad won't stand for it.'

'I'm sick of being overprotected, Sue. I'm not a

child now and I'm determined to have it out with him.'

'Well, rather you than me, but all right, I'll show you how to apply make-up. The kids have gone out to play so we've got the place to ourselves for a while. Just make sure you keep it to yourself, and you'll have to wash it off before you leave.' With her head cocked to one side, Sue studied Pet's face. 'With your looks, I reckon you could be a model. I always wanted to be an actress, and you could even try that.'

'Oh, no, I'd be too shy to go on stage. I didn't know you wanted to be an actress. What stopped you?'

'Marriage and kids. Oh, don't get me wrong, I love Bob, but having kids has ruined my figure.'

'No, surely not? I'd love to have a figure like yours.'

'Leave it out, Pet. My boobs have drooped something rotten.'

Sue got out her make-up bag and Pet smiled with delight, amazed at the array of cosmetics. There was panstick, face powder, eye shadows and lipsticks.

'Right, let's get on with it,' said Sue.

To begin, Pet was shown how to apply foundation, followed by powder and blusher. When it came to eye make-up, Pet found it harder than she'd expected. She spat on the block of mascara before coating the small brush, but when she tried to apply it to her lashes, the brush went into her eye. 'Ouch!' she cried, her eyes streaming.

'Don't rub it!' Sue cried. 'Dab it. Oh, blimey, too late – now you look like a bleedin' clown. Wash it off, love. We'll have to start again.'

Now that the stinging had eased, Petula had to laugh. It was true, with black mascara ringing her eyes, she did look funny. She rose to her feet, still giggling as she went to the bathroom, but the make-up was hard to get off, her eyes now stinging with soap.

At last, with the last vestiges of mascara removed, Petula was rubbing her face dry when she heard voices. She hung the towel on the rack, leaving the bathroom to find that Bob was home.

'Hello, Pet,' he said, but then frowned. 'Your eyes look red. Have you been crying?'

Pet felt a blush stain her cheeks and stuttered, 'No . . . no, of course not.'

'Are you sure you're all right?'

'Yes, I'm fine,' and grasping for a change of subject, she blurted, 'You're home early. I thought there was a meeting at the yard.'

'It was a short one.'

'What was it about?' she asked.

'It was nothing,' Bob said dismissively.

'You all had to be there, so it must have been something.'

'We're just thinking of expanding, that's all.'

Petula had no interest in the business, but her tactics had worked. Sue had now shoved the make-up back into the large satin bag, and thankfully Bob hadn't put two and two together. She loved all of her brothers, but they were overprotective, just like her father, and still treated her like a child. If any of the locals so much as gave her a funny look, they would rush to sort them out, so much so that over the years she had learned to keep her mouth shut. She thought that this would help her find friends, but it only made things worse and she was more avoided than ever.

The door flew open and Paul ran in, with Robby close behind. 'Dad,' he cried, throwing his arms around his father's leg, 'Robby kicked me.'

'Did he now?' said Bob, his eyes hardening as he looked at his elder son.

'Yes, and that's not all he's done,' Sue complained. 'He's been bloody murder all morning. First he nicked Paul's gobstopper and then when we went round to see Norma, he nearly killed Oliver's rabbit.'

'How did he do that?'

When Sue told him, Bob's face flushed with anger. 'You're old enough to know better, you little sod,' he said, raising his hand.

Petula said a hasty goodbye. Robby was going to be punished, and she didn't want to be around to witness the scene, even though he deserved it. 'I'll see you later,' she called, but had barely closed the door when she heard Robby's yelp of pain. With a wry expression she returned to number one, sure that the boy's backside would be sore for the rest of the day.

Petula found her mother still cleaning. The day stretched ahead, but worse was the thought of missing the dance at the youth club. Oh, she wanted to go, she really did, but not with one of her brothers turning up to escort her home. Her lips thinned, determined once again to have it out with her father when he came home.

Chapter Seven

Maurice walked home from the yard with Bob, the two of them discussing Danny's proposition. He was regretting his decision to go along with the plans, worried about the repercussions of treading on Garston's territory. As a child he had suffered from one illness after another, his school attendance patchy between bouts of asthma or conjunctivitis. When he'd been well enough to attend school, his brothers had protected him when there was any sign of trouble in the playground, encircling him and taking on anyone who wanted a fight.

He loved mathematics and had dreamed of becoming an accountant, but with so much time off school he had failed his exams. Things hadn't changed when he became an adult. His brothers still enjoyed a good fight but Maurice kept out of it, preferring to stay at home with his nose in books. He'd taken on the accounts for the family business and had once attended night school to gain qualifications, but his ambitions had been thwarted again when illness caused him to miss too many classes. Maurice pursed his lips. At least his role in the family business gave him a measure of respect with his brothers.

Maurice had stopped off at the newsagent's, and now paused before going into his house, hoping his wife was in a good mood. He was tired of Norma's nagging to leave Drapers Alley, unable to make her understand that without proper qualifications he would be hard-pressed to find a well-paid job. At the moment they enjoyed every comfort, and though the house was small, the council rent was low, enabling him to add regularly to their savings. One day he hoped to buy his own property, and to that end he had no intention of leaving the family firm. He just wished Norma would stop her constant carping. He knew she didn't get on with his mother, the old girl disgusted that Norma was already pregnant when they married. Yes, his mother was a prude, but if Norma tried harder, he was sure they could get on.

Maurice quietly opened the door. Unlike his brothers, he hadn't enjoyed much success with women and Norma had been only the second girl he'd taken out. At twenty, he'd still been a virgin, shocked and gratified when his fumbling attempts with Norma had been allowed to go all the way. Of course he hadn't been prepared, so Oliver had followed six months after their marriage, much to his mother's disgust. All right, Norma was older than he, but he didn't regret marrying her, and when he was up to it, they still had a good sex life – something he would rarely have enjoyed if he'd stayed single.

'Hello,' he said, walking to the kitchen, but one look at Norma's face made him wish he'd stayed out. 'What's up?'

'It's that bloody child next door. He threw Oliver's rabbit against the wall and it's a wonder he didn't kill it.'

'I suppose you mean Robby.'

'Of course I mean Robby. The boy's a menace, but Sue didn't even punish him.'

'Do you want me to have a word with Bob?'

Both then heard the sound of yelps through the thin adjoining wall and at last Norma smiled. 'Judging by that racket, I don't think it'll be necessary. If I'm not mistaken it sounds like the boy's getting a lathering.'

'Well, there you go then. Now, where's Oliver?'

'He's in the yard, no doubt checking on Shaker again. It really upset him, Maurice, and I'm just about sick of Robby's behaviour. Every time he shows his face there's trouble, but it got up Sue's nose when I told him off.'

'You can't blame her for that, love. It's up to her to sort Robby out – not you.'

Norma's eyes glinted with anger. 'So, you're taking

Sue's side as usual. Pretty Sue – sexy Sue. She's only got to bat her eyelashes and you go all aquiver.'

Experience had taught Maurice that there was only one way to deal with Norma when jealousy reared its head. He moved forward, pulling her into his arms. For a moment she was stiff, but as his lips kissed her neck, he felt the familiar tremble. 'There's only one woman who makes me go aquiver, love, and that's you,' he whispered. 'How about we pop upstairs?'

'Oh, Maurice, we can't. Oliver's only in the yard.'

'I'll just have to wait until tonight then,' he murmured, still nibbling at her neck. Norma might not be a beauty, but she didn't have a bad figure and he loved her long, auburn hair. A tent was forming in his trousers and, pressed against him, Norma could feel it, he was sure. 'See, it's you who turns me on,' he said huskily.

'Oh, get off me,' she complained, but Maurice could feel that the angry tension had left her body. Norma pushed him away, yet a small smile was now visible as she added, 'But as you say, there's always tonight. Now leave me in peace to get on with my housework.'

Maurice released her, and left the kitchen to take a seat in the living room. Taking up his newspaper, he scanned the pages. His imagination had been captured by a story that had appeared towards the end of April and he was hoping to read more about it. An American rocket had successfully reached the far side of the moon, but the mission to take television pictures of the lunar surface during the landing had been a washout when the internal power of the spacecraft failed. There was nothing further on the story and he felt a twinge of disappointment. The earlier rocket, launched in January, had missed the moon entirely, so surely actually reaching the moon's surface deserved a bit more coverage? What was the matter with journalists? Didn't they realise that one day this could lead to men actually walking on the moon? He shook his head in wonderment at the thought, his imagination fired up as he pondered what they'd find there.

'Hello, Dad.'

Maurice looked up from the newspaper. 'Hello, son. Is your rabbit all right?'

'Yes, but he seems a bit nervous.'

'After hitting a wall, I think that's to be expected.'

'I don't like Robby.'

As always when he looked at his son, Maurice felt a surge of pride. From the moment the boy had come into the world, he'd watched him like a hawk, fearing he'd pass his weaknesses to his son. Thankfully his fears proved unfounded. Oliver was sturdy, intelligent and a source of joy to both of his parents.

'Robby's your cousin – he's family. Though he's

a bit of a hooligan at the moment, I'm sure he'll grow out of it.'

Oliver didn't look convinced and, in truth, Maurice was doubtful too. Bob may have punished the boy, but nothing seemed to work. He knew his brother thought Oliver a sissy, a boy who wouldn't stand up for himself, but for Maurice it was a blessing. He wanted his son to grow up using his brains rather than his fists. He wanted him to make something of himself, and unlike him, to gain qualifications – something unheard of in the Draper family.

Maurice was glad that Oliver wasn't like Bob's elder son. Robby didn't take after Bob; in fact he was more like George, who had also enjoyed torturing animals as a child. Thankfully he had grown out of it, but a love of violence remained, and he got into a fight at every opportunity. The trouble was, George didn't know when to stop and Maurice feared that one day he'd kill someone. Oh, not with a weapon like Jack Garston. George didn't need that – not when he was capable of doing it with his fists and boots.

Unaware that his brother was thinking about him, George wasn't happy when he walked into a local pub for a lunchtime drink, and it showed, several customers looking at him warily. He'd agreed that he'd back Danny when the time came, but was now wondering if he'd been a bit hasty. It didn't pay to get into their father's bad books, but now that Danny had done just that, anything could happen. Bloody hell, when he retired the old man might even be so annoyed that he'd go over Danny's head, handing the running of the business over to Bob.

Danny had said he'd put his plans into action as soon as he took over, and would get rid of any brother who opposed them. Now, though, George was having doubts. The old man was no fool, and would probably put something in place to make sure it couldn't happen. Their father was a hard man, who always had to be in control. He ruled them with a rod of iron, yet he was fair, and George was sure that he'd take steps to ensure that the business remained a family concern when he stepped down. He might choose one of his sons to run the firm, but he would make sure that they all had equal shares.

Shit, George thought, his face blanching. All that could change if the old man found out about Danny's plans, *and* that he'd been daft enough to back them! Bloody hell, if that happened, they could both be out!

George ran a hand through his hair, grimacing. All this thinking was making his head hurt again. He scowled as he ordered a pint of beer and, obviously aware of his mood, the barman waived payment, sliding the glass nervously across the bar.

George drank deeply, afterwards wiping the back of his hand across his mouth as his eyes roamed the bar. Cigarette smoke hung in the air like fog, and on one table a game of dominoes was in progress. Not one person would give him eye contact and George's tension eased. Yeah, they knew who he was – knew he was a Draper and feared him, something he loved.

At the far end of the room he saw a couple of blokes playing darts so, hoping to put his thoughts about Danny and the business to one side, he walked up to the players. 'I'll give you a game.'

'You'll have to wait,' one of the men said. 'We ain't finished this match yet.'

George's eyes narrowed. He didn't recognise the bloke, but the other's face was familiar. It was Bernie Jackson and his fear was plain to see as he spoke to his mate.

'No, Vince, it's all right,' Bernie said. 'If George wants a game, that's fine. We'll start again.'

'You heard the man,' George snapped, and without further ado he walked up to the scoreboard, erasing the chalked running totals with a cloth.

'Oi! Fuck off! I said we ain't finished our game yet.'

George spun round to see Bernie Jackson grabbing his mate's arm, his voice a hiss of caution. 'Leave it, Vince. Don't you know who he is?'

'I don't give a shit if he's the Pope. He ain't got the right to muscle in on our game.'

This was all the excuse George needed for a fight and a surge of excitement blazed in his eyes. In two strides he was in Vince's face, fists pummelling his nose. Blood spurted everywhere and George loved it, the sight of it – the smell of it. He moved in again, fists raised.

'That's enough, George!'

George spun round to see the publican, Charlie Parkinson. The man was an ex-heavyweight boxer, well past his prime now, but George felt a measure of respect for the man. He was also a friend of his father's, and as George's eyes briefly flicked towards his prey again, he saw that Vince was trembling with fear.

'Huh, he ain't worth the bother. He's just a piece of shit.'

Charlie beckoned Bernie Jackson over, his voice quiet but firm. 'Get your mate out of here, and tell him to keep his mouth shut. Nobody touched him. He just walked into a door. Is that clear?'

'Yeah, as a bell,' Bernie said, then turning to George with a sheepish expression, 'Sorry, mate.'

George just nodded, ignoring Bernie as he urged Vince out of the pub. He snatched up his pint again, peeved that the fight had ended before he'd had time to vent his feelings. The pressure was still there – the feeling that his head was going to burst.

'How's your dad, George? I ain't seen him in a while.'

'He's fine. At Sandown races today and no doubt picking out a few nags to have a bet on.'

'And your mum?'

'She's good too.'

Charlie moved off to serve another customer whilst George leaned on the bar, staring into his pint. It was strange really, but after a fight he always felt randy, and though he'd only landed a few punches, he decided to go home. Linda was sure to be all right now, ready for him to give her a seeing-to. He may have missed out on turning that bastard into mincemeat, but a bit of sex was another way to let off steam.

He swallowed the pint then slammed the glass down as he called, 'See yer, Charlie.'

'Yeah, see you,' Charlie called back, and had George looked over his shoulder as he left the pub, he would have seen the look of relief on the land-lord's face.

Linda's mother smiled with delight as she opened the door. 'Hello, ducks.'

'Hello, Mum, how are you feeling?'

'I'm all right,' Enid Simpson replied. 'The warmer weather makes all the difference.'

Linda followed her mother to the kitchen, the lie evident as her mother hobbled in obvious pain to the nearest chair.

'Is your hip playing you up again?'

Enid dismissed the question. 'Sod my hip. How are you? Have you still got morning sickness?'

'Yeah, but I'm not feeling too bad at the moment.'

'You look tired, love. How is George treating you?'

Linda would have loved to blurt it all out – to tell her mother that she was frightened of her husband – that she feared his fists. Instead she lowered her eyes, knowing that there was no way she could worry her mother. Arthritis riddled Enid's body, her face lined with the daily grind of pain, but she never complained and Linda loved her deeply. She forced a smile. 'George treats me like a princess,' she lied, 'and he's dead chuffed about the baby.'

'Are you telling me the truth, Linda? When you come to see us you're always on your own and your dad was saying the same thing only the other day. We'd visit you, but to be honest, on the one occasion we called, George didn't seem pleased to see us.'

Linda fought for an excuse. 'George is busy, Mum. He works long hours and when he comes home he's worn out. You caught him at a bad time, that's all.'

'He must get some time off. It's Sunday tomorrow. Why don't you both come to us for dinner? Or we could come to you.'

Linda tensed, her thoughts racing. 'It's not a good time at the moment, Mum,' she lied. 'George is doing things around the house and we're all upside down. It's not that he doesn't want to visit you, it's just that he's too busy. He's the same with his mother. They live in the same street but he rarely bothers to pop in to see her.'

Enid acknowledged this with a nod of her head. 'Yeah, when I come to think of it, your father was the same. When my mother was alive I had to practically drag him to see her, and I could see that the whole time he was itching to leave.'

'Would you like me to make a cup of tea, Mum?' Linda asked, anxious to change the subject.

'That'd be nice, love. Your father should be home soon. He'll be pleased to see you.'

Linda was relieved when the conversation turned to the baby, her mother obviously delighted at the prospect of being a grandmother.

'I hope it's a boy,' she said.

'I don't mind what I have, as long as it's all right.'

'Is George's mum pleased about the baby?'

'Well, yes, I think so, but she hasn't said much. In fact, I hardly see her. Dan calls her Queen, and though it's a daft title, she does seem sort of distant and unapproachable.'

'What about your sisters-in-law? How do you get on with them?'

'I don't see much of them either. Yvonne seems a bit stuck-up, and so does Norma. Sue's all right, but to be honest, I prefer Ivy.'

'Ivy! Is she the niece? The one who looks as strong as an ox, with a face to match?'

'Oh, Mum, don't be cruel. I know she isn't much to look at, and the rest of the family don't seem to think much of her, but I think she's kind.'

'Yeah, sorry, love, it just sort of slipped out and as the saying goes, you can't judge a book by its cover. Anyway, back to your mother-in-law, and I'm sure she's nice too. You just need to get to know her, though I must admit she hardly said a word at your wedding. Still, unlike me, this isn't her first grandchild so I don't suppose she's as excited. I just wish my fingers would let me do some knitting, but I can't grip the needles. I made everything for you when you were a baby, and you should have seen the lovely shawl I crocheted . . .'

Enid rambled on, but Linda had heard it all before so hardly listened. As an only child she'd been spoiled, and hadn't appreciated how much love her parents showered on her until she'd left home at twenty to marry George. Before then she had found their love cloying, their expectations of her future restrictive. They had always shown great interest in her boyfriends, wanting her to marry one with prospects and insisting that she invited them home for inspection. Linda smiled ruefully. One boy, a bank clerk, particularly found favour, but he was weak, boring, and she'd resented the way her parents tried to push her into his arms. She had rebelled, breaking up with him to go out with George. Her parents had been horrified, but she wouldn't listen.

George was so different – rough, handsome, and exciting. He hadn't been soft like her other boyfriends, and when he held her in his arms his strength had made her shiver with delight. She had fallen in love with him – still loved him – but now, along with love, there was this awful fear.

'Hello, sweetheart.'

Linda spun round, her eyes lighting up. She ran across the room, throwing herself into her father's arms. She loved her mum, but it was her father who always showed affection, her mother more reticent.

'And how's my girl?' Ron Simpson asked.

'I'm fine, Dad.'

He was a small man, only an inch taller than his wife, their bodies equally thin. His light brown hair was thinning too, but his brown eyes twinkled as he stepped back to look his daughter up and down. 'I can't see any sign of a bump yet.'

'Give it a chance, Dad. I'm only three months gone.'

'Only six to go then,' he said. 'I hope you give me a grandson.'

'You're as bad as Mum,' Linda told him. 'What happens if it's a girl? Are you going to reject a grand-daughter?'

'No chance,' he said.

'Did you get it, Ron?' Enid asked.

'Yes, I did. It's in the hall.'

'I hope you got the right one.'

'Of course I did, woman.'

Enid struggled to her feet, beckoning Linda to follow her. 'We were hoping you'd be down to see us today, and it's just as well. There isn't much room in the hall so you'll need to take it home with you.'

Puzzled now, Linda walked behind her mother, her eyes rounding like saucers when she saw the shiny new carriage pram. The navy-blue, highly polished exterior gleamed, as did the chrome wheels.

'Oh, Mum,' she gasped.

'Now don't get all emotional. It isn't good for the baby,' Enid warned.

'But it must have cost the earth!'

'We want the best for our first grandchild, and other than you, who else have we got to spend our money on?'

'Yourselves,' Linda protested. 'You could have had a holiday with the money you spent on this pram.'

'I can't travel far, love, you know that. Now come on, don't cry. We thought you'd be thrilled to bits.'

'Oh, I am, Mum, I really am,' Linda choked as she dashed the tears from her eyes, 'but you paid out a lot of money for the wedding – and now this!'

'Huh, Dan Draper hardly let us put our hands into our pockets. All we paid for was your wedding dress and the flowers. Your father wasn't happy about it, I can tell you, but Dan Draper had to act the big man.'

'What's up? Don't you like it, sweetheart?' Ron Simpson asked as he joined them in the small hall.

'Of course I do. It's lovely,' Linda cried, her emotions all over the place. Her father's job as a bus conductor didn't pay a fortune and she knew the cost of this gift would have been overwhelming.

'That's all right then,' he said with a wink and a loving smile, 'but haven't you just made a pot of tea? One that's growing cold?'

'Oh, Dad . . .'

They returned to the kitchen where Linda got her feelings under control as she poured the tea. George might return that afternoon so she'd have to go soon, but was suddenly swamped with dread at the thought of leaving her parents' house. Here she was loved and felt safe. All the doubts about her marriage that she'd tried to quell forced themselves to the front of her mind. She was afraid to go home! Oh God, please let George be in a good mood.

Chapter Eight

When George left the pub at two thirty, he arrived home aroused and ready to take Linda upstairs. His brows creased. Where the hell was she?

'Linda!' he yelled.

There was no reply. Swiftly he ran upstairs to the bedroom, but finding it empty his mellow mood began to melt. It didn't take him long to look around the rest of the small house, then he strode next door to rap loudly on Ivy's knocker.

'Is Linda here?' he snapped.

'No, but she was around earlier,' Steve told him.

'Who is it?' Ivy shouted from inside.

'It's George. He's looking for Linda.'

There was a small pause before Ivy's voice rang out again: 'Try your mum's.'

George didn't bother to say goodbye, just turning on his heels to head for number one. He didn't bother to knock and walked in to find his mother on her knees washing the skirting boards.

'Have you seen Linda?' he asked.

Joan pushed herself up, giving him a look that George couldn't fathom. 'I haven't seen the girl, but from what Ivy tells me, your wife isn't too well. Not only that—'

'She's got a bit of morning sickness, that's all,' George interrupted.

As Petula came running downstairs, George asked, 'Have *you* seen Linda?'

'No, sorry.'

George saw Linda walking past the window and swiftly threw open the front door.

'Oi, you! Where have you been?' he shouted.

Linda halted in her tracks, her knuckles white as she gripped the handle of a huge carriage pram.

George moved forward, his eyes narrowed. 'What the bloody hell have you got there?'

Still Linda didn't speak and to George's annoyance his sister joined them.

'Oh, isn't it lovely?' Petula said when she saw the pram.

At last Linda spoke, her voice quivering. 'It . . . it's a present from my mum and dad.'

George's fists clenched. So, she'd been to see her parents, sneaking off without telling him. He couldn't stand Ron and Enid Simpson, the pair of them interfering old busybodies who had made it obvious from the start that they didn't think him good enough for their precious daughter. He'd been determined that once they married he'd make them pay, keeping Linda away from them as much as possible. Now, though, the cow had gone behind his back to pay them a visit.

He eyed the pram, seething. They must think he couldn't provide for Linda, or the coming child. To George it was like a slap in the face, his voice a growl as he said, 'That bloody thing will take up half the house. It's got to go.'

'Oh, no, don't say that,' Linda cried. 'We can keep it in the yard.'

'I said it's got to go!'

'Don't be silly, George,' said Pet. 'I know it's big, but you'll need a pram.'

'Who asked you?' George snapped and turning to Linda again he pointed towards their house. 'Home – now!'

He saw the frightened look that Linda shot towards Petula, but at least she obeyed him, pushing the pram to number five.

As soon as they went indoors, with Linda struggling to manoeuvre the pram through the house to the back yard, George's temper was let loose. He ran ahead of her into the kitchen, opening a drawer to grab the carving knife.

'I told you we don't want the fucking thing,' he yelled as, knife raised, he grabbed the pram, pushing Linda to one side as he sliced at the upholstery, the blade cutting through the material like butter.

Linda's scream was shrill, but George ignored her, the plush grey interior now in ribbons as he continued to slash again and again with the knife.

Pet stood on the pavement, watching George and Linda as they went inside number five. Linda had looked petrified, but surely George wouldn't hurt his wife? Involuntarily she began to walk towards their house, almost at the door when she heard the scream.

For a fraction of a second Pet froze, but then without thought she dashed inside, her eyes widening with horror. 'George! George, stop it! What are you doing? Stop it!'

He turned, the knife raised, and Pet blanched at the manic look on his face. Linda was white-faced too, rooted to the spot, but Pet knew they had to get out of there. She ran forward to grab Linda's arm.

'Come on,' she urged, dragging her outside.

In a few steps they were at Maurice's house. Pet thrust the door open, pushing Linda inside. 'Maurice! Maurice! George has lost it.'

'Yeah, I heard the racket.'

Linda swayed and it was Norma who took over, leading her to a chair. She then ran to fetch a glass of water, urging, 'Here, drink this.'

'What set George off?' Maurice asked as he watched his wife attending to Linda.

'Linda's parents have given her a lovely pram, but for some reason it upset George. I went into their place to find him shredding the inside of it with a knife. We've got to stop him, Maurice.'

Maurice shook his head, his breathing beginning to sound laboured. 'When George is in one of his moods, it's best to leave him to it.'

'But the pram!'

'It's too late to stop him now.'

'Are you all right, Maurice?' Norma asked. 'You're not having another asthma attack, are you?'

Petula had run to the nearest door, but now realised that Maurice would be the last one to intervene. Her father and Danny were out, and that only left Bob, but he wouldn't want to interfere either.

'Pet, take Linda down to your mother's,' Norma ordered. 'George wouldn't dare kick off there.'

Pet could see that Maurice was now gasping for air, but Linda looked awful too, her face deadly white.

'All right, we'll go,' Pet agreed, 'but I'll have to make sure we're in the clear first.'

'Listen, love, I don't want you hurt,' Maurice gasped, 'so be careful.'

Pet gingerly opened the door, stuck her head outside and then beckoned Linda. 'Come on, there's no sign of George.'

Linda looked terrified but rose to her feet. Taking her hand, both of them ran to number one.

Only moments later there was a knock on Maurice's door and he gasped with fear, but it was Bob who walked in.

'I've just seen Pet and Linda dashing past. What's going on?' he asked.

'George is kicking off,' Norma told him. 'Pet brought Linda in here but I told her to take the girl to her own house.'

'Is Pet all right?'

'Yes, but she's frightened of George and I don't blame her.'

'What set him off?'

Norma told him, ending with, 'Your brother's a bloody menace. Linda looked terrified . . . Pet too, and look at Maurice.'

'Not another asthma attack! Come on, Maurice, there's no need to get in a state. You know George. He'll be all right once he's gone off the boil.'

Maurice could only nod, whilst Norma bristled with anger. 'I've had just about enough for one day so he'd better not come knocking on our door. Oh, yes, Bob. Talking of menaces, I suppose Sue told you what Robby did to Oliver's rabbit?'

'Yes, she did, and I've given the boy a thrashing.'

'I'm glad to hear it, but as I've said before, Robby's getting out of hand.'

'Look, I know he's a little sod, but he's had a good hiding. If that doesn't do the trick, I'll come down even harder.'

'It'll need both of you to sort the boy out, but *she* lets him get away with murder.'

'Yeah, I know Sue can be a bit soft. I'll have a word – tell her that Robby needs a firmer hand.'

'Good, I'm glad to hear it,' Norma said, at last looking mollified.

'Norma, can I have a drink, please?' Maurice managed to gasp.

'Yes, all right.'

'Make one for Bob too,' Maurice wheezed, hoping that Bob wouldn't turn it down. He wanted him to stay for a while – wanted him there in case George turned up.

Joan looked up from her task as Petula and Linda almost fell into her living room.

'What's going on?' she snapped.

'It's George. He's gone mad. We ran to Maurice first, but he got upset so Norma told us to come here.'

'Gone mad! What are you talking about?'

'Linda's parents have given them a pram, but George is wrecking it.'

'Is he? Why's he doing that?'

'I don't know, Mum.'

Linda's face was wan, her body shaking. Joan asked sharply, 'Did my son hit you?'

'No . . . not this time.'

'Does that mean he's hit you in the past?'

'Yes,' she whispered, tears spurting and running down her cheeks.

Joan was ashamed of her son, sickened. Linda was pregnant and if George wasn't stopped she could lose the baby. It could be some time before Dan returned from the races, but she had to get Linda out of sight in case George came looking for her.

'It might be best if you stay out of the way for a while. You look exhausted, so why don't you go up to my room, have a lie-down? And don't worry, Dan will sort George out when he comes home.'

Linda's eyes flicked nervously to the window. 'Yes, all right,' she agreed.

Joan waited until she was out of sight before turning to Petula. 'Run next door, see if Danny's home, and if he is, tell him I want to see him. Just make sure that you stay out of George's way.'

Petula nodded, and as the girl ran outside, Joan hoped her eldest son was there. If George hadn't calmed down when he came looking for Linda, she doubted she'd be able to handle him.

Petula's mind was racing. George's behaviour had shocked her. She knew he had a temper, but had never actually witnessed his violence. When George lived at home his anger had been verbal, soon snuffed out by her father. Now, though, she was seeing another side of him, and it was one she feared. Was this how other people saw him?

Was this how he behaved outside of the alley? If so it could be another reason why they were shunned.

As a child Pet could remember the police turning up at the house, but her father and brothers had always explained it away by telling her that they had made a mistake. None of the family had ever been arrested, so she believed them, at least whilst she was at junior school. Doubts set in when she went to secondary school where some girls avoided her, making their reasons clear. When she'd asked questions, Maurice had been the only one who'd been a little more forthcoming, telling her that all the gossip concerned shady deals in the past. Nowadays, he had said, the family ran a respectable business and she had nothing to worry about.

Yet stories still reached her ears – whispers of her family being involved in fights and intimidation. She loved her father, her brothers, and didn't want to believe the gossip, but friendships had been hard to form. Over time there were three girls she considered friends, yet even so she was always the odd one out – the one who didn't enjoy the same freedom as them.

Yvonne's door was unlocked, like the others in the alley, but Pet rapped the letter box before going inside. 'Yvonne, is Danny home?'

'No, he isn't.' Yvonne looked at Pet's anxious face. 'What's wrong?'

'It's George. I'm surprised you haven't heard the racket.'

'I've been turning out the back bedroom so I didn't hear a thing. What's he been up to?'

Pet told her, then added, 'I think Mum's nervous that George will come looking for Linda.'

'I'll come back with you.'

Pet paled as they stepped outside to see George marching towards them. She gripped Yvonne's arm, her heart thumping with fear.

'Is Linda with Mum?' he snapped.

'Er . . . yes, but she isn't feeling well and went to lie down. She's asleep now, but when she wakes up, I'm sure she'll come home.'

'She'd better,' George warned, 'and you can tell her that from me.' With that he brushed past them, ignoring number one to march out of the alley.

'Thank God for that,' Yvonne said.

Pet told her mother what had happened, seeing her own relief reflected on her mother's face.

Joan sank onto a chair, shaking her head as she said, 'It ain't right, Yvonne. I shouldn't be nervous of my own son. Dan will have to sort him out. Ivy told me that he's been hitting Linda, but I didn't believe her. I've heard it from the horse's mouth now, though.'

'Dad has always told the boys that men who hit women are the lowest of the low. When he finds out about George, he'll go mad,' Pet warned.

She saw the women exchange looks, and then her mother said, 'You shouldn't be hearing this, Petula. Go to your room.'

'I'm not a child!'

'You're not an adult either. Now do as I say.'

Pet flung herself out, marched upstairs, and only just resisted the urge to slam her bedroom door. She sat on the edge of her bed, but only a moment later the door opened, Linda coming into the room.

'Oh, Petula,' she cried, moving to sit beside her. 'I . . . I want my mum.'

As Linda sobbed, Petula wrapped an arm around her and, despite what her mother had said, it was she who felt like the adult as she held this frightened young woman in her arms.

Chapter Nine

It was six o'clock and Dan wasn't in the best of moods as he made his way home. Not one of the horses he'd placed a bet on had come in, and he was considerably out of pocket. He had hoped to forget about Danny at Sandown, but he continued to intrude on his thoughts. He still couldn't believe that his son had suggested using kids. He was shocked to the core, and it hadn't helped when George seemed to go along with the idea.

Dan thought he knew his sons inside out – thought he had the business sorted and the future sewn up. When he retired, he'd planned for Danny to take over, but now he'd seen a side of his son that he didn't like and would have to have a rethink.

One by one Dan brought the boys to the front of his mind, starting with the youngest. Chris was a good boy with a keen brain. He had potential, and was able to hold his own in a fight, yet he didn't look for trouble. Yes, a good boy, but too young and, as yet, unsettled.

Next came George, and now Dan scowled. As a father, he knew he should love his sons equally, but with George he found that impossible. From the day the boy had been born Dan had sensed something bad in him. Not only did George lack intelligence, he also had a love of violence, wanting to provoke fights at every opportunity. He'd been forced to come down harder on George than any of the others – but maybe he'd calm down now that he was married and about to be a father. Dan nodded; marriage would be a stabilising influence. George was taking care of his wife, obviously worried about the morning sickness, and it was good to see that he had a softer side. There was still the problem of his intelligence, though, and worse, his lack of morals, making George totally unsuitable to run the business.

Dismissing George from his mind, Dan focused on Maurice. This son was definitely the brains of the family. He was capable of running things on the financial side, but he was weak, often ill, and hopeless when there were any signs of trouble from competitors. There had to be strong leadership and therefore he'd have to dismiss Maurice.

Bob seemed the obvious choice. He was the second eldest and next in line to Danny, but Dan had to dismiss him as successor too. Bob had none of the business acumen needed to run things. He could take orders, yet was incapable of giving them. Like Maurice, he'd be unable to keep the rest of his brothers in line.

Dan's problem was still unresolved as he drove into his garage, and his foul mood worsened when Joan pounced on him as soon as he walked in the door.

'Thank God you're home,' she cried. 'I've been dreading George showing his face before you got here.'

'What are you on about, woman?'

'Linda's upstairs and too frightened to go home. I don't blame the girl, not after what George has been up to . . .'

Dan's face darkened as Joan continued, her hands wringing with nerves. When she finally stopped gabbling, he snapped, 'Why didn't Danny sort him out?'

'I sent Petula to get him but he wasn't in.'

'And Chris?'

'I don't know where he is.'

'What about Bob and Maurice?'

'They didn't show their faces. When George kicked off, Pet dragged Linda into Maurice's house, but Norma sent them here. That's not all. Ivy came to see me this morning and she seemed to gain great pleasure from telling me that George has been hitting Linda. I didn't believe her, but Linda told me it's true.'

'He's what?' Dan thundered. He had no idea why George had shredded the interior of a brand-new pram, but that was nothing compared to laying into his pregnant wife. By God, he wasn't going to stand for that! 'Where's Petula?'

'I sent her upstairs to look in on Linda. The poor girl cried herself to sleep in Pet's arms.'

'Hello, Dad,' said Pet, her expression grim as she came into the room. 'Linda's still asleep, Mum, but I doubt she'll want to go home when she wakes up.'

'She'll have nothing to worry about once I've had a word with George,' Dan assured his wife and daughter.

'Oh, Dad, she was scared stiff. So was I. George was like a madman. He was using a knife on the pram and I was terrified he'd turn it on us.'

At his daughter's words, Dan's anger reached boiling point. He had always protected Pet, making sure that the alley was a safe haven, not just for her, but for all the family. Over the years he and the boys had made it plain that the alley was their domain, using fear and fists if necessary. It had worked and now, apart from Betty Fuller, only the police dared to enter without permission.

Dan's fists clenched. Pet had now been exposed to violence – not from an outsider, but from her own brother. Dan knew George had a temper, and struggled to keep it under control, but now his violence had overspilled into the alley. So much for marriage having a stabilising effect. Instead, with George no longer under his roof, the reverse had happened.

Through clenched teeth he hissed, 'I'll see if he's turned up yet.'

'Dan, your dinner's ready,' Joan called.

'Sod me fucking dinner,' he growled, slamming out of the house and striding to George's door. He found it locked, and hammered the wood with his fists, yelling, 'Open this bloody door!'

'He ain't in, Dad.'

Panting, Dan looked round to see Maurice, then another door opened and Bob appeared. Dan's lips curled in disgust as his sons walked to his side. 'Your sister was terrified and your mother's been going out of her mind with worry. Why didn't you two sort George out?'

Maurice said, 'Leave it out, Dad. You know what George is like when he loses it.'

'You pair of useless tarts! Rather than step in, you left Pet and your mother to face George.'

'No, Dad,' Bob protested, 'I'd have done something if he started on them, but he didn't. He left the alley, and between us we've been keeping an eye out in case he showed up again.'

Dan glared at Maurice. 'According to your mother, Pet brought Linda here, yet Norma couldn't get rid of them fast enough.'

'You can't blame Norma for that. She could see

I was having trouble breathing, and not only that, there's our kid to think about. You know as well as I do what George is capable of when he loses his rag. Do you really think I could have stopped him?'

Dad eyed his son, noting his narrow chest and arms that were a fraction of George's size. 'No, I don't suppose you could have done much,' he admitted. Maurice was a weakling, but there was no excuse for Bob. 'What about you, Bob? Where were you when all this was going on?'

'I was gonna do something, but George buggered off before I got the chance.'

Dan could see the shifty look in his son's eyes and wasn't fooled. If there was a fight Bob would wade in, but only if he had backup, and he always made sure that Danny or George had the front row. 'You could have gone to see if your mother needed any help.'

'When George went off I assumed she was all right.'

'How can she be all right when she's got a maniac for a son? Did the pair of you know that George has been hitting his wife?'

'What!' Bob spluttered. 'No, it's the first I've heard of it.'

'What about you, Maurice? You live next door and must have twigged something.'

'I've heard George yelling, but that's all. I can't believe he'd hit Linda. Are you sure you've got it right, Dad?'

'Yes, I'm sure,' Dan growled. 'Ivy told your mother before all this kicked off and now it's been confirmed by Linda.' He raised a hand to rake his fingers through his hair. Ivy should have come to him instead of upsetting Joan, and the girl knew that. He had hoped that by bringing her to Drapers Alley he could assuage his guilt – that he'd finally be able to let go of the past. But no, it still plagued him. 'Keep an eye out for George,' he told his sons, 'while I go and have a word with Ivy.'

Ivy opened the door to her Uncle Dan and stood to one side to let him in. She had watched the shenanigans in the alley with pleasure, only disappointed when George had stormed off and hadn't come back. Steve had wanted to see if her Auntie Joan was all right, but she had prevented him from going to number one, telling her daft husband that it was for George's brothers to sort out.

Uncle Dan looked upset, and that pleased her. 'You missed out on all the fun, Uncle Dan.'

'Fun! I'd hardly call it that,' he said, his expression hardening. 'I've told you this before, but you haven't listened. You know how bad your aunt's nerves are and that I don't want her worried. Instead of telling her about George, why didn't you come to me?'

'You weren't around and I was more concerned about Linda and the state she was in,' Ivy lied. She then took the opportunity to bait her uncle. 'You should

128

give Auntie Joan a bit more credit. She's stronger than you realise, in fact much stronger than my mother ever was. I know you keep Auntie Joan in the dark about certain things. Did you do the same with my mother?'

He paled, but recovered quickly. 'Of course not. I never had reason to keep anything from your mother.'

'Really?' she drawled. 'Well, my mistake then.' Ivy smiled thinly; sure she could see guilt written all over her uncle's features. Oh, he had kept a big thing from her mother, she was sure of it, and once again she was determined that one day she'd make him pay.

'Yes, well, despite what you think, your aunt isn't strong. As I've said before, I don't want her worried. In future, bring any concerns you have to me.'

Ivy bit her bottom lip, annoyed at her uncle's sharp tone. Her mother hadn't had the privilege of being free from worry, and despite Dan's so-called help, life had still been a struggle. They lived in poverty, while her uncle rose in power, opening a business to make even more money. She wanted to face him with it, but knew it would be a waste of time. He would deny it and she had no proof.

Taking a deep breath to stay calm she said, 'I hope you're going to sort George out.'

'Oh, I will. You can be sure of that.'

When her uncle left, Ivy closed the door. She wanted to see him unhappy – in fact she wanted to see all of the Drapers in misery – just as her mother had been before she died.

Dan marched back to number one, his guts churning. Sometimes he felt that Ivy knew something, but surely it wasn't possible? She'd been just a kid when his brother had been called up.

'Was he in?' Joan asked as he walked inside.

Dan saw Pet sitting at the table and just shook his head. Ivy's snide remarks had added fuel to the flames of his anger. He just wanted George to show his face so he could vent his feelings and as he began to pace the room his eyes returned again and again to the window as he kept a lookout for his son.

'Dan, you've got to calm down,' Joan said, moving to stand in front of him.

'Calm down! I'll fucking kill him,' he yelled, shoving his wife to one side.

As she staggered back, Joan's hip hit the side of the table and she yelped with pain but Dan was unaware of it as he continued to pace. He was also unaware that his daughter had fled upstairs.

Joan moved to stand in front of him again, laying a hand on his arm. 'Dan!' she begged. 'Dan, listen to me. Petula has seen enough for one day without you kicking off too. She saw you shove me and it frightened her. Now she's run upstairs.'

He stared down at his diminutive wife, her voice

penetrating his anger. 'Sorry, Queen. I didn't mean to push you so hard.'

'Yeah, I know that, but I dread to think what will happen if you confront George while you're in this mood.'

Dan knew that Joan was right. Pet had seen enough, yet when George turned up he'd have to sort him out and he doubted he'd be able to control his temper. Thoughts churning, Dan finally came up with a solution. 'Pet, come down here,' he called.

When Pet came downstairs, Dan saw that Linda was behind her. His temper almost overspilled again when he saw how frail his daughter-in-law looked and he had to fight to hide his feeling when he spoke to her. 'How are you, love?'

'I . . . I feel a bit better,' she said.

'Come and sit down, all of you,' Joan urged, and after going into the kitchen, she returned with plates of sausages, onion and mash. Dan was given his first, followed by Linda, Joan saying, 'You've got to eat, love. You're having a baby and need to keep your strength up.'

Dan saw how Linda's eyes flicked nervously to the door. He sat down, leaned across the table and laid his hand over hers. 'Don't worry. Leave George to me. I'll make sure he never touches you again.'

She looked back at him, her face devoid of colour. 'I . . . I'm not going back. I'd rather go to my mum's.'

'Oh, Linda, there's no need for that,' Joan said.

Linda's eyes filled with tears, her voice a wail. 'I want my mum.'

'All right, don't cry,' Dan placated. 'Eat your dinner and then I'll run you to your mother's house.'

'George won't be happy if he comes back to find her gone,' Joan warned as she gave Petula her dinner.

'I don't give a shit how George feels. Anyway, it's best that Linda is out of the way until I sort him out.'

He then turned to Pet, seeing that she was picking at her food too. Forcing a soft tone, Dan put his idea into action. 'Pet, didn't you say you wanted to go to the youth club tonight?'

'Yes, but it doesn't matter now.'

'Don't be daft. When you've finished your dinner, get yourself ready. I can drop you off at the club when I take Linda to her mother's.'

'No, it's all right, I don't want to go.'

'Why not?'

'I don't feel like it, and anyway, the other girls will laugh at me when one of my brothers turns up to escort me home.'

As planned, Dan said, 'All right, you can walk your-self home, but make sure you're in by ten fifteen.'

Pet's eyes widened. Dan knew he shouldn't lie to her, but like Linda, he wanted her well out of earshot when he confronted George. They wouldn't pick Pet up, but just to be on the safe side, she'd be followed home. If Chris showed his face, he'd assign that task to him.

Still Pet hesitated, but Dan urged, 'Come on, eat up, and then get your glad rags on.'

With a nod, Pet ate a little of her dinner. She then pushed her plate to one side before heading for her bedroom whilst Dan turned his attention back to Linda. With her face pale, hands shaking as she half-heartedly forked up a bit of mashed potato, she looked not much older than Pet. His son had a lot to answer for, and if he lost Linda it would be no more than he deserved. Her frailty so touched him that Dan wanted nothing more than to wring George's neck.

Only moments later the door was flung open. Linda gasped in fear, but it was Chris who walked in.

'Where the hell have you been?' Dan snapped.

'I went to Oxford Street to have a look around the shops, and then I had a drink with a mate.'

'You were needed here!'

'Why? What's going on?'

'George needs sorting out,' Dan said, and went on to tell Chris all that had happened.

'Bloody hell,' Chris gasped as his eyes flew to Linda. 'Are you all right?'

'No she bloody well isn't,' Dan growled.

Chris took a seat, picking up his cutlery as his mother laid a plate of food in front of him. 'Where's George now?'

'I dunno, but I'm taking Linda to her mother's. I'll be dropping Pet off at the youth club too.' Dan lowered his voice. 'I want you there when she comes out at around ten, but keep out of sight. I've told her that she can walk home on her own, so just trail her to make sure she's all right.'

'I can't. I've got a date tonight.'

'You'll do as I say.'

'Shit, Dad, can't you ask one of the others to meet Pet?'

'Oi, watch your language. There's ladies present.'

'Sorry, Mum – sorry, Linda.'

'Your father's one to talk. He hasn't stopped swearing since he walked in the door.'

Annoyed at the comment, Dan shot Joan a look, but she ignored him, turning on her heels to walk back into the kitchen. He frowned, wondering what had come over his wife, but then Chris spoke again.

'Dad, this is a first date – I'll look a right mug if I insist on dropping her home before ten.'

Dan pursed his lips, then after a small pause he said, 'Yeah, all right. I'll get Maurice or Bob to meet Pet, but stay in until I get back. George might turn up and I don't want your mother facing him on her own.'

Chris nodded, biting into a sausage with relish. 'I've arranged to meet Julie at eight. You're sure to be back before that.'

'Yeah, I will, and God help your brother when he decides to show his face.'

134

Chapter Ten

Pet stepped into her bedroom and closed the door. She felt that she was seeing her family for the first time, that a veil had been lifted from her eyes. Her brother George had terrified her, but she'd seen the madness in her father's eyes too. He had shoved her mother and she'd gone careering into the table, but he hadn't even noticed. If he'd been like that with her mother, she dreaded her father's reaction when George turned up. George deserved a telling-off – and more – but just how far would her father go?

What neither of her parents realised was that Linda had no intention of ever going back to George. Linda had confided in her before falling asleep on her bed, saying that she was now so frightened of George that she not only feared for herself, she feared for her unborn baby. Pet chewed her lower lip and wondered what to do. If she told her parents it would cause more friction, so maybe for the time being she should keep it to herself.

Pet moved to her wardrobe and took out a flared skirt and white blouse. The skirt looked all right, but the blouse, with its Peter Pan collar, looked prissy to her. At first she'd been surprised when her father suggested the dance, and even more so when he said she could walk home alone, but had soon realised why. He wanted her out of the way – making her even more frightened of what he'd do to George.

In any other circumstances she'd have been thrilled that for the first time she wasn't being escorted home like a kid, but her mood was low and she didn't feel a bit like dancing. Still, she decided, it would be better to go to the youth club than to be around when George faced the music.

Pet dressed, then studied her face in the mirror. She knew there wasn't a chance in hell that she'd be able to get out of the house wearing make-up, so she took a handbag that Sue had passed on to her and stuffed the lipstick inside, adding a block of mascara and blue eye shadow, which she had bought with her pocket money but never used. Until now, she thought, hoping she'd be able to apply the mascara without sticking the brush in her eye this time. Shoes were a problem. She only had pumps, whereas her friends would be wearing heels and she'd look childish beside them. With a sigh Pet brushed her hair, wishing she could style it like Sue's, but once again, her father would have a fit.

'You look nice,' Chris said approvingly as Pet went back downstairs.

'Yeah, you're as pretty as a picture,' Dan agreed.

Pet could see the tension in her father's face and wasn't fooled. He was hiding his anger – putting on a front – not just for her, but for Linda too. But it had worked. Linda was now calm and her face dry of tears.

'I'm ready, Dad,' she said as though wanting to be away before George appeared. She rose to her feet and, after saying a swift goodbye, they left the house, Linda looking fearfully behind her as they headed for the lockup.

'There's no need to be nervous,' Dan said, taking hold of her arm. 'George won't touch you again.'

Linda didn't reply and was visibly relieved when she had climbed into the back of the car. Pet sat next to her father, wondering if Linda would tell him that she wasn't coming back, but the girl said nothing during the journey.

They were soon at the youth club. Pet turned in her seat to look at Linda. 'Bye, and take care,' she said, feeling that her words were inadequate.

'Bye, Pet, and thanks,' Linda replied.

'Have a good time, but don't forget I want you home by ten fifteen.'

'Yes, Dad, I know.'

Pet climbed out of the car and shut the door behind her, waving to Linda as her father drove off.

She then went into the youth club with her head down and made straight for the cloakroom, relieved to get there before anyone saw her without make-up. The room was empty and, standing at the mirror, Pet applied eye shadow and mascara, pleased that she managed it without a problem. She finished with lipstick, and then, with a final pat to her hair, approached the hall.

Music was playing and quite a few girls dancing, but no boys. Some were standing watching the girls, whilst others were around the pool table at the far end of the room. Pet stood on the threshold of the dance floor, but then Wendy Baker spotted her and hurried to her side.

'Pet, I didn't expect you to come. You look nice – it's unusual to see you wearing make-up. Crumbs, your eyes look fabulous.'

'Thanks. You look nice too,' she replied, eyeing with envy Wendy's blue, full-skirted dress and the matching short bolero. Her mood began to lift, but as someone put on a recording of 'Moon River' by Andy Williams, Wendy frowned.

'Blimey, we can't dance to that. I can't see any of the boys asking us for a smooch.'

Wendy was wrong, Pet thought, as a tall, good-looking bloke ambled towards them. She didn't recognise him from school, and if anything he looked a bit too old for the club. His eyes were grey, his hair blond, and he was dressed in the motorcycle fashion of jeans with a black T-shirt. Wendy began to preen and simper, obviously certain that the young man was going to ask her to dance, but then both girls' eyes widened when he touched Pet's arm.

'Fancy a dance?' he asked.

Pet shot a glance at Wendy before she answered and saw that she looked annoyed. 'Er, no . . . no thanks.'

'Come on, I don't bite,' he urged.

Wendy spoke then, her words clipped. 'Go on, Pet, dance with him. I'm going back to join my *friends.*'

Pet was about to protest, but Wendy had marched off, whilst the young man put his arm around Pet's waist, drawing her into his arms. She went rigid, but then, as he began to move slowly, swaying to the music, she found herself responding.

'I heard your friend call you Pet. What's that short for?'

'It's just Pet,' she lied, unwilling to admit that she had the daft name of Petula. She glanced around the floor, embarrassed to see that they were the only ones dancing.

'My name's Tony. I haven't seen you before. Do you live around here?'

'I live about fifteen minutes' walk away.'

'That's not too bad,' he murmured, drawing her closer whilst crooning the words of the song softly in her ear.

This was the first time Pet had been held in a boy's arms and as he pulled her body imperceptibly closer to his, strange feelings assailed her. Embarrassed, she pulled back.

'I told you, I don't bite,' Tony said, but allowed the distance between them. 'I see you're a friend of Wendy's. Are you still at school too?'

'Yes, but I'll be leaving shortly.'

'You're just a kid.'

'I most certainly am not,' Pet protested.

'I love the way you speak,' he murmured, as he pulled her closer again.

They continued to dance, Tony saying no more until the record came to an end, when he released her. 'See you later,' he said abruptly, before walking off to join three other young men who were propping up the wall.

For a moment Pet stood in the middle of the dance floor, floundering and unsure of what to do, but then hurried to Wendy's side.

Wendy didn't speak, but Jane did. 'I see you've met our local heartthrob. But you want to be careful: Tony Thorn has got a bit of a reputation.'

'I only danced with him,' Pet said and, hoping to placate Wendy, she added, 'Anyway, he's not my type.'

'Huh, who do you think you're kidding?' Wendy snapped, and then turning to Jane she added, 'And as for reputations, his is nothing compared to Pet's family.'

'I've told you before, my family run a legitimate business now,' Pet protested.

'So you say, but it's not what we've heard.'

'Now then, Wendy,' said Jane, 'don't be nasty. Just because Tony danced with Pet, there's no need for sour grapes. We know he usually dances with you, but you know what he's like and I expect he saw Pet as fresh meat.'

Pet frowned, not sure that she liked being referred to as meat, but she couldn't resist a peek at Tony over her shoulder. He was lounging against the wall, but as their eyes met, he winked. The beat of music filled the hall and Pet flushed as Tony began to cross the floor in their direction. She quickly looked away, tense, but it was Wendy he spoke to.

'Come on, Wendy,' he invited.

With a triumphant grin, Wendy hit the dance floor, skirt swirling as she jived with Tony. For a moment they were the only two dancing, but then another couple joined them. Pet recognised the girl as one from her school, but not the boy, and though he looked a bit strange, he was a brilliant dancer.

'Who's that boy dancing with Josephine?' Pet shouted above the noise of the music.

'That's Ian, Tony's younger brother,' Susan answered.

'Younger brother? How old is Tony then?'

'He's eighteen.'

'Eighteen! Isn't he a bit old for the club?'

'Yes, but Ian's slow, retarded. He loves music and dance, so Tony always brings him.'

'That's nice.'

'Don't let that fool you,' Jane said. 'If you want my advice, you'll keep away from Tony Thorn.'

'Why?'

'He's just bad news, that's all.'

Jane's answer left Pet confused, but then she urged both Pet and Susan onto the dance floor. The girls were skilled dancers and Pet did her best to copy their moves, yet despite this she couldn't resist the occasional glance towards Tony and Wendy. Would he ask her to dance again? God, he was gorgeous and she hoped so.

Linda had hardly spoken during the journey, and when Dan dropped her off at her parents' house she had flown inside as though in fear of her life. Maybe he should have stopped to have a word with the girl's father, but instead, ashamed of his son and unable to defend him, he had driven off.

After parking his car, Dan went straight to Bob's house. 'Any sign of George?' he asked.

'No, he ain't shown his face,' Bob said as he stepped outside, pulling the door partially closed behind him.

'He'd better turn up soon, while Pet's out of the way. I want you there when she comes out of the club, but keep out of sight. Just trail her to make sure she arrives home safely.'

'Blimey, Dad, do I have to? Can't you ask Chris to do it?'

'He's busy.'

'What about Maurice?'

Dan's temper was close to the surface, and it didn't take much to set him off. 'I'm telling you to meet her, so just do it!'

Paling, Bob nodded in agreement, both then turning at the sound of footsteps. George had entered the alley, obviously unaware of his father's mood as he ambled towards them.

'Leave this to me,' Dan growled, hardly aware of Bob shooting inside and firmly closing his door.

'All right, Dad?' George asked.

'All right! Of course I'm not all right!'

'Why? What's up?'

Dan surged forward. He grabbed George, and despite his son's bulk, almost frogmarched him to number five.

'Here, what's going on?'

'Get inside,' Dan ordered.

George fumbled for his keys, and as he unlocked the door, Dan shoved him violently from behind, into the house.

'Bloody hell, Dad. Leave it out,' George cried as he staggered inside, only just able to remain on his feet.

Dan ignored his son's protests. He slammed the door behind them and glared at his son. 'You fucking worthless piece of shit.'

'Why? What have I done?'

Dan grew hot as he felt the blood pumping through his veins, barely able to control himself now as he screamed, 'Done! You've got the nerve to ask me what you've done! For one, you scared the life out of your sister *and* your mother, but worse, you fucking scumbag, you laid into your pregnant wife!'

'I didn't touch her,' George protested. 'I wrecked the pram, that's all.'

'Sod the pram . . . Linda told your mother that you've been hitting her.'

George shrugged. 'Yeah, well, I might give her a slap or two now and then, but it's nothing to make a fuss about, and no more than she deserves.'

At this, Dan's anger unleashed. His fists connected with his son's face again and again, putting all the force he could muster behind each blow. Dan heard George's grunts of pain but, intent on giving his son the lesson he deserved, he ignored them.

Dan didn't know when George began to return the punches, only aware as he staggered backwards that blood was pouring from his nose. 'You bastard!' he yelled, surging forward again, enraged that his son had dared to hit him.

As George continued to fight back, Dan began to tire, painfully aware that his son's strength was greater than his. The next few blows that George landed had Dan grunting in pain and each punch he tried to return became weaker than the last. For a moment he paused, gasping as he bent over, but then George's fist connected with his chin in a ferocious uppercut. Dan reeled backwards, hitting the floor with a thump that knocked the last of the breath out of his body.

Dazed, Dan looked up, trying to focus on his son as he lifted one arm, panting, 'Enough!'

It didn't stop George. Madness blazed in his eyes as he lifted a foot, the boot aimed at his father's kidneys. Pain tore through Dan's body, excruciating pain, but then he felt another kick, the sickening crunch as George's boot connected with his skull. Dan grunted, but then knew no more as he sank into a pit of darkness.

Chapter Eleven

Trancelike, George looked down on his father, but as a red mist cleared his eyes, he vigorously shook his head. Like a dog shaking off water, sweat sprayed around him, his mind foggy. What had happened? 'Dad! Dad!' he cried, dropping to his knees by his father's side.

There was nothing – not even a groan. George frantically tried to find a pulse, without success, and jumped to his feet in horror. No! No! His father couldn't be dead!

George became aware of blood dripping from his nose and raised his hand to wipe it away, his thoughts clearing. Yes, that was it. He had come home to find his father waiting for him, the old man furious because he'd hit Linda, so furious that he'd laid into him like a madman. He could remember his father's attack, the pain as each blow landed, then pressure mounting again in his head until he felt that his brain was going to explode. After that there was nothing – a black void.

Had he done this? Had he killed his own father? 'Dad!' he cried, once again dropping to his knees to shake his father's shoulder. 'Wake up! Come on – wake up!'

There was no response and George heard an unholy wail, hardly aware that it was issuing from his own mouth. 'It wasn't my fault, Dad! You shouldn't have gone for me like that! I only gave Linda a slap or two – that's all!' He leaned forward, his ear to his father's mouth. On hearing nothing, terror gripped his stomach like a vice.

George didn't know when his mind suddenly shifted but as though unable to face the horror of what he'd done, he now found himself calm as he reached out for someone else to blame. Linda! Linda and her big mouth! He jumped to his feet, running from the house, leaving the door wide open behind him as his boots pounded the pavement.

It was nearly ten o'clock and Pet's hopes were dashed. Tony hadn't asked her to dance again. He'd taken Wendy to the floor several times, but hadn't even glanced her way. It was her clothes, Pet was sure of it. Beside Wendy she looked prissy and plain, like a kid, whereas Wendy looked older than her years and very self-assured. None of the other boys had asked her to dance either, all of them avoiding not just her but, by association, her friends too.

She felt she had ruined their evening, and whilst Wendy was dancing with Tony she said, 'I . . . I'm sorry. It's my fault that you haven't been asked to dance. People are frightened of my family, but there's no need, and I wish they knew how wrong they are. I've spoiled things for you and shouldn't have come.'

'Yeah, well, don't worry about it,' Jane said. 'Anyway, the blokes are always like this.'

Pet doubted it was true, but as usual she couldn't help jumping to her family's defence. 'I know my father and brothers have got a reputation, but I don't know why. They're builders' merchants, that's all.'

She saw the swift glance that passed between Jane and Susan, but neither said anything.

Moments later Wendy left the floor, grinning as she joined them. 'That was the last dance and as usual, Tony made sure he had it with me.'

Pet hid her feelings, only saying, 'I'd best make a move or I'll be late home.'

The four girls left the hall together, but Pet would have to turn in the opposite direction to the others for her walk home. She glanced around, pleased that her father had kept his word and hadn't sent one of her brothers to meet her.

She said good night to her friends. Wendy was looking smug as Tony emerged with his brother, smiling in her direction.

'It's still early and Tony lives only over the road. Once he's dropped his brother off, I'm sure he'll be back to say a proper good night,' Wendy whispered, adding with a wink, 'if you know what I mean.'

Pet forced a smile as she said goodbye again. 'See you at school on Monday.'

'Yes, see you,' the girls echoed.

Pet gave a small wave as she walked away, but now her smile dropped. She had no chance with someone like Tony, but couldn't help dreaming, wondering what it would be like if she were the one he kissed good night.

She walked slowly. Had George turned up? Had her father sorted him out? God, she hoped so – hoped that peace had returned to the alley.

'Hello, Pet.'

With a start, Pet spun round, her eyes widening at the sight of Tony smiling down at her. 'Er . . . hello.'

'Do you mind if I walk you home?'

'No . . . no, of course not,' she stammered, glad that the darkness was hiding her blushes.

He tucked her arm in his, and as they passed under a streetlamp, she looked up at his face, her heart skipping a beat. He was so good-looking! She was so nervous, and desperately tried to think of something to say, but words failed her. Come on, she cajoled herself, say something. At last she stammered, 'Er . . . one of the girls told me that you're eighteen. What sort of work do you do?'

'Oh, a bit of this and a bit of that.'

Pet frowned. 'That sounds rather enigmatic.'

Tony laughed. 'Rather enigmatic! Now that's classy. As I said before, I love the way you speak. I've always had a soft spot for a posh twang.'

'Posh! I'm not posh.'

'Don't kid a kidder. I can't wait to see where you live.'

Pet almost stopped in her tracks. Goodness, she couldn't let Tony take her all the way home. Her father would go mad if he saw her with a boy – let alone her brothers. Her mind raced. She'd let him walk her part of the way, but then insist that he turn back. All she needed now was an excuse. 'My father insisted that I take elocution lessons, but I can assure you that we aren't posh. In fact, I'm afraid he's rather strict so it might be better if we part company on Lavender Hill.'

Tony smiled. 'Yeah, all right, I get the picture.'

They continued to walk, the conversation now turning to music. Pet was enthusiastic in her praise of Elvis Presley, thrilled to find that Tony was a fan too.

They discussed his records and with something in common, Pet found that her nerves had eased.

They had just turned onto Lavender Hill when Tony pulled into a recessed shop doorway, one that was deep and in total darkness.

'What . . . ?' Pet protested, but as Tony pulled her

into his arms, bending to kiss her neck, a wave of delicious feelings made her gasp. Only moments later, his lips found hers, but as his tongue snaked in her mouth, she didn't know how to react. Was she supposed to do it back? God, she felt so gauche, out of her depth. She tentatively tried, finding it strange, yet sort of nice too. The kiss seemed to go on for ever, but then Tony began to run his hands over her body, one touching her breast.

Instantly Pet tried to pull away, but Tony held her fast.

'No, no, let me go,' she protested.

'Come on,' he said huskily. 'You know you want it.'

'I said let me go!'

Tony abruptly released her, his tone scathing. 'I should have stuck with Wendy. At least she ain't a tease.'

Pet's eyes widened in the darkness. Was Tony inferring that Wendy let him go all the way? She drew herself upright, unaware of how haughty she sounded as she said, 'Unlike Wendy, I am *not* that type of girl. She may not be a tease, but she must be a tart.'

Tony chuckled. 'Oh, Pet,' he gasped, 'it's like I said. You've got class. Look, I'm sorry, but you can't blame a bloke for trying it on. Have I spoiled my chances or can I see you again?'

'I'll think about it,' she said, yet knowing full well that she'd jump at the chance of a date with Tony, despite his fumbling.

'Fair enough,' he said, as they moved out of the doorway. 'Now can I walk you a bit further, or are we close to where you live?'

'It isn't far so you'd best turn back. I live in Drapers Alley.'

'Bloody hell! Don't tell me that you're related to the Drapers!'

'Well, yes. Dan Draper is my father.'

'Jesus,' he groaned, 'of all the girls to choose from, I had to pick Dan Draper's daughter. Look, forget I asked you out. In fact, forget you ever saw me,' and on that abrupt note he hurried off without a backward glance.

'Tony . . . wait,' Pet called, but he didn't come back.

She saw him turn into a side street, out of sight now, and desolately she began to walk home again. She liked Tony a lot, but had seen the fear in his eyes when he realised who her father was.

Pet felt sick, at last facing her nightmare: the fact that all the gossip, the talk of her family being criminals, could be true. And not only that, judging by Tony's reaction, if they were criminals, they could be dangerous ones. No, no, it had all been in the past – it had to be . . .

As Pet drew near to Drapers Alley, all these thoughts were stripped from her mind when she saw an ambulance parked outside. Someone was being carried out of the alley! George! My God, what had her father done?

She ran – saw the family surrounding a stretcher and that her mother was sobbing.

'Mum! Mum! What happened?'

It was Bob who stepped in front of Pet, obscuring her view. 'Pet, go inside. You don't want to see this.'

'Oh God! What has Dad done to George?'

'It isn't George on the stretcher – it's Dad.'

'What? No, no!' she cried, pushing him aside, but her father was being loaded into the ambulance and it was too late for her to see anything. Her mother climbed inside, followed by Maurice, and then the doors closed. In seconds the ambulance sped away, lights flashing and the bell piercing the night air.

'Pet, I'm taking Dad's car,' Bob said. 'Yvonne and I are going to the hospital. You go to my place. Wait with Sue, and when Danny and Chris turn up tell them where we are.'

'I'm coming with you.'

'No, it's best you stay here.'

Pet's shoulders stiffened. 'He's my dad too and I've got a right to be there. Yvonne should be the one to stay behind. She can wait for Danny and Chris.'

'Mum will need Yvonne, love. You know that.'

Pet's stomach lurched. 'Why does Mum need Yvonne? Oh, Bob, don't tell me that Dad's dead?'

'No, he's still alive, but he's in a very bad way.'

'Then I'm coming with you,' Pet said firmly.

Yvonne spoke then. 'Pet's right, Bob, she should be there,' and turning to Sue she said brusquely, 'Keep an eye out. When Danny and Chris turn up, tell them what's happened.'

Sue looked momentarily annoyed, but then nodded. 'Yeah, all right.' She then took Norma's arm. 'Come on, girl, let's get you inside.'

Norma looked awful, her voice high. 'What if George turns up again?'

'Keep out of his way. Leave Danny or Chris to deal with him,' Bob said as he urged Pet and Yvonne forward.

Pet broke as she climbed into the car. 'Oh, Yvonne, I can't believe this is happening.'

'Don't cry, love. Your father's tough. He'll pull through, you'll see. Now come on, dry those tears. Your mother will need you to be strong.'

Strong? thought Pet. How can I be strong when my father might be dying?

Pet lost all track of time, and had no idea how long they had been sitting in the waiting room. Her mother was quiet, saying nothing, but Maurice was breathing heavily and Pet feared he was going to have a full-blown asthma attack.

As though aware of her eyes on him, he said, 'Don't worry, I'm all right. What about you? How are you doing?'

'I'm just worried sick about Dad.'

The door flew open and Chris came running into the waiting room, his face drawn with anxiety. 'What's going on? How's Dad?'

'We don't know,' Bob told him.

'We've been waiting for nearly an hour. It's about time someone came to tell us how he's doing,' Maurice complained.

Yvonne stood up. 'I'll see if I can find anyone.'

'Are you all right, Mum?' Chris asked as Yvonne left the room.

When his mother didn't reply, Chris sat down and placed his arm around her shoulder, but she shrugged him off. He shook his head, standing up again to move close to Bob, and though his voice was a hiss, Pet heard every word. 'What the hell happened? And where's Danny?'

'I'm not sure what happened, but going by Dad's injuries, I'd say that George kicked him in the head. As for where Danny is, your guess is as good as mine.'

'Kicked him in the head!' Pet cried. 'You didn't tell me that.'

Chris looked annoyed. 'What the hell is Pet doing here?'

'I told her not to come, but she wouldn't have it,' Bob said.

'You're the adult. You should have put your foot down.'

'Stop it!' Pet cried. 'Stop talking about me as if I'm not here.'

'All right, that's enough! Can't you see that you're upsetting Mum?' Maurice said.

They all looked at their mother, but she didn't look up, her hands wringing in her lap. 'You all right, Mum?' Chris asked again and when she didn't reply, he hissed, venomously, 'When George shows his face I'll fucking kill him.'

Yvonne came back, shaking her head as she said, 'The nurses can't tell me anything. We've got to wait for the doctor.'

'What's taking him so bloody long?' Maurice complained.

'I think they're still working on your father.'

'Bloody hell,' Bob murmured.

Time slowly passed, and their conversation was sporadic. Despite her fears, Pet found her eyes drooping, but when the door swung open at midnight, she sat up with a start. But it wasn't a doctor who walked in, it was Danny.

'What the hell's going on? How's Dad?'

'We're still waiting for news,' Maurice told him. 'The doc . . .'

Danny was gone before Maurice finished the sentence; his brothers hurrying after him.

'I expect Danny is going to see if he can find anything out, but like me, I doubt he'll have much luck,' Yvonne said. 'Can I get you anything, Mum? Would you like something to drink?'

Joan just shook her head, but at least there had been a reaction.

'What about you, Pet?' Yvonne offered.

'No, no, thanks. Oh, Yvonne, why is it taking so long?'

'I don't know, love, but we're sure to hear something soon.'

Danny came back into the room, trailing his brothers behind him. 'Fucking nurses,' he spat. 'They won't tell me anything.'

'Danny, please,' Yvonne begged. 'There's no point in losing your rag. The nurses do their best.'

'I want to know what happened, from the beginning,' Danny demanded. 'All I got was a garbled report from Sue about George attacking Dad.'

'That's about it,' Bob told him. 'I saw George running off and when I went round to his place I found Dad unconscious on the floor. He was in a state, so I called an ambulance.'

'There must be more to it than that.'

'George has been hitting Linda, and Dad was livid. He went round to sort him out, but don't ask me what happened after that because I wasn't there.'

Pet listened to this exchange, her stomach churning. George had attacked their father and beaten him. A sob escaped her throat.

Danny looked at her, his expression darkening. 'What the hell are you doing here?'

Pet just shook her head, too choked to reply.

'Chris, take her home.'

'No, Danny,' Pet begged. 'Please, I can't go home, I can't . . . not until I've found out how Dad is.'

Before Danny could say anything, the door opened.

'Mrs Draper?' a doctor asked as he walked into the room.

Joan stood up, her eyes suddenly clear. 'How is he?' she asked.

'Mr Draper is stable now, but he will have to remain in hospital until we can assess the extent of his injuries. He's obviously been badly beaten, and the police will have to be informed.'

'No,' Danny snapped. 'He wasn't beaten – he fell down the stairs.'

The doctor's bushy eyebrows rose. 'I find that unlikely.'

'My father will tell you the same thing.'

An expression crossed the doctor's face, one that Pet couldn't fathom, but then Danny spoke again.

'Can we see him?'

'Just for a few minutes and only two of you, please.'

Danny stepped forward and Joan leaned on his arm as they left the room. 'That's nice, ain't it?' Bob complained. 'Why Danny? Why not one of us?'

'He's the eldest,' Yvonne said.

Bob grunted but said nothing further, and they were back after only five minutes.

Pet, seeing how grey her mother looked, blurted out, 'How is he? How's Dad?'

It was Danny who answered. 'Dad's conscious, but he ain't right. When he tried to talk, he just sort of gibbered.'

'Oh, Danny, surely his brain hasn't been damaged?' Yvonne gasped.

As Joan's legs began to wobble, Chris hurried forward to take her other arm.

Pet's head was reeling. Did her father have brain damage? Was the knowledge of that what she had seen on the doctor's face?

Danny looked grim as he answered Yvonne. 'I don't know and the doctor said it's too early to tell. Dad needs more tests.'

'Mum's near collapse; we should get her home,' Chris said.

'No, no, I can't leave,' Joan protested.

'Mum, you heard the doctor,' Danny said. 'Dad's stable now, but as we can't see him again tonight, there's no point in staying. Now come on, you look exhausted and you won't be fit to see him in the morning unless you get a bit of kip.'

Joan allowed Chris and Danny to lead her from the room, Pet and the others following. Danny helped his mother into the front seat of his car, leaving Yvonne to climb into the back.

'Bob, drive Dad's car home,' Danny ordered. 'Take Maurice and Chris with you, then come round to my place.'

'Bloody hell, it's well after midnight. Can't it wait?' Bob complained.

'No it can't.'

'Danny, we're all worn out,' Maurice protested.

'Just do as you're told,' Danny growled.

Pet paused in the act of getting in beside Yvonne. Danny sounded harsh, but his tone was at odds with the expression on his face. If anything, he looked pleased. No, she had to be imagining it. Yet as he climbed into the car, she was sure he was smiling. Why? With all that had happened, how could Danny smile?

Chapter Twelve

Danny sat on the sofa, his trump card in his pocket. He was tired, but fought it off. There were things to sort out – and the sooner the better.

'Norma was none too pleased about me coming round here at this time of night. I got a right earful,' Maurice complained, 'but Ivy came up trumps. It was good of her to have that hot chocolate waiting for us and it went down a treat.'

'I got an earful too. Sue waited up but I couldn't tell her much and now she's gone to bed with the hump. I'm gonna get nothing but grief in the morning.'

'Who wears the trousers in your houses? My Yvonne does as she's told and I can't believe I'm hearing this.'

Both Bob and Maurice lowered their heads, whilst Danny said to Chris, 'If ever you decide to get married, make sure you rule the roost from day one. If you don't, you'll end up like this pair of dozy gits.'

'I can't believe you lot,' Chris said, shaking his

head in disgust. 'George nearly killed Dad, and here you are talking about your bloody wives.'

'Yeah, Chris is right,' said Danny. 'We need to get down to business. First, we don't want the police involved, so as I told the doc, Dad fell down the stairs. Second, we need to find George.'

'Too right we do,' Chris growled. 'He can't be allowed to get away with half killing Dad. When I get my hands on him – he's dead. Instead of sitting here, we should be out looking for him.'

Maurice yawned widely. 'Chris, from what Danny and the doctor told us, Dad's in a bad way. I feel the same as you about George, but it's after one in the morning and I can hardly keep my eyes open. It'd be a waste of time looking for him now. He's had plenty of time to get away and will be well out of the borough.'

'Maurice is right,' Danny said. 'George could be anywhere by now.'

'We can at least put the word out that we're looking for him,' Chris argued.

'We'll do that first thing in the morning. Maurice can run Mum to the hospital while the rest of us start the search.'

'No way,' Bob protested. 'I'll take Mum to the hospital. I want to see how Dad's doing.'

'Yeah, me too,' Chris agreed.

Danny wasn't going to stand for this. He was in charge now and the others had better get used to it. 'I said Maurice is taking her, and that's that. They won't let all of us in, so we'll go to the hospital after we've had a scout around for George.'

'Who gave you the right to tell us what to do?' Bob snapped. 'Dad is the head of this family, not you.'

'Now listen, and this goes for all of you. I saw Dad, and believe me it's going to take a long time before he's fit to run things again. In the meantime, I'll be taking over and you'll take your orders from me.'

Bob jumped up, his face red. 'No way! Until Dad tells us different, we've all got an equal say.'

Danny smiled thinly as he pulled out the document. 'Dad had this drawn up some time ago. This ain't his will – I admit I ain't privy to that – but for the time being this piece of paper is all I need. As you'll see, it states that if Dad is in any way incapacitated and unable to run the business, as the eldest son, I'm to take over.'

'How come we didn't know about it?' Bob asked.

Danny shrugged. 'You know Dad. He always does things on a need-to-know basis.'

'I bet you put the idea into his head.'

'Dad knows the score. In our game there are always risks and he saw the sense of my suggestion.'

'It ain't fucking right. In fact, if you ask me, Dad was livid about your idea of using children in films and I ain't so sure he'd want you running things now.'

163

'We had a chat and sorted it out. He agreed that as long as we stick to consensual sex, he's for it.'

'And we're supposed to believe that! When did you have this so-called chat?'

'Are you calling me a liar?'

'Come on, both of you, calm down,' Maurice urged as he scanned the document. 'Bob, if this is what Dad wants, then so be it. He obviously thinks that Danny is the one to hold the business together, and anyway, it's only until he's on his feet again.'

'Sod this,' Chris spat. 'I'm bushed. If we ain't doing anything until the morning, I'm going to bed. As for you running the business, Danny, it's fine with me.'

Danny hid his satisfaction. George didn't know it, but by putting the old man out of action, he'd done him a big favour. He'd now be able to put *all* his plans into action without any resistance. In the meantime, he issued his instructions again. 'Maurice, as I said, first thing in the morning I want you to run Mum to the hospital. Take Yvonne and Pet with you.'

'Norma and Sue might want to go.'

'Tough. Anyway, as I said before, they won't allow many visitors until Dad's out of intensive care.'

'How come Yvonne's going then?' Bob complained.

Danny, sick of Bob's constant carping, exhaled loudly. 'Mum's fond of Yvonne and she'll want her there.'

Bob was about to protest again, but Maurice broke

in, 'Danny's right, Bob, and anyway, with it being Sunday, Norma and Sue will have the kids to sort out.'

Danny stifled a yawn. He felt unusually tired, his eyes bleary with fatigue. 'Right, that's it for now. I'll see you in the morning.'

They all trooped out, and after closing the door behind them, Danny locked up. He went straight upstairs, undressed, but as he climbed in beside Yvonne, she stirred, saying, 'It was ages before you turned up at the hospital tonight. Where were you?'

'Doing a bit of business.'

'Is there someone else, Danny? Are you playing away again?'

'Of course not, you dozy mare.'

'I'm sure I could smell perfume on your shirt this morning.'

'For fuck's sake, Yvonne, leave it out. I don't need this. My dad's lying in a hospital bed, in a bad way, and I've got to take over the running of the business. There ain't another woman, so just shut up and let me get some kip.'

Danny heard Yvonne huff, but ignored it. He turned over, his back towards her, and closed his eyes, thoughts drifting. Yes, he had a tart on the side, but that's all she was, a tart. Yvonne was all right in bed, but she didn't like anything a bit different or kinky, whereas Rita had no such qualms. Still, he'd have to be a bit more careful, and the daft cow would have to stop smothering herself in cheap perfume.

Danny plumped up his pillow, his thoughts now turning to George. He'd always known that his brother was a mental case, yet even so, he'd never expected him to turn on the old man. If they found him, he'd have to be punished, but surely even George would have the sense to keep his head down.

George never reached Linda's parents' house. Instead he was slumped on a bench on Clapham Common. He didn't know when his brain had shifted again, but as he pounded the pavement, intent on sorting his wife out, the awful truth had returned to hit him. He had killed his father!

Hours had passed, and only the light from a distant lamp pierced the gloom. George had no idea what to do. He shivered. It was as though his life was over. He couldn't return to Drapers Alley. Ever! Yet it was all he knew. He would have to go away – far away from his brother's reach. He didn't care about Maurice or Bob, and he could even handle Chris if he had to. It was Danny he feared. Danny would kill him! Yet where could he go? Where would he be safe? Maybe he should turn himself in – maybe he should tell the police that he'd killed his father. They'd lock him up and in a cell he'd be out of Danny's reach. George groaned in despair. No, he couldn't do that. He'd get life for murder, and the thought of being locked in a cell for ever was unbearable.

For a moment he considered leaving the country, but as his addled brain turned, George realised it wasn't possible. He didn't have any money, or a passport. But there was money in Drapers Alley – plenty of it. Maybe he could find a way to get into his mother's house without detection. Yet dare he risk it?

Still he sat on the bench, his thoughts turning to Linda again. He'd made the biggest mistake in his life when he'd married her. It was her big mouth that had caused this and he felt like wringing her neck. No, don't be stupid, he told himself. He was in enough trouble. Fuck her! He never wanted to see her again and, as far as he was concerned, she and her unborn brat could rot in hell.

Finally, at three in the morning, realising he had no choice, George rose to his feet. To get away he had to have money, and if he had any chance of taking the hoard, he'd have to do it now.

George trudged home, but the closer he got to Drapers Alley, the more nervous he became. What if Danny was laying in wait?

As he entered the alley, George kept close to the wall, peering at the houses for signs of life. All were in darkness. George had one thing in his favour. When he'd married Linda and moved into number five, he had kept the key to his father's house and it remained on his fob.

Treading as softly as he could, he edged along the wall to number one, just about to put the key into the lock when he froze. His father was dead! Shit, what if he was laid out in the living room? In a cold sweat now, he remained rooted to the spot, but then a glimmer of reason returned. No, his dad wouldn't be laid out yet – it was too soon.

Carefully turning the key, George held his breath as he opened the door. The living room was empty, in darkness, and he crossed the room with his arms outstretched. He made it without bumping into anything and now headed for the bathroom. George still couldn't see a thing and had no other choice but to turn on the light so, pulling the door almost closed, he flicked the switch. For a moment he paused, his ears pricked, but hearing nothing he moved to the window. It was set back in the wall, with a plant on the windowsill that George carefully removed. He had always been in awe of how clever his dad was, and now as he fumbled under the sill for the hidden catch he recalled his amazement when he'd first been shown this secret hiding place.

His dad's idea had been ingenious, but now as George lifted the windowsill to pull out the long, metal box that fitted perfectly in the wall cavity, a sob escaped his lips. His dad was dead! He'd killed him! *Oh, Dad, I'm sorry. I didn't mean to do it. Oh, Dad, I'm never gonna see you again.* Grief hit George with such force that his legs caved beneath him. He slumped on the floor, the metal box cradled in his arms as he rocked back and forth.

George was immersed in an agony of grief, his back to the bathroom door and unaware that it had opened fully. Nor was he aware of anyone approaching him from behind until a hand grabbed his hair, pulling his head back. 'Wh . . . what . . .'

These were the last words George uttered as a knife sliced his throat, the cut deep. He opened his mouth, but could only gurgle as his blood spurted, splattering the walls. His head was pushed forward again, his chin now down as the rest of his life force drained onto his mother's immaculately polished lino.

Only minutes later, George's killer removed his body, dumping it in a place that wasn't far away, but one where it was unlikely to be discovered. Later, it would be hidden, but there wasn't time now. The effort of carrying George had almost drained his killer, but there was still the bathroom to clean up and time was short.

His killer hadn't anticipated that George's blood would spurt so far and it would take longer than expected to clean up, but every trace had to be removed. It seemed to take for ever, but finally it was done, and now there was only one thing left to do. The killer took the money, leaving the metal box wide open on the bathroom floor.

Chapter Thirteen

Joan was the first one up on Sunday morning. She hadn't expected to sleep, but surprisingly she'd gone off as soon as her head hit the pillow. Now, though, groggy but awake, her first thought was for her husband and all she wanted was to get to the hospital. Oh, Dan, Joan inwardly cried, please be all right. Please get better.

Chris emerged as she came out of her bedroom, his face grey. 'You look awful, Chris. Didn't you get any sleep?'

'Yeah, I slept. What about you? Are you all right?'

Joan forced a smile. Chris was a lovely lad, thoughtful and caring. He had always been her favourite, but ashamed of preferring one child over the others, she hid her feelings. 'I'm anxious to get back to the hospital.'

'Yeah, me too, but we should grab a bite to eat first. I'll give Pet a nudge while you make a pot of tea.'

Joan went downstairs and in the kitchen she placed the kettle on the gas before hurrying to the bathroom. On the threshold, she paused, her eyes on a metal box on the floor. Where had that come from? Something else looked odd, out of place, and at first she couldn't comprehend what it was, but then saw that her plant was on the floor too. Joan looked at the window and frowned. The sill looked odd, raised, and crossing the room she investigated what looked like a concealed compartment.

'Chris? Chris, come down here!'

In moments Chris was beside her. 'What's this?' she asked, 'and where did that metal box come from?'

For a second Chris didn't react, but then, his voice high, he said, 'Bloody hell, I'd best get Danny.'

'Wait,' Joan called, but Chris ignored her as he ran out.

Joan stared down into the cavity, her eyes then returning to the metal box. In minutes Chris was back, Danny behind him, his hair dishevelled.

'Mum, go back to the kitchen. Leave this to us,' Danny ordered.

'I've worked out where the box came from, but what was in it?'

'It was nothing, Mum. Just paperwork to do with the business, that's all.'

'But . . . but why was it hidden under the sill? And who took the papers?'

'Mum, please, we don't know, but there's nothing

to worry about, honest. Look, why don't you get yourself ready and Maurice will run you to the hospital?'

Danny's eyes were veiled and Joan could sense that he was hiding something, but in truth, she didn't want to know. It was bound to be something illegal, something her husband and sons were mixed up in, and as usual she buried her head in the sand. All she wanted was to find out how Dan was so, leaving them to it, she hurried to get dressed.

'That was quick thinking,' Chris hissed as soon as his mother was out of sight. 'Papers, that was a good one.'

'It's gone, Chris. All the money. Dad's savings, our savings, the business capital, gone!'

'Yeah, I can see that.'

'Was there any sign of a break-in?'

'No, I don't think so.'

'That's a bit odd. Didn't you hear anything?'

'Not a sound.'

'Are you sure?'

'Yeah, I'm sure. What are you trying to imply, Danny? Are you accusing me?'

'No, but why are you so touchy?'

'What do you expect? There was no sign of a forced entry so you must think it's an inside job.'

'No, Chris, I think George did it and I should have seen this coming. I should have realised that

George would need money to do a runner. We're well and truly in the shit now,' Danny moaned as he closed the box and returned it to its hiding place. 'Come on, the others will need to hear about this. You go to Bob's whilst I tell Maurice.'

'What's going on?' Pet asked as she came downstairs.

'Nothing for you to worry about,' Danny told her. 'Just get yourself ready and go with Mum to the hospital.'

'But—'

Danny and Chris both ignored their sister as they left the house, one going to number three and one to number four. Both looked grim as they knocked on the doors, and with Maurice the first to answer, Danny stepped inside.

'There was no need to knock me up. I'm getting ready,' Maurice said.

'Where's Norma?'

'She's still in bed.'

'Good. Now listen . . .'

As Danny told Maurice what had happened, he saw his brother's eyes widen in shock.

'What? It's all gone?'

'That's what I said. The bastard took the lot.'

'Blimey, I'm glad my savings are in a bank.'

'Mine were in the box.'

'Danny, I told you that money in the bank would have made a bit of interest.'

'Yeah, I know, but I never got round to it.'

'We had to hide the business capital, and now that it's gone we're in the shit. Bloody hell, Danny, we've got to get it back. We've got to find George.'

'Don't you think I know that? Oh, we'll find him, and when we do . . .' Danny left the sentence unfinished as he paced the small room. 'Look, for now we'll carry on as planned. You take Mum, Yvonne and Pet to the hospital while the rest of us have a scout round.'

Norma came downstairs, preventing further conversation.

Danny left, but as soon as he walked into his own house, Yvonne said, 'What did Chris want?'

'Someone broke in last night and nicked Dad's papers,' Danny lied.

'Papers? What papers?'

'Stuff to do with the business.'

Yvonne frowned. 'Why would anyone want them?'

'I don't know, and I ain't got time to worry about it now. Mum will want to get to the hospital so you'd best get a move on.'

Yvonne cocked her head to one side, her gaze intent. 'Danny, what's really going on?'

'Nothing! Now shut up about it and do as I said, get yourself ready.'

Yvonne did as she was told whilst Danny's thoughts raced. With their funds gone, they would need to make money, and fast. Hard porn was the answer, but how were they supposed to get it up and running without capital? If they didn't find George, he'd have to find a way. With six families to support, Danny knew he had no choice.

By ten o'clock, only two women remained in Drapers Alley. The events of last night had caused Sue and Norma to put their differences to one side, and with the kids playing outside, they sat gossiping at Norma's table.

'Have you seen Ivy this morning?' Sue asked.

'Yes, I saw her pass by earlier.'

'I was surprised that she waited up last night, and that she made them a chocolate drink. She's never had time for any of us, so why the switch?'

'Dan's her uncle so she's bound to be worried,' Norma said.

It was true that Ivy didn't have any time for them, but she didn't blame her. She was sickened by the Drapers too. As far as she was concerned, Maurice was the only decent one amongst them. She'd had enough and intended to push even harder to make him see sense. They had to get away from his family, from the alley, and the business. How he could allow Oliver to grow up in this environment was beyond her, but she wasn't going to allow her son to become tainted by this rotten family.

'Bob's gone off with the others to look for George. I wouldn't like to be in his shoes if they find him.'

'More violence – and what will it solve? Nothing. They should leave George to the police.'

'Leave it out, love. The Drapers take care of their own business and always have. They won't want the rozzers involved.'

'And what if Dan dies? That means that George has got away with murder.'

'Norma, don't say that! Bob told me that Dan was stable when they left the hospital last night.'

'Yes, but he's in intensive care and that means it's serious.'

'Oh, Norma, I hope Dan makes it. Bob would fall apart if anything happened to his dad. He's going to the hospital later and I wish I was going with him. He'll need me if the worst happens.'

'I doubt you'll be allowed to go. It seems Yvonne is the only daughter-in-law with that privilege.'

'Yeah, stuck-up cow.' Sue paused before saying, 'It's Petula I feel sorry for. She worships her dad and he spoils her rotten. She'll be in bits if anything happens to him.'

Norma wondered how Pet was coping. She was a nice girl, the only one of the Drapers she had any time for. Now, though, the girl had seen what her family was capable of, and her cosseted little world must be shattered. She doubted Pet would get much comfort from her mother. Joan was a cold fish, and from what she had seen last night, too wrapped up in her own world to worry about her daughter. 'Yes,

I feel sorry for Pet too. Now then, do you want another cup of tea?'

'I won't say no,' Sue replied. 'I've got a stack of ironing to do, but sod it, I'm not in the mood for housework.'

Norma smiled faintly. Sue was never in the mood for housework. Norma went through to the kitchen to make a fresh pot of tea, deciding her own cleaning could wait too. What did the house matter? She hated it, drawing no pleasure from her surroundings, and only kept it nice for Oliver's sake. Once again she was determined to leave Drapers Alley, and if Maurice wouldn't see sense, she'd leave without him, taking Oliver with her. Norma paused, biting her bottom lip. Yes, brave thoughts, but just where could they go? There was her parents' house, of course, but would they take her back? Yes, probably. They'd welcome her home, and as before, use her as a servant, someone to take care of them, but would they accept Oliver?

By eleven o'clock, her stomach awash with tea, Sue said, 'I wonder what time they'll all be back.'

'I don't know, and I expect they'll go again this evening.'

'Yeah, well, my place looks like a bomb's hit it so I'd best give it a quick tidy-up.'

Norma opened the street door, relieved to see that Oliver was happily playing football with his cousins, Robby for once behaving himself.

Sue stepped outside. 'Look,' she said, 'there's Ivy.'

Norma frowned. Ivy was coming into the alley from the other end so she wouldn't be passing their doors, but even from this distance she looked harassed. 'I wonder where she's been?'

'I dunno, but she looks a right mess,' Sue giggled.

'Hello, Ivy,' Norma said as the woman drew closer. 'What on earth have you been up to?'

'I've been down to our allotment.'

'I thought you left that to Steve?'

'Yeah, well, this is his only day off so I thought I'd give him a break. The allotment's been going to seed, and anyway, I don't mind a bit of hard work. Now if you don't mind, I need to clean myself up.'

On that note Ivy went inside and Sue's eyes rounded. 'Blimey, rather her than me.'

'Yes, well, unlike you, Ivy is built like an ox.'

'She's bigger than Steve, that's for sure. He's such a funny-looking bloke and I don't know what she sees in him.'

'With Ivy's looks, beggars can't be choosers. Anyway, see you later, Sue.'

'Yeah, see you,' Sue said, gyrating to her door.

Norma pursed her lips, feeling the usual surge of envy. Sue was so dainty, so sexy, but then Norma stiffened her shoulders. All right, she may not be as pretty as Sue, but after seeing Ivy, she at least felt feminine.

With a last glance along the alley, Norma went

inside, and though she tried to tackle her house-work, she couldn't get last night's events from her mind. George had almost beaten his father to death. How could a son do that to his own father? Bad blood, that was the problem, Norma decided, with Maurice the exception. She picked up a duster, running it over her sideboard, but then Oliver came charging in, a hand held over his eye. 'What happened?'

'Robby kicked the ball into my face.'

Norma took her son through to the kitchen where she bathed his eye, her jaws clenched in anger. Robby was a menace, another one with bad blood, an inher-ited love of violence. She just *wouldn't* have Oliver tainted. When Maurice came home she'd insist, once and for all, that they left Drapers Alley.

Ivy's lips were set as she walked into her house. There was no sign of Steve and the kids, but she could guess where they were. They'd be at the park, watching a local football match. Ivy scowled. She'd seen the way Sue and Norma had looked at her – disdain from Norma, and amusement from Sue. She hated them. Who were they to judge her? What did they know of her life? It was all right for pretty, petite Sue, and though Norma wasn't exactly an oil painting, she didn't draw pitying looks.

Ivy threw off her clothes, hastening to clean the dirt from her body, yet even when clean, she knew she'd still be ugly. From childhood she had suffered either pity or nastiness, and at school she'd been the butt of many cruel jokes. When she looked at her cousins, especially Petula, she couldn't understand why she was so different. Her parents had been good-looking; in fact her mother had been prettier than Auntie Joan, so why had she been born to look like an outcast amongst the Drapers? It wasn't fair, it really wasn't, and because of her looks she had known more humiliation than kindness since the day she was born.

Only her mother had loved her and Ivy still hadn't come to terms with her death. She had watched her suffer, longed to do something, anything to ease her pain, and without support from her so-called family, she had felt so alone. Auntie Joan hadn't come once, and though Uncle Dan had called occasionally, she could sense he had been itching to get away.

She had been heartbroken when her mother died, and when Steve came along she had grabbed at the chance for a little comfort, allowing him liberties from day one. Making love had helped her to drown out her sorrows. Marriage and kids followed, and though the boys were little buggers at times, she loved them dearly. All she wanted for them was a better life, and had watched their developing features with anxiety. Thankfully, they hadn't inherited her looks. Though they weren't exactly handsome, their features were even and both had Steve's lovely eyes.

Ivy thought about George and felt some satisfaction, a feeling at last of superiority. Yes, her boys might be naughty at times, but look what Auntie Joan had bred: a son who had beaten his father, and from what she had seen before he'd been carried off in an ambulance, Uncle Dan was in a terrible state. Good, Ivy thought. She hoped her uncle was in pain, pain that was worse than her mother had suffered. After all, it was no more than he deserved.

After cleaning herself up, Ivy heard voices in the alley, so quickly threw on fresh clothes and went outside. Sue and Norma were going into number one, which meant her Auntie Joan was back from the hospital. She ran to join them, her voice solicitous as she walked inside.

'Auntie Joan, what's the news on Uncle Dan? How's he doing?'

It was Maurice who answered. 'He's a bit better, but he's not out of the woods yet.'

'He looks dreadful,' Pet said, her eyes beginning to fill with tears, 'and he can't talk.'

'Come on now, buck up,' Yvonne said. 'The doctor said he's out of danger, and though it may take a while for him to recover, at least he's on the mend.'

As Joan flopped onto a chair, Maurice said, 'I think we all should leave now. Mum's just about had enough and needs to rest.'

Ivy's blood grew hot. They were at it again, pushing her out; well, she wouldn't rise to the bait. 'Auntie

Joan, is there anything I can do to help?' she said, whilst hoping the bloody woman would say no.

'No, it's all right, and as Maurice said, I would rather you all went home. My head is pounding and with everyone in here I feel like a sardine in a can.'

Ivy caught the look that Sue threw at Norma and guessed they were none too pleased to be chased out either.

'Yes, come on, let's leave Mum in peace,' Maurice said, taking his wife's arm to lead her outside. 'I'll be back later to run you to the hospital again, Mum.'

Ivy had no choice but to follow them. Her lips were set in a grim line, but she brightened up again when in her own home. It had happened at last, she was seeing the Drapers brought low. It sounded like her Uncle Dan was in a terrible state and she felt a surge of satisfaction.

Joan was glad when everyone left. She was unable to settle, almost out of her mind with worry. She'd do some housework, anything to fill her mind, and she'd start with the bathroom.

With a bucket of nice hot water, Joan was soon on her knees, scrubbing the bathroom linoleum. When she got to one corner she frowned to see that it had begun to lift, so rising to her feet she went to look for some glue.

With the tube in hand Joan went back to the bathroom, but as she raised the linoleum further to apply the glue, her eyes widened. The concrete floor and back of the linoleum were coated in something sticky. When she realised what it was Joan's hand went to her mouth in horror. Blood! But where had it come from?

'What are you doing, Mum?'

'Oh, Chris, you made me jump. Look, I've found blood on the floor.'

Chris bent to have a look, saying dismissively, 'It won't be blood, Mum, it must be something else. Look, leave it to me. I'll clean it up.'

'But—'

'No buts, Mum. You look worn out and shouldn't be doing housework. Now go on, make us both a cup of tea and I'll have this cleaned up in no time.'

Joan wanted to protest, but something in Chris's manner stilled her. Despite what he said, she was sure it was blood and couldn't understand where it had come from. Why had Chris denied it? Oh God, had Chris caught the robber in the act? Had there been a fight? But no, if that was the case surely Chris would have said something, and not only that, if he had caught the robber, Dan's papers wouldn't be missing. Joan's head began to buzz. Oh, she couldn't think straight. Dan was in hospital and that was enough to worry about. She didn't want to think about anything else – she didn't want to know what had happened, not when she was fearful of the answers.

Chapter Fourteen

Pet had noticed a change at school – more whispers, but also a difference in some of the other girls' behaviour. Instead of being nervous around her, there were some who openly made comments and asked questions. She was facing one now.

'How's your dad, Petula? Still rough, is he?' asked Kate, a girl who had previously shunned her.

'Yes, he's still in hospital.'

'And what about your brother George? We heard that he's gone missing. Has he turned up?'

'No, not yet.'

'My dad said that with your father in hospital and George missing, things are looking up. Your other brothers haven't got so much backup now.'

'What do you mean? Backup for what?'

'Leave it out. You know just what I mean.' And, turning away, she grabbed another girl's arm, both giggling as they walked across the playground.

Petula frowned, but then seeing Wendy walking

in the gate, she hurried over to her. She hated coming to school, wanting to be at her father's side until he got better, but her mother wouldn't let her take any time off.

'What's up, Pet?' asked Wendy.

'Oh, nothing, I just wish I could leave school after the summer term instead of waiting until the end of the year.'

'Yeah, me too. My mum's already put a word in for me at work and they said there's a job waiting for me.'

'Really! Where does your mum work?'

'In the sugar factory.'

Pet didn't envy Wendy. She didn't want to work in a factory, and still held on to her dream of working in an upmarket shop. But with her father so ill, any thoughts of getting a job when she left school had been pushed to one side. She remembered when she had gone to Sue for make-up lessons, thinking her mad to suggest that she could be a model, whereas Wendy definitely had the looks.

'I think you could be a model, Wendy.'

'Are you taking the mickey?'

'No, of course not.'

'Yeah, well, it's nice of you to say so. How's your dad?'

'He's still in a bad way.' Indicating Kate, she added, 'She asked me the same question, but it was funny, almost as if she enjoyed the fact that he's ill.'

'What do you expect? There are a lot of people around here who probably think the same.'

Pet wanted to protest, to defend her family, but once again she was assailed by doubts. Her father and brothers were supposed to be running a legitimate business but there was still gossip, and uppermost in her mind was the way Tony Thorn had acted when he found out that she was a Draper. Were they still criminals? Had she been a blind fool in allowing her father and brothers to fob her off? Her lips set into a thin line. Well, no more, she decided, determined to find out the truth.

'There they are,' Wendy said.

Pet turned to see Jane and Susan walking arm and arm through the gates, smiling when they saw them, but with the bell ringing there was no chance to chat as they made their way inside the building.

Despite putting the word out in Battersea and boroughs beyond, George hadn't been sighted. Over a month passed without finding him, and they had all but given up hope.

By mid-June a routine was in place in the alley. Maurice was the one who drove his mother to the hospital every day and, though Sue and Norma complained, it was always Yvonne who accompanied her.

Because she was at school during the day, Pet went with her mother in the evenings, usually accompanied by one of her brothers. With her father so ill, George still missing and her brothers so busy, she hadn't had a chance to question them about their activities so far, but she was keeping her eyes and ears open, hoping to snatch some information.

One Monday evening only Maurice was with them, and as Pet sat by the bed she couldn't understand why her father wasn't getting any better. He had changed so much. Instead of the strong man he had once been, in just this short time, he appeared shrunken, beaten and aged.

'What did you say, Dad?'

He tried to speak again, but there was only a stream of babble. Spittle began to run down his chin and Pet watched as her mother gently wiped it away.

'The doctor said you can come home next week, Dan.'

'What?' Pet said. 'Mum, why didn't you tell me? When did he say that? How can Dad come home when he still can't talk? Surely there's more they can do?'

There was another stream of babble as Dan tried to speak, one arm waving in frustration. Pet's eyes met those of her mother and she paled at her words.

'That's enough, Pet! Your father may not be able to speak, but he ain't deaf. Maurice,' she continued, 'take Pet outside. She's upsetting your father.'

'But—'

'Come on, Pet. You can see Dad's had enough now. Say goodbye and we'll wait in the car for Mum.'

Tears brimming, Pet bent over her father, kissing him on the forehead. 'Sorry, Dad, I didn't mean to upset you.'

'Just go,' Joan snapped.

Reluctantly Pet left the ward. 'Maurice, why didn't Mum tell me that Dad's coming home?'

'She only found out this afternoon, but you know now, so why all the fuss?'

'Because I sense that you're all hiding something from me and this is the last straw. Please, Maurice, I'm not a child. Tell me what's going on.'

Maurice stopped walking and turned to face her. 'Look, we didn't want to upset you and we hoped that Dad would recover, if only his speech.'

'But why isn't he getting any better?'

Maurice exhaled loudly, then said, 'All right, the others might not like it, but I'll give it to you straight. At first we were told that the kick to Dad's head had caused a swelling around the brain. We hoped that when it went down, he'd recover his speech. It looked hopeful, but then Dad had a stroke.'

'A stroke! Is that why his arm is so weak that he can't hold a pen?'

Maurice nodded. 'Yes, it affected one side of his body.'

'I can't believe you kept this from me!'

'As I said, we were hoping that he'd improve.

Come on, love, don't cry. After the beating it was touch and go for a while, and we nearly lost Dad. He may have had a stroke, but at least he's still alive.'

'Does . . . does this mean he'll never be able to speak again?'

'We don't know, Pet. I suppose there's always a chance.'

'He won't get any worse, will he?'

'As long as he doesn't have another stroke, I doubt it, and who knows, once he's home in familiar surroundings, he may improve.'

Pet clung to that hope.

Joan gripped Dan's hand, inwardly fighting her tears. Since the day she had met him, Dan had always protected her, shielded her, and she had leaned on his strength. Diminutive beside him, he had called her his Queen, and she loved him for it. Now, though, it felt as if the tables had turned and it was she who would have to be the carer, the protector. Somehow she had to keep him free from worry, free from stress. If she could do that, then maybe he'd get better.

As the eldest son, Danny would have to step in permanently. He would need to continue running the business, and she would have to ensure that if there were any problems, they didn't reach Dan's ears. It wouldn't be easy. The boys always came to their father if there were any problems. But no more!

She'd have a word with Danny, in fact with all of them. Their father had to have complete peace, and she'd see that he got just that.

As her determination to protect Dan rose, Joan was surprised at the well of strength she felt. Dan squeezed her hand and she said earnestly, meeting his eyes, 'It's all right, love. I'll look after you, I promise.'

He shook his head and as a stream of incomprehensible words issued from his mouth, Joan frowned; sure that she had caught one of them. Danny! Had he said 'Danny'? 'It's all right, love. Danny is taking care of everything. The business, the boys, the lot.'

Once again Dan tried to speak, his eyes wild as the bell rang to signal the end of visiting time.

'I've got to go now, Dan, but don't worry, everything is fine. As I said, Danny is taking care of everything. He's a good lad, and a chip off the old block.'

Dan became increasingly agitated and a nurse approached the bed, saying, 'You really must leave now, Mrs Draper. Your husband looks upset and I think he needs to rest.'

Joan tried to kiss Dan goodbye, but his good arm flapped as though pushing her away. She stood helplessly as the nurse took over.

'Come on now, Mr Draper,' the nurse said brusquely as she tidied the bed. 'Say goodbye to your wife and isn't it lovely that you're going home next week?'

Dan slumped, spent, and at last Joan was able to give him a swift kiss goodbye. 'I'll see you tomorrow, love.'

He didn't respond, his head turned away from her now. Joan left the ward, wondering what she had said to agitate him.

When Joan climbed into the car beside Maurice, Pet said, 'I'm sorry, Mum. I didn't mean to upset Dad.'

'Yes, well, he was still in a state when I left. When he comes home he's going to need complete quiet. I hope you realise that, my girl.'

'Yes, I know. Maurice told me about the stroke and when Dad comes home, I'll help you to look after him.'

'There's no need. I can cope, but just watch what you say in front of him.' Joan was surprised that Maurice had told Pet. It hadn't been her idea to keep the girl in the dark, but as usual, her brothers had wanted their little sister protected. Well, she'd have to grow up now, and though Joan didn't want any help with Dan's care, it was about time Pet learned how to do a bit of housework.

Joan settled in her seat as Maurice drove them home. Dan had seemed upset when Pet had asked a string of questions in front of him, but she was sure there was more to it than that. He had become worse when Pet left, and now Joan realised it was the mention of Danny that had started him off.

191

Yet surely that should have relieved him of any worry, not cause him to nearly have a fit.

'Maurice, did your father have a falling-out with Danny?'

'Er, no, Mum, not that I'm aware of. Why do you ask?'

'I'm probably imagining things, but he seemed to get out of his pram when I mentioned Danny's name.'

'He's probably just worried about the business.'

'Yeah, maybe,' Joan said, but somehow she thought there was more to it than that. She was then struck by a thought. Yes, that must be it. She'd have a word with Danny as soon as they arrived home.

Danny was turning over the things he needed to say. He'd called a meeting for nine o'clock that evening, and rather than return to the yard, he'd told Yvonne to disappear as soon as the boys came round. He didn't intend to discuss business in front of her, so she could bugger off next door to sit with his mother.

When there was a knock on the door, he was surprised to see his mother on the step. 'Hello, Mum. How's Dad?' he asked as she stepped inside.

'About the same, but something's worrying him. He became very agitated when I mentioned you and I've been thinking about it on the way home. I reckon it's because you haven't been to see him lately.

Your brothers all go, but when was the last time you went to the hospital?'

'I ain't been for over a week, but I've been busy. I've got the business to run, and since George took our capital, there's a lot to sort out.'

'What are you talking about? What capital? And when did George take it?'

Danny ran a hand over his face. 'Oh, shit, that just slipped out. Look, we didn't want you to know this, but I suppose I'll have to tell you now. That box you found on the bathroom floor, well, it had money in it: Dad's savings and capital for the business. George sneaked back and took the lot.'

He saw the blood drain from his mother's face. 'Mum, are you all right?'

There was a pause but then she said, 'I'm fine. It was just a shock, that's all. I don't know why you had to keep it from me in the first place. Mind you, I dread to think what your father will say when he finds out.' Her hand went to her mouth. 'Oh, listen to me, I'm not thinking straight. It would be best if we keep it from your father for now. The shock would be too much for him and might bring on another stroke.'

'Until he's on his feet and can talk again, we won't tell him, Mum.'

'Danny, I hate to say this, but he might never recover his speech, or be able to walk again. Now I know that you're busy, but you must find time to visit him.'

Danny hung his head, fighting for an excuse. Whenever he went to visit him, the old man got upset, and nowadays he avoided the hospital like the plague. Though his father couldn't talk coherently, Danny could guess what he was trying to say. He was out of favour and there was no way the old man would want him running things. It was just as well he couldn't talk, or it might be Maurice or Bob handling the business. If he went to see the old man when the others were there, they might twig and that was the last thing he wanted.

He met his mother's eyes now, the lie easy. 'I'm sorry, Mum, it's, well . . . it does my head in to see Dad like that.'

'I know it's hard, but go to see him, and when he comes home, I don't want him pressured. Have a word with the boys – tell them that if they have any problems they must bring them to you.'

'Yeah, all right.'

'If your father has complete peace, you never know, he might get better. In the meantime, I don't want him involved in running the business, so when you go to see him, don't mention it. Well, other than to say that everything is fine.'

Danny could see the change in his mother, the icy determination in her eyes. She no longer looked distant and remote. In fact, she looked like she was suddenly made of steel.

'Don't worry, Mum. We all want Dad to get better

and know we shouldn't worry him. I can look after the business for as long as it takes.'

'You're a good lad, and as I told your father, you're a chip off the old block.'

Yvonne had remained quiet during this exchange, but when Bob knocked on the door she rose to her feet. 'The boys want to talk business, so if it's all right with you, Mum, I'll come round to your place for a while.'

'I suppose so.'

When they had both left, Bob said, 'What did Mum want?'

'She wants to make sure that we don't pester Dad. When he comes home he's got to have peace and quiet so there's to be no business talk in front of him.'

When the others turned up, Danny repeated what their mother had said, and then it was on to business. 'I wanted to keep the hard porn strictly in the family, but with George taking our capital, it's impossible. I've come up with another idea and had a word with Eddy Woodman. He doesn't want to get involved in the making of hard porn, but he's agreed to let us use his equipment until we can buy our own.'

'That won't be for some time,' Maurice said. 'A decent camera won't be cheap, not to mention the gear for developing and splicing.'

'What about the girls, and the blokes, are they willing to take it up a notch?' asked Bob.

'Only one pair; the others don't want to know. I had a word with Lillie Ellington and she can supply what we need, but it's gonna cost a good few bob.'

'Why go through that old hag? Why can't you get a few girls off the street? There's plenty around Soho.'

'Use your head, Bob. We don't want anyone finding out about our setup or where it is. When Garston gets wind of what we're up to he's gonna put feelers out, and tarts like that won't keep their mouths shut. They'd soon blab to save their skins.'

'Lillie's crew would be the same.'

'No they won't. Lillie has her lot well under control. They know what would happen to them if they open their mouths.'

'I hope you're right,' Maurice said doubtfully, 'but I still think it's too risky.'

'Look, we've got to take a few risks if we want to make money. As I said before, we can soon hire some muscle if Garston gets wind of us.'

'Yeah, and that's gonna cost too,' Maurice complained.

'For the time being, we'll just have to tighten our belts a bit more. The most important thing is to get up and running, the sooner the better. In fact, I want to schedule our first shoot for Friday.'

'That soon?'

'Yes, Maurice, that soon,' Danny said. 'Me and Chris have been out and about and we've got advance orders.'

'What's on the agenda for tomorrow?' Chris asked.

'We've still got the usual stuff to make so I'll need you at Wimbledon. Maurice will be needed here to run Mum to the hospital, and Bob, I want you at the yard. There's a delivery of bricks and we can't leave that little weasel Steve to handle it on his own.'

'Why me?'

'For fuck's sake, just do it, Bob. It'll only be for a couple of hours and then you can join us at Wimbledon.'

Danny exhaled loudly, fed up with Bob's constant carping. He hadn't forgotten that Bob had tried to put him in the shit with the old man, but he'd get his revenge. What his brothers didn't know was that when the money came rolling in again, he intended to stash some away until he had the capital he needed. With the old man out of the way, he could go ahead with his plans to film kiddie porn. There was loads of money to be made, but he was going to keep his brothers out of the loop and ensure that all the profits were his. He'd already put a few feelers out, making discreet enquiries about getting hold of kids, and it had proved to be easier than expected.

Joan's mind was racing and she hardly listened as Yvonne chattered. She had been so intent on Dan that she had put the blood on the bathroom floor out of her mind, but after speaking to Danny and finding out that George had come back to take the money, her stomach was churning.

Had Chris caught George stealing it? Had he gone for him? Was it George's blood? No, no, of course it wasn't. Chris would never hurt his own brother. He was a good, kind lad, the best of the bunch. She was being silly and had to forget these daft suspicions.

'Are you all right? I don't think you've heard a word I've said.'

'What? Oh, sorry, Yvonne, I was miles away.'

'I said I'll help you when Dan comes home, but before then you'll have to think about where he's going to sleep.'

'Sleep! What do you mean?'

'Mum, he's going to be in a wheelchair. He won't be able to manage the stairs.'

Joan gave herself a mental shake. Dan was her main concern – his care when he came home. 'Yes, you're right, Yvonne. He'll have to sleep down here. I'll get a day bed, but it means getting rid of the sofa.'

'What a shame. And what about a commode? I know the toilet's downstairs, but it might be a job to wheel him through the kitchen to the bathroom.'

For the rest of the evening, Joan concentrated solely on Dan's homecoming, but when Chris came in, she just looked at him and her stomach did a somersault.

'Why are you looking at me like that, Mum?'

'Like what?'

'Like I've done something wrong.'

'Don't be silly, you're imagining things.' Yet even as she said these words, Joan knew she wasn't telling the truth. She did think that Chris had done something wrong, very wrong. Since the day that George had attacked his father, Chris hadn't been the same. There was something in his eyes that hadn't been there before, something deep, something haunted. Joan shuddered. The thought that her favourite son had done something to his brother, along with the fact that George had nearly killed his own father, was unbearable. She couldn't deal with it, she just couldn't, and as usual when unable to face things, she buried her head in the sand.

Chapter Fifteen

The following morning, Danny parked in the drive, and as he and Chris climbed out of the car, his eyes took in their surroundings. The spot in Wimbledon had been chosen for its location: down a narrow lane, it was well out of the way. There were no neighours to question the comings and goings, and they had put Pete Saunders in the cottage. He was an ex-con with a past, reclusive, grateful to work the small-holding, to grow vegetables, and to live rent free in return for his silence. He was the perfect foil should anyone decide to call, playing his part perfectly and acting like an eccentric old git if anyone asked questions. Not that many people had called over the years, but there were the meter readers, the occasional religious touts, and when there were local elections, the party candidates. So far the ploy had worked perfectly and Danny hoped it would continue to do so.

As they walked into the large barn, the high rafters hung with lighting, Danny interrupted the babble of voices. 'Right, let's get started,' he snapped, but he was pleased to see that the girls and their partners were ready. Bored with filming the soft stuff, and looking forward to making the real money-spinners, Danny just wanted to get it over with. He moved to inspect the set.

'We're nearly ready,' Eddy Woodman said as he tested the lighting with his meter.

A harem scene had been attempted with lots of soft draping, the bed covered with red satin sheets. Bright, embroidered silk cushions had been scattered along the headboard, but Danny shook his head, saying in disgust, 'You fucking morons. Since when did sheiks sleep in beds?'

'You and Chris are a bit late so we'd thought we'd get things moving,' Eddy protested, 'and it looks all right to me.'

Danny was about to explode again when Chris spoke.

'We're supposed to be in a desert, not a suburban bedroom, but it won't take long to put right. Give me a hand, Eddy. We'll take the mattress off the bed and put it on the floor. Set up a canvas backdrop and hang a few lamps around.'

'I'm supposed to be the cameraman, not the bloody labourer,' Eddy moaned. 'George used to do the humping.'

'Well, he ain't here, so just get on with it,' Danny snapped.

After one look at Danny's face, Eddy hurried to do his bidding, the task soon completed.

'It looks nice,' Andrea said as she preened in her mauve, chiffon costume.

With her midriff exposed and long shapely legs visible through the gauze trousers, Danny had to admit she looked tasty. Her long, dark, straight hair tumbled down her back, but the effect was spoiled by her chewing vigorously on gum.

'Have you looked at your part?' Danny asked.

'Yeah, it's a piece of cake. I'm dragged in, protesting, and when the sheik pulls off my veil I act scared. Then when he starts on me, I struggle for a little while before giving in. I then start to enjoy it and we get down to business.'

Danny exhaled loudly. 'Yeah, well, just make sure you ain't chewing that bloody gum.'

Andrea giggled and once again Danny was struck by how innocent she looked. Innocent – that was a bloody laugh. The girl was a tart, but she usually played her parts well. His eyes flicked to the so-called sheik, a bloke they used regularly. Tall, muscular and covered in tan-coloured panstick, he looked the part, and his costume wasn't bad either. He had played many roles but, like Andrea, he wanted to be on the stage. The soft-porn roles were just a way of making money whilst he waited for his big break.

At first Danny had loved the filming, finding

himself aroused every time he watched the action, and though they pretended otherwise, he knew his brothers had felt the same. Of course, unlike him, they went home to their wives, whereas he would call round to his latest girlfriend to indulge his fantasies. Some of the girls they used were on offer, but Danny wouldn't touch them with a bargepole. He'd never fancied going in after they'd been with someone else, and he wasn't about to start now, despite the inviting smile he got from Rusty, a redhead who made it obvious she fancied him.

'Right, let's get started,' he ordered.

Eddy checked the lighting again before moving behind the camera, saying to Danny as though it was an afterthought, 'How's your dad?'

'About the same, but he's coming home soon so things can get back to normal. Bob will be able to do the editing full time again, and Chris will here to handle the sets.'

With a few more tweaks to the scenery they were ready, and Danny stood behind Eddy as the camera began to roll. Andrea was dragged in by two blokes dressed up to look like eunuchs, her eyes wide with fear, her acting perfect as she got into the role. For once it went without a hitch, and Danny found his thoughts drifting, bored with seeing sex acted out.

He thought back to what his mother had said: that if the old man had peace and quiet, lack of stress, he might make a recovery. If that was the case, his father would be in charge again, but Danny loved being in control and didn't want to give it up.

By ten o'clock that evening, most of the residents of Drapers Alley were at home. In number six, the kids were in bed, and with only the gentle ticking of the mantel clock, all was quiet. Steve put down his newspaper, and then ran a hand over his face.

'Why haven't you been to visit your uncle?' he asked Ivy.

She shrugged. 'I haven't had the chance, and anyway, I haven't been asked. Maurice drives Joan and Yvonne up there every day, but I ain't been invited, and in the evenings it's the same. The boys and Pet go, but not one of them has given me a thought.'

'You could go on the bus.'

'Why should I get a bus when the others are all driven in style? Anyway, I ain't the only one who hasn't seen him. Sue and Norma haven't been either.'

'I still think it looks bad.'

'And I think it's bad that you've had to take a cut in your pay. After all, you're the one who does all the work at the yard and the others have hardly shown their faces lately. You should speak up for yourself. Tell Danny you want the same pay *and* a day off every week.'

'With Dan in hospital, the boys are busy. Things will get back to normal once he's home.'

'Don't count on it. Uncle Dan had a stroke so it's doubtful he'll ever be fit to run things again. Anyway, when the boys ain't at the hospital, they still ain't at the yard so I'd love to know where they go and what they get up to.'

'Search me,' Steve said, hoping that Ivy would stop quizzing him. He knew what the boys were up to – knew that when they weren't filming in Wimbledon, they were touting for business. Mind you, he was sure something else was in the wind, but so far he'd been kept in the dark. Despite Ivy telling him to complain, he knew better than to open his mouth. Dan might be ill and incapable of running the business, but his eldest son was even less approachable. Danny was throwing his weight about, snapping orders, with all of them expected to jump at his commands.

Steve's expression was wry. It could be worse. At least Danny had taken over and, though prone to violence, he was a pussycat compared to George. Steve wasn't sorry that George had disappeared off the face of the earth, and he had his own theory about that. He reckoned that George had jumped ship and gone abroad, well out of his brothers' reach.

'Steve, how do you feel about moving away from Drapers Alley?'

Steve's face stretched in disbelief. It was Ivy who had wanted to live here in the first place, but he'd move out again like a shot. 'Yeah, it would suit me, but what makes you think the council would rehouse us?'

'I don't know if they will, but it wouldn't do any harm to give them a try.'

'What's brought this on, Ivy?'

'Oh, I dunno. It's just that we don't fit in. I may have been born a Draper, but we're treated like outcasts. Linda was the only one who bothered with me, but now she's living with her parents again and I'm stuck on my own, day in, day out. Yvonne and Norma are snobs, and though Sue's as common as muck, she doesn't give me the time of day.'

Steve wanted to tell Ivy why – to tell her that it was her own fault – but if it meant getting out of Drapers Alley, he'd continue to keep his thoughts to himself. The truth was that instead of trying to make friends with any of them, Ivy made mischief, playing one off against the other. It had worked at first, but they had soon got wind of what she was up to and now they avoided her like the plague.

He shifted in his seat, smiling at the thought of leaving the alley. He could go back to totting, but in fact he'd do anything to earn a bob or two, anything but work for the Drapers. No more fear of getting stopped by the police – of them finding the bloody films he was delivering. He could be his own boss again!

'Get on to the council first thing in the morning, love,' he said, standing up to give his wife a swift hug.

'Yeah, I will, and I might even ask if we can be housed outside of the borough.'

'Suits me, love,' he said, winking before adding, 'and how about an early night?'

'All right, you're on.'

Steve smiled. Ivy may not be an oil painting, but beggars couldn't be choosers, and, with his loins stirring, he eagerly followed her upstairs.

Next door, Maurice was getting his usual earful from Norma, his voice tired as he answered, 'I've told you business is slow, and until things pick up you'll have to make do with what I can give you.'

'Make do! Do you think I can conjure shoes for Oliver out of thin air? Yes, I can cut down on food, bulk up with vegetables, but I can't force Oliver's feet into shoes that are now a size too small. You should be thankful that Oliver takes care of his shoes, unlike Sue's boys, so they last a good while. However, he can't help it when he grows out of them.'

'With what they cost, they should last. Anyway, can't you get him some cheap plimsolls for now? I used to wear them as a kid and they didn't do me any harm.'

'Are you mad?' Norma shrieked. 'They're only fit for PE, and I am *not* sending Oliver to school wearing plimsolls. You'll have to give me extra house-keeping this week and that's that!'

'Enough, Norma!' Maurice snapped. 'I'm sick to death of your demands! When you're not nagging me to leave Drapers Alley, you're on about money. You'll get what I give you and I don't want to hear another word about it!'

Maurice had to hide a smile when he saw the shock on his wife's face. Her mouth opened and closed, for once floundering for words. He rarely lost his temper, rarely stood up to her, in fact for a quiet life he seemed to spend most of his time placating Norma. It felt good to take a leaf out of Danny's book, but this thought was wiped out when Norma found her voice again.

She rose to her feet, her face red with anger. 'How dare you speak to me like that? I'm not asking for money for myself, I'm asking for money to buy *our* son a decent pair of shoes. I don't know what's come over you lately, but I won't be spoken to like a common fishwife.'

Maurice quickly broke in. It was all right for Danny to talk about controlling their wives, but if he didn't calm Norma down she'd go on and on until he couldn't stand it any more. 'All right, I apologise. I shouldn't have snapped at you like that. It's just that with Dad in hospital and the loss of trade at the yard, I'm feeling a bit stressed.'

Norma stood glaring at him, arms folded across her chest, but then exhaled loudly. 'All right, Maurice, I know you're under a lot of strain at the moment so I'll let it pass, but there is still the question of new shoes for Oliver.'

'I'll see what I can do,' he said, hoping that it would be sufficient to placate her for now. If only she'd be content with plimolls or a cheap pair of shoes, but no, Oliver always had to have the best. That had been fine in the past, and no doubt there'd be more money available soon, but for now they really did have to tighten the purse strings. His brothers' wives seemed to have accepted that, so why couldn't she?

Maurice found his chest wheezing as he took a breath. 'I really am bushed, Norma. If you don't mind, I think I'll go to bed.'

'I'll just tidy up, then I'll join you,' she said, her voice clipped.

Maurice wearily went upstairs, but as he undressed and climbed into bed, his chest was whistling, his breathing so laboured that he had to prop himself up on several pillows. He closed his eyes, finding that, as usual, his thoughts turned to his father. It was such a relief that the old man had survived George's beating, but it looked doubtful that he'd recover from the stroke. It meant that Danny would continue to be in charge, and now Maurice's chest heaved as he fought for air. He didn't trust Danny lately and was worried about where he was taking the business. Yes, they'd agreed to hard porn, and there was no doubt that they needed to make more money, but he couldn't dismiss his fears. Garston and other competitors weren't going to take the intrusion into their territory lightly and they were sure to retaliate. Under their father's leadership, they'd had little to worry about, with Drapers Alley a safe haven. Now, though, with taking on the hard stuff, all that could come to an end, and Maurice feared the future. His chest tightened and in panic he fought for air, sweat beading his forehead. For the first time he understood why Norma wanted to leave, and was horrified by the thought of Oliver in danger.

'Maurice, you look awful. Here, drink this.'

He turned his head, grateful for Norma's ministrations. Yes, she was a nag. Yes, she drove him mad sometimes, but when he was feeling like this, unable to breathe, his heart beating wildly in his chest, Norma always tended to him. Taking a cloth dipped in cool water, Norma bathed his forehead, whispering reassurances until at last he was able to fill his lungs with air.

'You poor darling. Are you feeling better now?'

'Yes, thanks, love.'

He watched now as Norma undressed and when she climbed into bed, she snuggled close. All right, he may not be the boss, unable to control his wife like Danny, but none of this mattered now as Maurice closed his eyes and drifted off to sleep.

* * *

210

Sue and Bob were still up, snuggled on the sofa as they listened to the radio. The room was untidy, a pile of ironing still untouched, but Bob hardly noticed as Sue ran a hand along his thigh.

'Was your dad any better this evening? Did he manage to say anything?'

'No, and as usual he seemed agitated. Mum thinks he wants to see Danny, but he didn't turn up.'

'Pet came to see me after school. She knows that your father had a stroke.'

'Yeah, Maurice told her, and Danny wasn't too pleased about it.'

'She isn't a child now, Bob.'

'She's still only fourteen.'

'Oh, for God's sake, Pet leaves school soon and it's about time you all let her grow up. She hates being treated like a child.'

Bob ran a hand over his face, changing the subject as he blurted out, 'Sue, I can't stand it that Danny's in charge. It ain't right, and I reckon we should all have an equal say in the running of the business.'

'It's only a builders' merchants. Surely it doesn't take much to run it.'

Bob swallowed. Blimey, he'd have to watch his mouth. 'Yeah, well, we should still have an equal say.'

'Never mind,' Sue consoled. 'Things could change. When your dad's home in familiar surroundings, he may get better.'

Sue continued to stroke his thigh and, glad of the distraction, Bob twisted in his seat. 'If you don't stop doing that I'll have to take you to bed. I wouldn't say no to a bit of slap and tickle.'

'I thought you'd never ask,' Sue said, smiling teasingly as she quickly stood up. 'Come on then, big boy, let's see what you're made of.'

Bob made a grab for her, and Sue squealed, giggling as he chased her upstairs.

Through the thin walls, Yvonne heard Sue's squeal and felt a surge of jealousy. For the first time in ages, Danny had come home early, but instead of the fun and games that she could hear next door, she felt only the pain of rejection. Danny had hardly spoken to her, and not long after ten he had gone to bed, saying he was tired and needed an early night. She had followed him upstairs, but he'd fallen asleep as soon as his head touched the pillow, whilst she had lain beside him, frustrated. It had been over a month since he had touched her, held her, or even kissed her, and now she was in despair. There was another woman, Yvonne was sure of it, and knew from past experience that he wouldn't make love to her until his affair ran its course. Was this one serious? Would he leave her?

Unable to sleep she had got up again, and after making herself a cup of cocoa, she sat alone in the living room. An hour passed, and still wide awake,

Yvonne rose to her feet to look out of the window. She pulled back the curtain, but as usual there was little to see, just the factory wall and the entrance to the alley. A shape appeared, and as it passed the bollard, she saw it was Chris. Yvonne frowned. It was late and she wondered where he had been, but then she shrugged. Unlike Danny, Chris was a single man, and a nice-looking one at that. Secretly, he was Yvonne's favourite brother-in-law. Chris was always polite, always thoughtful and, unlike Danny, she felt that when he finally settled down he'd be faithful. She stepped back from the window, knocking the small side table and sending her empty cup crashing to the floor. Swiftly Yvonne bent to clear up the mess, startled when she heard a voice.

'What are you doing? Why aren't you in bed?'

Yvonne looked up to see her husband framed in the doorway. 'I . . . I couldn't sleep so I came down to make myself a drink. I'm sorry I woke you.'

Instead of berating her, Danny said softly, 'Leave that until the morning. Come on – come to bed.'

Yvonne left the broken china where it was to follow Danny upstairs. She threw off her dressing gown, surprised when she got into bed to feel Danny's arms snaking around her. She turned her head, and in the soft glow from the bedside light, she saw his slow smile. Yvonne knew that look and felt a thrill of anticipation. Danny made love to her, slowly at first, but then with increasing passion.

Yvonne revelled in the feelings that he aroused, ones that were mixed with relief. Her fears dissolved. Danny may have been seeing another woman, but as always, he had come back to her.

Chris, the last member of the family to arrive home, carefully unlocked the door, trying to make as little noise as possible as he went upstairs. He didn't want to wake his mother, not when she was under so much strain lately. She had always been distant, remote, but he was seeing another side of her now. She was so focused and protective that it was like seeing a mother guarding her child, instead of a wife with her husband. Chris's lips tightened. She had never been protective of him. Instead, as a child, it had been his father he had to run to when he was upset or in trouble. He had longed to feel his mother's love, longed to be held in her arms, but when he had gone to her, she had pushed him away. Chris had never forgotten it and her rejection still haunted him. With older brothers he had hidden his feelings, knowing that if he cried they would have called him a sissy. Instead he had tried to toughen up, and when he was old enough his father had initiated him into the family business.

Chris felt a surge of pain. It broke his heart to see his father now – the man he had looked up to and admired, reduced to a babbling wreck. George had done that to him. George had all but destroyed their father.

His guts tightened and his heart rate rose as he moved past his mother's room. He wanted to fling open her bedroom door, to confide in her, but she would never understand. It was impossible. He had to keep his secret, not just from his mother, but from his whole family.

'Hello. You're late,' Pet said, stepping out of her bedroom. 'I can't sleep and I'm going downstairs to make a drink.'

Chris fought to pull himself together. 'Shush, you'll wake Mum.'

'Can we talk?'

'Yeah, all right,' Chris said as the two of them went quietly downstairs, and it was only when they were both sitting at the table that he spoke again. 'I'm surprised you're still awake. What do you want to talk about?'

'This family. Dad's ill in hospital and I know that he had a stroke. Until now, I've pushed everything else to the back of my mind, but he's coming home soon and I can't stop thinking about it.'

'Thinking about what?'

'The fact that Dad, and all of you, are criminals.'

'Don't be daft, that's all in the past.'

'Don't bother denying it, Chris.'

For the first time Chris saw the change in his sister. She looked harder, her eyes less innocent. He'd been so wrapped up in his father's recovery and the changes to the business, that he'd hardly noticed or given a thought to his little sister. 'What makes you think we're criminals?'

'It started with George and the way he treated his wife. I saw the violence, and Dad's reaction was just as bad. Then when I went to the dance at the youth club I met a chap, but as soon as he found out that I'm a Draper, he ran off, obviously scared out of his wits.'

'It's just as well. You're too young to be going out on dates.'

'Stop it! You're treating me like a child again. Tell me the truth, Chris. Just what is this family involved in? What made that chap run off like that?'

Chris lowered his eyes. For years they had kept Pet in ignorance, fobbing her off by telling her that they now ran a legit business, but she was growing up and blokes were starting to sniff around. With the family's reputation he wasn't surprised that one had bolted as soon as he found out that Pet was a Draper. Bugger it. He'd have to give her some sort of explanation, but it could hardly be the truth. 'Look, we ain't really criminals. Until recently we did a bit of money lending, and for a backhander we offered local business protection. That's all, Pet. If businesses didn't stump up, or anyone welshed on a loan, we sometimes had to be a bit heavy with them and it gave us a bit of a reputation.'

'Heavy. What does that mean? Did you beat them up, is that it?'

'Well, not exactly beat them up, but if they weren't wary of us, they'd have tried to get out of paying their dues.'

'Don't take me for a fool, Chris. What you're telling me is bad enough, but if it was true, I'm sure I would have heard about it. What are you really up to?'

Chris abruptly stood up. He had done his best, but he hadn't fooled Pet. He'd have to have a word with Danny. Maybe his brother could come up with something to fob her off, but he'd have to get to him in the morning before Pet did. In the meantime, he didn't want to face any more questions. 'Look, I've told you the truth, but if you don't believe me, ask Danny.'

'Oh, I will, but what about Mum? Did she know what you were up to?'

'Of course not. Dad ain't proud of what we did, but at the time the yard wasn't making enough to support six families so it's something we got into to make a few extra bob. Dad doesn't want Mum to know about it, so keep your mouth shut. Now it's late and I'm going to bed. With school in the morning, I suggest you do the same.'

'Yes, I'll go to bed, but you needn't think I've swallowed your lies. I'm not giving up until I hear the truth.'

Chris felt his temper flare. 'And what good would that do? If you find out the so-called truth, do you think it will make any difference? Do you think it will make your life any better? Believe me, it won't. You'd be better off remaining in ignorance.'

On that note, Chris turned on his heels, this time forgetting to tread quietly as he went upstairs. In his room, he threw off his clothes before flinging himself onto his bed. He'd made a mistake telling Pet that they were loan sharks, but he shouldn't have lost his temper. Maybe he should have told her that they were thieves, robbers, because even that would be preferable to her finding out what they really did. If she ever discovered their secret – his secret – he dreaded to think what her reaction would be. Despite saying she wasn't a child now, Pet was still innocent, untouched, and finding out that they were involved in the seedy world of porn could destroy her.

Chapter Sixteen

Chris had managed to talk to Danny before Pet was up the next morning, and now his brother was scowling. 'She's just a kid. Tell her to mind her own bleedin' business.'

'I don't think that'd work. Pet's growing up, and she's seen too much lately. She won't be fobbed off with the story I came up with.'

'I'm not surprised. Did you really expect her to believe that we offered protection and loans?'

'It was all I could come up with at the time.'

'Leave Pet to me. I'll have a word with her, but unlike you, I'll make sure she keeps her nose out of our affairs. Despite what you say, she's still just a kid, and a girl at that. What we men do to put bread on the table is none of her business and I'll make sure she understands that.'

Chris doubted that Pet would stand for it, but he kept his thoughts to himself. Danny had made it clear that he was running the show now, and that meant sorting out any problems within the family too. That was fine with Chris. He knew that he was considered to be Mr Nice Guy, and he wanted it to stay that way.

'Yeah, right, I'll leave Pet to you. Are we making another film today?'

'Yeah, I think we'll do a hospital theme. It seems apt, and a lot of men fantasise about nurses.'

'Ain't we done that before?'

'Yeah, but it was a while ago. To be honest, I'm running out of ideas. If you ask me, we've covered just about everything.'

'I don't suppose it would hurt to use all the themes again. We just have to rotate the girls and their partners and make a few adjustments to the storylines. What have you got in mind for the first hard-porn film?'

'It's got to be good, different; something that will top anything Garson has come up with. I was thinking of three in a bed.'

'Ain't that a bit old hat?'

'Not the threesome I've got in mind.'

Chris was about to ask more when Danny held a finger to his lips. 'Shush, Yvonne is on her way down. She's usually up at the crack of dawn, but I think I wore her out last night, if you know what I mean.' He gave a lewd wink.

'Morning, Yvonne,' Chris said, eyeing his sister-in-law as she walked into the room. She was wearing a long, pink candlewick dressing gown and looked thin, yet soft with her hair tousled and cheeks flushed.

'Hello, Chris. Goodness, look at the time. Why didn't you wake me, Danny?'

'It's only seven thirty and I was just about to, but then again, I was considering coming back to bed for another bit of slap and tickle.'

'Danny!' she exclaimed, the blush turning from pink to red before she almost ran into the kitchen, calling over her shoulder, 'I'll get your breakfast going.'

'I'm off,' Chris said. 'I'll see you later.'

Chris went back next door and found that his mother and Pet were up, both sitting at the table with a pot of tea and rack of toast already made.

'Where have you been?' Pet asked.

'I had a word with Danny about the arrangements for today.'

'Is that *all*, or did you discuss something else?'

'Just work,' Chris said before he sat down at the table, his eyes going to his mother. 'Are you all right, Mum?'

'Of course I am.'

'I expect you're looking forward to Dad coming home.'

'Yes, I am, but when he does there'll be some changes. I don't want your father to be worried about anything. If he has peace and quiet, he might get better. Petula, there's to be no more loud music, and you, Chris, I don't want to hear any business talk. Is that clear?'

'Yes.'

'Good. In fact, the more the pair of you stay out of his way, the better.'

Chris saw Pet's look of dismay, and felt the same. Now that his father had been cut down, felled, his mother had become strong. She was shutting him out as always, and from his father too. Well, he wasn't going to stand for that.

Pet was fuming. She had been to see Danny before leaving for school and he had told her in no uncertain terms to keep her nose out of the family business. Danny had never spoken to her like that before, his eyes hard and manner implacable. It was as if, as with George and her father, she was seeing him in a new light.

Since the day that George attacked their father, Pet felt as though everything had changed – that her life would never be the same again. She still didn't know what her family was mixed up in, but from what Chris had said, it was obviously some-thing illegal and dangerous. He'd lost his temper, saying she'd be better off not knowing. Yet that had only made her more determined to discover the truth, and now Pet's jaw jutted with determination.

Yet only moments later, she faltered. Did she really

want to know? If it was something really bad, how would she feel? Her father must be the leader, yet how could the man who loved and protected her be a criminal? Maybe it was better to remain in ignorance, to shut her eyes to what went on around her. For the first time in her life, Pet felt truly alone, and with this feeling the last vestige of childhood left her.

Pet reached the school gates, walking in to see first- and second-year kids running around as though they didn't have a care in the world. She felt remote from them, so much older now, and seeing two of her friends lounging against the wall, she traversed the playground to reach them.

Jane's expression lit up, her face animated. 'Pet, have you heard the news?'

'What news?'

'It's Wendy,' said Susan. 'She's pregnant.'

Pet gawked, and instantly a face sprang to her mind. 'Pregnant? Oh, my God. Who's the father? Was it that chap she danced with at the club?'

'If you mean Tony Thorn, no, it isn't his.'

'It was some bloke she was seeing on the sly, and her parents are going mad,' Susan said.

'Oh, poor Wendy. What is she going to do?' asked Pet.

'I think her parents want it adopted, but in the meantime, she isn't coming back to school,' said Jane. 'I don't blame her. If I was in her shoes I wouldn't be able to show my face.'

'But what if she doesn't want it adopted?'

'Well, Pet, I don't think she's got much choice,' said Susan. 'Oh, there's the bell. Come on, we'd better go in. We've got Miss Jones for history and you know what she's like if we're late.'

The three girls walked into the building, Pet's mind still on Wendy. Fourteen and pregnant – how awful. And then to have to have the baby adopted . . . She would be the talk of the school, the area, her life ruined. Pet knew what it was like to be talked about. All her life she had been shunned because she was a Draper, and her heart went out to poor Wendy Baker.

Danny looked at his watch. It was one o'clock and the film they were making was well underway. He moved over to Chris, saying quietly, 'I'm going to sort out the girls for our first hard-core film. You and Bob can finish up here.'

Danny left the building. In truth, he was going to the hospital and wanted to get there well ahead of his mother. He was tense as he drove off, gripping the steering wheel tightly. He cared about the old man, but didn't want him back in action. His father had always been the one in control, the one who made all the decisions, and Danny had lost count of the times he had suggested changes, only for his father to veto his ideas. The old man pretended to put them to the vote, but made it clear from the start whether he liked them or not. He was a wily old sod and knew that none of his sons would go against him. The last meeting had proved that.

Things had changed now, Danny thought. He was the one in control and didn't want to give it up. He loved it, but there was always the risk that his father would recover his speech, and if he did, there was no guarantee that he'd leave him in charge. Danny was determined to get through to his father, to make him understand that if he didn't want all his hard work over the years wasted he should leave him in control. Bob and Maurice were too weak, and Chris too young. Things would go to pot if the firm was taken out of his hands, and Danny was determined to tell the old man just that.

When he arrived at the hospital, Danny went to the ward, but as he walked in a nurse held up her hand. 'It isn't visiting time for another fifteen minutes.'

Danny used his charms, smiling ruefully at the nurse. 'I'm sorry, love, I must have got the visiting hours wrong. Look, I've had a long drive and I'm anxious to see my father. Surely it won't hurt if you let me in.'

'All right, but you're lucky. Matron just left and our ward sister is having her lunch.'

'Thanks, darling,' Danny said as he moved past the nurse.

His father was at the end of the ward, his bed the

last in the row, and as though his father was hard of hearing, Danny shouted, 'Hello, Dad.'

Dan's reaction was instantaneous. He tried to speak, his good arm waving as he spat out his odd gibberish.

'It's all right,' Danny placated. 'There's nothing to worry about. The business is fine and I'm looking after everything. I'm getting the other stuff we talked about up and running. We'll soon be making a mint and you'll be able to have that house in the country you've always wanted.'

He watched as his father struggled to sit up, the noise he was making now resembling that of a bellowing bull. Moments later something changed and, worried, Danny cried, 'Dad, Dad, are you all right? Nurse! Nurse!'

The nurse who had tried to bar his entry hurried down the ward. 'What happened?' she said as she reached the side of the bed.

Danny struggled to pull himself together. 'I . . . I don't know. He just sort of went funny, like he was having a fit.'

'I'll get the doctor.'

'Is he gonna be all right?'

'We'll know when the doctor has had a look at him. Now, please, wait outside,' the nurse said before closing the curtains around the bed.

Danny didn't need telling twice and almost ran out of the ward. He hovered outside, saw the doctor arrive and then he began to pace. He shouldn't have come. One look at him and his father became apoplectic. Bloody hell, all he'd tried to do was to reassure the old man, but instead he'd made things worse. He'd told him that the business was doing fine, said they'd make a mint producing hard porn . . . Danny paused, the blood draining from his face. Shit! Had his father thought he was talking about using kids? Oh God, what had he done? What if his father died? He'd have caused it!

Joan smiled when she saw Danny in the corridor, pleased that he had come to visit his father at last.

'Hello, Danny,' Yvonne said. 'I'm surprised to see you here during the day.'

'Me too,' Maurice said, obviously puzzled.

'I had a bit of time to kill, and as I was in the area I thought I'd pop in to see Dad.'

'Come on, let's go in,' Joan urged.

'We can't, Mum.'

'Why?' Joan asked, but something in Danny's expression caused her heart to thump with fear. 'What's wrong?'

'Dad was taken bad and the doctor's with him.'

'Bad! When?'

'It was only a little while ago. I had only been in there for a few minutes when he came over sort of funny.'

'Oh, Danny, don't tell me he's had another stroke!'

'I dunno, Mum. We'll have to wait and see what the doctor has to say.'

'But what brought it on?'

'Search me. I was just telling him that everything is fine with the business when he had some sort of fit.'

Joan felt her knees give way beneath her, grateful when Yvonne stepped forward to take her arm, saying gently, 'Come on, Mum, let's find you a seat. Danny will tell one of the nurses where we are.'

In a daze, Joan allowed herself to be led to a waiting room. She found herself silently praying. She knew the others were talking, but their voices washed over her as she begged for Dan's life.

At last the doctor appeared and Joan surged to her feet. 'How is my husband?'

'I'm afraid he's had another stroke.'

Joan managed to stay on her feet, but her voice was a croak. 'Is . . . is he going to be all right?'

The doctor's face was grave. 'We'll know more in twenty-four hours.'

'Can I see him?'

'For a few minutes and with only one other visitor.'

'Danny,' Joan said. She saw her son hesitate; saw the look of fear on his face. He looked so pale but she wasn't surprised. Like her, he was obviously worried sick about his father.

'No, it's all right. Maurice can go with you.'

'You're the eldest, Danny,' she said.

Danny appeared reluctant, but impatiently Joan urged him forward. When they walked into the ward the curtains were still around Dan's bed and for a moment Joan paused, fearful of what she'd find. She then drew in a huge gulp of air before moving forward to draw them back. With Danny just behind her she almost crept inside, her hand immediately going to her mouth in shock. Dan was unconscious, ashen, an oxygen mask covering his mouth.

'Oh, no. He looks awful.'

Joan turned panic-stricken eyes to her son, but saw a strange expression on his face, almost like one of relief, as he whispered, 'He's out for the count, Mum. Come on, we don't want to wake him up. You can come back later.'

'No, I can't leave him.'

Joan took Dan's hand. It felt cold, clammy, and after solicitously tucking it under the blanket, she bent to kiss his forehead.

'Come on, Mum,' Danny urged as he gripped her arm.

Joan's lips tightened in anger. Dan was her husband and she wanted to be there when he woke up. She glared at her son, annoyed that he was in such a hurry to go. 'We've only just got here.'

'The doctor said we can only stay for a few minutes.'

Joan was about to speak when the curtain was

pulled back. 'I'm sorry, Mrs Draper,' a nurse said, 'you really must leave now.'

'Can't I stay for five minutes?'

It wasn't the nurse who replied, it was Danny. 'No, Mum, you heard the nurse. We've got to go.'

'Why are you in such an all-fired hurry? You've hardly looked at your father.'

'I can't stand to see him like that.'

Joan could see the tension in her son's face and found her anger draining away. He loved his father and, yes, it was obviously breaking his heart to see him like this. She turned away to lean over Dan, her kiss soft above the oxygen mask.

'Don't leave me, Dan,' she whispered, her voice cracking. 'Come back to me.'

'You can see your husband again this evening,' the nurse said as she began to take Dan's blood pressure.

Her emotions in turmoil, Joan was only able to nod. Danny took her arm to lead her away from the ward.

'How is he?' Maurice asked when they joined the others.

'He wasn't conscious, so we don't know,' Danny told him. 'Now come on, let's get Mum home. She looks worn out and needs to rest before coming back this evening.'

As Danny took over, Joan felt a surge of gratitude. He was a good boy, and as she had said, a chip off the old block. He was taking care of her, just like his father. When Dan regained consciousness and she told him how good Danny had been, he'd be so proud of his eldest son.

It had been a fraught twenty-four hours, but at last Joan received the news she'd been waiting for. Dan would survive. His face looked dreadful, drooping on one side, with the right side of his paralysed body, further weakened. The doctor was doubtful now that Dan would ever make a full recovery. The second stroke had delayed his return home, but he was alive, and to Joan that was all that mattered.

With all her energies focused on her husband, Joan was hardly aware of what went on around her. She left everything to Danny, safe in the knowledge that he would continue to look after the family, and the business.

On Friday, Joan sat beside her husband, gripping his good hand. 'Hello, love.'

There was no response. None of his usual gibbering, no arm waving and sighing. Joan wiped the drool from the side of his mouth.

Loudly Maurice asked, 'How are you, Dad?'

'There's no need to shout,' Joan snapped. 'Your father isn't deaf.'

'I reckon it's a trait in your family,' the man from the next bed called. 'Your other son was just as bad, shouting at the poor bloke as though he's deaf.'

Joan was annoyed at the interruption, but puzzled too. 'What son? I don't know who you mean.'

'I'm talking about the one who came to see your husband just before he had another stroke.'

'Oh, you mean Danny. Why was he shouting?'

'Search me, but your hubby got really agitated when he saw him. Your son tried to calm him down. He told him that he was taking care of the business and there was nothing for him to worry about.'

'Yes, he's a good lad,' Joan said.

'If you ask me, these youngsters are all the same. They think that just because we're old, we've lost our marbles or we're hard of hearing. They forget that we fought for our country during the war. They should give us a bit more respect.'

Joan switched off as the man ranted on and on. Poor Danny, it must have been awful for him to see his father having another stroke.

She leaned forward, her voice soft. 'Oh, Dan, you'd be so proud of Danny. He makes sure I'm all right, taking care of me just like you did.'

There was a sound, a sort of groan and Joan felt a surge of hope. Dan had responded for the first time since his second stroke, and maybe there'd be other improvements soon.

Chapter Seventeen

It was now August and Danny was putting all his energies into the hard-core films. It was hot, and though the rafters were high, the barn felt stifling.

Danny's face was beaded with sweat, but his mind was set on the task in hand. He didn't want to think about his father – about what he'd done. The guilt swamped him, keeping him awake at night, until at last he decided there was only one thing he could do to assuage his guilt. His father hadn't got any better, and he'd been sent home last month, but from what Yvonne had told him, space was short now that he was in a wheelchair. He'd have to make sure they made lots of money, enough to ensure that his father had every comfort – even the house in the country that he'd dreamed of.

He looked through the camera, and as the two men and the girl got into position, he snapped his orders. 'Bob, check the lighting.'

'We could do with Maurice.'

'He's feeling rough today and anyway he's not a lot of help – so stop bloody carping and get on with it.'

Bob scowled but Danny ignored him. Chris came to stand behind the camera, having completed his work on the set, and at last they were ready to roll.

The girl had been told what to do, and when Danny said, 'Right, get on with it,' she went into action.

She was one of Lillie's girls and good – very good, Danny saw – but he'd watched some of Garston's films and it would have to be graphic to compete. As he'd instructed, one bloke was taking her from behind, but now it was time to up the action. Danny zoomed in, ready for a close-up of the oral sex. 'Right, Mary, take the other bloke in your mouth.'

Yes, it was graphic, but they needed more like this in the bag. The worry was getting to him, the responsibility, the need to make money, not for himself now, but for his father. He'd wanted to be in control, to run things, but now all his energies were focused on his old man, on his comfort. Danny knew that he'd caused his father's second stroke, knew it could have killed him, and once again the guilt overwhelmed him.

Late that night, Ivy was fidgeting nervously as she looked out of the window. The kids were tired, but she'd had to keep them up. Steve was chuffed, waiting for the off, as anxious as she was to leave Drapers Alley.

'I still can't believe we got this council exchange,' Steve said. 'It's bloody marvellous. I'd love to be around to see their faces when another family moves into this place.'

'Yeah, and Danny's when you ain't around to run the bloody yard,' said Ivy. She had waited until Auntie Joan's lights had gone out, and now regretted sneaking out to stick a note through her door. It would have been more satisfying to have just left without warning, but it was too late now. Mind, she hadn't told her the story about the exchange – just that they were leaving. Ivy smiled happily. There'd be little chance of them finding out where they had gone.

'I didn't even know that the council offered exchanges,' Steve said.

'Yeah, well, it's just as well that they do. Mind you, it wasn't easy. Most of the people on the list wanted the same area, but bigger places with more bedrooms. I was lucky to find a family in Kent who wanted to move to Battersea, *and* that they agreed to swap their place for Drapers Alley.'

'I still don't think that Dan will let them move in.'

Ivy shrugged. 'He ain't in a fit state to stop them. Anyway, he doesn't own this house, and as the council agreed the exchange nobody can stop them.'

'Danny might, and I wouldn't want to be in their shoes in the morning.'

'Look, the family used to live in this area, and if they haven't heard of the Drapers, it ain't our problem. The husband has been offered a good job in the brewery so they want to move back, and it's up to them to sort anyone out who wants to stop them.'

'Yeah, well, I wish them luck.'

Ivy risked a peek outside. The night was clear, the moon shining, yet she consoled herself with the thought that it wasn't far to the corner. If they went now they should make it unseen. 'I think we can risk it.'

'I hope you're right,' Steve said, 'but I still don't know why we're sneaking off like this.'

'For Gawd's sake, Steve, we talked about this. For one, you were too scared to tell Danny that you're leaving the yard, and secondly it's a way to pay him back for the way you've been treated. When we go without warning he'll be left in the shit with nobody to take your place.'

Steve scratched his head. 'Yeah, I suppose so, but it still seems a bit cloak and dagger.'

'What's cloak and dagger, Daddy?' Ernie asked.

It was Ivy who answered. 'It's an adventure. Now come on, kids, we're off. When we get outside I want you to scoot around the corner.'

Harry yawned and Ivy became impatient. 'Steve, you'll have to pick him up.'

'Leave it out. How am I supposed to do that *and* carry the suitcases?'

Ivy heaved a sigh. 'Ernie, I want you to hold Harry's hand, and make sure that he doesn't dawdle.'

'Why have we got to go? Why can't we stay here?'

'I've told you. We're moving to a new house, and when you see it, you'll love it. Now shut up about it, and as I said, hold Harry's hand.'

With that, Ivy picked up two suitcases, whilst Steve did the same. She took one last peek outside and then ushering the boys ahead of her, she urged them on as they all scooted out of the alley. Steve had been reluctant to use what little money they had saved to buy an old banger, but Ivy had told him that a car, even one that looked a bit of a wreck, was essential in the country. There'd be no buses to hop on, no underground trains, but despite the remoteness of the village, she couldn't wait to get there.

Steve found the old car hard to start and Ivy's nerves were jangling, but even so she was happy. After all this time everything she had hoped for had come to fruition. She had wanted to see her uncle brought low, and thanks to George he was suffering now, just as her mother had. Her Uncle Dan was finished, in a wheelchair, a gibbering wreck. Yes, it was time to leave Drapers Alley – time for her new life to begin.

When Joan got up the following morning, she saw the note that had been shoved through her letter box and ran to pick it up. It was from Ivy, to tell her that they had left the alley. Joan threw it down. It was a bit sudden, but in truth she didn't care. When she had first seen the note her heart had skipped, hoping it was from George, because despite what he had done he was still her son, and she couldn't help wondering where he was. It had been over three months now – three long months without news.

As though reading her mind, Pet asked, 'Mum, is that letter from George?'

Joan looked up, her eyes clouded for a moment. 'No, it's from Ivy to tell me that they've moved out.'

'What? But why would she leave without saying goodbye?'

'I don't know,' Joan said impatiently. She didn't care that Ivy had left the alley. She was just pleased to see the back of Dan's niece.

Hearing a soft groan, Joan went over to the day bed, smiling softly. 'Morning, love.'

There was no reply from Dan, just a wave of his good arm, and knowing what he wanted Joan said, 'Come on, Petula, give me a hand. Your dad wants to go to the bathroom.'

The morning routine began then, and Joan was glad of her daughter's help. She was at home from school during the summer holidays, which had been a godsend, but things would become difficult when she returned for her last term. Still, Joan thought, Yvonne was marvellous, always on hand to lend a hand, but it was a shame that she couldn't allow Danny in to see his father. One look at his eldest son and Dan went mad, so much so that she had been forced to tell Danny to stay away. She still didn't understand what caused it, but felt the only explanation could be that Dan resented that he was so helpless – that he was forced to let Danny take over running the business.

When Chris came downstairs half an hour later, Joan handed him Ivy's note, watching as his eyes widened.

'This doesn't make sense. Why has Ivy buggered off without saying anything?'

'Search me,' Joan said, 'but if you ask me it's good riddance to bad rubbish.'

Dan began to gibber and Joan wondered if he was upset that Ivy had left, but was distracted when Chris threw down the note.

'I'd better warn Danny that Steve won't be opening the yard,' he said.

'What about your breakfast?'

'I'll have it later.'

'Come on, Dan, calm down,' Joan urged as Chris hurried out. 'There's no need to take on just because Ivy's gone. She's a grown woman and not your responsibility. If you ask me you've done enough for her, and I ain't pleased that she didn't even bother to come to see you to say goodbye.'

'Dad, don't,' Petula said, taking her father's hand, and as usual, Dan responded immediately to his daughter, slumping ungainly in his chair.

'Petula, get the breakfast on and after that you can go upstairs to make our beds. Go on now, I can see to your father,' Joan snapped.

Petula did as she was told whilst Joan frowned, wondering why Dan always responded well to his daughter, but took no notice of her.

The brothers were at the yard. Danny, fuming, was unaware that a car was parked outside, the three men inside closely watching the entrance.

'I can't fucking believe this,' Danny said, his eyes sweeping over his brothers as he sat behind his dad's old desk. 'With Steve gone we're another man short – who's gonna do the bloody deliveries?'

'I know what dives in Soho have placed orders, so I can take the films out,' Chris offered. 'Are they already in the van?'

'Yeah, they're in the hidden compartment,' said Bob.

'All right. Chris, you take on the driving, and Bob, you'll have to handle the yard,' said Danny, shaking his head with annoyance. 'That just leaves me and Maurice in Wimbledon to handle the filming, but as soon as you've finished the deliveries, Chris, you can meet us there.'

'Why can't Maurice stay in the yard? I'd be more use at Wimbledon,' Bob complained.

'Oh, for fuck's sake, Bob, why do you have to question every decision I make? If we get a big order for building gear, Maurice ain't up to loading it on his own.'

'Yeah, yeah, all right.'

'Sorry, Bob,' said Maurice, his expression sheepish.

'Don't worry about it,' Bob said.

'Right, before we go, let's take a look at the books. How are we doing, Maurice?'

'We're doing all right, and profits are up on last month.'

Danny looked at Maurice's neat entries, somewhat mollified to see that he was right. Yes, things were looking up, but they still had to push harder. It wasn't going to be easy without Steve, and Danny was still annoyed that the git had buggered off without a word. He had no idea where he and Ivy had gone, but if he got his hands on Steve he'd wring his bloody neck.

The three men continued to watch the entrance. So far they had found out little and Jack Garston was growing impatient.

'If you ask me, this is a waste of time,' said one. 'We followed them here, and so far they ain't moved.'

'Are you gonna tell Garston that?' asked another, his wide-set shoulders straining the seams of his suit as he turned towards the back seat.

'Leave it out, of course not.'

The third man sniffed through a nose that had been broken, giving him a pug-faced look. He flexed his large muscular arms before speaking. 'Look, Garston wants us to teach them a lesson, but we need to get one of the Draper boys on his own. Now shut up and just keep watching.'

The sun was rising higher in the sky, all three sweltering and growing more impatient, but at last they saw movement. Two of the Draper boys were heading for a car, whilst another went to a van.

'He's on his own so we'll take him,' the pug-faced one said.

They waited until the van drove off and then followed, keeping a safe distance.

'The Drapers are mad to take on Garston,' the driver said. 'That's something they're soon gonna find out.'

'Yeah. Are we gonna take out his kneecaps like the last bloke?'

'No,' said the pug-faced one, 'it's gonna be in daylight and Garston said to just give him a warning. There'll be no shooters this time.'

They drove over the Thames, still keeping the van in sight, grinning when it eventually reached Soho. This was Garston's territory. He ruled this area and even if there were witnesses, not one of them would dare to say a word. On the rare occasions that anyone dared to cross Jack Garston, his revenge was swift, and so his reputation had grown. There was little he didn't have a hand in. He ran clubs, prostitutes, made hard-porn films, and had a protection racket that lined his coffers with even more money. He ran his empire on fear, his men knowing that they'd be taken out if they didn't obey his orders.

The van now turned into a side street, pulling up outside a sex shop, and the order was given to park behind it.

'Come on,' the pug-faced one said, slipping a knife out of his pocket. 'Grab him and hold him steady, while I mess up his pretty face.' Unaware that he'd been followed, Chris didn't stand a chance. He tried to fight off the men who held him, but two of them had him in a vicelike grip.

The pug-faced one leered, his face close to Chris's as he spat, 'This is a message from Jack Garston. He knows what you Drapers are up to, and wants you out.'

With that he moved back, a sickly grin on his face as he raised his hand, the knife slicing through Chris's cheek like butter. He ignored the scream, saying, 'Count yourself lucky that you're still alive. If you and your brothers don't stay out of Garston's territory, you won't be so lucky next time.'

They shoved Chris then, watching as he landed in the gutter, his face pouring blood. Laughing, they went back to their car and screeched away.

Chapter Eighteen

Danny and Maurice jumped into action as soon as they got the phone call, Danny breaking every speed limit as they drove to the hospital. Chris was already in the treatment room when they got there so Danny paced as he waited outside, whilst Maurice was slumped in a chair beside Bob.

The emergency department was packed, and Danny grimaced when he saw a couple of drunken tramps staggering in. He swiftly changed direction to avoid going near them, yet still their stench reached his nostrils, making them twitch with distaste. Since setting up the hard-porn side of the business in June, there'd been no sign of trouble and he cursed himself for not taking more precautions. From what Bob had told him, Chris's injury wasn't serious, but from now on they would have to raise their guard.

As Chris came out of the treatment room, his cheek covered in a wad of gauze, Maurice rose to his feet. 'Bloody hell, Mum's gonna have a fit when she sees him.'

Danny raised a hand to stroke his scar. 'It never did my reputation any harm.'

'Who did it, Chris? Was it Garston?' Maurice asked.

'Not personally, but a few of his mob.'

'So it's started, and this is probably just a warning. I reckon we should pack it in – get out now before Garston ups the stakes.'

'Leave it out, Maurice,' said Bob. 'We're just starting to rake in the money.'

'Yeah, and we can handle Garston,' said Danny.

Bob touched Chris's arm. 'How do you feel? Is it giving you gyp?'

'Nah, I'll survive. Now come on, let's get out of here.'

The four brothers left casualty, but as they climbed into Danny's car, Maurice continued to complain. 'I still think we should pack it in. What about you, Chris? What do you think? You're the one that got a kicking.'

'I'd hardly call it that. If I'd had a bit of backup, I'd have taken the bastards out.'

'It's my fault,' Danny admitted. 'Garston hasn't done a thing since we started up so I let myself become complacent. It was wrong to underestimate him and I should have seen it coming.'

'You haven't answered my question, Chris,'

Maurice persisted. 'Do you think we should pack it in?'

'No I don't. Stop acting like an old woman, Maurice. This is nothing – if we get a bit more muscle, we can handle Garston.'

'That'll cost an arm and a leg.'

'We'll find the money, so just shut up about it,' Danny said, shoving his foot onto the accelerator and screeching out of the car park.

Though Danny was watching the road, his mind was elsewhere, his thoughts on Garston and just how far the man would go to put them out of business. Well, sod him, because despite Maurice's carping, he wasn't about to give up. To make things right for his father, he needed money, lots of it, but so far almost everything they made went back into the business.

'It's not worth opening up the yard now, or going back to Wimbledon, so we might as well pack in for the day,' Danny said.

When they arrived home, Maurice was still acting like an old woman, looking nervously over his shoulder, and Danny shook his head in disgust. The alley was safe, but Maurice had always been a weakling, useless if there was any sign of trouble, all brains and no brawn.

As Bob and Maurice went into their houses, Chris said, 'Right, I'm going in to face the music. See you later, Danny.'

Danny knew there was no way he could go into his mother's house and just gave Chris a small wave. He had tried to see his father as soon as he came home from hospital, wanting to assure him that he wasn't going to use kids in the films. He hadn't been able to get a word in. When his father saw him he'd gone mad, bellowing like a maniac. His mother had rushed into the room, ordering him out, and telling him that he would have to stay away. Since then she had become like a sentinel, barring his entry. It cracked him up when Yvonne told him that his father wasn't getting any better and Danny knew that the conditions the old man lived in didn't help. He spent all of his time in the cramped living room, his outlook just a factory wall.

Danny felt swamped by depression. He wanted more for his father – decent accommodation and fresh country air – but they needed money to do that. It was getting so that every day was a fight, a fight to hold himself together, but he had to keep going, had to keep the business profitable. He owed his father – and big time.

'What happened to you?' Joan asked as soon as Chris walked in the door.

'I had a bit of an accident at the yard, that's all.'

Joan lifted the gauze to one side, seeing the cut and history repeating itself. Danny had once come home with a similar gash down his cheek. 'You've had stitches and that wound looks like it was caused by a knife.'

'It wasn't, Mum.'

Joan could see she wasn't going to get anything out of her son. Like the rest of the boys, he was secretive, but she was sure he'd been in a fight. Though she didn't want to admit it, Ivy leaving so suddenly had unsettled her. Like George she had just upped and gone. Though she would never be able to forgive her son for what he had done to his father, she couldn't help thinking about him. Had Chris attacked George? And if so, how badly? At times she wondered if she should talk to Danny about her fears, but then always decided against it. There had been enough trouble, enough violence, and anyway, maybe as Chris said, it hadn't been blood on the bathroom floor.

Joan pushed her fears to one side as usual, instead thinking about George's empty house. They had kept up the rent, and would continue to do so, making sure that another family didn't move into the alley, but there was still Ivy's house. She said in her note that she'd got an exchange, but so far nobody had moved into her house. It was bound to happen soon, though, but if strangers moved into the alley, they'd have to keep it away from Dan until they could be chased out. She was about to voice these thoughts to Chris, but then Dan began to grunt, his arm waving.

'What is it, love? Do you need the bathroom?'

When he made a bellowing sound, Chris said, 'I'll give you a hand, Mum.'

'Are you up to it?'

'Of course I am. It's only a cut.'

Joan was glad of the help. She still worried about Chris, the haunted look that was in his eyes, but Dan was her main concern. She could wheel him to the bathroom, but the effort of lifting him onto the toilet without help nearly broke her back. She had tried to get him to use a commode, but he had made his feelings plain even though he couldn't speak, becoming so agitated that she had feared he'd have another stroke. Joan closed her eyes at the thoughts that invaded her mind. She had prayed for Dan's survival and her prayers had been answered, but this wasn't Dan, not any more. He was now like a child, needing almost every-thing done for him. His days were spent just sitting in his wheelchair, his nights asleep on the day bed.

'Where's Pet?' Chris asked.

'She's in the kitchen making the dinner. I don't know what I'll do without her when she goes back to school in September.'

'You'll still have Yvonne to give you a hand, and what's the matter with Norma and Sue? They've offered to help out too.'

'I've told you before, I don't want those two in

here. Your dad is fond of Yvonne and doesn't mind her helping out, but he ain't so keen on the others.'

'Chris, what's wrong with your face?' Pet cried as she came into the room.

'I tripped over in the yard and caught my face on the edge of a pile of bricks.'

Pet's face paled. 'Oh, Chris . . .'

'Look, it's nothing. I don't know what all the fuss is about.'

There was a grunt, hand waving, and Joan berated herself. 'Come on, darling,' she said, 'let's get you to the bathroom.'

Dan closed his eyes in frustration. He hated being helpless, hated being trapped in a body that wouldn't respond. The worst thing was being taken to the bathroom, his wife having to help him onto the toilet and afterwards wiping his arse like a bloody baby. It wasn't dignified, and though Pet or Yvonne left the room as soon as he was lowered onto the toilet, he still felt that he was no longer a man, ashamed that either Yvonne, or worse Pet, would see his willie, or what was left of it.

He was useless now, incapable of speech, incapable of telling his wife that it wasn't the bathroom he wanted, it was to know what the bloody hell was going on. Chris had come in with his face cut, but Dan doubted it was an accident – more like the boys treading on Garston's toes. But what sort of films were they making? Now that he couldn't stop him, had Danny persuaded the others to use children?

There were times like this when his mind was clear, but others when he felt woolly, as though his brain wasn't functioning along with his body. Lately it was these woolly times that he sought, preferring it when he couldn't think clearly – couldn't worry about Danny and what he was doing with the business.

Dan groaned, unable to protest as he was wheeled to the bathroom. At least this time it was Chris who was helping and not his daughter. Pet was his pride and joy and he only felt calm when she was around him. Joan drove him mad, talking to him as if he was an imbecile, or talking over him as if he couldn't hear her every word.

He wasn't a bloody idiot, he still had a brain, but only Pet seemed capable of seeing this. Despite Joan telling the girl not to bother him, Pet would read him the morning paper, picking out articles that she knew he'd enjoy. His daughter was his one solace, but she'd be going back to school soon. Without her Dan knew that the house would close in around him, that he'd have to listen to his wife's inane chatter until she came home again.

'Here we go, Dan,' Joan said as she and Chris heaved him onto the toilet.

Dan bellowed in frustration, but as usual, he was ignored.

Chapter Nineteen

Summer passed, then came the autumn. One day at the beginning of November Pet was on Lavender Hill, shopping for her mother. She had little free time now, her days spent at school, evenings and weekends helping at home. She had given up trying to find out what her brothers were up to, preferring to believe that they were just running the family business. It was easier that way – easier than thinking about the alternative.

With her bags full of groceries she lugged them into the butcher's to join the queue, and her ears pricked when she heard two women gossiping ahead of her. They both reddened when they saw her, but Pet couldn't wait to get home, staggering indoors with her load to say excitedly, 'Mum, I've heard that Linda's had her baby.'

'Has she now?'

'Yes, and can I go to see her? Please, Mum.'

'You might not be welcome, and if you ask me,

if Linda wanted us to know, she'd have told us herself.'

'Oh, Mum, she's too frightened of George to come here.'

'Leave it out. She must know that he's missing.'

'You can't be sure of that. Please, can I go to see her?'

Pet watched her mother's lips purse, holding her breath, but at last she said, 'All right, I don't suppose it would hurt, but you'll have to ask Yvonne to call round to give me a hand with your dad.'

Pet ran to get her coat. She gave her father a swift kiss on the cheek and was about to hurry out when her mother called, 'Don't be long. We've got a lot to do today.'

'All right,' she said, swiftly closing the door behind her. After passing on her mother's message to Yvonne, she left the alley. It was cold and Pet stuffed her hands into her pockets, but she was also smiling. It was nice to have a bit of freedom. Oh, she didn't mind helping her mother, but it was all she did nowadays. She helped in the morning, after school and every weekend. In fact, this was the first time she'd been out on a Saturday for ages.

It was a long walk to Linda's house, and by the time she approached it, Pet was a little nervous. She was unsure of her welcome, and tentatively rang the doorbell.

Enid Simpson looked puzzled when she opened the door, her head cocked to one side.

'Mrs Simpson, it's me, Petula Draper. I've come to see the baby.'

'Petula. My goodness, I didn't recognise you – but then again, I've only seen you a couple of times.' She poked her head outside. 'You've come on your own?'

'My mother couldn't come. She can't leave my father.'

'Yes, well, I heard what happened to your dad. How is he?' Without waiting for a reply, Enid Simpson stood back. 'Oh look, you'd better come in.'

Pet followed the limping woman into the living room, but as soon as Linda saw her she jumped to her feet, the colour draining from her face.

'It's all right, Linda, she's on her own,' Enid said. 'She's come to see the baby,' and then turning to Pet, she added, 'As you can see, Linda is still a nervous wreck.'

'I heard that George was missing . . . but he hasn't turned up again, has he?' Linda gasped.

'No, no, we haven't seen him, and after what he did to my father, I doubt we ever will. My brothers have been searching for him, but he's nowhere to be found.'

'Are you telling the truth?' Enid snapped. 'Linda has filed for divorce, but without knowing where he is, it isn't going to be easy. Are you sure you haven't got his address?'

Pet shifted uncomfortably, wishing now that she hadn't come. 'I'm telling the truth, Mrs Simpson. We really don't know where George is.'

'You can't be sure that he won't come back. Please, Pet, make sure he stays away from me. I don't want him near my baby!'

'Linda, you've got to calm down. It's no wonder that you can't breast-feed. Now isn't it time for Louisa's bottle?'

Her mother's words seemed to have some effect. Linda looked to a crib that was placed near the fire. 'Yes, she's just waking up.'

'All right, I'll make her bottle.'

'I'll do it, Mum. I can see that your hip's playing up.'

'I can manage. What about you, Petula, can I get you anything?'

'No, thank you, Mrs Simpson.' As the woman left, Linda moved to take the baby from the crib.

'Louisa,' said Pet. 'It's a lovely name.'

Holding the baby, Linda seemed calm, and sitting down, she moved the shawl aside to reveal the baby's face. 'It was my grandmother's name.'

'She's beautiful,' Pet whispered. 'Can . . . can I hold her?'

Linda swiftly held the baby close to her chest. 'No, no, you can't, and anyway, I think she needs changing.'

'I won't hurt her.'

'You're a Draper, aren't you? Oh, I'm sorry, please don't look at me like that. It . . . it's just that since having the baby my emotions seem to be all over the place. One minute I'm fine, then the next I find myself down in the dumps. Look, come and sit down and once I've changed Louisa you can hold her.'

Pet perched on the edge of the sofa, watching as Linda changed the baby's nappy. When the pin was in place, she held her out. 'Here, you can have her now, but make sure that you support her head.'

With the baby in her arms, Pet smiled. Louisa was so pretty, and after all her nephews, this was her first niece.

'I wrote to tell Ivy that I've had the baby and she replied this morning,' Linda said, nodding towards a letter on the table. 'She certainly seems to have taken to life in the country.'

'Ivy! You're in touch with Ivy?'

'Well, yes, of course I am. We saw a lot of each other when I lived in the alley, and we're still friends, even if distant ones.'

'We haven't heard a word from her since she left.'

'I know, she told me, but she always speaks well of you, Pet.'

Ivy had left without saying goodbye, and it had always puzzled Pet. Her mother refused to talk about it and her brothers were the same. It was obvious that they didn't have any time for Ivy, but she didn't know why. Ivy had always been nice to her, as had

Steve, and she missed Ernie and Harry, even though they were a pair of scallywags.

'I'd like to write to Ivy. Can I have her address?'

Linda shook her head. 'I'm sorry, but Ivy has asked me not to pass it on.'

'But why?'

Linda was quiet for a moment, small teeth chewing on her lower lip, then said, 'Look, all I know is that she doesn't want anything to do with you Drapers.' The baby began to whimper, then cry, so Linda took her from Pet's arms. 'She's hungry and I don't know why it's taking my mother so long to make her bottle. I'll be back in a tick.'

When Linda left the room, Pet's eyes were drawn to the envelope on the table. She leaned forward, picking it up, and after just a moment's hesitation, she drew out the letter. Her eyes had only scanned the address when the door opened again, and guiltily she looked at Linda.

'Oh, how could you? Ivy will go mad if she finds out.'

'I . . . I'm sorry.'

'Did you see the address?'

'Yes, but that's all.'

'You mustn't tell Ivy. Don't write to her, and for God's sake don't tell anyone else that you know where she is.'

'But why?'

'What's going on?' Enid asked as she walked into the room.

'It's Pet, she read my letter.'

Enid's lips curled. 'What do you expect? She's a Draper, ain't she, and they're all the same.'

'But . . . but I didn't mean any harm.'

'Look at the state of my daughter! If you ask me, you've done enough harm just by coming here. I shouldn't have let you in and now I want you to leave. Tell your mother and the rest of your family that they're not welcome here, and you, miss, don't show your face at my door again.'

Pet fled the room, wrenched open the front door, ran outside, and kept on running until she was out of breath. Oh, it had been awful, dreadful. All right, she shouldn't have looked at Linda's letter, but surely they had overreacted?

By the time Pet arrived home, she had calmed down and looked composed as she walked inside.

'Oh, Pet, I'm glad you're back,' Yvonne said, her upper lip beaded with perspiration. 'I'm not feeling too well and think I've caught a chill, but I didn't want to leave your mum to manage on her own. How was Linda? Did you see the baby?'

'Yes, I saw her, and Linda has called her Louisa.'

'That's nice. Anyway, I'm off.'

Her mother waited until the door had closed behind Yvonne, and then said, 'Babies are always a touchy subject with Yvonne, and if you ask me, she's got more than a chill. I thought the poor girl was gonna pass out. Now then, tell me what happened at Linda's.'

Pet hesitated. If she told her mother the truth, it would only cause more bad feelings, so instead just said, 'There's not much to tell. Linda was fine and I saw the baby, but I didn't stay long.'

'Did she know that George is missing?'

'Yes, but she's still frightened that he'll turn up so I doubt she'll come here.'

'Well, with your father ill I can't leave him to go there, so I don't suppose I'll see the baby. Now then, come on, Pet, the bedrooms need turning out so you'd better make a start.'

Pet said nothing. She knew her mother had little time for her brothers' children, so wasn't surprised that she was showing little interest in the new baby.

She went over to her father, saying, 'I'll just get the bedrooms sorted and then I'll read you the paper.'

He managed a lopsided smile, but then hearing her mother's huff of impatience, Pet hurried upstairs. As she stripped her mother's bed, Pet's mood was low. She couldn't help thinking about Linda and the baby. Louisa was her niece, but it was unlikely that she'd ever see her again. Unexpectedly her eyes filled with tears.

* * *

As Pet went upstairs, Joan was glad to leave the bedrooms to her daughter. Pet was still turning out to be a godsend, helping her after school and at weekends. She'd be leaving school soon and, instead of her getting a job, Joan had decided that she could stay at home, helping out full time. In the meantime, Yvonne was good, coming round every day to give her a hand, but with Danny and her own house to look after, it didn't seem fair. When Pet was at home all day, it would no longer be necessary, and it would be nice not to feel beholden to her daughter-in-law. Norma and Sue still offered to muck in too, but she didn't want those two floozies in her house, chatting all the time and upsetting Dan. She hardly saw them these days and that suited her fine. She didn't want Dan disturbed any more than necessary, and that meant keeping her grandchildren out too, but with Paul's birthday coming up later this month, she'd better think about getting him a present.

She didn't want to think about Linda, or the baby, but was unable to push them from her mind. George was a father now, with a daughter, but unless he turned up again the child would grow up without ever knowing him. It didn't seem right somehow, and surely one day, he'd show his face.

Chapter Twenty

Steve Rawlings thanked his lucky stars that they'd left Drapers Alley. He hadn't gone back to totting, but didn't mind. Almost as soon as they'd moved in, their nearest neighbour told him about a job going on a local farm. He'd been doubtful at first, but had taken it on, and he'd found that he loved it. Though it was early in November, there had been a dusting of snow and the farmer had shaken his head, forecasting a hard winter with worse to come.

Steve trudged home, glad to arrive. In the porch he kicked off his boots before going into the living room to find Ivy sitting by the fire. The room was a mess, the housework untouched.

'What's the matter, love?' he asked, sinking onto a chair opposite her.

'Nothing's the matter.'

'Come on, Ivy. I know you ain't yourself.'

'It's nothing, just a bit of a tummy ache, that's all. I think it was that pie I ate last night.'

'You've been down in the dumps lately. If you're not ill, what is it? Did that letter from Linda to say that she's had her baby unsettle you?'

'No, but we got on well and there's times when I miss her.'

Steve frowned, sure there was more to Ivy's funny moods than that. 'Do you regret leaving Drapers Alley?'

'Leave it out, of course I don't.'

'I wonder how the family that swapped with us are getting on.'

'They didn't move into the alley.'

'What? How come we still got the swap?'

Ivy looked into the fire, then said, 'If you remember, they had already moved back to Battersea, living with the woman's mother until the exchange was agreed. It had just gone through when the mother was taken seriously ill. She needed constant care so they decided to stay with her instead of moving into our place.'

'Oh, yeah, and how do you know all this?'

'I got it from the old biddy in the village post office. She was a friend of the family and said that they're still in touch.'

'So our old place could still be empty.'

'I've no idea, but with a shortage of housing, I doubt it.'

'I wonder if they've found George.'

'Bad pennies always turn up. Anyway, why are you so interested?'

Steve shrugged. 'I'm not, but they're still your family.'

'You and the boys are my family. As far as I'm concerned, I don't care if I never set eyes on the Drapers again.'

'You've never told me why you hate them so much.'

Ivy looked into Steve's eyes, her expression thoughtful for a moment, but then she said, 'I don't suppose it would hurt to tell you now. When my father died, I was just a kid, but Uncle Dan took me and my mother under his wing. He would turn up in his posh car, flashing his money by topping up my mother's war widow's pension. I grew up hearing the gossip about the Drapers – that they were thieves, my father and Uncle Dan both good at cracking safes. It was when he bought the builders' merchants that I became suspicious of my Uncle Dan's so-called generosity, even more so when I became an adult and he continued to help me.'

'Suspicious of what?' Steve asked.

'Where do you think he got the money to start up the business?'

'I have no idea, but what's that got to do with anything?'

'It's got everything to do with it. You see, I think he got the money from the last job he did with my father, but instead of coming back from the war to his share, my father was killed in action. Uncle Dan

263

should have given the money to my mother – money that would have ensured that she died in comfort instead of poverty. But no, he didn't do that. Instead he must have kept the lot.'

Steve shook his head. 'I think you're wrong. Dan might have done some dodgy things, but to him family is everything. He's got a code, a strict one, and though he might rob others, he would never rob his own.'

'OK, so what happened to the money from the last job he did with my father?'

Steve was quiet as he ruminated on Ivy's words. Then he said, 'Ivy, you were a child when your father was called up. How do you know they did a job?'

'When my dad was killed in action, Uncle Dan came round to see us. I was supposed to be in bed, but I sneaked downstairs and heard them talking. My mother was in a terrible state, crying, but then mentioned that at least she wouldn't have to struggle financially to bring me up. My Uncle Dan told her that the job hadn't been successful – that there wasn't any money.'

'Well, there's your answer then. It sounds to me like they didn't manage to pull it off.'

'If they didn't pull it off, where did he get all that money from?'

'Ivy, he didn't start up the yard for years, and I doubt it was the only job he did. No doubt he had a good few bob stashed away.'

'Exactly! I'm sure they pulled off other jobs before my father was called up. If my Uncle Dan had money stashed away, why didn't my father?'

Steve scratched his head. 'Yeah, well, you've got me there.'

'I'll tell you why. My uncle always handled the finances, so I think he kept my father's stash. Even if the last job was a washout, there still should have been cash for my mother, but we never saw a penny. When she died, Uncle Dan played the kind uncle, and when we got married he got us our house in Drapers Alley. Why do you think he did all that?'

'Well, you're his niece and he's big on looking after his family.'

'If you ask me, it was more like guilt.'

Steve stared into the fire. He still couldn't believe that Dan Draper would rob his own brother, but had to admit that it all sounded suspicious. He turned back to Ivy. 'If you're so sure about this, why didn't you confront your Uncle Dan?'

'Because I didn't have any proof, but when I used to bait him – to hint – I could tell that I had him rattled. I wanted to pay him back, to make him suffer, but then lo and behold, George did it for me.'

'Yeah, well, Dan certainly suffered. George nearly killed him.'

'When it happened, when I knew the state Uncle Dan was in, all my anger sort of left me. I hated the alley then, and everyone in it. I just wanted out, and thank God we got the exchange.'

'I'm with you there. I didn't like working for them, Ivy. I used to shit myself every time I went out on a delivery.'

Ivy's eyes narrowed. 'If you were only delivering building materials, I don't see why. Come on, Steve, we're never going to see the Drapers again so you can tell me what they were really up to.'

Steve looked into the fire, ruminating again. Surely there'd be no harm in telling her now. 'All right, Ivy, I suppose you deserve the truth. You thought they were doing jobs, robberies, but in fact they made money from porn. It was my job to deliver it.'

'Porn! My God, I can't believe it.'

'It's the truth, Ivy. They've got a place in Wimbledon where they make the films.'

'What sort of place?'

Steve told her where it was and about the setup, but then she suddenly slumped forward, clutching her tummy.

'What is it, love? Are you all right?'

The boys came running through the door, their cheeks rosy from the cold air. They loved playing outside and it was impossible to keep them in. Steve saw the effort Ivy made to straighten herself up, her face the colour of dough. 'I reckon you should see the doctor.'

'What's the matter, Mum?' Ernie asked.

'Nothing, love, it's just a bit of indigestion, that's all. Now, let's get you cleaned up before dinner.'

Steve could see what an effort it was for Ivy to stand up, and placed a staying hand on her arm. 'Let me get the stink of the farmyard off and then I'll see to them.'

'No, I can manage.'

She ushered the boys from the room, leaving Steve frowning. He wasn't convinced that Ivy had indigestion, sure there was more to it than that. She could be so stubborn at times and it drove him mad, but like it or not, he was going to make sure that she saw a doctor.

Chapter Twenty-one

The weekend passed and, in Drapers Alley, Yvonne still felt ill. She did her best to hide it as she placed Danny's dinner on the table, then sat opposite him. He had changed so much since taking over from his father. He had lost weight, his cheeks gaunt, and she knew he wasn't sleeping well. He often turned to her for sex, but that was different too, almost as if he was using it for comfort. Yet why? He had the responsibility of running the yard, but with three brothers to help him, surely there wasn't that much to worry about. Yvonne knew that business had been slow for a while and money tight, but with talk of some sort of expansion, things were sure to improve. She had tried talking to him about it, but he snapped her head off if she made any mention of business.

'Are you still feeling rough?' Danny asked.

'No, I'm fine now,' she lied, changing the subject. 'Danny, are you going round to see Linda's baby?'

'No, why should I?'

'She's your niece.'

'So what?' he said, his voice lacking interest as he pushed his plate to one side, his meal hardly touched. 'I've got to go out again for a couple of hours.'

'Oh, Danny, not again. It's already eight o'clock and you're hardly in these days.'

'Don't start, Yvonne. I've got a business to run, orders to get. I might be late, so don't wait up.'

Yvonne wanted to protest, to tell him to stop taking her for a mug. The yard was closed now, as were most businesses, so how could he be chasing orders?

When a scream pierced the air, Yvonne's eyes widened, then both she and Danny rushed outside, just in time to see Bob's younger son fleeing down the alley like a scalded cat.

Sue and Bob must have heard the scream too, Bob yelling, 'Paul! Paul, wait! Come here!'

As Paul disappeared past the bollards, Bob set out in pursuit.

'What happened? Did you see anything?' Sue gasped.

'We just heard a scream,' Yvonne told her.

'Where's Robby?' Sue cried, her eyes scanning the alley, but it was Bob who appeared, holding Paul's hand as he walked towards them.

'He's all right. He's just got a bit of a burn, that's all. A banger went off while he was holding it.'

'It was Robby,' wailed Paul. 'He lit the banger then he gave it to me, but I didn't have time to throw it before it went off.'

'Where is he?' Bob asked.

'I dunno. Oooh, Mum, my hand hurts.'

'Come on, let's get you sorted,' Sue said. 'And as for you, Bob, I ain't happy that you bought the kids those bangers. If you ask me, they're dangerous.'

'Leave it out, it's fireworks night and all the kids play with them.'

'I think I agree with Sue,' said Yvonne. 'They're far too young to be playing with fireworks. Oh, look, there's Robby.'

'I'll leave you to sort him out,' Sue said to Bob, before taking Paul inside.

The boy had come into the alley and ran towards them. 'Is Paul all right?'

'No he isn't, and well you know it, you little sod. Now get inside,' Bob snapped.

'I didn't do nuffin', Robby protested, crying out as Bob grabbed him by the ear to drag him indoors.

'They shouldn't have matches, let alone fireworks,' Yvonne said as she and Danny went back to their own house.

'Half the kids in the area have penny bangers,' Danny said as he picked up his coat. 'Right, I'm off, and as I said, don't wait up.'

Yvonne nodded, unhappy but knowing better than to complain again. She still didn't feel right, and hadn't for some time, despite telling Danny that she felt fine. Maybe she should see the doctor, but what could she tell him? She wasn't in pain. It was just that she felt so drained. But knowing old Doc Addison, she thought he'd just prescribe a tonic.

Danny headed for his car. When Chris had been knifed in August, he knew it could be the start of a turf war, and had wanted to retaliate, to show Garston that the Drapers couldn't be messed with. He'd tried to be prepared, to find out all he could about Garston, his operation and the muscle behind him, but despite putting out feelers for months, it was still proving impossible. Time and time again he came up against a wall of silence and it was driving him mad. In the meantime he had put precautions in place, making films but only delivering them once a month, sending Chris out with a bit of hired muscle.

So far there hadn't been any more trouble, but Danny doubted it could last. He climbed into his car. All he had found out so far was that Garston was rarely seen, but he wasn't ready to give up yet, and at last Danny had got a whisper of a contact. The bloke was someone he knew from years ago, one he was told had worked for Garston recently. Whether Bert Mills was willing to talk remained to be seen, but Danny was prepared to pay for information.

There was thick smoke in the air from many bonfires, and the occasional rocket shot up into the sky before bursting into a shower of sparks as Danny drove to Tooting. When he walked into the pub he saw it was nearly empty, but the man he was looking for was propping up the bar.

'Hello, Bert. What are you drinking?'

'Danny! Blimey, long time no see. What are you doing in this neck of the woods?'

'I was hoping for a little chat.'

'Oh, yeah, what about?'

'Tell me what you're drinking first.'

'Bitter, mate. I'll have a pint of bitter.'

Danny waited until the landlord had pulled two pints, but after paying, the publican still hovered within hearing distance.

'Come and sit down, Bert,' Danny said, indicating a table.

Once seated, Danny leaned forward, saying softly, 'What can you tell me about Garston?'

'I can't tell you anything, Danny.'

'I'll make it worth your while.'

'If I open my mouth I wouldn't live long enough to spend it.'

'He wouldn't know the info came from you.'

'Huh, you don't know Jack Garston. He's got eyes and ears everywhere and, believe me, he'd find out.'

'Look, all I need to know is where he's based, and how much backup he's got.'

'Danny, I don't know what you're up to, but you don't want to cross Garston.'

'One of his mob knifed my brother and I ain't standing for that.'

'Yeah, well, I'm sorry to hear that, but I still can't tell you anything.'

'Yes you can, Bert, and before you say no again, remember – I can be just as nasty as Garston.'

Bert paled, but shook his head. 'Yeah, you frighten me, Danny, but not as much as Garston.' He then rose to his feet, his pint of beer untouched as he walked back to the bar where he leaned forward, saying something to the landlord.

The landlord's eyes shot towards Danny, and when Danny saw him walk to the back of the bar to make a phone call, he knew it was time to leave. Bert had obviously opened his mouth and now Garston would know he'd been trying to suss him out. Danny walked out of the bar, determined that one day, when Bert was least expecting it, he'd make him pay for dobbing him in.

Bert Mills had been ordered to the club. He'd been nervous around Danny Draper, but that was nothing compared to how he felt now.

Jack Garston sat behind his desk in the back room, his eyes rock hard. 'What did Draper want?'

'He was trying to find out about your operation.'

'What did you tell him?'

'Nothing, Jack.'

'Are you sure about that? I hear that you and Draper go back a while.'

As Jack's cold eyes bored into his, Bert felt like

prey. He had to convince the man or he'd be dead meat. 'Yeah, I know him, but I ain't seen him for years. I didn't say a word, Jack. I swear. I warned him off, that was all.'

Garston's smile was thin. 'All right, Bert, relax. Sit yourself down and we'll have a little chat. Rick here will get you a drink. Whisky, is it?'

'Yeah, thanks,' Bert said, still tense as he sat down. Rick was one of Garston's henchmen, known for his love of pulling out his victims' fingernails. Bert moved his hands to his lap as though this small act could protect them, but Rick went to the bar, pouring the drinks. Garston seemed satisfied, but Bert knew better than to let down his guard. The man didn't look like a villain. Short and overweight, he could appear benign, fooling anyone who wasn't aware of his reputation, but if crossed the change was instantaneous. He became a vicious monster, and there were those who had found this out to their cost.

Garston lit a fat cigar, his cheeks puffing like bellows, then ordered Bert, 'Tell me what you know about the Drapers.'

As Rick put a shot of whisky in front of him, Bert instantly picked the glass up, swallowing the lot in one gulp. 'As I said, I ain't seen them in years so I can't tell you what they get up to nowadays. They've been rumoured to have done a few jobs, but then Dan Draper bought a yard, becoming respectable.

Mind you, knowing the Drapers the business could be a front, but I don't know what for.'

'I do, and you ain't telling me anything that I don't know already. The Drapers need another lesson, a hard one. Tell me about the family, what makes them tick.'

'There ain't much I can tell you, except that they look after their own. The alley where they live is a bit like a fortress and nobody goes in there without invitation.'

'More stuff I already know, and it's not what I'm looking for. I want a weakness. For instance, what matters most to Dan Draper?'

Bert frowned, wondering what he could give Garston to get the man off his back. 'There's been talk that he ain't what he used to be, but in my time I know his daughter was his pride and joy.'

'His daughter,' Garston drawled, gimlet-eyed as he sucked deeply on his cigar. Then he smiled. 'All right, Bert, you've told me what I need to know. You can go now.'

Bert didn't need telling twice and hastily rose to his feet. 'Thanks, Jack.'

Garston waved him away and Bert almost ran from the room. There was a stripper on stage but so anxious was he to leave he didn't pause to take in the act. He didn't know what the Drapers had done to make an enemy of Jack Garston, but it looked like the daughter was going to pay the price.

Chapter Twenty-two

At the end of the week, Danny faced his brothers. 'I can't get any information on Garston. I've been asking around and I've tried everything – threats, bribes – but nobody will talk.'

'Shouldn't that tell you something?'

'Like what, Maurice?'

'It's obvious. If they won't talk to you, despite your threats, they're more afraid of Garston than us. As I've said before, we should get out now before he pulls another stunt.'

Chris fingered his cheek, his scar a match with Danny's. 'I owe Garston for this and I'm looking forward to his next move.'

'Yeah, well, you might just get your chance,' Danny told him. 'I had a chat with a geezer on Monday, and I think the fact that I was asking questions has got back to Garston. It might stir things up, and with any luck it'll force him to show his hand. I'm coming with you on the next delivery. If his henchmen show their faces, it could lead us back to Garston, and that's just what I want.'

'I don't like it, Danny. We should stick to soft porn.'

'And make peanuts, Maurice?'

'I'd hardly call it peanuts. We were doing all right – in fact more than all right.'

'You were the one who said that our profits were unlikely to increase.'

'Yes, I know, but we were still making good money.'

'I can't believe I'm hearing this! Garston has only made one move against us and you're acting like a frightened tart. The man just needs a taste of his own medicine. Once he gets it, he'll back off.'

'And if he doesn't?'

'We'll cross that bridge when we come to it. In the meantime, Maurice, we've got films to make. I think you're up to running the yard, so you stay here.'

'I can't handle the heavy lifting on my own, you know that. And what if Garston makes a move on this place? Have you thought about that?'

Danny's brow furrowed. 'To be honest, no, but you've got a point. It's no secret we own this business, but I've been more concerned about him finding our base in Wimbledon. All right, we'll get someone who can handle themselves to work here. In the meantime, I'll leave Bob with you.'

Maurice looked mollified, and after sorting out a few more things, Danny and Chris left to go to Wimbledon. As he drove, Danny kept his eyes peeled, but there was no sign of a tail. If Garston wanted to go up against them again, he'd make sure the man suffered for it. Nobody messed with the Drapers and got away with it.

Later that day, Pet was walking home from school. She found herself thinking about Linda and the awful things her mother had said, and the fact that Ivy didn't want any of them to know her address. Before forgetting it, she had scribbled it down in her diary, and though Pet knew she couldn't write to her cousin, at least she knew where she was. Maybe one day she would get in touch with Ivy, try to bring about some sort of reconciliation, but for now she would have to be content with that.

Pet's thoughts shifted. She would be leaving school soon, and had wanted to work in a shop, but with her father ill, and George gone, maybe she could help in some way with the family business. She had never thought much about the work involved at the yard, but by the amount of time her brothers spent running the place, it must be doing all right. There must be lots of paperwork such as orders, invoices, and perhaps they'd let her take over the office work. It would be lovely if she could prove everyone wrong – to find that nowadays her brothers really were respectable, and running a thriving family business.

Pet shivered as she was blasted by the cold wind. A van pulled up just ahead of her but, deep in thought, she hardly noticed. As she drew level the back doors flew open and two men jumped out. Startled out of her reveries, Pet saw them running towards her, but before she could react, they grabbed her, lifting her off her feet, and tossed her into the back of the van.

The doors slammed and then they were hurtling off down the road with Pet on the floor where they had thrown her. Dazed and bruised, she managed to turn her head, frightened out of her wits when she saw one of the men edging towards her.

'No . . . no,' she whimpered, 'please . . . don't—' Her words were cut off as sticky tape was stuck roughly across her mouth.

She was then hauled onto one of the long seats, one man next to her, and the other opposite. All she could see was his flint-like grey eyes, boring into hers. She looked away, petrified, but then the man next to her reached out to grip her thigh with his rough hand. Pet had never known such gut-wrenching terror – terror that caused her bladder to release.

'Fuck me, she's wet herself.'

'What do you expect, she's just a kid.'

'Yeah, but I can see why he wants her – she's a bit tasty. When she's cleaned up, I wouldn't mind a sample myself.'

'He'd kill you.'

Pet felt strange, giddy, her head buzzing. Her vision dimmed, pinpricks of lights floating before her eyes – and then she knew no more.

'She's passed out.'

'We're nearly there. He wants her in the basement.'

'Then what's he gonna do with her? Is he going to put her on the game?'

'She's been snatched as a warning to the Drapers. After that, I've got no idea, but I guess we'll find out soon enough.'

Yvonne had just taken off her coat when there was a knock on her door. She had been to the doctor's and was still in shock. But she was also surprised by her mother-in-law walking in. Joan rarely left the house now, leaving Pet to do all the shopping whilst she took care of Dan.

'Pet's late home from school. It isn't like her and I'm getting worried.'

'Perhaps she went to a friend's house,' Yvonne suggested.

'No, she wouldn't do that. She always comes straight home. Look, I've got to get back to Dan. Can you let the boys know and maybe they'll have a scout around to see if they can find her?'

'All right, I'll ring the yard.'

'Thanks, love,' Joan said.

Bob answered Yvonne's call. 'Is Danny around, Bob?'

'Er, no.'

'Do you know where he is?'

'I think he's out doing a bit of business.'

'What about Chris?'

'He's with Danny, but what's wrong? It ain't like you to ring the yard. Is there a problem? Is my dad all right?'

'Yes, but your mum's worried about Pet. She hasn't arrived home from school.'

'What! But it's gone five. Hang on, it's Paul's birthday and Sue has laid on a bit of a spread. Perhaps Pet's at my place.'

'I'll pop down there, but I don't think it's likely.'

'Have a look anyway. If she's not there, give me another ring.'

Yvonne replaced the receiver and then ran along to Sue's house. She rapped on the letter box before going inside to find that the birthday tea was over. The boys were playing on the rug in front of the fire, but Paul jumped to his feet when he saw her.

'Look what I've got,' he cried, running over to show her a fire engine.

Sue came out of the kitchen, wiping her hands on a tea towel. 'Yes, and it was your auntie who gave it to you, so say thank you.'

'Fanks, Auntie.'

'It's from your Uncle Danny too, but I'm glad you like it. What else did you get for your birthday?'

Paul ran back to the rug, and bending down he picked up a car. 'I got this from Petula.'

'He's car mad and we got him that,' Sue said as she nodded towards a big yellow dumper truck on the rug. 'Norma and Maurice gave him a puzzle, and his gran, practical as ever, gave him a new woolly hat, scarf and gloves.'

'Have you seen Petula?'

'Not since she dropped Paul's present off before she went to school.' Sue's head cocked to one side. 'Why, is there a problem?'

'She hasn't come home yet and Joan's worried.'

'Flaming hell, it's only just after five. What's all the fuss about?'

'She should have been home by now.'

'Huh, so she's a bit late, and to be honest, I don't blame her. When she ain't at school she's stuck indoors cooking and cleaning. It's no life for a girl who's coming up fifteen. If you ask me it's about time she was let off the apron strings.'

'Sue, I couldn't agree more, but the fact is, Petula always comes straight home. This is unlike her and you can't blame Joan for being worried.'

'She's probably just rebelling a bit, and it's about time too. If Joan would let us all give her a hand, Pet could have a bit more freedom.'

'Mum, tell Robby, he's nicked my car.'

'Robby, give it back to him.'

Yvonne said hastily, 'I'd best get back.'

282

'Mum . . .'

Yvonne scooted out to the sound of Paul's wail, leaving Sue to sort out her sons. She rang the yard and then went to her mother-in-law's. 'Bob and Maurice are locking up. They'll be here soon.'

'What about Danny and Chris?'

'They weren't there.'

Dan's good arm was waving as he made strange sounds without forming any coherent words. 'I think he's worried about Petula too,' Joan said, walking across to stroke his hair. 'Don't fret, love.'

It was awful to see Dan's distress, and Yvonne was touched by Joan's tenderness. He may not be able to communicate, but this proved he knew exactly what was going on around him. Petula might be nearly fifteen, but she hadn't had the sense to warn her mother that she might be late home. Dan was so upset and Yvonne couldn't help feeling annoyed at the girl's thoughtlessness.

By eleven that night, there was still no sign of Petula. The boys had been out for hours, Danny and Chris looking in one direction, Maurice and Bob in the other.

When they returned to Drapers Alley, Yvonne came flying out of number one. 'Did you find her?'

'Does it look like it?' Danny said.

'Your dad's been in such a state that your mum had to call the doctor. He's been sedated now, but if he wakes up to find that Petula is still missing, I dread to think what will happen.'

'Do you think I don't know that?'

'Where did you look?'

'Everywhere, and before you ask, yes, we tried all the hospitals.'

'Maybe we should tell the police.'

'Leave it out, Yvonne.'

'Danny, think about it. The police have got resources that we haven't.'

'Yvonne's got a point,' Maurice said, and though it was freezing, sweat beaded his brow.

Danny was struggling to hold himself together. He'd hoped his suspicions were unfounded, but the longer Pet was missing, the more his guts churned. When his mother appeared, he couldn't meet her eyes.

'Oh, Danny, where is she?'

'I don't know, but don't worry, we'll find her.'

'Mum, you look awful,' Chris said, 'and it's freezing out here.'

'Yes, come on, let's get you inside,' Yvonne urged.

'You won't stop looking?'

'Of course we won't,' Danny said, a hard knot of worry like a rock in his stomach. He had wanted to stir Garston up, to force his hand, but hadn't expected the bastard to strike out at his family.

He waited until Yvonne and his mother had returned inside before voicing his thoughts to his brothers. 'I think Garston's got her.'

'I've been thinking the same,' Chris said. 'But if that was the case, surely he'd have been in touch?'

'Maybe he wants to make us sweat for a while.'

'I told you we should pack it in but none of you would have it. Now look what's happened. If he's got Pet, fuck knows what he'll do to her.'

Danny glared at Maurice. 'I'm in charge so this is down to me, but if the bastard so much as lays a finger on her – he's dead.'

'Yeah, you're in charge, but you should have listened to me – made Chris and Bob listen to me. But no, Danny, you had to stir things up, had to act Mr Big and now look what's happened.'

'Look, this isn't achieving anything,' said Chris. 'We need to concentrate on finding Pet. Have you any idea where Garston might be holding her?'

Danny shook his head. 'Do you think I'd be standing here if I did?'

Maurice moved to lean against the wall, his breathing tortured, and it was Bob who said, 'You look awful, Maurice. Go home and leave this to us.'

Maurice nodded. 'All right, but if Pet hasn't turned up by morning, I'm coming out with you again.'

As Maurice went into his house, Bob said, 'What are we going to do now, Danny?'

'We'll just have to wait for Garston to get in touch.'

'Until we know for sure that he's got her, we should keep looking,' Chris urged.

'Yes, all right,' Danny agreed, but his guts were

telling him it would be a waste of time. Garston had his sister. Pet's innocent face swam before his eyes. The thought of Garston touching her sickened him. *I'll kill him*, his mind screamed, his anger the only thing that was holding him together.

Pet couldn't stop shaking. The tape had been ripped from her mouth and then she'd been shoved into a back room and onto a bare bed, the mattress filthy and stained. She had been so cold, but then seeing a dirty quilt on the floor she had snatched it up, sitting with it wrapped around her whilst the smell of her own urine assailed her nostrils. In despair she had frantically looked for a way to escape, but the only window was barred. Hours passed. She didn't know why she'd been snatched, but terrifying thoughts assailed her mind. Oh God, what were they going to do to her?

She swallowed, her throat parched. In the next room she could hear the occasional sound of muffled voices, but so far she had been left alone.

When the door opened, Pet stiffened in fear as a man walked towards her, menacing in his balaclava. She cowered, but his voice was surprisingly gentle.

'Here, I've brought you a drink.'

As he held out a mug, Pet snatched it, gulping down the water as though it were nectar.

'Why . . . why am I here?'

'You'll find out soon enough.'

'Please . . . please let me go.'

'Sorry, I can't do that.'

Pet frowned, sure that she had heard his voice before. 'Do . . . do I know you?'

He shook his head, glancing behind him as another man entered the room.

'What's this?' he snapped. 'Having a taster, are you?'

'No, I just gave her a drink, that's all.'

'Good, 'cos I'm first.'

'No, she ain't to be touched.'

'Unless you tell him, he ain't likely to find out. Come on, let's have a bit of fun.'

Pet screamed, trying to scramble away as the man grabbed her.

'He probably wants a virgin, have you thought of that?'

'Fuck, she stinks to high heaven.'

'If you touch her, he'll kill you.'

'Keep your hair on. With her stinking of piss I don't fancy her anyway. Shame, though; cleaned up she'd be a bit of all right.'

'Yes, she is rather nice,' a voice said.

Both men spun around, the man who had grabbed Pet holding up his hands as though in surrender. 'We didn't touch her, honest.'

'Yes, but from what I heard, it's thanks to Tony.'

Pet was still shaking as she looked at the third man to enter the room. He was short, tubby and wearing a three-piece suit. Unlike the other two, his face wasn't covered, and, as he looked at her, his smile was kindly.

'Are you all right, my dear?'

'Please . . . I want to go home.'

'Well, that's up to your brothers.'

'My . . . my brothers?'

'Don't look so surprised. Surely you know what your brothers have been up to?'

'N-no.'

'Really? Well, maybe I should put you in the picture.' He laughed. 'Oh, pardon the pun, but then again, looking at you, perhaps I *should* feature you in one of my films.'

Pet stared at the man. He didn't look menacing and he was talking about films, but what did that have to do with her brothers? 'I . . . I don't understand. My family supply building materials. They don't make films.'

The man's demeanour changed, his voice a snarl. 'Bring her upstairs.'

Before Pet could react she was dragged off the bed, each man taking an arm and pulling her towards a narrow wooden staircase. She was so afraid that her legs could barely support her.

Oh God, help me.

She was hauled upstairs, barely taking in the opulent hall before she was dragged into another room.

'Sit her down,' the fat man said, 'and then set up the projector.'

Pet was forced onto a plush sofa, cowering as the fat man sat next to her. 'Now, my dear,' he said, his demeanour once again benign, 'the films that I'm going to show you were made by your brothers, and are the reason why you're here.'

'Ready, boss.'

'Good,' he said, his voice once again hardening as he snapped, 'Turn off the lights and roll it.'

The room was plunged into darkness and then almost immediately a film was showing on a screen in front of Pet. At first, confused, she couldn't understand what was happening, but then as it unfolded she watched it in horror. A woman was thrown onto a bed, her wrists tied to the posts. She struggled, screaming as a man began to do things to her that made the bile rise in Pet's throat. She didn't know much about the sex act, only what her friends had told her, but this – this was awful. He was raping her! Oh God, it was terrible! Unable to watch any more, she turned her head away.

The fat man tittered. 'Don't worry, my dear, I'm sure they're only acting.' His voice then changed as he snapped, 'Run the next one.'

'No . . . no . . .' Pet whimpered as the film unfolded. This time it was a child being raped, the little girl crying out for her mother in terror. No – no, she couldn't watch it. 'Oh, please, please, turn it off.'

'Yes, I think that's enough, and anyway, my dear, I can't stand the smell of you for much longer.'

'She pissed herself.'

'Yes, Gary, I think that's obvious. Now then, Miss Draper, as I said, the films were made by your brothers.'

'No . . . no, I don't believe you.'

'Oh, I can assure you it's true. I've known about their operation for some time – in fact since they started production. It was fine when they stuck to making nice little soft-porn films – something that holds no interest for me – but, you see, they became greedy.'

Pet shook her head against his words. It couldn't be true, it just couldn't.

His voice droned on. 'I tried to warn them off, but it seems that scarring your brother's cheek wasn't enough.'

'You! You did that to Chris.'

'Ah, I see I've got your attention at last. My, you are a pretty little thing,' he mused. 'It would be a shame if I had to hand you back, but then again, I don't really have to.'

Pet cringed in fear as his pudgy hand reached out to stroke her leg. He then snapped, 'Tony, get her cleaned up and then for now, take her back to the basement.'

'What do you want me to do, boss?' the other man asked.

'I haven't forgotten what I heard downstairs. Get out of my sight and I'll deal with you later.'

'Come on, on your feet,' she was ordered as the other man grabbed her arm.

'Leave me alone.'

'Ah, that's nice, Tony; she's got a bit of spunk. If the Drapers don't learn their lesson she'll make a nice little addition to my stars, and I've got just the film in mind.'

Pet was dragged out of the room and then upstairs to a bathroom.

'Go on, get cleaned up.'

He made no move to leave, and arms folded defensively, Pet stammered, 'Not . . . not till you go.'

'All right, but don't try anything. I'll be back with some clean togs.'

As he left, Pet looked frantically around, but there wasn't a window, no means of escape. She sank down onto the cold tiles, sobbing.

Only minutes later the door opened and clothes were thrown onto the floor beside her.

'Come on, get a move on, and then get those on.'

Pet was unable to stop the sobs that racked her body. She sank onto her side, curling into a ball.

The man crouched down beside her, his voice surprisingly soft. 'Come on, your brothers ain't daft. As long as they play ball, you'll be out of here.'

As he reached out to touch her, Pet scrambled away.

There was a soft laugh. 'Still the innocent, I see. Still just a kid.'

His words sparked a memory. Tony! It was Tony Thorn, the boy she had met at the youth club. With a spark of hope she sat up. 'I . . . I know who you are. Please, Tony, please let me go.'

'I can't. Garston would kill me.'

'Oh, please, Tony . . . pleeease.'

'Look, I've told you, as long as your brothers play ball, you'll be all right.'

'But they don't make those horrible films.'

'They do, and they were idiots to take on Garston. Now come on, have a quick wash and get dressed. If I don't get you back to the basement we could both be in trouble.'

Pet was unresisting as Tony hauled her up, but when he didn't leave she just stared at him.

He sighed with exasperation. 'It ain't me you've got to worry about, but all right, I'll wait outside.' As he went out of the door he hissed, 'Get a move on.'

Pet washed. Though she hated the low-cut, tight black dress she'd been given, at least it was preferable to the smelly clothes she discarded. Her mind was racing. Despite refusing at first, surely she could persuade Tony to help her?

When Pet tried the handle she found that the door wasn't locked, but Tony was waiting outside. He urged her forward, down one flight of stairs, and then through a door that led to the basement.

'Tony, please, you've got to help me.'

'I've told you, I can't,' Tony said as he pulled off his balaclava, adding ruefully, 'Now that you've clocked me, wearing this is a waste of time.'

'Tony, please, there's been some sort of awful mistake. That man must have got it wrong. My brothers wouldn't be mixed up in . . . in . . .'

'Porn,' Tony finished for her. 'Garston's got eyes and ears everywhere and he doesn't make mistakes. As soon as there's a snifter of something, he hears about it. Take your brother Danny, for instance. As soon as he asked about getting hold of kids, Garston heard about it. Oh shit, you ain't gonna faint on me, are you? Look, sit down, bend over and take deep breaths.'

Her head swimming, Pet staggered to a chair. She had wanted to know what her brothers were involved in, expecting some sort of crime, but she had never in her wildest imaginings thought it would be as horrendous as this. Children – they used children to make those terrible films. It couldn't be true, it just couldn't.

'Here, drink this,' Tony urged, holding out a mug of water.

Pet gulped it down, and then at the sound of a door opening, Tony snatched up his balaclava, hastily pulling it on.

'Is everything all right down here?' Jack Garston asked as he appeared at the foot of the stairs.

'Yes, Mr Garston. She's no trouble.'

'I'm glad to hear it,' he said, his smile soft as he turned to Pet. 'Unfortunately, I won't be able to savour your lovely delights tonight, my dear. There's a problem at one of my clubs I have to deal with.' He turned to Tony again, his manner instantly changing. 'She should be in the back room. Put her in there and keep your hands to yourself. Do I make myself clear?'

'Yes, Mr Garston.'

With a sickly leer, Garston focused on Pet again. 'Good night, my dear, sleep well.'

Tony took Pet's arm, urging her to her feet as the man left. When it was all clear, he ripped off his mask again. 'At least you're safe for tonight. You'd better try to get some sleep.'

'Safe! What . . . what do you mean?'

'It's best you don't know.'

Garston's words spun in her mind. He wanted to savour her delights. The images she had seen on the film flashed into her mind. Oh, no, surely he wasn't going to rape her! 'Tony, I'm begging you. Don't let him touch me. Please . . . let me go.'

'There's nothing I can do. Garston is a nasty piece of work, as nasty as they come. You cross him at your cost, as your brothers have found out. I can't let you go, Pet. I've told you. He'd kill me.'

'Why do you work for him?'

''Cos I was a mug and didn't know what I was getting into. I only started out as a bouncer at one of his clubs, but then he started giving me other work to do and you don't say no to Jack Garston. Take tonight, for instance. You could have knocked me down with a feather when I was ordered to snatch you.'

'Why did you do it then?'

'Oh, grow up, Pet. I've told you why. When he says jump, you do it, and quickly.'

'You could leave. You don't have to work for him. Please, Tony, if you can't let me go, at least tell my brothers where I am.'

'Oh, yeah, and how am I supposed to do that without Garston finding out?'

Pet shook her head in despair. 'I don't know, but please, you must do something. You can't leave me here for that man to . . . to rape me.'

'Look, this is down to your brothers – not me. They shouldn't have crossed into Garston's territory. They should have listened to his warning, but they didn't and now you're paying the price. Now shut up about it and get some sleep.'

On that note, Tony left the room and Pet heard the key turn in the lock. Despair washed over her as she sank back on the bed, sobbing with fear as she clutched the filthy quilt around her.

Chapter Twenty-three

The brothers trooped home in the early hours of the morning. A light still shone in number one, but the other houses were in darkness.

'Do you think knocking up that publican will work, Danny? Do you think he'll pass on our message?' Chris asked.

'When I talked to Bert Mills in the pub, the landlord was doing his best to earwig. I saw him making a phone call, so I reckon he's one of Garston's narks. Anyway, trying to get a message to Garston is better than sitting around sweating until he decides to contact us.'

Chris yawned, exhausted, but he doubted he'd be able to sleep.

Yvonne emerged from number one, her face drawn with anxiety.

'Any luck?' she asked.

'No, but come on, we'd better try to get some sleep,' Danny told her.

Chris looked at the street door, dreading going inside. He knew his mother would be awake and waiting for news, but there was nothing he could say to put her mind at rest. He took a deep breath and walked in.

The room was almost in darkness with just the glow from the fire, aided by the solitary flicker of a single candle on the mantelpiece. Chris saw his mother huddled in a chair with a blanket wrapped around her, and then looking at the day bed, he saw that his father was asleep.

'You haven't found her?' his mother whispered.

'No, but we'll look again in the morning. Why don't you go to bed?'

'How can I sleep when I don't know what's happened to Petula? Oh, Chris, what if a nutter has got hold of her?'

His father stirred and she looked anxiously towards him. Chris waited until he settled again, then whispered, 'Don't think the worst, Mum. We'll find her, you'll see.'

'I hope you're right, son, because if you don't, I think this will just about finish your dad off.'

There was a soft groan and once again she looked towards the day bed, hissing, 'We don't want to wake him. You'd best get some sleep too.'

Chris was relieved to creep upstairs. Yes, a nutter probably had Pet, a nutter called Jack Garston. Inwardly he cursed Danny, cursed himself for agreeing to make hard porn. If anything happened to Pet, it would be their fault. Shivering, he undressed and then, flinging back the blankets, he dived into bed, the icy sheets momentarily taking his breath away.

Chris wished he had Phil's body to snuggle up to, but he had to keep it a secret. He was sick of sneaking around, of hiding the truth, and had planned to leave home. He had the money, but one thing after another seemed to stand in his way. His father was still too ill, his mother worn out looking after him, and now to top it all, Pet had been snatched.

Chris rolled onto his side, clutching a pillow. Who was he kidding? If they found out, he'd lose his family – something he just couldn't face. They'd think he was weird, perverted and would never accept it – never!

Danny couldn't sleep. He lay with his back to Yvonne, images of his sister and what might be happening to her haunting his mind. He had never expected Garston to hit out at his family. In doing that, the man had broken the unwritten rules.

Yet as he turned over, flinging an arm around Yvonne, he knew that with Garston's reputation, he should have been prepared. There were no excuses. He'd been the one who had stirred the man up. This was down to him – his pride, his ambition, and his greed.

'Can't you sleep, Danny?'

'No, I'm worried about Pet.'

'Yeah, me too. I still think you should tell the police that she's missing.'

With a huff of annoyance Danny rolled onto his back. 'There's no need to involve the police. We'll find her.'

'But you've already been searching for hours and she hasn't turned up. What if someone's got hold of her?'

'All right, don't go on about it. If we don't find her tomorrow, I'll tell the police,' Danny snapped. He knew it was a lie, but at least it would placate Yvonne for the time being. With any luck Garston would get his message and once he knew they'd agreed to stop production, he'd let Pet go.

'Do you want me to make you a hot drink? It might help you to sleep.'

Danny ignored the question, breathing heavily to feign sleep. He heard Yvonne's soft sigh and then she flung an arm around him, snuggling close. Danny lay unmoving. If anything happened to Pet, he knew he'd never be able to live with himself. For the first time in his life, Danny found he was taking a look at himself – and not liking what he saw.

Maurice wasn't faring any better. He'd stayed up until his brothers returned again, but on finding that they hadn't found Pet, he sneaked upstairs, careful not to wake Norma as he climbed into bed. He felt dreadful and fought to control his ragged breathing. What if Danny was right? What if Pet was in Garston's hands? His chest tightened until he was wheezing in pain, his mind plagued by fear. When they first ventured into Garston territory, he'd feared the future, feared for Oliver's safety. Pet had been snatched, but it could just as easily have been his son.

Mentally he assessed his financial situation. Things had been tight after George had nicked the money, and though at first they'd all had to take a pay cut, things had started to look up. Even during the lean time and Norma's nagging, he hadn't dipped into his savings. For years he'd been putting regular amounts in a bank, money for the house he hoped to buy one day, and if Oliver continued to do well at school, he was salting money away for the boy's university expenses. It might be a silly dream to think that the boy would ever attend university, but nevertheless he'd been determined to be prepared.

Maurice didn't want to leave the alley and his family, but he had to put his son's safety first. He had the finances, if necessary, but he just hoped it wouldn't come to that. First things first, though – they were going to look for Pet again in the morning and he had to get some sleep. Asthma attack or not, he was determined to join in the search.

* * *

Bob was scowling as he got into bed. Yvonne had waited up, so why couldn't Sue? She was supposed to be fond of Pet, but obviously not enough to keep her awake.

He closed his eyes, but couldn't stop thinking about Petula. He shouldn't have listened to Danny, shouldn't have agreed to upping the ante. If they had stayed out of Garston's territory none of this would have happened.

'Did you find her?'

'No,' he said, wrapping his arms around his wife. 'I thought you were asleep.'

'I dozed off for a while, but I can't settle. Do you think she's run away?'

'No, Pet wouldn't do that.'

'She's had a rotten life since your father came home, so I wouldn't be so sure. If your mother wasn't so stubborn and had let me help, Pet could have had a bit more freedom.'

'Don't start now, Sue. I'm knackered and I need some kip.'

'Yeah, but take tonight, for instance. I went along to see your mum, but as usual she wouldn't let me in. Honestly, Bob, she drives me mad. I only wanted to help . . . to see if there was anything I can do, but she more or less shut the door in my face. Of course, Yvonne was there, Miss Goody Two-Shoes allowed admittance.'

'For Gawd's sake, change the record,' Bob snapped

as he flung himself over onto his back. 'I ain't listening to any more of this. My sister's missing and I'm worried sick. We're going out looking again in the morning and I've got to get some sleep.'

Thankfully Sue didn't say anything else, just huffed with annoyance as she yanked the blankets over herself. Bob closed his eyes, but it was an hour later before he finally managed to doze into an uneasy sleep.

By five in the morning, only one person in Drapers Alley remained awake. Joan was uncomfortable in the chair, but she was too worried about Dan to go upstairs. He was restless, and occasionally he groaned in his sleep.

She stood up, her knees and hips stiff. She had kept the fire going, and now, as quietly as possible, she picked up the poker to stir the coals. God, she was parched, but she daren't make a cup of tea. With Dan so fidgety, the least bit of noise could wake him.

Joan went into the kitchen, knowing she'd have to be content with a cup of water. It was freezing and she shivered. Was Pet cold too? Was she lying somewhere, injured? Joan returned to the living room where she sat in her chair again, drawing the blanket around her legs. She dreaded the dawn, dreaded how Dan would react when he woke to find that Pet was still missing.

Chapter Twenty-four

'Now then, Tony, you aren't supposed to be asleep.'

Tony jumped to his feet, woozy. 'Sorry, Mr Garston, but I only dozed off for a couple of minutes.' He quickly glanced at his watch, amazed to see that it was eight in the morning. Bloody hell, he'd been asleep for hours!

'Get the girl.'

Still woozy but trying to hide it, Tony did as he was told. He flung open the door to see Pet asleep on the bed, the quilt tangled around her.

'Come on you, get up!'

She woke, and though at first she looked dazed, groggy, her eyes suddenly widened with fear. 'Wh . . . what?'

Jack Garston walked into the room. 'Good morning, my dear, I hope you slept well. My, your brothers must be worried about you. It seems that they've sent me a message. They've agreed to stop production in return for getting you back.'

303

Tony saw the relief that surged in her eyes. She shakily got off the bed. 'Does . . . does this mean I can go?'

'Of course, but all in good time. Your brothers have caused me considerable time, effort and expense, so I think I deserve a little compensation – don't you?' He then turned, snapping out, 'Tony, take her upstairs to my room.'

Tony saw the colour drain from Pet's face, the fear in her eyes. 'Come on,' he said, grabbing her arm.

'No . . . no!' she cried, resisting him.

Tony hated this but, with no choice, he dragged her out of the room and upstairs, feeling like he was taking an innocent lamb to slaughter.

Jack Garston went ahead and, reaching his bedroom, he opened the door. 'Put her inside and then go. Wait downstairs.'

Pet clung to him, her eyes wide in appeal. 'Oh, Tony, please help me, ohhh, please . . .' but unable to stand it, Tony shook her off, almost running from the room.

Garston closed the door, and before Tony was out of earshot, he heard Pet's terrified screams. He tensed, but knowing there was nothing he could do, he continued to the basement. He'd seen and done some rotten things in the past, followed orders, but nothing had ever affected him like this. He felt sickened. Jack Garston was exacting his revenge of the

Drapers, but Pet hadn't done anything wrong. It was her bloody brothers who deserved to suffer, not her. God, he'd had enough, he was getting out, but he'd have to find somewhere well out of Garston's reach.

Tony sat in the basement, trying not to think about what was happening to Pet. Over an hour passed, time in which he filled his mind by planning how he was going to get away from Jack Garston. The door opened, and he stood up, trying to hide his feelings when he saw Pet. She looked awful, like a broken doll.

'You can take her home now, Tony. Drop her off close to where she lives, and, as you worked all night, you can have the rest of the day off.'

Unable to look at the man, Tony could only just about grind out the words, 'Thanks, Mr Garston.'

'Goodbye, my dear,' Garston said, but it drew no response from Pet. She stood as still as a statue, her eyes distant, unfocused.

Tony knew he had to get out of there before he did something silly. He wanted to smash the man in the face, to wipe the supercilious smile from his lips. He grabbed the van keys, threw Pet's stinking coat around her shoulders, and then snapped, 'Come on, you.'

Pet didn't move, so he took her arm, pulling her forward. She moved woodenly but he managed to get her outside and up the basement steps. Tony then bundled her in the van, driving off with his foot down hard on the accelerator. Once around the corner, he flicked a glance at Pet. 'Are you all right?'

She didn't answer, and though Tony tried again, there was no response. He gave up, concentrating on the road as he drove her to Battersea.

When Tony pulled up near the alley, Pet didn't move, so, jumping out, he went round to the passenger side, opening the door.

'Come on, Pet, you're home now.'

Still no response, so he reached up, gently urging her out and onto the pavement. 'Look, you've only got to walk through there,' he said, turning her round and pointing at the alley.

Bloody hell, Tony thought, it was like talking to a plank of wood. He turned her back to face him, looking into her eyes. 'Pet, you've got to go home. Your parents must be worried sick.'

There wasn't a flicker of response and seeing the dead look in Pet's eyes, he felt swamped with guilt. He'd heard rumours about Garston's appetites, his strange fancies, but too scared to disobey the man, he'd led Pet to his bedroom. He should have flattened the slimy git, stopped him from laying his filthy hands on Pet, but he'd done nothing!

'Come on, you're safe now,' he said, giving her shoulders a small shake.

When she didn't react, Tony dropped his hands

to his sides, his mind racing. He couldn't take her into the alley – the Drapers would kill him – yet his guilt made him feel that he couldn't just leave her standing like a zombie on the pavement. It was no good, he couldn't look into those dead eyes any longer. Tony turned her round again, giving her a gentle shove forward. 'Go home!'

Pet took a few steps and, his fingers crossed that she'd keep on walking, Tony jumped into the van, his foot like a diver's boot on the accelerator as he screeched away.

They were going out to search again, but Maurice wasn't ready and was holding them up. Whilst waiting, Chris decided to pop to the local shop for some cigarettes. He hurried out of the alley, saw a van speeding off, and then paused.

No, it couldn't be! His heart missed a beat. 'Pet! Pet!' he cried, running up to her. 'My God, are you all right?'

Pet was walking woodenly, her face expression-less.

'Oh, Pet, what has he done to you?'

She still didn't react, her eyes fixed ahead as she took one slow step after another.

Chris took her arm. 'Come on, Pet, let's get you home. We've been going out of our minds and we were out half the night looking for you.'

There was still no response, but thankfully she

kept moving, until at last Chris was able to urge her inside.

'Mum,' he called. 'Look.'

'Pet. Oh my God, Pet!'

Chris watched as his mother hurried forward, her face alight, only to pause when she saw her daughter's face. 'What is it, love? What's wrong?'

'Come on, talk to us,' Chris urged.

She stood like a statue and for the first time Chris noticed her clothes. Her coat was over her shoulders, but beneath it she was wearing a black dress, which thankfully his mother hadn't noticed. The smell reached him then, his nostrils twitching.

'Chris, her coat stinks,' his mother cried. 'I think she must have wet herself.'

Pet remained unmoving, her face pale, frozen, like alabaster.

'What's the matter with her, Chris?' but then as Dan began to wave his arm as he tried to speak, she hurried to his side. 'Look, love, I told you not to worry. Petula's here. She's come home.'

'Pet, come and sit by the fire,' Chris urged. 'You look frozen.'

Gently he led her forward, pushing her gently onto a chair. 'I think she's in some sort of shock, Mum. Maybe we should get the doc to have a look at her.'

He watched as his mother pursed her lips. She then shook her head saying, 'No, not yet. Let's see if she snaps out of it first. Pop next door and ask

Yvonne to come round. She can look after Pet, whilst I see to your dad.'

Chris nodded, taking a last look at his sister before he left. She was sitting stiffly, her eyes fixed, distant. His jaws worked in anger. What had Garston done to her?

He hurried next door to find that Danny and Bob were still waiting for Maurice. 'We can call off the search. When I went to buy some fags, I found Pet just outside the alley.'

'What? Is she all right?'

'I don't know, Danny. Physically she looks all right, but she seems a bit weird.'

'I'm going to see her,' Bob said, almost running out of the door.

'Yeah, me too,' said Danny.

'Hold on, Danny, you know how Dad reacts when he sees you.'

'I don't give a shit. I'm going to see Pet.'

'Mum asked me to fetch Yvonne. She needs a bit of help.'

'Yvonne!' Danny yelled, and as she came hurrying downstairs he said, 'Pet's turned up and Mum wants you to give her a hand.'

Danny didn't wait for his wife as he hurried out, but Yvonne was quick too, not far behind him as he went into number one. Chris took up the rear, but as soon as his father saw Danny, he went wild.

'You'll have to go, Danny,' cried Yvonne.

309

'Not till I've seen Pet,' he argued, ignoring the ranting sounds his father was making.

Chris saw that Pet was unmoved by what was going on around her, her face expressionless.

'Danny, go,' he heard his mother shout. 'Do you want your father to have another stroke!'

With a shake of his head, Danny pushed Bob to one side to kneel in front of Pet, his voice frantic. 'Where have you been, Pet? What happened?'

Pet didn't answer, and as Dan's noises increased in volume, Yvonne cried, 'Danny, please, you must go.'

As Danny straightened, Chris saw an expression on his brother's face that he had never seen before. Danny looked utterly dejected, broken. Without a word he walked across the room and out of the house, his shoulders bent like an old man's.

Yvonne had seen Danny's reactions too, and frowned, but with Dan playing up, she had to concentrate on helping her mother-in-law.

'Come on, love,' Joan urged. 'If you don't calm down I'll have to get the doctor to give you a sedative again.'

Dan moaned, his good arm waving to indicate his wheelchair.

'All right, we'll get you up,' Joan told him. 'Bob, there are too many people around your father so you'd best go, but you can come back later. Chris, you can give me a hand.'

'What about Pet?'

'Yvonne will see to her.'

Bob gently stroked Pet's hair, his face white with anxiety. 'Mum, can't I stay with her?'

'She needs cleaning up, so leave her to Yvonne.'

Bob bit on his bottom lip and for a moment Yvonne thought he was going to argue, but thankfully he gave Pet's hair a final stroke, saying as he left, 'If she's still like this in an hour or two, you should call the doctor.'

Chris and Joan hauled Dan up and into his wheelchair. He was still jabbering, whilst Joan answered as if she could understand his every word. 'Yes, I'll wheel you over to Pet, but not until you calm down.'

Dan became quiet at last, and as Joan pushed him across the room until his chair was close to his daughter, Yvonne saw that one side of his face twisted into the parody of a smile. His good arm shook as he reached out, his hand finally resting on Pet's arm. She didn't respond to his touch, didn't turn her head to look at her father, and once again Dan began to jabber, but softly, as though consoling his beloved child.

Yvonne's eyes filled with tears. Pet looked dreadful. Where had she been? What had happened to her?

'Look at her, Mum. I still think the doc should take a look at her,' Chris urged.

'She was frozen when you brought her in, and if

she was out all night in this weather, no wonder she's in such a state. A nice hot bath might bring her round. If that doesn't work, we'll call the surgery.' Joan became brusque. 'Right, Dan, let's get you to the bathroom first.'

Chris helped his mother, whilst Yvonne kneeled down in front of Pet. 'Oh, love, what's the matter? Were you in an accident? Are you hurt?'

Pet didn't respond, and Yvonne's nose wrinkled. The child stank, her coat filthy and creased. Maybe she'd been run over, left lying somewhere, but surely if that was the case, someone would have seen her?

'Come on, darling, let's get you out of that coat,' Yvonne urged, gently unravelling it from Pet's shoulders. There was no resistance and Yvonne fought tears. Pet looked traumatised, as though she had faced something so dreadful that she had died inside. Oh God, please – not that! Underneath the coat, Pet was wearing a dress that Yvonne hadn't seen before. She frowned, but was then distracted as Joan wheeled Dan back into the room.

'Right, the bathroom's free for Pet.'

'Come on, love,' Yvonne urged, but Pet didn't move.

Chris took her arm, gently pulling her up, and as though a puppet on strings, she rose to her feet. Yvonne took over then, finding as she took Pet's arm that the girl moved forward without resistance.

'Mum, I need a word with Danny,' Chris said. 'Can you manage without me now?'

'Yes, I'll be fine.'

When they reached the bathroom, Yvonne found that Pet just stood there as she ran a hot bath. She threw in some bath salts, then said, 'It's ready.'

Pet didn't move and Yvonne floundered. She would have to undress her, but it didn't feel right, an intrusion. Softly urging, Yvonne managed to peel down the dress, her eyes widening. Pet's small breasts were bruised and covered in bite marks. Oh God! Oh, no! As gently as possible she continued to pull the dress down, finding to her horror that Pet was naked underneath. There were more bruises around her thighs, but worse, traces of blood on the insides of her legs. Tears overspilled now, running down Yvonne's cheeks. Pet had been raped, and by the looks of it, violently. Who had done this to her? It must have been a maniac, a monster!

Chapter Twenty-five

'You saw the state Pet was in,' Bob said. 'I told Sue that she's been in some sort of accident, but I can't see her swallowing that for long. What do you think Garston did to her, Danny?'

'Ain't it bleeding obvious?'

Yes, it *was* obvious, Chris thought, his temper flaring. 'When I get my hands on Garston I'll slit his fucking throat.'

'You'll do nothing,' Danny said quietly, but his manner was subdued, as though just talking was an effort. 'This is down to me to sort out.'

Chris had expected Danny to go off on one, to rant and rave at Garston. Instead he appeared deflated, his voice lacking conviction. 'No, Danny, I'm not having that. When you find Garston, I want to be there. You saw Pet, and I want to make sure he suffers for what he did to her.'

'Yeah, I'm with Chris,' Bob said. 'Pet may be able to tell us where she was held, and then we'll have Garston.'

'You're both forgetting something,' said Danny. 'What do you think will happen when Pet starts to talk?'

'Well, as I said, hopefully she'll be able to lead us to Garston.'

'That's not what I'm getting at, Bob. When Pet does open her mouth, who do you think she'll talk to?'

'Oh, shit!' Chris exclaimed, suddenly understanding what Danny was getting at. 'Mum, or maybe Yvonne.'

'Yeah, that's right.'

Bob cottoned on too, his voice high with anxiety. 'Do you think Garston told her about us?'

'Yeah, probably.'

'That . . . that means Pet knows, and if she talks . . .' Bob's voice trailed off before it rose again. 'It's our fault that Garston snatched Pet, but we've got to keep her quiet, Danny.'

'And how are we supposed to do that?'

'We could get to her first. Have a word with her.'

'I could give it a go,' Chris suggested.

Danny shrugged. 'I suppose you could give it a try, but you'll have to do it out of Mum, Dad and Yvonne's hearing.'

'She didn't seem to take in a word of what was said to her. What if she doesn't listen?' Bob asked.

'If she doesn't, then our wives will probably find out about our little sideline.'

Bob ran a hand through his hair in agitation. 'I'd better warn Maurice.'

'He's still rough so it might be best to leave it for now,' Chris suggested. 'What about the yard, Danny? We usually open until one o'clock on a Saturday.'

Danny said nothing, his gaze once again distant.

'Danny, did you hear what I said?'

'Yeah, but don't bother to open up. We'll all meet up there after Chris has had a chat with Pet.'

Chris met Bob's eyes, but his brother just shrugged before saying, 'I'd best get back to Sue,' and on that note he gave one last glance at Danny before walking out.

'I'll go and have a talk to Pet and let's hope I can convince her to keep her mouth shut,' Chris said. There was no response from Danny, leaving Chris seriously worried about his brother. 'Danny, I'm off,' he said, yet as he walked to number one, he knew that Danny's state of mind was the least of his concerns at the moment. If he couldn't get through to Pet and she opened her mouth, the shit really was going to hit the fan.

Yvonne found a dressing gown on the back of the door, and after helping Pet to put it on, she led her out of the bathroom. Her mother-in-law's eyes were wide in appeal, and Dan was quiet, both looking at her expectantly.

'She's all right, ain't she, Yvonne? Tell me she's all right. She . . . she ain't been touched?'

Joan had been through so much and it showed. Since Dan had come home, the weight had fallen off her from the heavy burden of his care. The fact that her own son had beaten his father half to death could have destroyed her, but instead she had surprised them all with her strength. Yet Yvonne felt it was a tenuous strength, one that could crack under the strain.

Fearing both their reactions, Yvonne blurted out, 'She's fine, well, other than a few bruises. I think she's been in some sort of accident and maybe that's why she's in shock. She could have been laying somewhere, injured.'

'But you said she's only got a few bruises. What about her head? Did you check her head?'

'Yes, and don't worry, it's fine. There's not even a sign of a bump.'

When Yvonne saw her mother-in-law sag with relief, she felt a little less guilty about her lies. 'Do you want me to take her up to bed?'

'Yes, good idea, a bit of kip might be just what she needs.'

Pet was still in a trance as Yvonne led her upstairs, where she tucked her into bed like a child. As Yvonne sat down beside Pet, she realised that she shouldn't have lied to her in-laws. All it had done was to put off the inevitable. When Pet came out of this shock, they would find out the truth and it could destroy Dan. He adored his daughter and had always kept her protected, innocent, but now . . .

'Oh, Pet, if you can hear me, please, don't tell your parents what happened to you. It would break their hearts.'

Pet didn't respond, but her eyes closed and her breathing became regular as she fell asleep. Yvonne crept out of the room, going downstairs to see that Chris had returned.

'How is she?' he asked.

'She's asleep,' Yvonne told him, then saying, 'Mum, if you can manage without me, I'll pop home for a while.'

'Yeah, that's fine, love, and thanks for your help.'

Yvonne called goodbye and then hurried out, worried about Danny and anxious to see if he was all right.

She was relieved to find Danny alone. He was sitting on the sofa, his eyes closed. Drained, exhausted, her usual stamina gone, Yvonne felt like sinking down beside him. She'd had a good night's sleep, but lately that didn't seem to make any difference. Now she fretted, wondering what to do. Should she tell Danny the truth, tell him that Pet had been raped? Maybe it would be better to leave it for now, to wait until Danny was more like himself.

His eyes opened. 'How is she?' His tone was listless.

'She's in bed – asleep,' and worried about Danny's reaction if she told him that Pet had been raped, she added, 'I . . . I think she must have been in some sort of accident.'

'Yeah, one called Jack Garston.'

'What? Who's he?'

Danny rose abruptly to his feet. 'I'm going to the yard. I'll see you later.'

'Wait . . .' The door slammed and Yvonne was left, her question unanswered.

Danny knocked on Maurice's door. Norma opened it, her face showing her annoyance as she stood back to let him in.

'I need a word with Maurice.'

'He's still having trouble with his breathing.'

Danny stepped inside to find Maurice slumped in a chair, his face beaded with perspiration. 'We're all meeting up at the yard. Do you think you're up to it?'

'I doubt it,' Norma snapped. 'When Bob told us about Pet's accident, this is what happened. And let me tell you, it hasn't helped that your mother turned him away. He's got just as much right as the rest of you to see his sister.'

'It's all right, Norma, just leave it, will you?' Maurice gasped. 'How is she, Danny?'

'From what I saw, she's in a bad way.'

'What are we planning to do?'

'Nothing. *We're* doing nothing. This is all down to me – my fault.'

'What are you saying?' Norma cried. 'How can Pet's accident be your fault?'

With his head all over the place, Danny realised that he'd said too much in front of Norma. Yet what did it matter? What did any of it matter now? When Pet opened her mouth, they'd all find out. 'As I said, Maurice, we're meeting up at the yard. If you can make it, we'll talk then.' He walked abruptly out, closing the door behind him.

With his head down, Danny strode out of Drapers Alley. One look at Pet and he knew what had been done to her – knew that Garston had sent one last message before releasing her. Instead of rage, instead of wanting to find Garston to ring his bloody neck, Danny had felt only self-loathing. Pet was only fourteen – a child – and the realisation hit him like a blow to the solar plexus. He had wanted to use kids in porn. Kids even younger than Pet. He was a sick bastard – as sick as Garston.

Chris came downstairs, shaking his head. 'It's no good, Mum, she's still sort of out of it. I've got to go to the yard. Can you manage without me?'

'I expect Yvonne will come round again to give me a hand. You go, I'll be fine.'

When Chris left, Joan flopped onto a chair, but soon after when Dan drifted off to sleep she went upstairs, quietly walking into Pet's bedroom. She found her daughter awake, laying flat on her back, her eyes fixed on the ceiling.

'Are you all right, love?'

Pet didn't answer and, frowning, Joan sat on the side of the bed. She reached out, running her hands over Pet's head, parting her hair, but as Yvonne had said, there was no sign of any injury. Yet something had to be wrong for Pet to be in this peculiar state. Maybe if she talked to her she'd elicit some response.

'I can't tell you how pleased we are that you've come home. When you went missing, your poor dad got in a right old state. I had to get the doctor out to give him a sedative. He's having a bit of a kip now, but did you see how pleased he was to see you? You're the apple of his eye, so thank God you've come home safe and sound.'

Joan paused, but Pet didn't even blink. She reached out again to stroke her daughter's hair, finding that the action felt alien. Like the boys, she hadn't shown Petula any affection, and didn't really know how to start now. Yvonne said that Petula hadn't been touched, and it had been such a relief. If Dan thought anyone had laid a hand on his daughter, he'd go mad.

When there was still no response, Joan frowned. There may not be any sign of a head injury, but despite a nice hot bath and a bit of kip, Pet was still in this strange state.

'I'm going to ring the surgery, Petula. I think you need to see a doctor,' she said, hurrying out of the room.

Chris shook his head as he looked at his brothers. 'I tried, but talking to Pet is like talking to a stone wall. She seems to be sort of comatose.'

'The longer she stays like that the better,' Bob said.

Maurice knew he had to stay calm. He too feared what would happen when Pet began to talk, but he was sickened by Bob's remark. 'I don't know how you can say that. Surely you don't want her to stay in that state?'

'I didn't mean it, I'm just spouting, but we've told you what might happen when she opens her mouth and I'm worried sick.'

'Don't you think I am too?'

'Look, this isn't getting us anywhere,' Chris said.

Maurice looked at Danny. 'Any ideas?' Danny just shook his head and Maurice frowned. There was something wrong. Danny hadn't spoken since the meeting began. He was slumped behind the desk, his face downcast. 'What's up, Danny?'

'I'm finished – we're finished.'

'Come on, don't talk like that,' Maurice cajoled. 'We can't be sure that Garston said anything to Pet. We may be in the clear.'

There was a defeatist tone to Danny's voice. 'I doubt that.'

'I think we've got to consider the worst-case scenario,' said Chris. 'Either we wait to see what Pet has to say, or you prepare your wives and Mum for what she might tell them.'

'Leave it out!' Bob protested. 'Oh, yeah, I can see it now. By the way, Sue, I think you should know that we make porn films. One of our rivals wanted us to stop production, so he kidnapped and raped Pet as a warning.'

'All right, there's no need for sarcasm. If you've got a better idea, let's hear it.'

'I haven't got any ideas.'

'Right then, if you don't want to prepare them, I don't think we've got much choice,' Chris said. 'We'll just have to wait and see what happens when Pet comes out of shock. In the meantime I want to find Garston. He can't get away with what he did to our sister.'

'I've told you, leave Garston to me.'

Maurice stared at Danny worriedly. 'Wouldn't it be better to back off? If you go after Garston, he's going to retaliate and you've seen what he's done to Pet. If you stir things up again he could snatch one of our kids.'

'Bloody hell,' said Bob, 'I hadn't thought of that.'

'We should stop making films, close down the Wimbledon operation,' Maurice urged. 'It'll show Garston that we're no longer a threat.'

'No,' snapped Chris. 'We should go after Garston

– take him out, finish him and then there'll be no need to stop production.'

'I told you, Garston's mine,' Danny murmured.

Maurice knew that he wouldn't be able to talk them out of it. They wanted revenge and so it would go on, the violence, the turf war. He gulped in air, his mind racing. He knew what he had to do – that he had no choice. Not only did he fear for Oliver's safety, he feared for his marriage too. He had never taken Norma's threats about leaving him seriously, but if she found out about the porn business it would finish their marriage. Yvonne and Sue might cope, both aware that the Drapers were no angels, but Norma was different. She came from a different background, had different standards. She'd be horrified, disgusted.

It would be hard to leave his family, but Maurice knew now he had to act quickly, before Danny and Chris went after Garston. He began to breathe heavily, feigning illness. 'Sorry, but I feel a bit rough. I think I'd best go home.'

Danny said nothing, his head still down, and it was Chris who answered, 'Yeah, all right, but we'll need to talk again.'

Maurice continued to gasp for breath as he left. If possible he'd tell his parents and his brothers that he was leaving, but he wanted to be packed and ready first. Then they would just go, before anyone could persuade him to stay.

*   *   *

Another hour passed, but nothing was resolved.

Fed up with going round and round in circles, Bob said, 'Look, this is just a waste of time.'

'Yeah, you're right,' Chris said. 'Come on, we might as well go home.'

Danny didn't argue, his face set as he rose to his feet. They locked the yard, all climbing into Danny's car and heading back to Drapers Alley, each preoccupied with his own thoughts.

When they arrived, Bob had no sooner put his foot inside his house when Sue started.

'Your mother drives me mad, Bob. I only wanted to find out how Pet is, but she wouldn't let me in.'

'When I saw Pet earlier she was in a terrible state. No doubt Mum and Yvonne think she needs a bit of peace and quiet.'

'Bob, for God's sake, I care about your sister and I want to see her. I'm your wife, part of the family, but I'm treated like an outcast. Norma is too, and she's just as fed up with it. We're kept out of your mother's house as though we're contagious.'

'Don't be daft, it ain't like that. Dad's upset about Pet, and Mum's just doing her best to keep him calm, that's all. She looks worn out these days, and now this has happened. You should cut her a bit of slack.'

'If she's worn out, she should accept me and Norma's offer to help. We'd muck in, but she'll only allow Yvonne to give her a hand.'

'For Gawd's sake, I've only just got in the door. Do you have to keep going on and on about it?'

'I don't keep on about it, but what about the boys? When was the last time they saw their grandfather?'

'Where are the kids?'

'Playing in the yard, but don't try to change the subject.'

'Look, with half his face paralysed, my dad looks funny. As Mum said, it might scare them if they saw him, and that would upset Dad.'

'Is that why he's kept a virtual prisoner?'

'Prisoner! What are you on about now?'

'Your dad hasn't been outside the door since he came home. He's got a wheelchair, so there's no need for it.'

'Sue, I know my dad, and believe me, he wouldn't want anyone to see him the way he is now. If he wants to go out, he'll let Mum know.'

'How's he supposed to do that?'

'He'd point to the fucking door, you silly cow!'

Sue gasped, her neck stretching. 'Don't swear at me, and I ain't a silly cow.'

Bob had to smile at the indignant expression on Sue's face. He hated arguments, his voice now placatory. 'All right, don't get your knickers in a twist. I'm sorry. It's just that I'm tired and worried about Pet. I was going to grab a bite to eat and then go to see how she is.'

'Oh, yes, and unlike me you'll have no trouble getting past your mother.'

'Sue, my sister is in a bad way, but all you're going on about is my mother. Sod it, I'm going to see how Pet's doing.'

Bob marched out of the house, but when he got to his mother's she opened the door, her face white with anxiety. 'What's up, Mum?'

'I've rung the surgery, asked for a doctor to come out to see Pet, but as it's Saturday, it may be a while before one turns up. Your dad's been playing up too, but he's dozed off at last so I won't invite you in in case it wakes him up.'

'All right, Mum,' Bob said. 'I'll come back later,' and as the door closed he turned to make his way back home, fed up and knowing that when he got there, Sue would start nagging again. His stomach churned. Yes, she might be in a mood now, but if she found out about the porn all hell would be let loose.

Chapter Twenty-six

Sue finally calmed down, and later that day, with the kids playing in the yard, Bob was dozing in his chair when there was a knock on his door. He opened his eyes, blinking away sleep as Maurice walked in.

'Bob,' he said, face wan, 'I've got something to tell you.'

Instantly awake now, Bob's stomach jolted. 'What is it? Have you been to see Pet? Has she said anything?'

'No, I haven't seen her yet. I . . . I've come to tell you that I'm leaving.'

'What . . . ?'

'I'm out, Bob. We're all packed and once I've said goodbye to everyone, we're going.'

Bob stared at Maurice, unable to think coherently, able only to splutter, 'But . . . but why?'

Maurice flicked a glance at Sue before asking, 'Can we talk outside?'

She reared up. 'That's it – shut me out as if I'm not a part of this family.'

'Sue, please, not now,' Bob said before walking outside with Maurice, closing the door behind him. 'Now what's this all about? Why are you leaving?'

'I should think it's obvious. Danny and Chris ain't gonna let Garston get away with what he did to Pet, and as I said at the meeting, I'm worried about Oliver. I've had it, Bob. I'm sick of living like this. I'm sick of the violence, and I'm shit scared of Jack Garston.'

Bob's temper flared. 'You can't do this, Maurice. You can't just leave like this. Dad's still in a state, and it's obvious that Pet's been raped, but all you seem to care about is yourself.'

'There's nothing I can do to help Dad, or Pet. If there's trouble with Garston, you know I'd be useless. All I'm fit for is looking after the books, and it's not just myself I'm thinking about – it's my son!'

'We could talk to Danny and Chris – persuade them to leave Garston alone.'

Maurice shook his head. 'They'll never agree, but it's not only that, Bob. If Pet opens her mouth, Norma will find out what we've been up to. She'll leave me, Bob, and she'll take Oliver with her.'

'But where will you go? And what about Mum? She ain't gonna like it.'

'Dad's the most important person in Mum's life and he always has been. She has no time for Norma, or Oliver, so I doubt she'll miss us. As for where we're going, well, until I can sort something out, we'll find digs.'

With a sigh of exasperation, Bob said, 'I can't believe this. Since George put Dad in hospital, it feels like this family is falling apart.'

'I may be leaving Drapers Alley, but you're all still my family and I'll keep in touch.'

Bob could see the sadness in his brother's eyes, could hear that his chest was staring to wheeze, and his anger seeped away. 'What about the yard – the books?'

'You, Chris and Danny will manage. Keeping the books for the yard is a doddle and as for the other books – I'll leave them with Danny.'

'Look, I can understand why you want to go, but isn't there anything I can do to persuade you to stay?'

'No, Bob. I'm sorry, but I can't risk staying and . . . and if you don't mind, I'd rather you kept out of the way when I tell the others.'

'Danny's gonna do his nut,' Bob warned.

'Yeah, I know.'

Bob impulsively wrapped his arms around his brother and, obviously unused to displays of brotherly affection, Maurice momentarily stiffened, but then Bob felt his embrace returned. 'Promise me you'll stay in touch, Maurice.'

'Of course I will,' he said, his voice gruff with emotion. Then with a forced smile, he walked to Danny's house.

Bob went back inside to find Sue waiting, her arms folded across her chest.

'What's going on? Why are they leaving?'

'I dunno, love.'

'Don't give me that. I ain't that stupid. It's obvious that Maurice is doing a runner. Are the police after him? Will they be after you?'

'No, of course not.'

'Then why are they leaving?'

'I've told you! I don't know.'

'Sod you then. I'm going round to see Norma.' And with that Sue marched out of the house.

Bob flopped onto a chair. It had happened so quickly that he couldn't take it in. Maurice was leaving, running off, and though he was upset, he couldn't really blame him. Pet was bound to open her mouth and when she did they'd all be in deep, deep mire.

When Maurice told Danny, he waited for the explosion, amazed when it didn't come.

Danny just shrugged. 'I'm surprised, but I can see why.'

Maurice frowned. He'd expected Danny to do his nut, but instead he remained slumped on the sofa. 'What's wrong, Danny?'

'Nothing's wrong,' he replied, at last rising to his feet. 'I don't suppose I can persuade you to stay?'

'No, sorry. Even if you and Chris agree to leave

Garston alone, I can't risk Norma finding out about the other stuff.'

'I've already decided to close down Wimbledon.'

'Do the others know?'

'Not yet.'

'I feel rotten for buggering off, but you don't need me, Danny. As I told Bob, I only look after the books and you can handle them,' Maurice said as he pulled them out of his pocket. 'This one is for the yard, but keep the other one out of sight.'

'What will you do for money?'

'I've got a few bob stashed away, and I can always look for a job.'

'Are you staying in the area?'

'I don't know, Danny. I haven't thought that far ahead.'

'You'll keep in touch?'

'Yes, of course I will.'

Yvonne walked in from the kitchen, frowning. 'I couldn't help overhearing some of what's been said. It sounds like you're running away, Maurice, but why?'

'Keep out of this, Yvonne,' Danny said.

'But—'

Maurice swiftly broke in, 'Look, I've got to go. Bye, Danny. Bye, Yvonne.'

Danny nodded, his voice hoarse as he said, 'Let me know where you are.'

Maurice gulped, finding saying goodbye to his

family agonising. Memories of his childhood flashed into his mind; the way his brothers had always looked after him, stood up for him, but now he felt like a rat deserting a sinking ship. 'I'm sorry, Danny,' he gasped.

'There's no need, mate. You warned against Garston in the first place, but I wouldn't listen. This is all down to me – my fault that you've been forced to do this.'

Maurice could feel his chest tightening. A full-blown asthma attack could delay his departure and that was the last thing he wanted. He shook his brother's hand, said goodbye and then quickly left.

Now outside, Maurice drew air into his lungs, trying to prepare himself as he knocked on his mother's door. She opened it, her expression harassed.

'Not now, Maurice. The doctor has just arrived to take a look at Pet, and your father's playing up a bit.'

'But, Mum—'

'Come back later.'

Maurice opened his mouth to protest again, but found the door shut in his face. He paled. The doctor was there. Would he be able to get Pet to talk? Yet how could he leave without saying goodbye to his parents, and Chris? For a moment he remained outside his mother's door, but then he turned swiftly, heading for Bob's house. He had to get Norma away from the alley before Pet opened her mouth, but once they had settled, he could come back to visit them without her.

When Bob opened the door his face lit up. 'Maurice! Have you changed your mind?'

'No, but the doctor's with Pet and Mum wouldn't let me in. I can't hang around, Bob. Will you tell her – and Chris?'

'Yeah, all right, but what excuse am I supposed to make?'

'If the doc gets through to Pet, I doubt you'll need one.'

'Oh shit, I hadn't thought of that.'

'If she still isn't talking, I suppose you can blame Norma. Tell Mum that she wanted to leave the alley.'

'All right, but she's still going to think it's odd that you left without saying goodbye.'

'I know and I'm sorry to lay this on you.'

'What did Danny say?'

'Not much. Only that he's going to close Wimbledon down, and then he said he doesn't blame me for leaving.'

'Close down? But why? I don't know what's up with Danny. We can still make soft porn.'

'He ain't himself, that's for sure.' Maurice looked at his mother's door, his heartbeat increasing. What if Pet was talking? 'Look, I've got to go, Bob.'

'I couldn't tell Sue why you're leaving, so she went round to see Norma. What excuse did you give her?'

'None. She's been nagging me for years to leave the alley, so I just told her that if she didn't stop asking questions, we'd stay. So far it's done the trick, but I'll have to come up with something to shut her up.'

'Sue thinks the police are after us.'

'I must go, Bob.'

'You'll let me know where you are?'

'Of course I will.'

Maurice found himself wrapped in an embrace again. He returned the pressure, almost cracking up as he gently pushed his brother away. 'Bye, matc,' and before Bob could answer, he hurried off.

When he walked inside his own house, Maurice found Sue and Norma facing each other like combatants.

'Maurice, will you please tell Sue that I don't know why we're leaving.'

'That's right.'

'She seems to think that we're running from the police. Is that why?'

'Look, Norma, you've been nagging me for years to get out of Drapers Alley and now you've got your wish. I have my reasons for leaving and you'll just have to trust me on this.'

'Sue's right, isn't she? It's the police – they're after you.'

'No, Norma, the police aren't after me. Now either we leave right away or we stay, and for good.' Maurice hoped this continued threat would be enough to silence his wife. It had been the one he used throughout the afternoon whenever she began to ask questions. She'd initially been thrilled when he told her they were leaving, happy at first to begin packing, but it hadn't lasted long. She wanted to know why they had to go in such a hurry without the chance to arrange a van for the furniture. He told her that once they'd settled he'd get the removals sorted out, and thankfully that had been enough to mollify her, but now Sue was stirring things up again.

'Leave it out, Maurice,' Sue snapped. 'You can't expect Norma to just leave without knowing why. And what about Oliver? How does he feel about it?'

'Sue, I don't want to fall out with you, but this is none of your business.' He turned to Norma. 'Well, what's it to be? Are we going, or are we staying?'

For a moment there was only silence, but then with a small nod, Norma said, 'We're going.'

'Where's Oliver?'

'He's upstairs, sulking. He doesn't want to go.'

Maurice shook his head in exasperation. When he told Oliver that they were moving, he'd been more upset about leaving his rabbit than his cousins. He was an only child, used to playing alone when the other boys weren't around. Maurice had found a box, stuffed Shaker inside, and just hoped that they could sneak the animal into digs. It had been worth it to see the smile on his son's face.

'Oliver,' Maurice called.

When the boy came reluctantly downstairs, Maurice kneeled in front of him. 'Look, son, we've got to go now. Do you want to pop round to say goodbye to your cousins?'

Oliver shook his head, only saying sulkily, 'No.'

Sue sniffed, and then tears began to roll down her cheeks. 'Oh, I can't believe this is happening. Paul's gonna miss him something rotten.'

'We'll stay in touch,' Maurice consoled and, knowing that he couldn't stand much more of this, he picked up two of their cases. 'Right, let's go. Oliver, you carry Shaker, and, Norma, can you manage a couple of cases? We've only got to hump them around to the car.'

'Yes, all right,' she said, her voice subdued as she added, 'Good . . . goodbye, Sue. I'll ring you. I promise.'

Maurice took one last look around the living room, finding his feet leaden as they left the house. There was no sign of Danny, but Bob was on his doorstep. Sue ran into his arms, sobbing, but after giving her a swift hug he gently disengaged himself.

'Go inside, love. See to the boys,' he urged.

With a strangled gasp she nodded, whilst Bob moved to take the cases out of Norma's hands. 'I'll carry these,' he said.

They walked silently to the garages, passing the two empty houses, one that had been George's, the other Ivy's. There would be three empty now. When they came to the end of the alley, Maurice found that he couldn't look back, his emotions barely under control.

He loaded the luggage into the car, knowing that if he looked at Bob it would be his downfall. Somehow he had to build a new life, but the thought of doing it without the support of his family was overwhelming. Norma climbed into the passenger seat, Oliver in the back, and almost choking, Maurice got behind the wheel. He started the engine, gasped, 'See you, Bob,' and then drove away, before his brother had a chance to answer.

Chapter Twenty-seven

When the doctor arrived, Chris hurriedly said that he was going out, and bolted, shutting the door behind him.

Dr Addison could see that Joan Draper was worried about leaving her husband on his own, but nevertheless she showed him upstairs.

When he saw the young girl lying on the bed, he cleared his throat. 'Would you stay whilst I examine your daughter?'

'But my husband . . .'

'I'm sure he'll be fine for a few minutes,' he said dismissively, going on to examine Petula.

He was appalled by the girl's injuries and examined her as gently as possible, but it wasn't only her physical injuries that concerned him, there was her mental state too.

'Do you know who did this to your daughter?' he asked, replacing the blankets.

There was no reply and he turned to see that Joan

Draper was white-faced, clinging to the end of the bed as she gasped, 'No! Oh, Doctor, I didn't realise that she's been . . . been touched. Petula arrived home this morning after being missing all night. My . . . my daughter-in-law said that she must have been in some sort of minor accident, that's all.'

'Yes, well, as you've now seen, your daughter has been touched, and violently.'

'Is . . . is that why she won't talk?'

'She's suffered an horrendous ordeal, so dreadful that her mind has closed down. I've seen this reaction before and if there's no response in forty-eight hours, she'll need to be admitted to hospital. I'll call again on Monday to see if there's any improvement. If you think she needs to see a doctor before then, call the surgery and you'll be put through to the locum service.'

'Please, my husband mustn't know that she's been . . . been . . .' Joan Draper floundered, unable to say the word. 'I don't think he could stand it, Doctor. He'd go mad.'

'Yes, I can understand that, but there may be consequences.'

'What do you mean?'

Dr Addison cleared his throat. This was difficult, but the signs would have to be looked for. 'What I'm trying to say is that you will need to keep an eye on your daughter's menstrual cycle.'

Joan Draper stared at him, ashen-faced. 'You . . . you don't mean that she could be pre . . . pregnant.'

'It's too soon to say, but there is always the possibility.'

'Oh, God,' she gasped. 'No, please, not that.'

'My advice is just a precaution.'

As they left the room he could see that Joan Draper was making a supreme effort to bring herself under control. Dan Draper was awake when they went back downstairs, and she even managed a parody of a smile.

'Petula's going to be fine, Dan. Ain't that right, Doctor?'

'Yes, well, I'll have another look at her on Monday.'

'See, Dan, I told you not to worry.'

Dr Addison saw the look of relief on the man's twisted face. He said goodbye, his expression grim as he left. The girl's injuries had been dreadful and he wondered if the police had been informed.

Chris strode quickly down Lavender Hill, anxious to get to Phil – anxious for comfort. He felt as though everything was falling apart. Danny had lost it, and not only that, none of his brothers had been concerned about their mother, about how she'd be affected if Pet opened her mouth. All they'd been concerned about was their wives. They'd forgotten that the old man had been involved with the porn from the start – all right, not the hard stuff – but even so, how would his mother take it if she found out? She had always been a bit of a

341

prude, narrow-minded, not slow to show her disgust when Maurice had got Norma in the family way. She disapproved of Sue too, calling her a tart, and though she had put up with the old man when he swore, she would never allow a smutty joke. Would she turn against the old man if she found out about the porn? Yes, of course she would, and she'd turn against him too, against all of them.

Since his father's beating and George's disappearance, Chris had already sensed that his mother had changed towards him. At first she had seemed edgy, nervous around him and unable to meet his eyes, but when he'd questioned her she had denied that anything was wrong. At first he'd been shit scared that she'd found out who he was seeing, but had soon realised that it couldn't be that. If his mother knew, if any of his family knew, they'd have confronted him. His fear of discovery had served to make him extra careful when he sneaked off.

Thankfully, nowadays his mother seemed to have relaxed a little bit, but if she discovered that they'd been making porn, how would she react? Would she throw him out? He dreaded facing it, seeing the disgust on her face. Maybe he should get out now, leave before the shit hit the fan. Even though he hated the idea, it was better than the alternative.

Feeling desolate at the thought of leaving his mother, when Chris reached Phil's house he banged on the door, relieved when it was opened almost immediately.

'Chris, what's the matter, love? Come here, come to Mummy.'

Gratefully Chris fell into arms that enfolded him – comforted him.

Yvonne was puzzled and concerned. When she had told Danny about Pet, he had mentioned Jack Garston, and now when Maurice called round to say he was leaving, the same name had come up again.

'Danny, who is Jack Garston? Is he a copper?'

Danny didn't look at her, only saying shortly, 'No.'

'I don't understand. If he isn't a copper, why has Maurice been forced to leave?'

'Yvonne, you don't want to know. Just keep out of it.'

'Danny, please, I do need to know what's going on. It's important. Are the police after you too? Will you be doing a runner? Will *we* be doing a runner?'

'We ain't going anywhere.'

Yvonne heaved a sigh of relief, but it was short-lived. If this man Garston wasn't a copper, then who was he? God, she was worried sick. Danny seemed depressed, morose. All right, he had good reason to be upset. He adored Pet and it must have been a shock to see her in that state, yet she was sure there was more to it than that.

Yvonne was still hugging her news to herself. She had been itching to tell Danny, hoping it would snap him out of his depression, but then Pet had gone missing, making it an impossible time. She reached out, touching his arm. 'Danny, please talk to me. Tell me what's going on.'

'Yvonne, just leave me alone. I ain't in the mood for this.' And Danny leaned forward, burying his face in his hands.

Yvonne wanted to comfort him, to hold him. She hadn't planned it this way, but now she blurted out, 'Danny, I've got some wonderful news. I'm pregnant.'

He sat bolt upright, his eyes wide as he turned to look at her. 'You're what?'

Yvonne smiled softly. 'I'm having a baby, Danny. We're having a baby. I've been feeling rough for some time now and finally went to see the doctor on the same day that Pet went missing. When he told me that I'm four months pregnant, you could have knocked me down with a feather. I mean, I had no idea, especially as I've been having my periods. The show was small, but it just didn't occur to me that I might be having a baby.'

She had anticipated this moment so many times, expecting to see joy on Danny's face, but instead he jumped to his feet, his face the colour of chalk.

'No . . . no, you can't be.'

Yvonne touched her stomach. It had hardly

increased in size so was it any wonder that Danny didn't believe her? 'I know it doesn't show, but I am, really I am. Oh, Danny, what's wrong? I thought you'd be pleased.'

'I ain't fit to be a father.'

'Don't be silly, of course you are. You'll make a wonderful father.'

'You must be joking. I'm a bastard, Yvonne – a sick bastard.'

'I . . . I don't understand.'

Danny raked both hands through his hair, his expression wild. 'All right, you wanted to know, so I'll tell you. When I've finished, I won't blame you if you walk out of that door for good.'

He sat down again, his voice hesitant at first, but as it grew in strength, Yvonne wanted to put her hands over her ears, to shut out his words. She felt sick, bile rising to her throat, but this time it was nothing to do with her pregnancy.

'Please, I don't want to hear any more.'

It didn't stop Danny; nothing did. On and on he went, spewing out all the disgusting things he had done until Yvonne couldn't stand it. She fled, running upstairs where she slammed the bedroom door behind her. Wildly she grabbed a suitcase from under the bed, throwing clothes haphazardly inside.

Yvonne had always known that Danny was a bit of a rogue, that the Drapers were involved in shady deals, but never in her wildest imaginings had she expected to hear that they produced filthy, disgusting films.

She had lost count of Danny's affairs, of the times she had forgiven him, but just how many of his so-called porn stars had he slept with? Her stomach churning, Yvonne closed the suitcase before lifting it from the bed.

When she carried it downstairs Danny was on his feet, but he didn't say a word as she walked towards the door. It was the look on his face that stilled her. He stood unmoving, looking utterly crushed, broken, and in that moment Yvonne knew she couldn't do it. Despite every sickening thing he had told her, she couldn't leave him. She loved him – she always had and always would.

She turned round and, without a word, walked back upstairs, tears rolling down her cheeks.

Chapter Twenty-eight

Next door, Bob dreaded going to see his mother, but Sue's questions finally drove him out. He paused outside Danny's door. Maybe he could have a word with his brother first and between the two of them, they could come up with an excuse for Maurice's departure.

'Danny,' he said as he walked straight in, 'Maurice didn't get a chance to say goodbye to Mum or Chris. I've got to tell them that he's gone. Chris will guess why, but Mum's gonna do her nut. Any ideas?'

Danny's voice was lacklustre. 'No, sorry.'

'Come on, Danny, buck up. We need to sort this out.'

'Bob, just leave me alone, will you?'

'You're supposed to be in charge, the one who's running things.'

'Not any more.'

'But—'

'Since I took over the firm, all I've done is fuck things up. You're in charge now.'

'I don't want to be in charge, but if I was I'd make sure that we leave Jack Garston alone. Maurice left because he's shit scared of him and, to be honest, now that I've had time to think about it, I feel the same.'

'Fine, we'll leave him alone. I'm finished with porn, with the lot of it.'

'Danny, you can't just bale out. What about Wimbledon?'

'Close it down.'

'Chris won't like that.'

'You're in charge now. You sort him out.'

'Danny, come on – don't leave all this to me. What am I supposed to tell Mum? And not only that, the doctor has been to see Pet. What if she's opened her mouth?'

'I dunno, Bob. I've told Yvonne the truth and, as I said, you can sort the rest out.'

'You've what? But she might tell Sue.'

Danny just shrugged and Bob's temper flared. 'You could have bloody warned me.'

'Yeah, sorry, but I don't think she'll say anything to Sue.'

'How did she take it?'

'Badly, but at least she's still here.'

'What about Mum? Do you think she'll tell Mum?'

'I dunno. She might.'

'Shit, Danny, you'll have to stop her.'

'What's the point?'

'What's the matter with you? As you said, you're the one who fucked everything up and you've got to sort it out.'

At last Bob got some response. Danny rose to his feet, but instead of annoyance, his voice rang with despair. 'Don't you think I know that, Bob? But I can't do anything . . . it's too late. Pet's in that state because of me. The firm's had it because of me. I'm finished, we're finished, and there's nothing – nothing I can do about it.'

Bob had never seen Danny in this state. He'd always played the big man, issuing orders, so sure that they could play Garston at his own game and win. He glared at his brother. 'Right, well, sod you then, but I'll tell you this: when Mum finds out, I'm not taking the blame. As you said, it was your idea, and you can take the fall, not me.' Bob spun on his heels and marched out of Danny's house, slamming the door behind him.

Without a thought he strode to his mother's house, rapping the letter box, and when she opened the door he said quickly, 'Mum, Maurice and Norma have gone. They've moved out of the alley.'

'What? Don't be daft. Come on, come inside, but keep your voice down. Your father has just dozed off again. It's all he seems to do lately.'

Bob stepped inside to see his father in his wheel-chair, head back and mouth hanging open. 'Is he all right?'

'Yes, but he's been in a state about Pet and it's worn him out,' she whispered, beckoning Bob through to the kitchen.

'Where's Chris?'

'Out as usual. That boy's hardly around these days.'

'How's Pet?'

'Oh, Bob, I don't know how to tell you this, but . . . but she's been raped.'

Although he and his brothers had guessed this, Bob feigned shock. 'What? Who did it, Mum? Has she said?'

'No, she hasn't opened her mouth, but it was bad, Bob, really bad. The bastard needs catching, castrating.'

'We'll sort it out, Mum.'

'Yes, I know you will, but come on, what's this about Maurice?'

'I told you. He's moved out.'

'Of course he hasn't. He came down to see me a little while ago, but with the doctor here I told him to come back later.'

'He couldn't wait, Mum. He asked me to say goodbye and to tell you that he'll be in touch once he's settled.'

'Maurice has never said anything about moving before. Now you're telling me he's just upped and gone without saying goodbye – without seeing his father?'

Bob nodded, dreading his mother's questions.

'Why has he left in such an all-fired hurry?'

'I dunno, but I think it was Norma. She's been nagging him for ages to get out of the alley.'

As his mother looked up at him, it was as if he could see the wheels turning in her mind, but then there was a cry from the living room.

'Your father's awake. Don't say anything in front of him. He's had enough for one day. It'll have to keep until tomorrow, and if he's up to it I'll break it to him then.'

Bob heaved a sigh of relief as he followed her into the living room. 'Hello, Dad.'

His father's good arm waved, and seeing his mother moving to wipe the spittle from his chin, Bob said, 'I'll leave you to it, Mum. I'll see you later.' Before she could respond, he shot out of the door.

Bob knew that Sue would start on him again as soon as he walked in the door, but with only spare change in his pocket, he couldn't disappear to the pub. So far Pet hadn't told anyone what had happened to her, but he knew it was just a matter of time. It was going to come out, either through Pet or Yvonne, and there was nothing he could do to stop it. With no choice, Bob knew he'd have to tell Sue. He'd wait until the kids were in bed, and that would give him time to rehearse what he was going to say.

* * *

At eight o'clock, Bob sat down next to Sue. 'Er . . . we need to talk.'

'You're telling me. I want to know what's going on, but so far talking to you has been like trying to get blood out of stone. I want to know why Maurice has left, and don't try to fob me off again.'

'All right, but this ain't gonna be easy so hear me out before you do your nut.'

Bob took a deep breath before starting at the beginning. As his tale progressed he saw Sue's eyes widen with shock. When he got to the part about making hard-core films, he placed the blame at Danny's door.

'It was Danny's idea. He said there was big money in it, and so we got sucked in. We knew that we'd be going into Garston's territory, but Danny was sure we could handle him.'

Sue leaned back, her head down, and then it was Bob's turn to widen his eyes as she spoke without anger. 'It sounds to me like Danny got too greedy – as though everything was fine until you got into the other stuff.'

'Yeah, that's right.'

'So what happened next?'

'To warn us off, Garston snatched Pet and bloody hell, Sue, you should see what he's done to her.'

'You told me that she was in an accident, now you're saying that this man took her. Oh God, what did he do to her?'

Bob gulped. 'She was raped and it was violent – so bad that she's been sort of struck dumb.'

The colour drained from Sue's face, her voice quivering. 'Oh, no, poor Pet. I wish I could go to see her but I know your mum won't let me in.'

'When things calm down, I'm sure she will.'

'I doubt it. Oh, poor Pet,' she cried again. 'That Garston must be a right bastard and I hope you're going to sort him out.'

'He's a nasty piece of work and he's got a lot of backup.'

'Sod his backup. He raped Pet and he needs a good kicking,' Sue said, her eyes filling with tears. She became quiet then, sniffing and shaking her head with distress.

Bob said nothing, his eyes downcast, and then dashing the tears from her cheeks, Sue said she was going to make them a drink. When she came back from the kitchen, clutching two glasses of whisky, she downed hers quickly, coughing as the liquid hit her throat.

'Do you feel better now?' Bob asked.

'Yeah, but it's been a bit of a shock. I'm upset about Pet, and I suppose I should be annoyed about the porn, but strangely enough, I'm not. Blimey, dirty films. I never would have guessed. You should have told me. I could have been in some of them.'

'I can't believe this! You're my wife, the mother

of my children and you expect me to let you appear in porn films?'

'Calm down, love, I didn't mean the really dirty ones.'

'Leave it out, Sue. I wouldn't have you flaunting your body for everyone to see.'

'Yeah, well, I was only kidding.'

He smiled, mollified, and in truth relieved that Sue had taken it so well. 'I'm glad to hear it.'

'Does Yvonne know about the porn – and what about your mother?'

'Yvonne does now, but only because Danny told her. My mother doesn't know, and if she finds out I dread to think how she'll take it.'

'I'd like to be around when she finds out. It'll knock Her Highness off of her throne, that's for sure.'

'Don't be like that, Sue.'

'What do you expect? You know your mother treats me like a bleedin' leper. Not only that, she hardly bothers with the boys.'

'With Dad in that state, she's got a lot on her plate.'

'You always make excuses for her and it gets right up my nose.'

'For Gawd's sake, Sue, I've just told you about Pet and Jack Garston, but you seem more interested in my mother.'

'Yeah, yeah, you're right and I'm sickened about

what Garston did to your sister. You said Maurice did a runner because he's scared of Garston, but there must be more to it than that.'

'If we take on Garston, anything could happen. Maurice was worried that next time he might snatch Oliver.'

'What! Bloody hell! If that's the case – what about our boys?'

'If we leave Garston alone and if we stay out of the game, I think we'll be all right. Danny's agreed, but I don't know about Chris.'

Sue lost it then, her voice rising in anger. 'You fucking idiot! How could you put our kids at risk?'

'But I've told you, it wasn't me. It was Danny's idea. He's the one that got us in this mess.'

'You'll have to talk to Chris. Make sure he doesn't go after Garston.'

'Yeah, don't worry, I will. Chris won't want the kids harmed so he'll see sense. Come on, love, calm down, everything is going to be all right.'

With a huff, Sue sat down again. Bob pulled her close, nuzzling her neck.

'Pack it in,' she said, but as he carried on, her voice became husky. 'Porn, blimey, and I bet you enjoyed making those films. Describe one.'

'What?'

'Go on. I need something to take my mind off Pet and what that bastard did to her. Tell me about one of the films you made. Did you join in the action?'

'No, of course not. There's only one woman who turns me on.'

'I bet it was a laugh, though. Come on, let's have an early night and you can tell me all about it.'

Bob had expected a rollicking – worse – but Sue had surprised him. She had got out of her pram only over the kids, but now that he'd assured her that they'd be fine, she was getting all frisky. Blimey, he thought as he followed her upstairs, what a woman.

Chapter Twenty-nine

On Sunday, Pet came out of her stupor at four in the morning, her body bathed in sweat. She'd been having a nightmare and tried to fight it off, but as her mind cleared it was worse, the memory of what had happened hitting her with force. She curled into a ball, reliving it, sobbing. Jack Garston had been a monster, doing unspeakable things, the pain more than she could bear. He had laughed at her screams, relished it when she fought, slapping, pinching, forcing himself inside her even though she had cried out in agony. It didn't stop then, there was more to come, but when he had thrown her over onto her stomach, the pain as he entered had been so excruciating that something weird happened. She felt as though she was leaving her body, floating away, distant from all that followed. Until now! *No, I don't want to think about it!* But it was no good, the horror played over and over again in her mind. Her body felt filthy, dirty, degraded. *Oh God, oh please, I just want to die. Let me die.*

Sobbing, she flung back the blankets, uncaring of the cold as she ran downstairs and into the bathroom. With water gushing into the bath Pet climbed in. Then, taking a scrubbing brush, she attacked her body, on and on, scrubbing, hardly feeling the hard bristles or the pain. Only when she was red raw did her hands finally become still. Tears ran down her cheeks. It was no good. She still felt filthy, defiled, and she doubted that she'd ever feel clean again.

In despair she climbed out of the lukewarm water, dried herself and got back in her nightdress, walking with leaden feet to the living room. In the dim light she saw her father, his arm waving, and with a sob of anguish she ran across the room, throwing herself down beside him on the narrow day bed. 'Oh, Dad, Dad . . .' she wailed.

As his sweaty arm wrapped around her, Pet stiffened, but this was her father, a man who had always looked after her, protected her and one she didn't have to fear. She lay against him, and though he couldn't form words, she knew from the sounds he was making that he was trying to soothe her. The fire was still glowing in the hearth, banked up with nuggets of coke, the warmth and her father's murmurs finally lulling her to sleep.

Pet woke again three hours later, and the first face she saw was her brother's. He was leaning over her, gently shaking her shoulder. It all came flooding back, the films she'd been shown, the awful things she had seen. 'Get away from me!'

'Pet, it's all right. It's me, Chris.'

Unable to bear his touch, she shrugged off his hand, remembering almost word for word the things that Jack Garston and Tony Thorn had said about her brothers. She looked at Chris, saw the scar on his cheek, evidence of Garston's warning, but they hadn't listened. She'd been raped because of them, made to pay the price for their refusal to stop making those awful films.

Pet saw her mother walking into the room, a frown on her face as she took in the scene. 'What's going on? Pet, what are you doing on your father's bed?'

Pet rose to her feet, shivering. She couldn't speak, couldn't tell her mother about the terrible films she'd seen, one in which a child had been raped, or what Jack Garston had done to her. Pet was swamped with shame. She should have fought harder, found something, anything, to smash over his head. With a small sob she fled the room, running upstairs to the sanctuary of her bedroom where, almost leaping into bed, she drew the blankets over her head. She wanted to shut out the world – an evil world she no longer wanted to live in.

'Did she speak to you, Chris? Did she say anything?'

Chris stared at his mother, heart pounding in his

chest. Pet had come out of that strange stupor and now it was only a matter of time before it all came pouring out. 'Er . . . yeah, but I didn't catch what she said. I'll go and see if she's all right.'

'Come through to the kitchen first,' she hissed.

Chris frowned, but did as his mother asked, his face stretching when she spoke again.

'You didn't come in until after I was in bed last night, so I couldn't tell you what happened when the doctor examined Pet. Oh, Chris, I don't know how to tell you this, but she . . . she was raped. I can see you're shocked, but listen, we've got to keep this from your father. You know how he feels about Pet, and if he found out, well, I dread to think what will happen.'

'Did she say who did it?'

'No, she still wouldn't say a word, but if she's talking now, somehow we've got to make sure that she doesn't say anything in front of your father.'

'All right, Mum, I'll do my best,' Chris said.

'There's one more thing. Maybe *you* can tell me why Maurice and Norma buggered off without even saying goodbye.'

'What! Bloody hell, this is news to me. When did they leave?'

'It must have been when the doctor was here, and if you ask me, it's a bit funny. Bob said that Norma's been nagging him for ages to go, but why now and in such an all-fired hurry? Doesn't he care about his sister? Doesn't he care about his family? If you ask me, there's something going on – something that Bob didn't want to tell me. Now come on, you must know.'

'I don't. Maurice didn't say anything to me and I'm as surprised as you.'

He saw his mother's eyes narrowing suspiciously. Saying that he wouldn't be long, Chris hurried upstairs. He was shocked to hear that Maurice had left so suddenly, and was angry too. How could he go now – just when they all needed to pull together? He'd have a word with Danny and Bob later, but first he had to sort Pet out.

Chris found her buried under a mound of blankets. 'Pet, it's me, Chris, are you OK?'

The mound moved, but there was no reply. 'Pet, please, love, we need to talk.'

Once again there was only silence, but Chris knew she could hear him. 'Listen, when I get hold of Jack Garston, I'll slit his bloody throat.'

Still silence, but Chris continued, hoping that his words would get through. 'Mum knows that you were raped, but you can't tell her who did it, or why. She won't be able to take it. She'd crack up. There's Dad too – he'll go mad if he finds out that you've been touched. It might cause him to have another stroke. Mum's worried sick and she doesn't want him to find out.'

He heard a small sob and tried to move the

blankets aside but she fought him, keeping them tight over her head. 'Pet, come on, don't be like this.'

At last her head popped out, but the look on her face made Chris reel backward. Her eyes blazed with hate, spittle flying out of her mouth as she yelled venomously, 'Get away from me! Yes, he raped me, hurt me, and it's all your fault, but you don't seem to care about me. You're just scared that Mum might find out what her precious sons have been up to!'

'No, Pet, it isn't like that. Of course we care, and I've told you, the bastard will be made to pay for what he did to you. Come on, surely you know that we didn't want this to happen. We had no idea that Jack Garston would go this far.'

'He warned you, he told me, and your cheek is proof of that.'

'Yes, I admit he warned us off and we should have listened.'

As though she hadn't heard him, Pet's voice rose again. 'He made me watch your films. There was one with a little girl in it and she was only about ten years old. It was awful – she was terrified. How could you do that to her? My God, you're animals. You're monsters. You're as bad as him! I hate you, I hate all of you.'

'I don't know what you're talking about. What little girl?'

'The one in the film. A film you made!'

'Leave it out, Pet. It wasn't one of ours. We don't use kids. We'd never do that.'

'I don't believe you.'

'Listen to me. All right, I admit we make porn films, but we would never use children. I swear on my life, Pet, I promise you. I don't know what Garston showed you, but it wasn't one of ours.'

The anger seemed to drain from Pet, replaced by heart-rending sobs. She began to rock backwards and forwards as tears streamed down her face. Chris could hardly stand to see her pain and impulsively he leaned forward to drag her into his arms.

'No, no, don't touch me,' she cried, fighting off his hands. 'Go away. Leave me alone!'

'I can't, Pet, not until you promise me that you won't tell Mum, or speak about being raped in front of Dad. He couldn't take it, Pet, and you know that.'

'All right – all right!' she screamed. 'I won't say anything. Now get out. Get out of my room.'

Chris rose to his feet, relieved that she was going to keep her mouth shut, but hating himself for what they had done to their sister. Yet he hated Jack Garston more. Somehow he'd find the man – and when he did . . .

'Chris – Chris, can you come down? I need a hand with your father.'

'I'm coming,' he called back.

Pet was still crying and he didn't want to leave

her, but she refused to look at him, instead lying down whilst pulling the blankets back over her head.

He found his mother in the kitchen, her face anxious. 'Close the door,' she said, and when Chris had done so she asked, 'Petula was shouting. What did she say?'

'She's upset, but don't worry, she won't say anything in front of Dad.'

'Oh, thank goodness, but as I said, Chris, whoever did that to Petula was a monster, a maniac. He needs catching, locking up and the key thrown away.'

'Don't worry, Mum. I'll have a word with Danny and we'll sort it out.'

'Yes, I know you will. Now come on, we'd best get your father to the bathroom.'

Chris glanced at the clock. It was still early, but after giving his mum a hand he wanted a word with Danny and Bob. They had a lot to sort out – starting with Jack Garston.

Pet remained buried under the blankets until she heard Chris leave. As soon as he had touched her, images of Jack Garston rose in her mind, the things she'd been forced to watch, the things he had done to her. It had been awful, dreadful, but oh . . . that poor little girl.

Pet's stomach lurched. Oh God, her mother knew that she'd been raped! She would ask questions. She'd want to know how it happened and who did it. Chris had asked her not to say anything, but there had been no need. She couldn't tell her mother – couldn't speak about the disgusting things that Garston had done to her body.

She shifted, sore, bruised, unable to forget the things that Garston had said about her brothers. At first she refused to believe him, but had finally accepted the truth. Like Garston, like that monster, they made those films, peddled porn. Chris had said they didn't use children and she prayed it was true. The other film had been bad enough and now she shivered. Would Garston add his final warning? A warning that made her stomach chum. After he had raped her he had laughed, taking great delight in telling her that the whole act had been filmed.

Pet licked her lips, her mouth dry and throat parched. Her stomach was empty, hollow, and she couldn't remember the last time she had eaten. She wanted to go downstairs for a drink, but feared facing her mother, knowing that out of her father's hearing, the questions would start.

At last, unable to stand her thirst any longer, Pet threw back the blankets and rose to her feet. There was only one thing she could do. She'd go downstairs and if her mother asked questions, she'd pretend she had no memory of what had happened. But, oh, if only that were true!

* * *

Danny was up, but was still in his dressing gown when Chris walked in.

Danny saw his brother's eyes flick to Yvonne before he said, 'Danny, we need to talk.'

The older brother ran a hand over his face, saying tiredly, 'Bob's in charge now. Speak to him.'

'Leave it out, Danny, we've got things to sort out,' Chris protested, his eyes once again flicking to Yvonne.

'It's all right. Yvonne knows everything – about Garston, about the porn. I told her last night.'

'Why did you do that? Why jump the gun? I've sorted Pet out and she's agreed to keep her mouth shut, but now you've gone and told Yvonne. What if she tells Mum?'

'She won't,' Danny said. 'Ain't that right, Yvonne?'

'Yes, that's right,' Yvonne snapped, her back stiff as she walked out of the room.

They had barely spoken last night, Yvonne saying only that she didn't want anyone to know about the baby yet. Baby! He didn't want to be a father – he wasn't fit to be a father. A wave of despair washed over him. He didn't want to think. All he wanted to do was sleep.

'Garston showed Pet a film using kids and told her it was one of ours.'

It didn't surprise Danny. Nothing Garston did could surprise him now. He shrugged, saying nothing.

'Come on, Danny, this had gone far enough. Snap out of it. You can't leave everything to me and Bob. We've got Garston to sort out.'

Danny just wanted Chris to leave. He said tiredly, 'Bob wants us to back off, and I think he's right. I'm finished with it, Chris, finished with Garston and porn.'

'You don't mean that, and what's all this about Maurice leaving?'

'Ask Bob.'

'For God's sake, Danny, what's the matter with you?'

Danny felt tears stinging his eyes, and he rose to his feet, ashamed, just shaking his head as he went upstairs.

Chris was dismayed, unable to believe that this was Danny. Big Danny, tough Danny, the one who took over, who ran things.

He turned, walked out and went to Bob's house, saying without preamble as he went in, 'Bob, what's going on? Danny said you're in charge.'

'Yeah, I know. I think he's lost it, Chris.'

'You're telling me. Where's Sue? We need to talk.'

'She's giving the kids a bath.'

'What's this about Maurice leaving?'

'You can't blame him, Chris. He was shit scared.'

'There was no need for him to do a runner. I've had a word with Pet and she's agreed to keep her mouth shut.'

'Bloody hell, that's good, but Maurice was just as freaked about Garston. Listen, Chris, if we go after him things will only get worse. Maurice was worried about him going for Oliver next, and to be honest I feel the same. It ain't worth it, Chris. It ain't worth putting my boys at risk.'

Chris closed his eyes for a moment, gathering his thoughts. He knew that Bob was right, but it stuck in his craw to let Garston get away with it. 'All right, Bob, we'll leave him alone for now, but I ain't happy about it.'

'Thanks, mate. I'll tell Sue and it will put her mind at rest.'

'She knows about Garston?'

'Yeah, I told her everything, and other than worrying about the boys, she took it really well.'

'She'd better keep her mouth shut around Mum.'

'Of course she will – she ain't daft.'

'We need to tell Maurice that's he's in the clear. Did he leave an address?'

'No, but he said that he'd be in touch as soon as they're settled.'

'That's good,' Chris said. 'In the meantime we're still got the business to run. Danny said he wants out of porn, but he's sure to come round.'

'I want out too.'

'But why? We can still make the soft stuff.'

Bob shook his head. 'I don't want to risk it. Too much has happened, Chris – too much has changed.

The old codes have gone, and Garston has proved that. If we go on making porn, we might step on another bastard's toes, one as bad as him.'

'We can handle them. We've done it before.'

'I told you, things are changing and there's too many wanting in on the game now. These new crews will do anything to put us out of business and I ain't risking my boys.'

Chris moved a few magazines from a chair before sitting down. He couldn't carry on without his brothers, and anyway, maybe Bob was right, maybe it was time to pack it all in. All they'd have left was the yard, but that didn't make enough to support them all. For years it had just been a front, with them selling just enough building materials to keep it ticking over, but surely it could be made profitable.

'All right, Bob, with the rest of you wanting out, I don't think I've got any choice. That leaves just the yard. We need to make it work, need to increase profits. Any ideas?'

'Leave it out, Chris. I ain't got a clue.'

'Do you know how much money we've got in the kitty?'

'Maurice looked after the books, but after ploughing everything back in to buy equipment, I don't think there's much.'

'What about the premises in Wimbledon? Could we sell the place?'

'No, it's in Dad's name so we couldn't do that without his agreement.'

'With Dad in that state, we won't be able to get it.' Chris was quiet for a while, his thoughts turning, finally coming up with an idea. 'If we get more stock, add more lines, it'll increase profits.'

'Yeah, good idea, but with sod all in the kitty, how are we supposed to pay for it?'

If they wanted to build up the business, Chris knew he'd have to do something. He heaved a sigh. 'I've got a few bob stashed away. I suppose we'll have to use that.'

'Blimey, how did you manage that?'

'Unlike you, I haven't got a wife and kids to support so I've managed to save a fair bit.'

'If it wasn't for George,' Bob complained, 'none of this would have happened. We had plenty in the kitty before he nicked the lot.'

'Yeah, well, we'll need to think about what sort of lines to add, and then source the best prices.'

'All right, Chris, we'll get on to it first thing tomorrow.'

Chris nodded, feeling he was more in charge than Bob as he walked out. Until Danny pulled himself together, they'd have to manage without him. He still wasn't happy that Maurice had left, but until he came back, there was one family fewer to support.

Chapter Thirty

Ten days passed, and Pet had withdrawn into herself. Unable to stand the memories, her body was mending, but not her mind. She ate, she drank, tried to help her mother, but she hardly spoke.

'Petula, I need some shopping. Here's a list.'

She stared at her mother in horror. Out? She didn't want to go out. What if Garston was out there? What if he was lying in wait to snatch her again?

'Don't gawk at me like that. It's about time you stirred yourself, and a bit of fresh air will do you good.'

Pet shook her head, her voice a hoarse whisper. 'I . . . I can't.'

'Don't be silly. I'm only asking you to go to the local shops. You can't spend the rest of your life stuck indoors.'

'But—'

'No buts, Petula. Now get your coat on and make sure the butcher doesn't fob you off with all fat on the belly of pork.'

Pet looked to her father, but he had dozed off, something he did more and more frequently. When awake he always seemed to want her close, something she knew annoyed her mother. Yet she drew comfort from him – from his lopsided smile and the love she saw in his eyes.

'Yes, that's right, take a good look at your father. The way you're carrying on is worrying the life out of him and it's got to stop. All right, I know you've had a rough time of it, but for your dad's sake you've got to pull yourself together. Now come on, it can start with a walk to the shops.'

Pet found her coat thrust into her arms, and reluctantly putting it on, she took the list. Her teeth bit into her lower lip as she looked at the door, but then her mother opened it, gesturing her outside. Hesitantly she stepped into the alley, the door closing immediately behind her. There was no one in sight, the alley empty, but still she shivered with fear. Slowly Pet walked to the end, skirting the bollards. When turning the corner she almost clung to the walls as she scuttled to the shops. Once she had felt safe, protected, but not any more. Now she only felt exposed and vulnerable.

The butcher's was her first stop – Mr Pearson, a rotund, red-faced man who was always cheery. 'Hello, Petula, what can I get you?'

'M-Mum wants a belly of pork.'

He nodded, his gaze keen. Why was he looking

at her like that? Did she look different? Did he know? Feeling a wave of self-disgust, she lowered her face. He unhooked the meat, wrapped it and, fumbling for the money, Pet grabbed the parcel and ran out of the shop.

Petula hadn't been gone long when Yvonne called round. Joan found it hard to forget that her daughter-in-law had lied to her about Petula being raped, but there were times when she still needed help with Dan and he had to come first.

'I saw out of the window that you've managed to get Petula to go out,' Yvonne said.

Joan placed the kettle onto the stove, then shook her head, her expression when she turned one of worry. 'She hardly opens her mouth, Yvonne. I've tried talking to her, but she clams up. She still insists that she can't remember what happened, but I find that hard to believe.'

'Maybe it's for the best. It would be a terrible memory, so it might be better to stop pushing her.'

'Yes, you could be right, and at least this way I haven't got to worry about her saying anything in front of Dan. Mind you, she's still funny with Chris, and when Bob makes a rare visit, she ignores him too. I don't get it, Yvonne. I mean, why be funny with them?'

Unable to admit that she knew why, Yvonne lowered her eyes. Poor Pet, she had been through hell because of her brothers and it was no wonder she hated them. She fumbled for an answer, only able to murmur, 'I don't know why, but I'm sure she'll come round. It's her birthday in a couple of weeks, but I'm not sure what to get her.'

'I'll give Chris the money to buy her something nice, and I hope it cheers her up because the way she's carrying on is worrying the life out of Dan. Come to that, you're looking a bit peaky too. Are you all right?'

'Yes, I'm fine,' Yvonne lied, but in truth, since Danny had told her about being involved in porn, she had hardly slept. Just the thought of it made her feel ill – the films, the easy women, and knowing Danny, he had sampled them all. They were finished with it now, yet it still had the power to turn her stomach. If she hadn't been pregnant, would she have left him? No, she admitted, she loved him too much and the thought of life without him was unbearable. There was also the increasing worry about his mental state. Danny needed her now. He didn't go out, didn't wash, shave or dress. Instead he spent most of the day flopped on the sofa. So far she'd been able to hide this behaviour from her mother-in-law, yet she was desperate to confide in someone. Bob and Chris knew, but they were so busy trying to make a go of the yard that they hardly came round. When they did call they tried to make Danny snap out of it – tried to get him to take an interest in the business – but he just didn't want to know.

'At least I've got one less thing to worry about,' Joan said. 'Petula had a show yesterday.'

'Did she? Oh, that's good.'

Once again, Yvonne lowered her eyes. Until Danny showed some interest in the baby, she didn't feel she could tell anyone that she was pregnant. She had waited so long for the moment, pictured it, telling everyone the joyous news with Danny playing his role as the proud father to be. If he would just snap out of this depression, it could still be that way. She was still hardly showing, but Christmas was only a few weeks away and it would be a wonderful time to break the news. After all the dreadful things that had happened lately, it was sure to lift everyone's spirits.

Chris and Bob were at the yard, discussing the new stock they had ordered. Without much competition in the area, they had decided to give a section of the building over to decorating supplies, with a range of wallpapers, paints and all the accoutrements needed by anyone in that trade. Stock had also been low on building materials, and now Bob smiled as he spoke to his brother.

'I don't know how you managed to save that much money, but we'd have been stumped without it. I just hope we make a go of this or you'll have no chance of getting it back.'

'The advertising should do the trick, and I've got an appointment with that developer on Monday. If we can offer him a good deal, he may buy all his materials from us.'

'Fingers crossed you can manage to strike a deal. It might just make Danny sit up and take notice. We've got all this shelving to erect for the new shop, and with the stock coming in, we could do with a hand.'

'It's about time we heard from Maurice.'

'Yes, I know, but let's face it – he wouldn't be much use with the hard graft.'

'He still should have been in touch.'

'Is Mum going on about it again?'

'A bit, but she's more worried about Pet. To tell you the truth, I dread going home nowadays. As soon as I walk in you can cut the atmosphere with a knife, and Mum can't understand why Pet is giving me the cold shoulder.'

'Pet's the same with me, and though I want to see Dad, I avoid popping in as much as possible. Still, you can't blame Pet for not wanting to talk to us.'

'I know. And change the subject because it still gets to me that Garston got away with it.'

'To be honest, I'm just glad that we're out of the game. We may not make a fortune, but at least we haven't got to worry about him, his kind, or the Vice Squad. Mind you,' Bob continued, shaking his head in bewilderment, 'my Sue never ceases to amaze me. With Christmas just over a month away I told her not to spend too much on presents, and instead of getting the hump she just said that we're mad to stop making the soft porn.'

'Yeah, well, she may be right. We made good money out of it.'

'If you're thinking of starting up again, you can count me out.'

'Keep your hair on. It was just a passing thought, that's all.'

Bob nodded, his voice clipped as he said, 'Good. Now come on, let's get on with this shelving or we'll have nowhere to put the new stock when it arrives.'

'It's being delivered on Monday, so let's hope I'm not too long with that developer. If I'm not back in time you'll be handling it on your own.'

'This is bloody ridiculous. We need an extra hand and I reckon we should have another go at Danny. We should tell him that if he wants to keep taking a cut, he'll have to do his share of the work.'

'Yeah, good idea. I just hope he listens this time.'

'He'd better,' Bob growled. 'I'm sick of doing all the work while he sits at home all day, doing sod all.'

Joan jumped as the door was thrown open, Petula darting into the room.

'What on earth's the matter?'

Obviously out of breath, Petula's chest heaved as she dumped the shopping bags onto the table. She then fled upstairs, but with Dan looking bewildered, Joan was unable to follow her daughter.

'Don't worry, Dan. I'm sure she's all right.'

He shook his head, babbling, good hand pointing to the stairs. 'All right, I'll go after her,' Joan placated, and though reluctant to leave Dan on his own, she knew it would be the only way to calm him down.

Joan's tread was heavy as she climbed the stairs. With all that had happened, she sometimes felt over-whelmed, her nerves almost at breaking point. It had been an awful year, one dreadful event after another. In May, George had almost beaten his father to death, and this had been followed by Dan having two strokes. She had no idea where George was, and try as she might, fearing it was his, she couldn't put out of her mind the blood on the bathroom floor. Following that, Ivy had left, but that was no loss, and then there was Chris. The boy wasn't the same, obviously hiding something, and then there had been that dreadful cut on his cheek.

Joan drew a breath. Her daughter had then been raped, and the strain of trying to keep it from Dan was wearing her down. He was suspicious; she was sure of it, his eyes always anxious when he looked at Petula.

Joan paused at the top of the stairs. Maurice had been next, leaving the alley without even saying goodbye. She knew that Norma had had a hand in it, but the speed of their departure still worried her. But first and foremost was Dan. She had to keep him calm, free from worry, and now as she opened her daughter's bedroom door, Joan was so worried about Dan that she didn't realise how hard her voice sounded.

'Petula, I don't know what's going on, but you've upset your father again. Did something happen when you were out? Is that it?'

Petula's face was hidden as she shook her head.

'Something must have upset you or you wouldn't have come home in that state.'

'They . . . they were all looking at me. They . . . they must know.'

'I don't know who you're talking about, but other than this family, nobody knows what happened to you.'

Joan saw tears on her daughter's cheeks and, despite Yvonne's advice, she said, 'Look, love, I know it must have been terrible, but you've got to stop bottling it up. If you'd only talk about it, tell me what happened, I'm sure it would help.'

'I . . . I can't. I don't remember.'

Worried about leaving Dan on his own any longer, Joan sighed in exasperation. 'Well, one way or another, as I said earlier, you've got to pull yourself together. It's upsetting your dad and it's got to stop. He needs to see that you're all right, so come on, come downstairs, and for God's sake, try to put a smile on your face.'

With obvious reluctance, Petula stood up and wiped the tears from her face. Joan was relieved when she followed her downstairs. 'See, Dan, I told you that Petula's all right. Old Pearson tried to fob her off with a bit of dodgy meat and they had a bit of a falling-out. Ain't that right, Petula?'

Joan held her breath, her eyes on her daughter. Petula's smile was thin, but at least it was visible as she nodded in agreement.

Dan beckoned Petula to his side, and still with the thin smile on her face, Pet pulled a chair close to the fire before sitting next to him. Joan heaved a sigh of relief. He looked calm now, at peace, but nowadays he was only really content when he had Petula close by.

Bob and Chris closed the yard and, though worn out after a hard day's graft, they went straight to see Danny.

As usual he was slumped on the sofa and, as Yvonne went to make them a cup of tea, Bob said, 'Look, Danny, me and Chris have had enough. Chris has sunk all his savings into the yard and we've got a lot of stock coming in. We can't manage on our own and need a hand.'

When Danny didn't respond, Chris took over. 'You've got to do your share. You can't just sit there while me and Bob do all the work.'

Danny still said nothing, and now Bob exploded. 'We've been working our guts out all day and we're knackered, but look at you, sitting there like a lump of bloody lard with Yvonne waiting on you hand and foot. Well I've had it, Danny. Either you do your share, or you can forget taking a cut of the profits.'

With a small shrug, Danny said, 'Fair enough.'

Yvonne came into the room and, judging by the worried look on her face, Chris guessed that she had heard everything. His temper also snapped. 'You're a selfish bastard, Danny. You're so wrapped up in your own misery that you haven't given a thought to Yvonne. She's stuck by you, but you don't deserve her. With no money coming in, what's next? Will you send her out to work to keep you?'

At last it seemed that something had got through to Danny. Both brothers stared at him in shock as his chest began to heave and a strangled sob escaped his throat. They had never seen Danny cry and were shocked, but Yvonne ran forward to throw herself beside him on the sofa.

She pulled him into her arms. 'Don't, Danny, don't. It's all right. We'll be all right.'

'Oh, Yvonne, Yvonne . . .'

For a while there were only the sounds of Danny's heaving sobs and Yvonne's soft murmurings.

Maybe it was the catalyst their brother needed, but

Bob felt awful. He hadn't expected Danny to break down like this. 'Sorry, Danny,' he said sheepishly. 'We shouldn't have gone off on one, but, well, it's just that we're at the end of our tether.'

Yvonne looked up, saying softly, 'Would you mind leaving now?'

'Yeah, all right,' Chris said. 'Come on, Bob, let's go.'

They walked out, Danny still sobbing in Yvonne's arms.

'I didn't expect Danny to react like that,' Chris said.

'Nor me, but he needed something to snap him out of that bloody depression.'

'Yeah, and who knows, he might soon be back to throwing his weight around as usual.'

Bob frowned. 'He needn't think he can start playing the big boss again. It's us that came up with the ideas for the yard, and from now on we should have an equal say in running it.'

'We will, and as it'll be a new year soon, maybe we can make it a year that's a fresh start for all of us.'

'I'll drink to that,' Bob said, 'but I'd best go in for my dinner first or Sue will have my guts for garters.'

'I don't doubt it. I'll have some grub too, and then if you're up for a drink, I'll meet you in the Nag's Head.'

A new year, 1963, Chris thought as he waved to

Bob before going indoors. Mind you, there was still Christmas to face. Danny might be on the mend now, but it was still going to be difficult. There'd be no big family get-together this year, no parties, and unless Maurice got in touch, it would be another dampener on the proceedings. Come on, Maurice, he silently urged. Surely you're not too busy to pick up a phone.

Maurice wasn't too busy to get in touch with his family, he was just too ill. The first digs they had found had been awful, the room damp and heating scarce. Norma had been murder, constantly nagging, constantly questioning why they had left Drapers Alley, and only his attacks of asthma had made her shut up. Shortly after, they found this flat in Balham, but once again he had been struck down, this time with the flu. The flat was quite spacious, with the added bonus of being furnished, though of course Norma carped about wanting her own things. The landlord had agreed to let them have their own furniture, but until he was on his feet again, Maurice couldn't make arrangements to pick it up.

Norma was trying to get him to eat, but he shook his head, turning his mouth away.

'Come on, Maurice, just a little more.'

He ached, his whole body ached, and with his temperature fluctuating, he was one minute hot, the next cold. 'No, I don't want it.'

The bedroom door flew open, Oliver running into the room. 'Dad, I can't work out how to do this sum. Will you help me?'

'Oliver, not now. Your father isn't up to it.'

'It's all right,' Maurice protested, struggling to sit straighter in the bed.

'Don't get too close to your father. I don't want you going down with the flu too,' Norma warned, walking over to her son to take the exercise book from his hand.

When she handed it to him, Maurice frowned as he looked at the sum. It was long division and he could see where Oliver had gone wrong. 'Do you like your new school?'

'It's all right.' Then, adding on a rush: 'Dad, can I have a bike for Christmas?'

'If you can work out where you've gone wrong with this sum, without my help, then yes, you can.'

'Cor, thanks, Dad,' Oliver cried with a hop of excitement.

Norma returned the book and when Oliver ran from the room she asked, 'Can we afford a bike, Maurice?'

'Yes, don't worry, we're not short of money yet. Mind you, I'll have to look for a job as soon as I'm on my feet again.'

'What have you got in mind?'

'I don't know, but there's sure to be something I can do,' Maurice said, trying to sound optimistic, though he doubted he'd find much that paid more than twelve quid a week. He was tired, his head aching. For years he'd kept the family books, earned good money too, but now he feared the future.

Chapter Thirty-one

Yvonne was happy, happier than she'd been in a long time. A month had passed and Danny was more like his old self, though there was still a change in his personality. Where he had always been self-assured, dominant, he was now softer and she rather liked him this way. He now pulled his weight at the yard, going in every day, and even his relationship with his brothers had changed. There was a camaraderie now that had been lacking before, and from what Danny had told her, things were going well with the business.

She hurried into the alley, clutching her shopping bags, glad to get inside out of the cold. She'd have a hot drink before popping next door to help Joan, but had only just taken her coat off when the door opened again.

Sue walked in with the children trailing behind. 'Watcha, Yvonne. It's bleedin' freezing out there and too cold for the kids to play outside. Now they've broken up from school they're under my feet all day and it's driving me mad. I thought those pea-soup smogs we had in early December were bad enough, but I think this snow is worse.'

Yvonne smiled at the boys, and though Paul smiled back, Robby just scowled as she asked, 'What do you want Father Christmas to bring you?'

'There's no such thing as Father Christmas.'

'Yes there is,' Paul protested.

'Only babies believe in Father Christmas.'

'I'm not a baby.'

'Yes you are.'

'Please, boys, don't start,' Sue begged. 'You've been bickering since you got out of bed and you're giving me a headache.'

Yvonne walked over to the sideboard where she pulled out some paper and a couple of pencils. 'Come on, sit at the table and if you can draw me a nice picture, I might just find some chocolate for you.'

Sue smiled gratefully as the boys did Yvonne's bidding, then said, 'Have you got Pet's Christmas present?'

'Yes, I found her a nice cardigan.'

'What about your Christmas shopping? Have you finished?'

'Almost,' Yvonne said, indicating her shopping bags. 'There's still the chicken, but I've got it on order and I'll pick it up on Christmas Eve along with my vegetables.'

'Things are still a bit tight, and I only gave Pet some bath salts for her birthday, not that I was allowed in to number one to see her. I had to rely on Bob to pass them on. Pet never pops in to see me now either, and I haven't got a clue what to get her for Christmas. How is she? Is she any better?'

'No, not really. She hardly talks and I know it's getting Joan down.'

'Have you been invited for Christmas dinner?'

'Of course we haven't. With the way Dan reacts, it's impossible.'

'Yeah, it's funny the way he's taken against Danny. We haven't been invited either, but I can't say I'm surprised. How do you feel about us coming here?'

Yvonne's mind raced. Sue never cooked a Christmas dinner if she could get out of it, but maybe it wouldn't be so bad having them here. She was itching to break the news that she was pregnant and it would be nice to have them to join in the celebration. 'Yes, all right.'

'Mind you, it might get up old face-ache's nose,' Sue said, smiling widely.

'Oh, Sue, don't be cruel,' Yvonne cried, annoyed that the thought of upsetting Joan seemed to be giving Sue pleasure. 'With all that's happened she's got little to be happy about these days.'

'Look, Auntie Yvonne,' Paul cried, waving his picture as he ran to her side.

Yvonne smiled at his drawing of a Christmas tree,

complete with an angel on the top. 'It's lovely, darling.'

'What about mine?' Robby said as he too proffered a picture, but his angel looked as though it was hanging by its neck instead of perched on top.

Yvonne hid her distaste, saying only, 'Yours is lovely too.'

'Can we have our chocolate now?'

Yvonne went into the kitchen, returning with a bar of chocolate, which she broke in half, handing it to the boys.

Only Paul said thank you, but Sue didn't admonish Robby as the boy stuffed it into his mouth. She then cocked her head to one side, musing, 'I could get Pet some make-up. She once got me to show her how to put it on.'

'I don't know,' Yvonne said, shaking her head doubtfully. 'Pet doesn't seem to care about her appearance now. The poor girl went through hell and there's no sign of her getting over it.'

'Why did Auntie Pet go to hell, Mummy? What's hell?'

'Gawd, little pigs with big ears,' Sue said. 'Come on, time to go. I still think I'll get Pet some make-up. You never know, it might cheer her up. There's nothing like a bit of powder and paint to make a woman feel better.'

Yvonne made no comment, just saying goodbye as she closed the door. It would take more than powder and paint to put the smile back on Pet's face, and though it saddened her to see the girl in such a state, she was at a loss to know how to help her.

In the yard, Danny was arranging stock whilst Bob served a customer. Chris was outside with the fork-lift, loading the order onto the customer's van. He'd also come up trumps, securing them a deal with a large, local builder, but things were slowing down on the run-up to Christmas. Still, their profits were good, but without Chris putting cash into the business none of this would have been possible. They had come to an agreement, with Chris taking a bit extra each month until the money he'd put in was repaid.

Danny felt as though he had come out of a dark tunnel, his brother's words last month finally breaking through the mire of guilt and self-loathing that had swamped him. Chris was right, Yvonne had stood by him and it *was* more than he deserved. He'd been a bastard, a sick bastard, and would never forgive himself for what happened to Pet, but he knew now that he had to pull himself together for Yvonne's sake. He hadn't wanted to be a father, felt he didn't deserve to be a father, but when his brothers had gone, leaving him and Yvonne to have a good talk, he couldn't fail to see how much having a baby meant to her.

Reaching up, Danny placed rolls of wallpaper onto the rack. He had always wanted to be the boss, the big man, but now found himself happy just to work at the yard. He was also enjoying a burgeoning, easy relationship with his brothers. Along with that he felt more optimistic about the future. In the past, they had only just kept the yard ticking over, but now they could make a real go of it. Of course, they would never be rich, but they'd still enjoy a good living standard. It saddened him that the old man's dream of living in the country would never happen, but if they gave Mum an extra cut each month, he could have every comfort. Anyway, Danny consoled himself, his mother wouldn't want to live in a big house. She'd work herself to death keeping it clean, and with the old man to look after, she'd be happier in Drapers Alley.

'Danny, have you got a minute?' asked Bob.

'Yeah, I'm coming,' he called back, placing the last roll of wallpaper on the rack.

'We've just had a call from Mr Larson. He's starting another project in the new year and wants to place an advance order. It's huge, Danny, and I'm not sure if we can fill it.'

Chris came in, rubbing his hands. 'It's bloody freezing out there.'

'Chris, as I've just told Danny, we've got a bit of a problem. Larson wants to place a huge order.'

'How's that a problem?'

'I'm not sure if we can afford to fill it. Look,' he said, pushing the scribbled order towards Chris.

Chris whistled, his brows shooting up. 'Blimey. But if we don't fill it he'll go elsewhere and I doubt we'd get another customer like him. He's the biggest builder in the area. All our other customers are small fry in comparison.'

'Maybe we could try the bank – get a loan,' Danny offered.

'Yeah, good idea,' Bob said.

'You said he wants this order for the new year. We'd never get a loan through in time,' Chris said. He chewed on his lower lip, eyes downcast, before saying, 'There's only one thing for it. I'll just have to dib up the last of my savings.'

'You've got more?' Bob asked, voice high with surprise.

'It'll clean me out, but yes.'

Danny stared at Chris, hating the way his mind was working, but unable to quell his suspicions. Chris had already sunk a fair amount of money into the business, but was now offering more. Yes, he was a single man, but it was still going some to have that amount in savings. His mind went back to the morning they had found the empty cash box in the bathroom. He had blamed George, was sure it was George, but could remember how touchy Chris had been. No, no, it couldn't have been Chris. He was mad even to think it, yet was unable to stop himself from blurting out, 'How did you manage to save so much money?'

'It wasn't hard. Mum only takes my keep and, unlike you, I didn't keep my money in the cash box. Like Maurice, I put mine in the bank, earning a bit of interest.'

'I didn't know that. You never said, nor did Dad, so I assumed you kept your savings in with ours.'

'Yeah, well, it's just as well I didn't.'

'When we were struggling to raise money for the Wimbledon operation, you didn't offer to put money in. Why do it now?'

'Because this is legit – safe – and anyway, the yard is all we've got left. Why all the questions, Danny?'

'I was just wondering, that's all.'

It was Bob who broke the tension. 'Well, all I can say is thanks, Chris. This order will well and truly put us on our feet, and I might just celebrate by buying Sue a bottle of her favourite perfume for Christmas. Now come on, let's grab ourselves a cup of tea while we've got the chance.'

'Yeah, I'm all for that,' Danny said, and, knowing now that his suspicions had been unfounded, he threw a placatory arm around Chris's shoulder. He'd been daft to think that Chris had stolen the money – it was George, it had to be. 'Whose turn is it to make the brew?'

'Yours,' Chris said, walking through with him to the office.

'Here, I've got a good one,' Bob said whilst Danny filled the kettle.

'Go on then, let's hear it,' Chris said.

'What do you call a camel with three humps?'

'I dunno,' Chris said, 'but no doubt you'll tell us.'

'Humphrey.'

Danny couldn't help laughing. 'You silly sod,' he spluttered, 'but at least it was clean for a change.'

Chris laughed too, then said, 'Here, Bob, I've got one for Sue, but don't worry, it's another clean one.'

'Oh, yeah, go on then.'

'How did the blonde burn her ear?'

'I dunno.'

'The phone rang while she was ironing.'

Laughter rang out in the office and Danny felt a surge of relief. Because of his stupid suspicions he had almost blown the good relationship he now enjoyed with his brothers. He wouldn't make the same mistake again.

Pet sat close to the fire. Her father was opposite, dozing again, yet she drew comfort from his presence. She knew her state of mind upset him, and tried her best to hide her feelings, but it was so hard.

The front door opened, Yvonne bright-eyed as she walked in. 'God, it's bitter out there. Christmas will be here in less than a week and I reckon it could be a white one.'

Pet said nothing but listened to the conversation.

'Don't talk to me about Christmas,' her mother was saying. 'It won't be the same, and with just the four of us for dinner it hardly seems worth the effort. Not only that, we still haven't heard from Maurice.'

'I'm sure he'll be in touch soon,' Yvonne consoled.

'I hope you're right. Oh, Yvonne, Christmas was once such a happy time, but now there's nothing to celebrate.'

'Don't cry,' Yvonne pleaded. 'We have got something to celebrate. I wasn't going to say anything until Christmas Day, but I can't keep it to myself any longer. Me and Danny, well, we're going to have a baby. We're so happy, Mum.'

Pet felt as though all the blood had rushed to her face. She had kept her mouth shut, said nothing, bottling all the horror inside, but now images of the film she had been shown flashed in her mind. The little girl, the terror she had seen on her face. Chris had denied that they used children . . . but what if it was true?

Pet felt bile rise in her throat. Danny was happy – how dare he be happy! Something snapped inside her mind, all the horror, all the hate rushing forward as she jumped to her feet. 'No! No, you can't be having a baby. Danny isn't fit to be a father!'

'What are you talking about?' Joan cried. 'Don't be silly, Petula.'

'Him – them – my brothers. They make porn films using children! They're sick. They're monsters.'

'What? Yvonne, I think she's gone mad. I think she's lost her mind!'

Pet was unaware that her father had awoken, finding that now she had started, she couldn't stop, the words pouring from her mouth. 'They tried to take over Jack Garston's territory. He warned them but they wouldn't stop, so he took me and he made me watch their films and . . . and then he raped me.'

The bellow stopped Pet's outburst. Her father was making unholy sounds and she spun around, horrified that he had heard.

'Dan, Dan, it's all right,' Joan cried, rushing towards him, but then he flopped and her voice rose to a screech: 'Get an ambulance! Yvonne, get help. I think he's had another stroke.'

Pet stood frozen, but as Yvonne ran to the telephone, her mother turned, her eyes blazing as she spat, 'Get out of my sight. You've caused this, you and your lies.'

With a hand held over her mouth, Pet fled the room, running upstairs to throw herself onto the bed. Because of her big mouth – because she'd blurted it all out – her father was having another stroke. *Oh, Dad, Dad, please be all right.*

Pet had no idea how long she lay there, her mind in torment, before she heard the ambulance men arriving. Terrified for her father, she ran back downstairs. They were working on him, but from the look on their faces, she feared it was too late. One shook his head, and Pet stood helpless as her mother fell to pieces, wailing, her hands tearing at her hair.

She ran forward, trying to stay her hands. 'Mum, Mum, don't.'

She was pushed away as her mother turned to Yvonne, throwing herself into her arms. 'He's gone, Yvonne. My Dan's dead.'

The words hit Pet then like a blow to her stomach and, unable to bear it, she fled the room again. No! No, her father couldn't be dead! He just couldn't.

'What are you doing?' Joan cried as the ambulance men began to heave Dan onto a stretcher.

'We're taking him to hospital.'

Joan's face lit up. 'He's alive! Oh God, I thought he was dead.'

'I'm sorry, missus, he is, but he still needs to be seen by a doctor to ascertain the cause of death.'

'But can't he stay here? I can get our own doctor.'

'I'm afraid not. You see we were called out, so we have to follow through. You'll need to come with us because they'll want to talk to you about his medical history.'

Joan became aware of Yvonne urging her into a coat, and as they walked outside she said something, but Joan found she couldn't reply. Her stomach was so twisted with grief that she could barely put one foot in front of the other. Along with the grief came guilt. There had been times when she'd be so overwhelmed with exhaustion that she had wished Dan hadn't survived the second stroke. Yet now that he was gone, she just wanted him back, her life empty and meaningless without him.

Hardly aware of Yvonne beside her, Joan climbed into the ambulance, moving straight to Dan's side. His face looked different, at peace, and as she reached out to touch his cold cheek, she felt tears pouring from her eyes. *Oh, Dan – Dan, come back to me. I can't go on without you, I just can't.*

Chapter Thirty-two

Yvonne had made a frantic call to the yard, so when the three brothers ran into the hospital room soon afterwards, she knew that they must have broken all speed limits to get there.

'What happened?' Danny asked.

Yvonne drew them to one side, her voice a whisper. 'Pet finally snapped. She spilled it all out – about you, the porn, saying that you used children in the films.'

'But I spoke to her, told her it isn't true,' Chris hissed.

'She still spat it out, including that she'd been raped. Your dad, well, he went mad.'

Danny shook his head, his voice betraying his pain. 'I can't believe he's dead.'

'I know, Danny,' Yvonne consoled. 'It was so quick, so sudden.'

'I warned Pet that this might happen and I was right,' Chris said, his face ashen. 'Where is she?'

'She's still at home. Your mother turned on her, blamed her.'

'So Mum knows everything?' Bob said.

Yvonne nodded, her voice still low. 'Yes, but I'm not sure that she believed her.'

'Yeah, well, Pet should have kept her mouth shut.'

'Oh, Bob, how can you say that?' Yvonne protested. 'Pet's just a kid, and none of what happened was her fault.'

'Yvonne's right,' said Danny, 'it's all down to us, but come on, we can work this out later. For now, we had better see to Mum.'

'The doctors have spoken to her and confirmed your dad's death. If you can get her on her feet, we can leave.'

'I'd like to see Dad first,' Chris said.

Bob nodded. 'Yeah, me too.'

Danny walked across to his mother and, taking a seat beside her, took her hand. 'Mum, we're going to see Dad. Do you want to come with us?'

'He's dead, Danny.'

'I know, Mum, I know.'

'Yvonne, can you ask one of the nurses where my father is?' Danny urged.

She went across to one of the nurses to be told that Dan hadn't been moved yet. Bidding them all to follow her, the nurse led them into a side room.

All three brothers broke down when they saw their father, as though until now they hadn't accepted his death. It was painful to see them trying to be manly, trying to fight tears, with only Danny succeeding. Chris was the most badly affected, openly sobbing as he looked at his father, and Yvonne could see that her mother-in-law was close to collapse.

'Danny, I think we should get your mum home,' she urged.

He nodded, gently leading her away, and in a solemn procession they exited the room. Danny left his mother in the care of Bob and Chris whilst he went to speak to a nurse. Yvonne followed him, surprised by Danny's strength and presence of mind as he asked about the arrangements. Somehow she had expected Danny to fall apart again, that the depression he had suffered would make him mentally weak, but instead he had rallied, taking control.

'Yes, if you contact an undertaker,' the nurse told him, 'he can make all the necessary arrangements to have your father moved to a funeral parlour.'

Danny thanked her, and when he and Yvonne joined the others, Danny took his mother's arm to lead her gently out of the building to his car. Bob, the largest of them, sat in the front, and the rest of them in the back.

Yvonne reached out to clasp her mother-in-law's hand, finding it freezing. There was no returning pressure, Joan sitting as still as a statue during the journey home.

They parked and walked into Drapers Alley, Danny and Chris on each side of their mother. She still said nothing, and this continued as they entered number one. Joan went across the room to sit by the hearth, her face like chalk.

Danny poked the fire into life before adding a shovelful of coal. 'Are you all right, Mum?' he asked.

There was no reply, but when Joan looked at Dan's empty wheelchair she broke, placing both hands over her face as her body shook with sobs. 'Oh, Dan . . . Dan.'

It was obviously too much for Bob. With tears in his eyes he said, 'I'd best go and tell Sue.' With that he hurried out the door, closing it behind him.

Chris now stood next to his mother, his hand on her shoulder, obviously fighting tears too. Unable to watch the scene any longer, Yvonne went through to the kitchen. She felt helpless to comfort them and so did the only thing she could think of: she filled the kettle to make a cup of tea.

When Yvonne returned, she saw Danny sitting at the table, and Chris still close to his mother. Pet was nowhere in sight and Yvonne's heart went out to her. She was just a kid, and after what happened to her was it any wonder that she was unable to keep it bottled up inside?

Danny had his head in his hands, hardly aware of her when she placed a cup of tea beside him, and after giving one to Chris and her mother-in-law, Yvonne went upstairs.

Pet heard voices but, too afraid to face her mother, she remained in her room, huddled under the blankets for warmth.

Her door opened and Yvonne crossed the room to perch on the edge of the bed. 'How are you doing, love?' she asked.

The sympathy in Yvonne's voice was too much for Pet, and with tears flooding her eyes she cried, 'Mum said it's my fault, and she's right. Chris warned me and I should have kept my mouth shut, but I didn't and now . . . now . . . Oh, Yvonne, my dad's dead.'

'No, Pet, no. It's not your fault. After what you went through it was unfair to expect you to keep it locked inside. No wonder you broke down, love, and nobody blames you.'

'My mother does.'

'She's in a state, Pet. I'm sure she'll come round when she has had time to think about it.'

'I told her about my brothers too, about the . . . the porn. Did . . . did you know about it, Yvonne?'

'Not until recently, and when Danny told me I was shocked to the core. At first, I was going to leave him, but then I found that I couldn't. All right, I know that making porn films is awful, but when you think about it, there are worse things. They didn't hurt anyone, kill anyone, and—'

The image flashed into Pet's mind again, one that she found it impossible to forget. 'That man Garston, he made me watch a film,' Pet broke in. 'He said that my brothers made it . . .' She stopped, unable to go on.

'That must have been dreadful. For the life of me I'll never understand why men want to watch them, but honestly, nobody gets hurt in the making of them. It's just acting, Pet.'

'I was hurt, and the little girl I saw wasn't acting. She was screaming, terrified.'

'Oh God, the poor child,' Yvonne cried. 'But, Pet, I swear, your brothers didn't use children. Surely you know them better than that?'

No, Pet thought, she didn't know her brothers. The view she'd once had of them was an illusion. As tears continued to fall, she wanted the one man she felt safe with, one who looked at her with love in his eyes and who managed a lopsided smile every time he saw her. 'Oh, Yvonne, I want my dad. He can't be dead . . . he can't . . .' And as Yvonne's arms wrapped around her, Pet clung on as though she were drowning.

'Bloody hell, Bob, it must have been a bit sudden,' Sue said. 'I didn't hear or see anything, but the kids have been playing up, making a racket all morning, so it ain't surprising. What happened? Did he have another stroke?'

'Yeah,' Bob croaked, going on to tell her what Yvonne had said.

'Well, I can't say I'm surprised. From what you've told me, Pet must have been like a time bomb waiting to go off. But saying you used kids – that was terrible. What about your mum? Has she said anything? Has she mentioned it?'

'No, not yet, and I don't know what we're going to say when she does.'

'You wouldn't use children. I know you better than that, and your mother does too. As for the other stuff, if you ask me there was no harm in it, and she might see it that way too.'

'Leave it out, Sue. You know what a prude my mother is, and not only that, we've got to keep it from her that my dad was involved. It'd be too much. With what she's had to put up with lately it'd be the last straw. She'd go bloody mad.'

Sue hid her thoughts. Yes, the old cow was a prude, acting all high and mighty. It would bring her down a peg or two to know that her precious husband had been involved. Blimey, she'd love to see the expression on the old girl's face if it came out. They might try to hide it from her, but Sue knew she could put a spanner in the works.

There was no love between Sue and her sanctimonious mother-in-law, but Sue knew it wasn't her fault. She had tried, but from the start Joan had looked down on her, treated her like a tart, an outcast in the family. It was payback time, and nice to have something over on her mother-in-law at last. She'd leave it for a month or two, maybe wait until the old girl got over her grief, but as soon as she got on her high horse again, she'd let it slip.

'Oh, Sue, I can't believe he's dead,' Bob cried as his eyes filled with tears again.

Sue made the effort, wrapping her arms around her husband whilst she murmured, 'Oh, love, don't cry.'

Both boys came running in, their eyes widening. 'Why is Dad crying, Mum?' Robby asked.

Deciding it was better to tell them, she moved away from Bob, saying softly, 'He's upset because . . . well, because Granddad has passed away.'

The boys looked puzzled, but as they hadn't seen their grandfather for so long, it wasn't surprising. She tried again. 'He's dead. Dan, your granddad, is dead.'

Bob began to sob now and Paul ran to his side, grabbing his hand. 'It's all right, Dad. Oliver's rabbit was dead but then he woke up again.'

'Don't be daft,' Robby sneered. 'Shaker wasn't dead, he was just knocked out.'

'Shut up, Robby,' Sue snapped.

'Can I have a rabbit for Christmas?'

Unable to believe her ears, Sue glared at Robby. 'I can't believe you. I've just told you that your granddad's dead and you're asking me for a bleedin' rabbit.'

She heard a gasp and spun round to see Bob running upstairs. It was no surprise that he was taking his dad's death so badly, but Christmas wasn't far off and it would certainly put the kibosh on any celebrations. There was little chance of having Christmas dinner with Yvonne and Danny now. Bugger it, she'd have to make some sort of effort for the kids' sake, but would Bob be able to do the same?

Danny and Yvonne went home in the early evening, glad that Chris was there to keep an eye on Joan. She had finally stopped crying, but her face was still etched with pain. Yvonne had been unable to persuade Pet to come downstairs, the girl too frightened to face her mother. It broke Yvonne's heart to see Pet so lost, so alone, but finally she had left her, determined to do something about it, no matter what the consequences.

The house was cold when they went inside but Danny quickly lit a fire. He then sat down, deep in thought, but after a while, to Yvonne's surprise, he brought up the very subject.

'What do you think I should do?' he asked. 'I know you said Mum didn't believe Pet when she told her about the porn, but that was in the heat of the moment. Once she's over the shock and it begins to sink in, she's bound to start asking questions.'

'I think it's time to tell your mother the truth.

Pet's been through enough and she's so alone, Danny. Your mother blames her for your dad's death, but if she knew why Pet snapped and blurted it all out – if she knew what the poor kid has been through – I'm sure she'd forgive her.'

'Blimey, Yvonne, I can't tell my mother the truth now. You saw how fragile she is. I don't think she could take it.'

'So Pet's got to suffer. Don't you think she's suffered enough, Danny? Come on, you said it yourself, sooner or later your mother is bound to start asking questions. What if she aims them at Pet?'

'I hadn't thought of that. With Dad gone, Pet has no reason to keep her mouth shut and she might tell Mum that we use kids again.'

'I told her you didn't and I think she believed me. Even so, it would be fairer if the rest of it came from you.'

'Yeah, you're right, but I dread to think how Mum will take it. Maybe it can wait until after the funeral . . . And talking of the funeral, it's still got to be arranged. Mum isn't up to it, so I suppose it's down to me.'

'I doubt it can be held until after Christmas.'

As Danny looked at her Yvonne could see the pain in his eyes. She feared that he'd break down again, sink back into depression so, feeling the baby moving, she took his hand to lay it on her stomach. 'Can you feel it, love? The baby's kicking and it's so strong I reckon we've got a footballer in there.'

'You think it's a boy?'

'I don't know, love. We'll just have to wait and see.'

'My son,' he mused, 'or maybe my daughter.'

Yvonne heard the note of awe in his voice, but then his arms went around her as finally he broke, crying for his father, for the man he had been apart from for so long and who he would never see again.

Joan was glad when Yvonne and Danny left, relieved too when Chris finally went upstairs. She moved across the room to lie on Dan's day bed, feeling the indent of his body. With a sob she picked up his pillow, sniffing it to find his special smell. She felt lost, bereft. Dan had been her life – she was bound to him – and when he became helpless she had given herself to looking after him. She buried her face in the pillow, trying to muffle her sobs. If Chris heard her crying he would come downstairs again. He would try to comfort her, but there was no comfort.

She heard footfalls on the stairs and in the dim light saw Petula coming into the room. Joan held her breath, but thankfully her daughter didn't see her lying there as she went through the kitchen to the bathroom. Seeing Petula brought it all back: the look on Dan's face when Petula shouted that she'd been raped, the other things she had said about the boys that Joan couldn't bear to think about. It couldn't be true, it just couldn't. Petula must have gone mad, her sick mind conjuring up this fantasy because she couldn't remember what had really happened.

Petula was coming back, passing like a ghost through the room, and once again Joan held her breath, thankful that her daughter didn't see her. The house became silent again, Joan clutching the pillow as though it was a lifeline.

She cried on and off for what felt like hours, until finally, with a hiccuping sob, she stopped. She felt drained, empty, as if a part of her had died with Dan – that he had taken her heart with him, the two of them inseparable, even in death.

Finally, exhausted, she drifted off to sleep.

Chapter Thirty-three

When Pet woke up on Saturday morning, her first thought was for her father. She had spent most of the past three days alone in her room, unable to face the hate she could see in her mother's eyes. She huddled in her bed against the cold, haunted every night by nightmares. Oh, she was so thirsty, parched, so she quickly dressed, shivering as she tried to pluck up the courage to go downstairs.

Pet paused at the top of the stairs, but her thirst drove her down and she had just reached the living room when the front door was flung open.

Bob dashed in. 'Where's Mum?' he asked as his eyes scanned the room.

'In the bathroom,' Chris told him.

'How is she?'

'About the same. She gets up, washes, dresses, but it's as if she's on automatic. If you speak to her, she hardly listens, and her eyes have still got that vacant look about them.'

'What about you, Pet? How are you doing?'

Pet said nothing. She felt sickened, betrayed by her brothers, and ignored them as she went through to the kitchen. She filled the teapot and poured herself a cup of tea, quickly gulping it down. Then, hearing the bathroom door opening, she hurried out, about to return upstairs, when Bob's voice stilled her.

'Mum, there you are,' he said. 'I've just had a call from Maurice. I . . . I told him about Dad and he's on his way to see you. I had to get dressed before I came to tell you, so he should be here any minute now.'

She didn't respond, her gaze now fixed on the flames as they licked up the chimney.

'Did you hear what I said, Mum?'

'Yes, I heard you.'

'Maurice is living in Balham now and he hasn't been in touch because he's been ill. He had the flu, a really bad bout and ended up in hospital with pneumonia. Don't worry, he's on his feet again now. I'll just tell Danny that Maurice is on his way, and then I'll be back.'

As he hurried out, Chris accompanying him, Pet slumped onto a chair, the room silent. Her mother suddenly turned, their eyes locking. Her mother's gaze was long, hard, unfathomable and, unable to look away, Pet found her own eyes filling with tears.

'Petula—' Joan began, but then the door opened

to let in a blast of cold air as Danny, Yvonne and Bob trooped into the room.

'Bob just told us that Maurice is on his way,' Danny said.

Pet stood up, hurrying upstairs. Her stomach had lurched at the look in her mother's eyes, the accusation, the loathing. Yvonne had said that her brothers didn't blame her, but her mother still did. Oh, if only she had kept her mouth shut, hadn't blurted it all out. No wonder her mother hated her.

She felt so alone, an outcast with nobody she could turn to for comfort. At one time she would have gone to her brothers or their wives, but now she didn't want to be near them. It was their involvement in porn that had led to Garston taking his revenge on her – and every time she looked at them it all came flooding back. She longed to get away, far away, never to have to see them again. It was fear of the outside world that held her back, yet even if she found the courage to leave, she had nowhere to go, no family outside Drapers Alley.

Pet pulled the blankets around her, longing for the warmth of the fire. She couldn't go downstairs, her mother didn't want her around, and her brothers would be there. She burrowed further under the blankets, yearning for her father. She knew that Danny had arranged the funeral, but her mother didn't want her there. She'd be forced to stay at home, a home where she was no longer welcome. *Oh, Dad, Dad, I won't even get the chance to say goodbye.*

Minutes passed, but then Pet heard voices and guessed that Maurice had arrived. She didn't want to see him and hoped he didn't venture up to her room. He'd been involved too; they had all been involved. Like Ivy, he had left without saying goodbye . . . Pet's thoughts came to a standstill, her eyes suddenly widening. She *did* have somewhere to go, but would they take her in?

Pet looked around her tiny room. She knew that her mother would never forgive her, that unless she found the courage to leave Drapers Alley, this room would become her prison. Oh, but surely anything would be better than this. Finally, her mind made up, she began to stuff clothes into a bag.

Danny watched his mother's face as Maurice walked to her side, but she hardly reacted.

'Hello, Mum.'

She said nothing, and to break the tension Danny said, 'Blimey, Maurice, you look as thin as a rake.'

'Yeah, you look terrible,' Bob agreed.

Still his mother didn't move and Danny regarded her worriedly. She looked so old now, no longer plump, her face lined with wrinkles.

'You look frozen, Maurice. I'll make you a hot drink,' said Yvonne.

As his wife walked through to the kitchen, Danny said, 'I'm glad you're here, Maurice. I've made all the arrangements but the funeral can't be held until after Christmas.'

Maurice's voice was abrupt, 'When and where is it?'

'On the fourth of January at eleven in the morning, and we're using St Jude's.'

Maurice nodded before sitting opposite his mother, his hands held out to the fire as he said, 'Are you all right, Mum?'

Slowly she turned to look at him, her eyes suddenly clear, but when she spoke her tone was bitter. 'So, you've decided to show your face at last.'

'I'd have come sooner, but I've been ill, Mum, in hospital.'

'I'd still like to know why you went off without saying a word.'

'I came to say goodbye, but you wouldn't let me in and I couldn't hang around. Norma's been nagging for years, and if I didn't go with her, she'd have gone without me.'

'Yes, that's what Bob said, but I think there's more to it than that.' Her eyes suddenly flicked around the room, briefly settling on Danny, Chris and Bob, before they returned to the fire.

Danny found that he was holding his breath.

There had been suspicion in his mother's eyes when she had looked at them, but thankfully the moment seemed to have passed. He knew he would have to tell her, but not now – he couldn't face it now.

Yvonne came back into the room carrying a tray, and about to set it down when someone thumped loudly on the front door. Danny shot his brothers a look before opening it, but before he could react, two men pushed their way in, followed by several uniformed police.

'What the hell . . . ?'

The men flicked out identity cards, and though one spoke, both were smiling triumphantly. 'We have a warrant for the arrest of Mr Daniel Edward Draper.'

'What the fuck are you talking about?' Danny yelled. 'My father's dead.'

The smile dropped, but the man's eyes narrowed shrewdly. 'Dead, you say? Have you a copy of the death certificate?'

'Danny, what's going on?'

He turned to see his mother on her feet, her face white with shock. 'It's all right, Mum. There's been some sort of mistake, but don't worry, I'll sort it out.' He then grabbed the document from the mantelpiece, shoving it under the officer's nose. 'Read it, and when you've finished – *get out!*'

'Hold your horses,' the officer said. 'We'd still like

416

you and your brothers to accompany us to the station.'

'What for?' Danny snapped.

'Acting on information received, we obtained a search warrant for premises in Wimbledon where evidence of pornographic material was found.'

'For fuck's sake, Danny, I thought you closed the place down,' Chris yelled.

All of Danny's old nature rose to the surface as he yelled, 'Shut up!' He glared at his brother, but then saw Pet, hovering on the threshold of the room. She had her coat on, was holding a bag, obviously ready for flight. The copper's words sank in. *Acting on information received*. Spittle flew out of his mouth. 'You! You did this. I'll fucking kill you . . .'

Pet made a run for it, but as Danny reached out, his arms were grabbed, forced behind his back. 'Get off me,' he yelled, but it was too late, she was nearly out of the door. 'Come back, you bitch,' he screamed but, forcibly held, he could do nothing to stop her.

Pet fled the house and kept on running, her chest heaving until finally she was forced to stop. She walked then, rapidly, heading for Clapham Junction train station. Her mind was in turmoil, her heart thumping wildly in her chest. Danny thought she had been to the police. He said he would kill her and the look on his face had been manic. Oh, but she hadn't told the police, even though at times she had been so haunted by the little girl in the film that she had wanted to do something, anything to bring about her rescue. Yet she had done nothing, a coward, afraid that if she reported Jack Garston he'd come after her again.

The wind was bitter, stinging her cheeks, her fingers numb as she gripped the bag. A part of her wanted to go back, to run home again, but even as the thought crossed her mind, Pet knew it was impossible. Even if she could convince them that she hadn't been to the police, her mother's hate remained and it was no more than she deserved.

Frozen to the core now, Pet went into the post office, taking out money from her savings account. From there, it wasn't far to the station, but with a change of trains she knew it would be a long time before she reached her destination.

When a train arrived, Pet climbed aboard, barely thawing out before she had to get off again. On the second train she settled down for a longer journey, hardly noticing the passing scenery as her mind twisted and turned.

Finally, as the train pulled into her station, Pet stood up, her mind at last still. She had left, doubted she'd go back, but with no idea of what the future held, it was with trepidation that she began the last leg of her journey.

After asking directions, Pet started to walk, footsore

and weary by the time she turned into a lane, thick with snow. It was lined with trees, their branches skeletal, the sky a blanket of grey, heavy with more snow. Pet trudged along, both mentally and physically exhausted as she finally approached the house. When she opened the little wooden gate, the path lay clear ahead, and reaching the front door, she knocked, standing back a little as the door opened.

A face peered out at her, one that at first frowned, but then looked worried. 'Pet, oh my God, what on earth are you doing here?'

'Oh, Ivy, please, can I stay with you? I haven't got anywhere else to go.'

Pet was drawn inside, the fire acting like a magnet as she staggered, frozen, towards it. When Ivy spoke, she turned, but instead of a welcome on her cousin's face, she saw what looked like apprehension.

'Pet, how did you find me? Does anyone else know that you're here?'

'I took the address from Linda, but I didn't give it to anyone else.' Her voice cracked when she said, 'Oh, Ivy, my dad's dead.'

'What? When? Oh Gawd, I'm all of a dither. Look, sit down and I'll make us both a drink.'

As Ivy left the room, Pet sat by the hearth, taking in her surroundings. It was a nice room, chintzy and cosy, with brass ornaments reflecting the glow from the fire. A Christmas tree stood in one corner, sparkling with tinsel and baubles. Paper chains festooned the ceiling, each corner holding a bunch of coloured balloons. She leaned her head back, closing her eyes until her cousin returned.

'Right,' Ivy said, handing Pet a cup and saucer before taking a seat on the opposite side of the hearth. 'I think you had better start at the beginning.'

And Pet did, spilling it all out, her voice quivering with emotion until at last she was spent, ending with, 'I was ready to leave, but when the police turned up Danny must have thought I'd called them. He said he'd kill me. I had to run, Ivy, I had to get away.'

'Oh, you poor kid,' Ivy said. She was quiet for a moment, her head low, but then she looked up. 'All right, love, you can stay here, but only if you promise not to tell anyone where you are. I don't want any of that lot turning up here.'

'Oh, Ivy, I won't, I promise, and thank you . . . thank you so much for taking me in.'

Ivy suddenly grimaced, doubling over to clutch her stomach.

'What's wrong? Are you all right?'

'Yeah, yeah, it's just a bit of cramp, that's all,' she said through clenched teeth.

'Can I get you anything?'

Ivy sat up again, shaking her head. 'No, I'm fine now. Come on, let's get you sorted out,' and pushing herself to her feet, she beckoned Pet to follow her.

They went upstairs where, throwing open a

bedroom door, Ivy said, 'I'll double the boys up and then you can have this room. We'll just have to move Harry's clothes and toys.'

'Oh, Ivy, he won't like that.'

'He won't mind. The boys used to share a room in Drapers Alley and, to be honest, I think they miss it. Nine times out of ten when I come to wake Harry up, I find him in Ernie's room, asleep on the bottom bunk . . .' Ivy groaned, doubling over again as she sank onto the single bed.

'Ivy!' Pet cried.

'It's all right, it's just cramp again. It's my time of the month.'

Pet knew what it was like to suffer painful cramps, but she had never been as bad as this. 'Look, if you show me what things to move, I can manage on my own.'

'All right, love, I won't say no. You'll find clean sheets in the airing cupboard on the landing, but you look a bit bushed too, so just change the bed for now and we'll sort the rest tomorrow. While you're doing that, I'll get the spuds on the boil for dinner.'

'Is Steve at work?'

'He had to go in this morning, but now he's taken the boys into town to get some last-minute Christmas shopping.'

'Where does he work?'

'On a farm. I never thought he'd take to it, but he loves it.'

'Ivy, I know you said I can stay, but what about Steve?'

'He won't mind and the boys will be dead chuffed to see you. Right, I'm off and I'll see you downstairs.'

As Ivy left, Pet looked around the room. It was nice, under the eaves with a sloping ceiling and a little leaded window. She was so relieved that Ivy was letting her stay, but it was so quiet, so strange here that for a moment she felt a wave of desolation. She had a little money left in her Post Office book, but she couldn't expect Ivy to keep her indefinitely. If she could find a job, anything to pay her way, she wouldn't be a burden.

After changing the bed, Pet went downstairs to find Ivy sitting in front of the fire.

'The spuds are cooking,' she said, 'and I've lit the oven to heat up the casserole.'

'Is there anything I can do?' Pet asked, but then the front door opened, and with a flurry of cold air Steve and the boys rushed in.

Steve drew to a halt, his face registering his surprise. 'Blimey, Pet. What are you doing here?'

'She's come to stay for a while. I'll tell you about it later, but it can wait for now.'

'Look, Ernie, it's Auntie Pet,' Harry cried, the five-year-old hopping with excitement.

Pet gave them a hug, but then Ivy said, 'All right, boys, no doubt you're hungry, so go and wash your hands while I dish up dinner.'

Ernie grinned widely, green eyes just like his father's, twinkling. Pet smiled back at him, feeling a little happier. They were pleased to see her, welcomed her, and at last she felt like she was part of a family again.

Chapter Thirty-four

In Drapers Alley, Yvonne was unable to sit still. She paced the floor, wringing her hands whilst her mother-in-law sat staring into the fire. It was eight in the evening when the door opened and Sue walked in.

'The boys are asleep, but I can't leave them on their own for long. Is there any news?'

'No, nothing,' Yvonne told her. 'I went down to the station, but they wouldn't let me see Danny. All I was told was that he was still being questioned.'

Yvonne was startled when her mother-in-law suddenly rose to her feet. 'I didn't want to believe Petula – I thought she'd lost her mind – but now I know that she was telling the truth. I've got to find her. Where do you think she's gone?'

'I don't know, Mum, she could be anywhere. She was ready to go when the police came so she must have had something planned.'

'As far as I'm concerned, she'd better stay away,' Sue

snapped. 'I used to think a lot of Pet, but she's a grass and if I get my hands on her I'll bloody kill her.'

'Oh no you won't,' Joan snapped. 'Since the boys were taken for questioning I've been sitting here, turning it all over in my mind, and I'm sickened by the lot of you. When Dan died, I went into a sort of stupor and like a fool I blamed Petula. My God, what I've put that poor girl through doesn't bear thinking about. Porn – my sons making porn! It's disgusting, and you two must have known about it. Get out of my house, go on, get out, and don't show your faces in here again.'

'Don't come the high and mighty with us,' Sue yelled. 'From what Yvonne told me, the police had an arrest warrant for Dan.'

'That was a mistake. My Dan would never be mixed up in porn.'

'Don't kid yourself,' Sue snapped. 'He was up to his eyeballs in it from the beginning and don't tell me that you haven't worked that out for yourself, and let me tell you—'

'Come on, Sue, leave it. Can't you see she's had enough?' Yvonne urged, taking Sue's arm.

Joan looked awful, her skin the colour of putty.

'I've hardly started, but don't worry, I'm going. I can't risk leaving the kids for much longer.' Sue's eyes snapped to Joan again. 'Oh, yes, and talking about my boys, they're your grandsons but you hardly know they exist.'

'Get out!'

Sue threw Joan a look of disgust before leaving, but Yvonne remained, only for Joan to say, 'And you can get out too.'

'Oh, Mum, don't say that. I can't leave you like this. Look, I'll make us both a cup of tea.'

Yvonne hurried through to the kitchen, stiff with tension as she made a brew. She moved slowly, hoping that by the time it was made, her mother-in-law would have calmed down. When it was ready she tentatively carried it through to the living room, only to find that Joan still glared at her angrily.

'You knew, didn't you – knew that the boys were mixed up in porn, and worse, from what Petula said, they use kids?'

'No, Mum, no, they would never do that. Pet got it wrong and she knows that now.'

'Huh, and I'm supposed to believe you?' Joan snapped. 'Well, I don't. You lied to me about Petula. You said she hadn't been raped, or are you going to say she got that wrong too? No, of course you can't. When the doctor examined her, I saw the state of her with my own eyes.'

'I was just trying to protect you – to protect Dan.'

'Sue said that Dan was mixed up in making mucky films too. Is that true?'

Yvonne was saved from answering when the front door opened again, Danny and Chris walking in.

With a gasp Yvonne ran into her husband's arms. 'Oh, Danny, Danny.'

'It's all right, we're in the clear. The premises are in Dad's name so they don't have any proof that we were involved.'

'But Chris said that you hadn't closed down.'

With a rueful smile Chris said, 'Yeah, me and my big mouth, but at the end of the day it didn't matter. All they found was the equipment and a few reels of films that hadn't been distributed. As Danny said, the place is in Dad's name so there was nothing to tie it directly to us.'

Danny frowned as he looked at his mother. 'You look awful, Mum, but don't worry. It's all over now.'

'All over?' she snapped. 'How can it be over when my daughter has run off and I don't know where she is? Sue tells me that your father was wrapped up in porn too. I want the truth, Danny, and from the beginning.'

Danny ran both hands over his face. 'Mum, it's been a long day and we're bushed. Can't this wait until tomorrow?'

'No, it can't. I want the truth – and now!'

'All right, calm down. I'll tell you, but sit down first.'

She glared at him, but nevertheless sat down. 'Right, let's hear it.'

'Danny, no . . .' Chris warned.

Danny ignored him. 'Dad was past cracking safes,

Mum, and it was my idea to make porn films. He wasn't interested at first, but I talked him round.' Danny paused to take a breath, then went on to tell his mother everything, finally saying, 'So you see, Pet was snatched because we went into Jack Garston's territory.'

Joan looked stunned. Then she suddenly reared to her feet, screeching, 'Get out! Get out of my house!'

'What?'

'You heard me!' And turning to Chris she shrieked, 'And that goes for you too.'

'Mum, calm down.'

'Calm down? You expect me to calm down? Your father was sick, you're sick, the lot of you. Now go, get out of my house!'

Yvonne could see that her mother-in-law was near breaking point, her chest heaving as she glared at them. 'Come on, Danny,' she urged. 'Your mother's had enough for one day.'

For a moment she thought he was going to argue, but then he nodded. 'Yeah, come on, Chris. Yvonne's right.'

Yvonne shivered as they walked outside, pulling her cardigan around her chest.

'You should have kept your mouth shut, Danny,' Chris spat.

'She had to know sometime.'

'She took it badly,' said Chris, 'and I'm not surprised.'

'She'll come round,' Yvonne placated, 'and in the meantime, Chris, you're welcome to stay with us.'

'No thanks.'

'But where will you sleep?'

'Don't worry about me. I'll sort something out.'

'What happened to Maurice?'

'He went straight home, and Gawd knows what he's gonna tell Norma. Anyway, I'm off,' he said, stuffing his hands into his pockets as he walked out of the alley.

When they went indoors, Danny lit the fire. Then, sighing heavily, he said, 'I made a right mess of that. Maybe I should go back. I don't like leaving Mum in that state.'

'No, not yet. She's been through enough and needs time to calm down. Leave her to sleep on it, love.'

As the fire took hold, Danny slumped onto the sofa. Yvonne sat beside him, taking a deep breath before voicing her thoughts. 'Danny, I've been thinking about Pet.'

'Grassing on us didn't do her any good. As I said, the place is in Dad's name so they've got nothing on us.'

'That's just it. Didn't the police say that acting on information received, they searched the premises?'

'Yeah, that's right.'

'Danny, think about it. Jack Garston showed Pet some films, told her they were yours, but not where you made them. She knew nothing about the premises so how could she have dobbed you in?'

Danny frowned, but as the penny dropped, he jumped to his feet. 'Bloody hell, you're right. It couldn't have been Pet.' He rubbed a hand across his forehead. 'But if it wasn't her – who was it?'

Yvonne shook her head, unable to give him an answer, whilst Danny began to pace the room.

'Jack Garston!' he suddenly yelled. 'It must have been him. Wait till I get my hands on that bastard.'

Yvonne's stomach clenched. 'No, Danny, no. Think, you've got to think. If you go after Garston he'll retaliate. Last time he took Pet, and you know what he did to her. What if this time he takes me, or one of the kids?'

'He wouldn't fucking dare.'

Yvonne jumped to her feet, but feeling a surge of dizziness she sank back onto the sofa. It had been a dreadful day, and now this. She felt sick, nauseous, her nerves at breaking point.

'Yvonne, what is it? What's wrong?'

Though she hated herself for doing it – hated using it as a weapon – Yvonne knew she had no choice. She had to stop Danny from going after Garston. 'It . . . it's my blood pressure. The doctor warned me that it's high. He . . . he said it can be dangerous, both for me and the baby. I'm supposed to rest and avoid stress.'

'Right, come on then,' Danny said, leaning over to heave her into his arms. 'Let's get you up to bed.'

'Please, Danny,' Yvonne begged as she leaned her

head on his shoulder. 'Please don't go after Garston. I'm frightened – scared of what he'll do.'

She felt his arms tighten around her and tensed, but then he said, 'All right, don't get upset. I'll leave him alone for now.'

Yvonne raised her head to look at Danny's face. 'For now', he had said. She sighed, knowing from his expression that for the time being, she'd have to be content with that.

Sue snuggled up to Bob, relieved that he was home and in the clear. 'They kept you at the station for bloody hours,' she complained. 'I went to your mum's to see if there was any news, but the old cow chucked me out.'

'Why did she do that?'

'Ain't it obvious? She knows about the porn now and said she's disgusted with the lot of us.'

'She's upset, love, but I'm sure she doesn't blame you.'

'Huh, knowing your mother she probably thinks I put you up to it,' Sue said as her eyes flicked round the room. She had made a bit of an effort for the kids' sake, putting up a few decorations, but even so, it was going to be a lousy Christmas. Mind you, she consoled herself, they'd be all right next year. When Dan's will was read, Bob was sure to get a chunk of the business and it must be worth a pretty penny.

'Have you seen your dad's will?'

'Leave it out. Mum's been in too much of a state to think about the will – we all have. I think she's got it, but it can wait until after the funeral.'

Sue hid her disappointment, but it wasn't the only thing that was disappointing her lately. She ran her hand along Bob's leg, but there was no response. He wasn't interested and hadn't been since his father died, but maybe she could try something else to tickle his fancy. 'Bob,' she said, leading up to it, 'it'll be Christmas Eve in a couple of days and we'll have to make a bit of an effort for the kids.'

'It doesn't seem right.'

'It isn't fair to ruin their Christmas. I'm not asking for much, just that we let them put out a mince pie for Father Christmas and some milk for the reindeers as usual.'

'Yeah, all right.'

'I don't expect you to dress up as Santa this year, but what about your Christmas treat? Instead of waiting, you can have it now if you like.'

'You've still got the outfit?'

'Of course I have. I'll go and put it on.'

'Not tonight, love. I'm bushed and I ain't in the mood.'

'You don't want Santa's little helper?' she asked as she ran her hand along the inside of Bob's leg.

'Leave off, love,' he said, moving her hand away

as he stood up. 'I'm knackered and I think I'll have an early night. Are you coming?'

'There ain't much chance of that these days,' she snapped.

'Trust you to take it the wrong way. I meant are you coming to bed?' but then seeing the funny side, he began to laugh.

Sue found it infectious, the pair of them soon doubled up with mirth. Sue didn't know what caused it, but as though the laughter had released something in Bob, the tension that had lined his face dissipated. He held out his hand, and with a wink said, 'Come on then, let's see you in that outfit.'

Sue didn't need telling twice. Giggling, she ran upstairs, but she didn't have time to put the pixie costume on before Bob grabbed her, pulling her onto the bed.

Joan sat alone in a silent house. Now, instead of grief, she felt only anger. Dan had been mixed up in porn and her stomach churned. He had ruled the boys and the business, one that she now knew was just a front. Oh, she had known that Dan was a bit of a rogue when she married him, but despite that she had admired his morals, the code that he lived by. Women, he always said, were to be respected, protected, looked after, and it was something he had instilled in his sons. Or so she had thought. Her teeth ground together. How could using women to make disgusting pornographic films be respecting them? And children – Pet said they used children. It was awful, dreadful. Oh God, what an idiot she'd been, a blind fool. The man she had loved, looked up to, had turned out to be a sick monster.

She glanced at the clock, worried about her daughter and hating herself for what she had put her through. Petula had been raped, violently, but she had hardly shown her an ounce of sympathy, her concern only for Dan and that he didn't find out.

The poor girl had held it all inside, eating away at her, and was it any wonder that it had all burst out? She had blamed her daughter for Dan's death, and maybe him hearing about the rape had been the catalyst, but in truth she knew that Dan had been going downhill for a while.

Joan sat wringing her hands. Danny had threatened to kill Petula. The poor girl must be so frightened, hiding, but Joan didn't blame her for going to the police. If she had known what they were up to, she'd have done the same. They were sick, disgusting, using poor children to make those awful films.

There was only one thing Joan wanted now and that was to have her daughter safely home again. She'd never been much of a mother, had treated her daughter badly, but now she just wanted the chance to make it up to her.

Oh, Pet, where are you? her mind cried out. You're all I have left now. Please come home. Don't be frightened. I'll make sure that Danny doesn't lay a hand on you, that nobody ever lays a hand on you again. It'll be just you and me, Pet, and as far as I'm concerned, the rest of them can rot in hell.

Joan's mind twisted and turned, wondering how she could find her daughter, until, exhausted, she fell asleep where she was sitting, the fire slowly dying until at last it went out.

Chapter Thirty-five

When Pet awoke in a strange room the following morning, for a moment she was disorientated, but then it all came flooding back: her father's death, her mother's hate, the police turning up, and Danny – Danny blaming her, threatening to kill her. Tears stung her eyes, but then, hearing the sound of giggling, she forced them away as her door was thrown open.

Harry and Ernie tumbled into the room. 'Auntie Pet, Auntie Pet, are you getting up?' Ernie urged.

'It looks like it,' she said, throwing back the covers. It was still dark outside and she had no idea of the time, but if the boys were awake, it must mean that Ivy and Steve were up too. 'Let me get dressed and then I'll come downstairs.'

'Yeah, all right, but don't be long,' Ernie cried, his eyes alight with excitement. 'It's snowing again, Auntie Pet, and Mum said that as soon as it's light we can build a snowman. Will you help us?'

'Of course I will.'

'Yippee,' Harry shouted, the two boys scampered out.

Pet went to the bathroom and after a quick wash she threw on some clothes before running downstairs to find the boys and Ivy in the kitchen. It was a nice room, far bigger than the kitchens in Drapers Alley, with an oak table and chairs in the centre and a large dresser against one wall, lined with blue willow-pattern china.

'Morning, love,' Ivy said. 'Help yourself to a cup of tea, and what would you like for breakfast?'

'I don't mind. Anything will do,' Pet said, reaching out for the teapot as she sat at the table.

'The boys usually have something hot and they want beans on toast this morning. Will that do?'

'Yes, and thanks. Where's Steve?'

'He's gone to work. I know it's Sunday, but the livestock still need sorting out. He's got Christmas Day off, but that's all.'

Pet paused in the act of pouring a cup of tea. She could see that Ivy was in pain, but obviously making a supreme effort to hide it. Pet frowned, sure that this was more than cramp. Ivy looked ill, really ill, and now putting the teapot down, she rose to her feet.

'Ivy, sit down. I want to make myself useful so I'll cook the breakfast.'

'There's no need.'

'Please, you took me in and it will make me feel better if you let me help.'

For a moment Ivy hesitated, but then she sat at the table, her hands clutching her stomach. 'All right, I won't say no. You'll find bread in the bin and beans in that cupboard over there.'

Pet opened the cupboard and frowned. It was dirty inside, very dirty. She took out the beans before turning to Ivy. 'Where's the tin opener?'

'In that drawer,' she indicated.

The cutlery drawer was dirty too, some knives and forks still showing remnants of food. She found the tin opener, her eyes involuntarily meeting Ivy's as she turned.

'I know, Pet, I know,' she murmured. 'The housework is getting on top of me, and I'll be glad of your help. If you ask me, your turning up will prove to be a godsend.'

Pet frowned, wondering what Ivy meant, but saw that Harry and Ernie were still, listening to the conversation. 'Right, boys, one piece of toast or two?'

'Two, please,' they chorused.

Pet found a saucepan, unable to help noticing that though the kitchen appeared clean on the surface, inside every cupboard it was a different story. Something was very wrong with Ivy, she was sure of it, and if her cousin wouldn't tell her what the problem was, she'd ask Steve. In the meantime she would do all she could to help Ivy, starting with the breakfast.

Chris left Phil's house and as he passed Arding and Hobbs, he glanced in the windows at their Christmas displays. Chris sniffed, fighting his emotions. It was going to be awful, the first Christmas without his father, and unless his mother let him back in, he'd be without her too. He could have stayed where he was, but Phil was constantly nagging about bringing their relationship into the open and it was driving him mad. He couldn't do it – couldn't face his family's reaction. If they found out they would never understand, and not only that, locally he'd be a laughing stock.

At last, his feet feeling like blocks of ice, Chris turned into Drapers Alley, fumbling for his key, but as he tried to turn it in the lock, it wouldn't move. His mother must have put the catch down, but as she was alone in the house he wasn't surprised, so lifting the door knocker, he rapped several times.

When she didn't come to the door he lifted the letter box, calling, 'Mum, come on, open up. It's bloody freezing out here.'

Through the narrow gap he could see that she was sitting by the fire, but she didn't move. 'Mum. Come on. Open the door!'

'What's going on?' Danny called from next door, his head poking out of an upstairs window.

'It's Mum. I can see her through the letter box, but she won't let me in.'

'Is she all right?'

'I dunno,' Chris called, bending down to peer through the letter box again. He frowned, standing up to call out, 'She ain't moving.'

'Hold on, I'm coming down.'

In what felt like moments, Danny was beside him, thumping loudly on the door. 'Come on, Mum, open this door.'

With a tut of impatience he too peered through the letter box. 'Yeah, I can see her, but you're right, she ain't moving.' His brow creased with anxiety and then, lifting the letter box again, he shouted, 'Mum, if you don't open this door I'm gonna kick it in.'

The door opened, their mother glaring at them as she spat, 'Don't you dare kick my door.' She stood in front of them, arms folded across her chest to bar their entry.

'Come on, Mum, let me in,' Chris urged.

'I don't want you in my house, any of you. My daughter is the only decent child I've got, but you threatened her, Danny, and now she'll never come home.'

'We'll find her, Mum, we'll put it right. She didn't grass on us, I know that now.'

'She didn't? What makes you think that?' Chris asked.

'I'll explain later,' Danny told him.

'Mum, what about my stuff?' Chris urged. 'I need clean clothes.'

'All right, you can come in to pack, but then, until you find Petula, I don't want to see your face again.'

Chris stepped inside and when his mother slammed the door in Danny's face, he said, 'Mum, come on, there's no need for that.'

'Just get your stuff and then get out.'

'Can't we at least talk about it?'

'I don't want to talk. I just want to see the back of you. Now either you go upstairs to pack, or you get out now.'

With a sigh Chris went up to his room. With his mother in this mood there was no point in arguing with her, but surely in another twenty-four hours she'd come round. He packed a case, and with his dark suit over his arm he returned downstairs. 'I'm going now, Mum.'

'Good.'

'I don't like leaving you on your own.'

'Find my daughter and I won't be. Now go on, bugger off.'

His head low, Chris left and went straight to Danny's house, saying as he went in, 'There's no talking to her.'

'We'll just have to find Pet.'

441

'She could be anywhere, Danny, and with your threat hanging over her head, she'll be keeping her head down. But what's this about her not grassing on us?'

'As Yvonne pointed out, Pet didn't know about our place in Wimbledon so it couldn't have been her.'

'Bloody hell, but if she didn't, who did?'

'I don't know, but my first guess is Jack Garston.'

Chris knew he'd have to kip down in Danny's for now, but uppermost in his mind was Jack Garston. He'd find the bastard, and when he did . . .

Maurice arrived at nine thirty and got the same reception. His mother opened the door, told him to bugger off and then slammed it in his face. He didn't really want to see Danny, but there were things to be sorted that couldn't wait. He went next door to find that Bob and Chris were there, the pair of them sitting on Danny's sofa.

'Mum wouldn't let me in,' Maurice said as he took a seat by the fire.

'She won't let any of us in, and she chucked Chris out,' Danny told him, going on to relate all that had happened when they returned from the police station.

Maurice's breath wheezed in his chest. 'So, it's all out in the open. No wonder she wouldn't let me in.'

'What about Norma? Did you tell her that we were taken in for questioning?' Bob asked.

'No, I just said that I spent the day with Mum.'

'What excuse did you come up with for leaving the alley?'

'None, and I don't intend to. Just the threat of us coming back is enough to shut her up.'

'My Sue knows all about it and instead of doing her nut, she took it well. Yvonne knows too, ain't that right, Danny?'

'Yes, she does. Maybe you should tell your wife, Maurice. It's bound to come out sooner or later and it'll be better coming from you.'

Maurice wanted to spit in Danny's face, but hid his feelings. 'No, Danny. I know Norma, and if she finds out it'll be the end of my marriage. We're in the clear; we're not involved in making films any more, so as long as I keep her away from the alley, there's no need to tell her.'

'What about Dad's funeral? We can tell Sue and Yvonne to keep their mouths shut around Norma, but we can't say the same for Mum.'

'I'll come alone.'

'How will you manage that?'

'I doubt Norma will want to come, so it won't be hard.'

'How are you managing for money?' Danny asked.

'I've still got a fair bit saved, and I'll get a job after Christmas.'

'What about the yard?' Bob asked. 'Dad has probably split it between us, so even if you don't want to join us in running it, you'll still be entitled to a share of the profits.'

'I haven't given Dad's will a thought,' Maurice lied, 'and anyway, until it's read, we won't know how we stand.'

'Yeah, well, none of us have mentioned it to Mum yet. She's been in such a state that we decided to leave it until after the funeral.'

'Look, forget about the will,' Chris said impatiently. 'You seem to have forgotten that we've got to find Pet.'

Danny nodded. 'Yes, Chris is right, and as I told Bob earlier, it wasn't Pet who grassed on us. I reckon it was Jack Garston, but now Pet thinks I'm after her and I feel like shit.'

Maurice frowned. 'I doubt it was Garston. If word got out that he's a grass, he'd be finished. Not only that, Garston had no reason to dob us in. We're out of the game now and he knows it.'

'Yeah,' Bob said, 'Maurice is right.'

'All right, so it wasn't Garston,' said Danny. 'We'll just have to find out who it was, and then sort him out, but for now we need to put our heads together to find Pet.'

'What about her friends? She could be with one of them,' Bob suggested.

'I know where one lives, a girl called Jane, but that's all,' Chris said.

Danny rose to his feet. 'Right, let's start there.'

'Do you mind if I leave you to it?' Maurice asked. 'I'm still a bit rough and the cold weather really gets to my chest.'

'Yeah, go on home. We can manage,' Danny told him. 'I'll just pop upstairs to tell Yvonne what we're up to, and then we can leave.'

'I'll tell Sue,' Bob said, saying goodbye to Maurice before he hurried out.

Maurice turned to Chris. 'If Mum doesn't change her mind, you could move into George's place.'

'No, I don't fancy that. Too many memories,' Chris said.

Maurice frowned at his cryptic reply, but then Danny came downstairs, wrapped up against the cold in his camel coat and carrying brown leather gloves.

'Right, let's go,' he said.

As they walked outside snow was falling and Maurice shivered. He said a hasty goodbye, calling to his brothers that he'd see them the next day before hurrying out of the alley to his car.

Maurice drove off, his mood low. He'd told his brothers that he hadn't given his father's will a thought, but it wasn't true. In fact he was disappointed that they were waiting until after the funeral to read it.

On Lavender Hill, the traffic lights turned to red. Maurice pulled up automatically, his mind hardly on the road. Since leaving the alley he'd been constantly worried about the future, but on hearing of his father's death the burden had lifted. He would receive an inheritance, and had mentally calculated the business assets. There was the yard and the small-holding in Wimbledon, both worth a lot of money. They could be sold, the money shared, and his worries would be over.

Maurice gripped the steering wheel, fighting off feelings of guilt. Yes, he was sad when his father died, but since having two strokes and coming home from hospital, his mother had guarded him so well that Maurice had hardly seen him. It had saddened him that his father had been left helpless, half alive, a shadow of the man he used to be. When he had stopped holding the reins of the family business, it had gone to pieces, and most of that had been down to Danny. The distance from his family had given Maurice time to think, for his resentment to build. It had been Danny's ambitions, his obsession with making money that had put Oliver at risk, forcing Maurice to leave the alley. He had managed to hide his feelings this morning, but just looking at Danny sickened him.

Once he had his inheritance, Maurice was deter-mined to start a new life, somewhere where there was no chance of Norma ever finding out about his past. If it wasn't for his health, they could have emigrated, but they could still move to the other end of the country, maybe Devon or Cornwall, where they could buy some sort of small business, a tea shop or one selling souvenirs. They might never be rich, but he would be his own boss without the worry of finding employment. He wouldn't miss Danny, though he'd miss the rest of the family, but once away from London he would never have to worry about losing his wife and son again.

Danny, Chris and Bob were propping up the bar in a local pub, all drinking shorts. They had been to see Jane, but the girl said she hadn't seen Pet and didn't know where she was. She had given them a couple of other addresses to try, but again they drew blanks.

'That's it then,' Bob said. 'We've been everywhere, and put out the word, but nobody's seen her.'

Danny downed his third whisky. 'She can't be walking the streets in this weather. Somebody must have taken her in.'

'I still can't get over the reception we got when we tried Linda's parents' place. I thought the old boy was going to have a fit when he saw us,' said Chris.

'Yeah, and I thought Linda was going to pass out,' Bob said as he waved his glass at the barman to indicate another round.

Danny shrugged. 'It was worth a try, and once

Linda knew that we weren't interested in her baby, she calmed down, especially when we told her that there's still no sign of George.'

As another drink was put in front of Chris he threw it down his throat, then said, 'Shit, I dread telling Mum that we ain't found Pet.'

'You and me both,' Danny said, waving his glass and adding, 'but a few more of these might help.'

By closing time, all three were drunk, none bothering that Danny was in no fit state to drive as they got into his car. After a few fumbled attempts Danny managed to find the ignition, and though mounting the pavement at every corner, he somehow managed to drive home.

They staggered into the alley, propping each other up, and stopped outside their mother's door.

Chris was swaying on his feet but managed to rattle the letter box. He shook his head, trying to focus, and when the door was flung open he slurred, 'We've tried, Mum, but we couldn't find her. Can I come in now?'

'No you bloody well can't. I've told you, find my daughter, and until you do, you can bugger off,' she shouted, slamming the door shut.

'Blimey, I never thought I'd see the day,' Bob chuckled. 'Mum's starting to swear like a trooper.'

'Ish not funny,' Chris slurred.

'Sod you then, I'm going home,' Bob said, taking his arm from around Danny to stumble to his own front door.

Danny held Chris up as they went into his house, where he heaved his brother onto the sofa, almost falling as he sank down beside him. He was drunk, but seeing his mother had sobered him a little. Yvonne came into the room from the kitchen, her face anxious.

'Did you find Pet?'

He shook his head. 'No, but we'll keep looking.'

Her eyes flicked to Chris and he grinned inanely. 'Watcha, Yvonne.'

'Have you been drinking?'

'We only had a few, love,' Danny told her, his eyes drooping until, unable to keep them open any longer, he sank back and in moments was asleep.

When Chris did the same, Yvonne shook her head before returning to the kitchen. They were supposed to be looking for Petula, but instead they had been in the pub, and judging by the look of them they'd been drinking since opening time. She wanted to talk to Danny about Christmas, but now it would have to wait until he sobered up.

It was Christmas Eve tomorrow, her order waiting to be picked up, but how could she cook a Christmas dinner knowing that her mother-in-law was alone next door? Then there was the funeral to face. Two cars had been ordered, but with Joan feeling the way she did, would she refuse to travel to the cemetery with her sons? It was a mess, everything was a mess and the last thing she needed was her husband coming home drunk. Her head began to thump, and tiredly she rubbed her forehead. It was no good, she'd have to lie down. So, having poured a glass of water, Yvonne carried it upstairs. Drunk or sober, Danny would have to sort it out. She'd had enough.

Chapter Thirty-six

Pet was dusting the living room, but paused to look out of the window. The landscape was white, a blanket of snow thick on the ground. It had been snowing heavily since Christmas, and according to the weather forecast, there was no sign of a let-up.

Today was her father's funeral, the thought of it almost more than she could bear. When the door opened, Pet spun round to see Ivy coming into the room, her cousin frowning when she looked at her.

'Are you all right, Pet?'

'It's today – my father's funeral.'

'Blimey, no wonder you look upset. Come on, leave the housework and I'll make us both a nice cup of hot chocolate. Honestly, you're just like your mother, always on the go, but for once, give it a rest.'

'I'd rather keep busy.'

Ivy grimaced, her hands involuntarily rubbing her tummy. 'Bloody ulcer,' she complained, 'and that jollop the doctor gave me is a waste of time.'

Pet frowned as she looked at Ivy. 'I think you've lost more weight.'

'There isn't much I can eat that doesn't give me gyp so is it any wonder?'

'No, I suppose not,' said Pet, 'but if the medicine isn't helping, maybe you should go back to see the doctor.'

'It'd be a waste of time. The old quack is well past it, and if you ask me, he should retire. I reckon his eyesight is going and when I told him about the pains in my tummy he asked a few questions, but didn't examine me before saying it's an ulcer.'

Pet hadn't been close to Ivy when they had lived in Drapers Alley, but living with her now had proved a revelation. Ivy was kind, a good mother, her marriage a happy one.

When Pet had asked Steve about Ivy's constant pain he'd told her it was an ulcer, but Pet knew nothing about them, only seeing how debilitating the pain could be. She did all she could to help Ivy, taking on the housework and sometimes the cooking, pleased to be useful. It helped to keep busy, helped to keep thoughts of her family at bay, but at night, alone in her room, it was impossible.

Ivy's clock struck the hour, and seeing the time, Pet's eyes filled with tears. It was happening now, her father was being buried. She felt a touch on her arm, the duster pulled from her hand.

'Come on, Pet,' Ivy said, her voice unusually gentle. 'I said leave the housework.'

'Oh, Ivy, I should be there. I should be at his funeral.'

'I know, love, I know,' Ivy murmured, pulling Pet into her arms and holding her whilst she cried.

Danny's face was grim as he listened to Yvonne. It had been a lousy Christmas and New Year, culminating in this, his father's funeral. His mother still wouldn't have anything to do with them, stubbornly spending Christmas Day alone, and only that morning had she conceded to let Yvonne in the door.

'She doesn't want you or anyone else in the car with her,' Yvonne said when she returned, 'but she finally agreed that we can follow.'

'What about the service?'

'She wants to sit alone in the chapel.'

'This is bloody ridiculous.'

'I know, and I did the best I could, but it's like talking to a brick wall.' Tears suddenly filled Yvonne's eyes. 'We used to be so close, Danny, but now your mum hates me.'

'She'll come round, love, you'll see.'

'No, Danny, I don't think so. She's so bitter and I don't know what she meant, but she said something about the lot of us having a shock coming. Oh, look at the time. The cars will be here soon so I'd better get changed.'

Danny was already in his suit, with white shirt and black tie. Chris was upstairs putting his on, but he'd have to warn Bob that they would have to use the second car, one that had been booked to take the wives and children to the service. 'All right, and while you're getting ready, I'll pop round to tell Bob about the arrangements.'

When Danny went into his brother's, his overcoat flung around his shoulders, he saw that the kids were ready, both Robby and Paul dressed smartly and, like him, wearing black ties. Sue was wearing a black coat, but to him her hat looked frivolous, perched on the side of her head with a small veil covering her eyes.

'Any sign of Maurice?' she asked.

'No, not yet,' Danny told her as Bob came downstairs. 'Mum doesn't want any of us in the car with her so we've got to follow. Seven of us won't fit in the second car, so you go in that with Maurice, Sue and the boys. I'll take Yvonne in my car.'

'So, Mum finally let you in,' Bob said.

'No, not me, it was Yvonne.'

Sue's lips curled in derision. 'Huh, I might have guessed.'

The door opened, Maurice saying as he walked in, 'I saw the cars outside the alley and there's a bloke in a top hat knocking on Mum's door.'

'Right, I'll get Yvonne and Chris,' Danny said, hurrying next door.

Soon everyone was on the pavement, all eyes gaping as their mother walked outside. Instead of black, she was wearing a fawn-coloured coat with a wide-brimmed hat in the same shade, the outfit more suited to a wedding than a funeral.

'She said we had a shock coming and this must be it,' Yvonne whispered.

'What's her game? Look at her – it's bloody disgusting,' Sue snapped.

Without a backward glance Joan walked out of the alley, the rest of them following. Danny glanced at the hearse; saw the flowers surrounding his father's coffin before quickly looking away. He fought to pull himself together and, telling the others to get into the second car, he hustled Yvonne to the lockup to get his.

Danny needn't have hurried. With his top hat under his arm, and umbrella held out in front of him, the funeral director stepped in front of the hearse, slowly walking in front of it, the cars moving behind at a snail's pace. Danny waited until he could slot in behind the second car, and as he drove slowly along he saw that the pavement was lined with locals solemnly watching the small procession pass. He was pleased to see that they were showing their respects, and though they had held his father in fear, many had turned to him when they had a problem.

When the hearse turned onto Lavender Hill the funeral director hopped into the front, the car picking up pace. At last they reached the chapel where they all stood silently as the coffin was carried in. Then their mother was beckoned forward, dry-eyed as she walked straight to the first pew. The others then followed, all shuffling into the row behind her, but before the service could start, Robby's voice echoed as he piped, 'Nanny, is Granddad in that box?'

His mother didn't turn, but Danny saw that her shoulders had begun to shake. He wanted to run to her, to offer comfort, but then to his horror he heard a titter of laughter. His mother wasn't crying, she was laughing. My God, she was actually laughing!

When the chapel service was over Joan walked to the cemetery, aware that the rest of them were close behind, but ignoring them. It was freezing, snow laying on the ground, the path slippery underfoot. When they reached the graveside, Joan saw the way the vicar looked at her, his disapproval plain, his expression pompous. Who was he to judge her? What did he know of her life, her disillusion? All right, she wasn't wearing black, the mark of respect, but Dan didn't deserve respect, only contempt.

Robby began to run around and, bending down, he scooped up a handful of snow to throw at his brother. Bob restrained the boy, shaking his shoulders before pulling him to stand beside them at the graveside.

Joan wasn't listening as the vicar began his into-nation, her mind on her plans. As she had told Yvonne, they were in for a shock. When this was over she'd allow them in her house for one last time and then, if her plan worked, she would never have to see the lot of them again.

Joan was brought back to the present as Danny threw a flower into the grave where it landed on top of Dan's coffin. As the others did the same, Joan saw the vicar moving towards her. She didn't want to hear his platitudes, his talk of Dan being in a better place. Huh, she just hoped it wasn't true because as far as she was concerned her husband should rot in hell.

Joan ignored the vicar's outstretched hand, turning instead to head for the car that was to take her home. She was ready now, ready for the confrontation, her mouth set in a grim line as she settled back in her seat.

It wasn't a long drive, hardly time for her feet to thaw before Joan got out of the car, only pausing long enough to thank the man who had held the door open. In a few minutes she was indoors, and though she had banked up the fire, it had burned low. She hurried to add more coal. Taking off her coat, she stuffed her feet into slippers whilst her eyes flew to the document tucked behind the clock on the mantel-piece. She waited then, looking out of the window, until shortly after they all walked into the alley.

Joan flung the front door open. 'Danny, Bob, Maurice, Chris,' she snapped, 'I want to talk to you. Not you, Sue,' she ordered as the woman moved forward, dragging the boys. 'Nor you, Yvonne.'

Sue shot daggers, but Joan didn't care. Yvonne looked sad and for a moment Joan almost wavered. She was fond of Danny's wife, more than fond, and if just one of them could remain, she would want it to be Yvonne.

Joan walked back inside, the boys following her, with Chris, the last in, closing the door.

'Right, this is your father's will,' she said as she took the document from behind the clock, 'and I suggest you sit down before I read it.'

They each took a seat, all looking at her expectantly, so taking a deep breath, she began. 'Before I read the will, I'd like to know how I stand financially. How is the yard doing?'

'Mum, I know that Dad wouldn't want you to worry about the business,' Danny said. 'You can leave all that to us. The yard's doing all right and we'll see that you're taken care of as usual.'

Joan smiled thinly, her eyes sweeping over her sons as she opened the document. 'I was with your father when this was drawn up. It's been in my possession ever since, and before you ask, it's the only will he made. Now I won't go into all the legal jargon, or read it word for word, as the sooner you get out of here the better. All you need to know is that everything, your father's entire estate, has been left to me.'

'What?' Maurice cried. 'But he can't do that. What about us?'

'You are mentioned, all of you. Your father says that he'd like you to run the business, continuing to take a cut of the profits each month as wages.'

'But we thought he'd share it between us,' Maurice protested.

Joan's eyes swept over her sons again. Maurice was the only one who had spoken; the others looked at her in stunned silence. 'If I had predeceased your father, then yes, the estate would have been shared equally between you, but I didn't die first, *he did*.' Joan smiled thinly again. 'Mind you, your father still thought he had it covered – that one day his precious sons would get their inheritance.'

Danny spoke at last, to ask, 'What do you mean, Mum?'

'At your father's insistence, my will was drawn up at the same time as his, and he made sure that I named you all as my beneficiaries.'

Joan now stood up. Drawing another document from behind the clock, she held it up, speaking to her husband as though he was there, in the room. 'See this, Dan? It's my will. You thought you were infallible, that you'd always be able to control me, the meek, biddable little wife. Well, let's see you control this,' she shouted as she threw her will onto the fire, watching with satisfaction as it was taken by the flames and devoured. 'They'll get nothing from me – *nothing*.'

'Mum, what are you doing? Have you lost your mind?' Danny shouted.

'No,' Joan spat, 'I haven't lost my mind. In fact, for the first time in my life, I'm seeing things clearly, thinking for myself.'

'Mum, come on, calm down,' Chris urged. 'If you carry on like this you'll make yourself ill.'

'Looking at you lot is enough to make me ill, but I ain't finished yet so you'd better sit down again.'

'Look, Mum, let's talk calmly,' Chris said as he took a seat. 'I don't care about Dad's will, or yours, but he did say that he wants us to look after you, to run the business, and that suits me fine.'

'I own the yard now and there's no way on earth I'd let you lot run it,' Joan snapped. 'In fact there'll be no business to run. I'm going to sell it.'

'You're going to do what? But you can't,' Danny cried.

'Oh yes I can, Danny. I can do what I like.'

'Look, is this about Pet? Because if it is, give us a chance to find her.'

'I gave you a chance.'

'She could be anywhere. We need more time.'

'No, Danny, with your threat hanging over her head, like George, she's gone. She'll never come back

460

unless you lot are out of the way, and with this in mind, I've got a proposition for you.'

'What sort of proposition?' Maurice asked.

'As I said, I'm selling the yard, but there's still that other place, the one in Wimbledon. I want nothing to do with it. In fact, the thought of it makes me sick to my stomach. Now I'm going to make you an offer, and you'd better take it because it's the only one you're going to get.' Joan paused, but saw that Maurice had leaned forward, his face eager with anticipation.

'Go on, Mum,' he urged.

'All right, let's get down to business,' she said curtly. 'I want you all out of Drapers Alley and, once gone, I don't want to ever see your faces again. If you agree to go I'll give you that place in Wimbledon. You can sell it and split the profits between you.'

Maurice looked delighted. 'Blimey, thanks, Mum.'

'Hold on, Maurice,' said Bob. 'It's all right for you, you've got a flat, but where are we supposed to live?'

'Come on, it wouldn't be the end of the world. I found a place and you can do the same.'

'Mum, please, don't do this,' Chris begged. 'We're out of the porn game now and we'll never go back to it. I had to put all my savings into the yard to expand our stock and it's just starting to pay dividends.'

'You'll get your money back.'

'But I can't leave the alley, Mum. Who'll look after you?'

'Look after me? You? Don't make me laugh. I can look after myself and I don't need a sick disgusting animal that used children to make pornographic films living under my roof.'

'We didn't use kids. We'd never do that. Tell her, Danny.'

'He's telling the truth, Mum.'

'Even if I believed you, which I don't, it wouldn't make any difference. You still made other films and you can't deny that. Now are you going to accept my offer or not? Because if you don't, you'll end up with nothing.'

'We'll accept it,' Maurice hastily said.

Danny's temper spilled over. 'Maurice, are you out of your mind? Of course we're not accepting it.'

'If we don't, as Mum said, we'll end up without a penny.'

Joan watched as her eldest son ran a hand through his hair, obviously trying to calm down before he met her eyes. 'Mum, I know you're upset, but this is silly. Surely you don't really want us to leave the alley.'

'Yes I do, and my mind's made up. In fact, I don't want any of you to put a foot inside *my* yard again.'

'It won't run itself, Mum. If you close down you won't have any money coming in.'

'I told you, I'm selling it, and if you must know, the sale's already in hand.'

'I can't believe you're doing this,' Danny groaned. 'Mum, at least give us time to think about it.'

'Oh, I know your game, Danny. You're trying to stall me, hoping I'll change my mind, but I won't, you can be sure of that. Now you've got one hour, and after that you either accept my offer or you can forget it. Now bugger off, the lot of you.'

'Come on, Danny, you can see she means it,' Maurice urged.

As Danny looked at her, Joan kept her head high, her expression hard. At last, with a sigh of exasperation he turned to march out, his brothers behind him.

Joan was glad to see the back of them and slumped in her chair. Her plan *had* to work, it just had to, or Petula would never come home. She closed her eyes, praying silently as she waited for her sons to make their decision.

Bob said he'd talk to Sue and hurried into his own house, his face white as he broke the news.

'So your father left you nothing, not even a few bob?'

'That's right.'

'But your mum's offering to give you the premises in Wimbledon?'

'Yeah, but as I said, only if we move out of the alley.'

'That suits me fine.'

'Do you really mean that? It means finding somewhere else to live, but by the time the money is split between four of us, I don't know how much we'll get.'

'Of course I bloody mean it, now shut up and give me time to think.' Sue was quiet, her eyes narrowed. Then she said, 'I reckon you'd get a good few thousand, and if you pool it with your brothers, what's to stop you starting up your own business? With your contacts you could carry on supplying building materials. You'd only have to find premises and buy in stock.'

Bob's face lit up. 'Sue, you're a genius. I'll go and put it to the others.'

He hurried next door and without preamble said, 'Sue's had a great idea. If we take Mum's offer and sell Wimbledon, we could start up our own business.'

'Count me out,' said Maurice. 'I've got my own plans.'

'That still leaves three of us,' Bob said eagerly.

'None of you seems to be thinking about your mother,' Yvonne protested. 'If we leave the alley it'll be empty. She'll be all on her own.'

'It's what she wants – she made that clear,' Maurice said.

'We can't do it, we can't just leave,' Chris said.

'If you stay in the borough,' Maurice argued, 'you can keep an eye on her and, who knows, she might eventually come round.'

'Yeah, Maurice is right,' said Bob, 'and anyway,

I don't think we've got much choice. If we don't take the offer, we'll all be left with nothing.'

'I've just thought of something,' said Chris. 'Even if we agree to take up Mum's offer, we've still got to sell Wimbledon and that could take time, maybe months, and it would give us a chance to bring her round.'

'Bloody hell, I hadn't thought of that,' said Bob, 'but if it takes that long to sell, what will we do for money? Shit, I'll have to get a job, work for someone else, and I don't know about you lot, but I don't fancy that.'

So far Danny had just listened, but now he said, 'It's funny really, almost like fate, if you believe in all that rubbish. The last time I was at Wimbledon it was to tell Pete Saunders that we were closing down, but he didn't seem surprised. When I told him that he could stay on at the cottage for a while, he said he'd already been looking round for another place.'

'Hang on, Danny. How could Pete have known in advance that we were closing down?' asked Chris.

'With all that was going on at the time, I wasn't myself, and to be honest it sort of went over my head. He said something about a big developer sniffing around, looking to buy the land, and that he was looking for another place in case we took the bloke's offer.'

'What offer?' asked Maurice.

'Pete gave me a letter that had been delivered to

the cottage, but as I said, I was in a bit of a state and hardly looked at it.'

'Blimey, talk about luck,' Maurice said, then asked eagerly, 'Where's the letter, Danny?'

'I dunno.'

'Think, Danny. Did you leave it at the cottage or bring it home?'

'At the time it didn't seem important so I've no idea. I might have just stuffed it in my pocket.'

'Try the sideboard, Danny,' Yvonne suggested. 'You usually clear your pockets when you take off your jacket so you might have put it in the drawer, the one that you keep locked.'

'Yeah, all right,' Danny said, taking out a bunch of keys to find the small one that fitted the drawer. He walked over to the sideboard, saying as he unlocked it, 'I doubt it's here, though.'

They all watched as Danny pulled out papers. Then, finding a book, he said, 'Blimey, the hooky business accounts. I should have destroyed these. If the police had warrants to search this place, it would have left us in the shit.'

'Give it to me,' Maurice urged. 'I'll burn it now.'

Danny handed the book to Maurice, watching as his brother threw it onto the fire.

'It seems sort of symbolic,' he murmured, 'our old lives going up in flames.' He shrugged and returned to his search. 'Got it,' he said at last, pulling out an envelope.

'Give it here, Danny,' Maurice urged, and after scanning the contents he said, 'This is too good an offer to turn down, but we don't know if he's still interested. Give him a ring, Danny.'

'Are you all sure about this?' Danny asked. 'Do we really want to take Mum's offer?'

'I do,' said Maurice, 'and if you ask me, we'd be mad not to.'

'Yeah, and as my Sue said, it'll give us the chance to set up our own business.'

'What about you, Chris?'

'You seem to have made up your minds, so I don't suppose I've got much choice.'

'Right, the decision's made,' Danny said.

Moving to the telephone, he dialled the number. They all listened, hearing only one side of the conversation, but even from that it soon became clear that Danny had struck a deal.

He finally replaced the receiver, turning to say, 'We're on. There's only the legal stuff to be sorted now.'

'Blimey, you were right, Danny. Talk about fate,' Bob said.

Only Yvonne and Chris looked doubtful, Chris saying, 'That's it then. Once it's all finalised, we're all going, but it still doesn't seem right to leave Mum.'

'I feel the same,' said Yvonne.

'Bloody hell, Yvonne, do you think I'm happy

about it?' Danny snapped. 'But as Bob pointed out, if we don't take Mum's offer we're stuck with nothing. Like him, I'd have to get a job to pay the rent, but doing what? Without any skills I'd be down to labouring on a building site or something like that, and earning shit money. Is that what you want?'

'No, no, of course not, but—'

Before Yvonne had finished speaking, Danny interrupted, turning to look at Chris. 'What about you? Once the money is in place, do you want to come in with me and Bob, or do you want to go it alone?'

'I don't know. I'll need to think about it.'

'Please yourself, but don't take too long about it,' Danny said, obviously fired with enthusiasm as he continued, 'because after telling Mum that we'll accept her offer, me and Bob are going to start looking for some decent premises. Ain't that right, Bob?'

'Yeah, and somewhere else to live.'

Danny glanced at his watch. 'The hour is nearly up so let's get back to Mum's.'

Only Chris hesitated, but Maurice said quietly, 'Come on, Chris. It'll all work out, you'll see. This is a fresh start for all of us, a chance to make something of our lives. I want to start up a little business and if you don't go in with Danny and Bob, you could do the same. If you make it a success, make Mum proud, she's bound to come round.'

Chris still hesitated, but as though Maurice's words had touched his heart, he at last nodded. 'Yeah, you're right. Mum's disgusted with the lot of us and until I can give her something to be proud of, she's never going to forgive me. Not only that, if I can find a business that's close by, I can still keep an eye on her.'

Danny knocked on his mother's door, she opened it and they stepped inside. Chris's eyes flicked along the alley and settled on George's house. So much had happened in such a short time, but it had all started there. Chris shivered, looking swiftly away. He was the last to walk into his mother's house, wondering if it would be for the last time.

Chapter Thirty-seven

By March, everyone was sick of snow. It had been the worst winter that anyone could remember, with the River Thames freezing over in places, but at last a thaw was settling in.

Petula filled a hot-water bottle, firmly screwing on the top before taking it upstairs. She didn't care about the weather, was unaware that in Ivy's garden the tips of daffodils were poking through. Pet's only concern was for her cousin. They had watched her go downhill, until finally, that morning, Steve had put his foot down, insisting that she saw the doctor again. With Ivy in so much pain, Steve had demanded a house call.

Now, as Pet pushed open the bedroom door, she said, 'Here, I've brought you a hot-water bottle. The doctor should be here soon.'

'I bet the old quack wasn't happy about being called out,' Ivy said, but her voice was weak, the pain wearing her down.

Pet tucked the hot-water bottle under the blankets and then heard a knock on the front door. 'That must be him now.'

When she hurried back downstairs, Pet opened the front door to find a young man on the front step, his eyes crinkling at the corners when he smiled. 'Dr Finch is down with the flu. I'm Dr Davidson, his locum.'

'Oh, right, you'd better come in,' Pet said. She led him upstairs, saying, 'My cousin is in a lot of pain. Dr Finch said she has an ulcer, but she's getting worse and the medicine he prescribed doesn't help.'

As they walked into the bedroom, Ivy struggled unsuccessfully to sit up.

'Good morning, Mrs Rawlings,' the doctor said. 'I'm Dr Finch's locum. My name is Dr Davidson, and this young lady tells me that you have an ulcer.'

'Yeah, that's right, and it's bloody killing me.'

'Right, let's take a look at you.'

Pet remained whilst the doctor carried out his examination, and though he frowned, his voice remained impassive as he said, 'I'd like to send you for a few tests. If you have a telephone, I'll ring the hospital now.'

'Tests? What sort of tests?'

'An X-ray, bloods and maybe a barium meal.' He turned brusquely to Pet. 'Do you have a telephone?'

'Yes, it's downstairs.'

He followed Pet, saying as he picked up the

receiver, 'I'll arrange for an ambulance to take Mrs Rawlings to the local hospital. With any luck there'll be one available.'

'What? You want her to go now?'

'Yes, that's right,' he said, hastily dialling the number.

As she picked up on the doctor's urgency, Pet's stomach lurched. 'It . . . it isn't an ulcer?'

The call went through, Pet's question unanswered.

In Drapers Alley, Joan read the letter again before screwing it up and throwing it onto the fire. She didn't care what the council said, because when the time came, she wasn't budging from the alley. It explained why the rest of the houses remained empty, the alley now looking run down and desolate, but until her daughter came home, she was staying put.

Grim-faced, she put on her coat and after tying a headscarf around her head Joan stepped outside. The snow was thawing, the pavement mushy but, deep in thought, she hardly noticed. The sale had gone through on the yard, and after making sure that Chris was paid off, the rest was safely in the bank. Her new will was drawn up and the solicitor wanted her at his office to sign it. She had hated making a will the first time, feeling that it was like tempting fate, but in the end, with Dan going first, fate had been on her side.

It rankled that the boys had done all right from the deal she had struck with them, but she just wanted rid of them and had no choice. Petula was her only concern now – her need to make it up to her daughter. At least when anything happened to her, Joan thought, her daughter would do all right, her new will made out in Petula's favour.

Danny and Bob had started up on their own as builders' merchants, but she had no idea what Maurice was up to. To her annoyance, when old Bill Tweedy retired Chris had bought his shop, her son now living on the corner of Aspen Street to remain within spitting distance. He usually called round on a Wednesday afternoon and, sick of telling him to bugger off, she was glad that the solicitor's appointment coincided with his visit. Joan sighed. Though loath to admit it, she was lonely, sorely tempted at times to let Chris in, but she couldn't do that, not after what he had been involved in.

She had hoped that when her sons left, Petula would show her face, but so far there was no sign of her. Of course it didn't help that Chris's shop was just around the corner, but as it was Danny who had made the threats, she still hoped, still prayed, for her daughter to come home before it was too late.

Few people spoke to Joan, but she had kept herself to herself for years so it wasn't surprising. Yet now, as she turned into Aspen Street, she saw that Betty

Fuller was standing on her doorstep, deep in conversation with her neighbour. They went back years and at one time Betty had been after Dan. He hadn't been interested, and at the time Joan had been thrilled that, instead of Betty, he had chosen her. Thrilled – yes, she'd been thrilled, but now she had lived to regret it.

Betty broke off her conversation when she saw her, but Joan didn't miss the wink that she threw at her neighbour before she spoke. 'Watcha, Joan. We were just talking about Chris and we're wondering how you feel about his friend – you know, the one that works in his shop.'

'Sorry, can't stop,' Joan said.

'You should have a word with him. He's making himself a laughing stock.'

'I don't know what you're talking about,' Joan snapped as she hurried away, yet even so, her curiosity was piqued. Chris, a laughing stock? But why? Oh, what did it matter? She was finished with him, with all of them. All she wanted was her daughter, but it had been so long now, months since Petula had run away. Would she ever come back? Oh, please, God, she must.

Danny was bent over a battered desk, adding up columns in the account book, his tongue sticking out of the corner of his mouth in concentration. Maurice had always handled the accounts and this was new territory for him. At last they balanced and, leaning back, he smiled with satisfaction. They were doing all right, and though it had taken a bit of wrangling, they had managed to hold on to their biggest customer, his order now filled. Chris had told him that his mother had sold the yard as a going concern, and that would mean competition, but so far, with the promise of discounts, they had managed to bring all their old customers with them.

It was a shame that Chris had decided to go it alone, and now Danny's face straightened. In a million years he had never expected Chris to turn soft, buying a piddling little corner shop to be close to their mother. Not only that, he'd begun to hear rumours, ridiculous ones that needed to be snuffed out. Chris was a Draper, a name that still meant something in the borough, and he wasn't going to stand for the local gossip turning his brother, and by association them, into a pervert and a laughing stock.

Danny scowled. He might be out of the porn game and running a truly legit business, but he was still a Draper, still his father's son, and still wanted the respect that the name deserved.

Bob came into the office, grinning widely. 'Dick Larson's had me in stitches. He told me a couple of really good ones.'

'Go on then.'

'What do you call a donkey with three legs?'

'All right, tell me.'

'A wonkey.'

Danny just chuckled, before saying, 'Rubbish. He must have got that one out of a Christmas cracker.'

'All right then. What did the elephant say to the naked man?'

'I dunno.'

'How do you suck up water with that dangly little thing?'

Danny laughed. 'Better.'

'A snail goes into a pub, but it's against policy to serve snails so the barman kicks him out. A year later the snail comes in again, looks up at the barman and says, "What did you do that for?"'

This time Danny roared. 'Yeah, I like that one.'

Bob saw the account book lying open on the desk. 'How are we doing?'

'Considering that we've only been up and running for just over a month, we're doing fine, but I want to talk to you about Chris and the local gossip.'

'Danny, I've told you, it's rubbish.'

'I know it's rubbish, but someone is spreading this shit and I ain't standing for it. We may have left the alley but we're still Drapers and the locals need to remember that.'

'Yeah, well, once we've had a quiet word in a few people's ears, it's bound to stop.'

'It'd better,' Danny growled.

'Talking about the alley, I wonder how Mum's doing.'

'Chris said she still won't let him in, but he'll keep trying.'

'Maybe Yvonne could give it a go.'

'She had a rough time when the baby came early. She isn't ready for a run-in with Mum.'

'Sending Sue round would be a waste of time. Those two have never seen eye to eye. I suppose we'll just have to leave it to Chris to make a breakthrough. Still, at least Yvonne and Sue are getting on well, the pair of them as thick as thieves now.'

'Sue was brilliant when Yvonne came home with Danny junior, and with him being so tiny, Yvonne was a nervous wreck. It was good of Sue to help out, and anyway, with us living in the upstairs flat, and you down, it's just as well they get on.'

Bob grinned. 'It was a bit of luck finding that house, and with it already divided into two flats, it's ideal. Sue prefers it to Drapers Alley, and the kids love the garden.'

Danny yawned. 'He may have been early, but my boy was screaming his lungs out last night.'

'Yeah, I heard him and it's a wonder Maurice didn't hear him in Devon. Has he been in touch with you yet?'

'No, but at least I hear how he's getting on through you. I think he blames me for everything and, to be honest, he's right.'

'He'll come round. Last time he rang me he said

that Oliver has taken to country life like a duck to water.'

Despite the lack of sleep, Danny smiled. He knew how it felt to have a son now, his boy his pride and joy. He had never wanted kids, but that had changed the instant he saw Danny junior. The urge to find Garston, to take revenge, had left him, his one desire now to provide a secure future for his son. At one time he had let depression swamp him, and he was still ashamed of his weakness. He was back to his old self now, and he'd show his son what it meant to be a Draper. Legit or not, he would make sure the name still brought the respect it deserved.

'Customers,' Bob said.

Danny closed the account book and, Bob ahead of him, left the tiny office. Yes, he thought, they were doing all right, the proceeds from Wimbledon setting them all up, but there was still something unfinished. They still hadn't found Petula.

Chapter Thirty-eight

Pet's stomach churned as she listened to Steve. It couldn't be true. It just couldn't.

'Does . . . does Ivy know?'

'Yes, she knows.'

Pet had to ask, swallowing deeply before saying, 'How . . . how long?'

'From what the doctor said, there's no way of knowing. It could be weeks, months. If it had been found earlier, there may have been a chance, but it's too far advanced now and it . . . it's spread to her bones.'

'Can't they do something . . . anything?'

'No,' Steve replied, his eyes moist and, raising his arm, he cuffed at them with the sleeve of his jumper.

Pet was crying now too. Ivy had been in hospital for two weeks, undergoing test after test, but she had never expected this – never expected to hear that her cousin was dying. Since Ivy had taken her in, they had become close, a relationship forming that had been absent in Drapers Alley. She had seen Ivy battling with her pain, trying to pretend that she was fine in front of the boys, always trying to be cheerful. Oh God, the boys! They were going to lose their mother. The thought was unbearable and, sobbing now, Pet buried her face in her hands.

It was quiet for a while, but then Steve said, 'Pet, she wants to come home. I tried to talk her out of it, but she won't have it. The thing is, she's going to need looking after. I know you're only fifteen, and it's a lot to ask, but do you think you could take it on?'

'I'll try,' Pet said, rubbing the tears from her cheeks.

'You'll have a bit of help with the district nurse calling in every day.'

'What about Harry and Ernie?'

'They'll be at school most of the day, and . . . and maybe I can get one of the neighbours to give you a hand, perhaps take them on after school until I come home.'

'Yes, that could work.'

They were quiet again then, both with their own thoughts. Pet was still reeling with shock, fighting tears. Without hesitation she had agreed to look after Ivy, but had no idea what to do, what care her cousin would need. She owed it to Ivy, wanted to help her cousin to repay her kindness, but what if she made a mess of it? What if she couldn't cope? With a sob she prayed for strength – strength to be there for Ivy and the strength to watch her die.

Phil had just cuddled him again and Chris was red-faced as he served a customer. The two old biddies standing in the queue were looking at them with disgust, whispering, and Chris knew that he'd been a fool, an idiot, for agreeing to let Phil work with him in the shop.

No matter how many times he warned Phil he was ignored. But determined to have it out once and for all, Chris waited until the shop emptied. Then he said, 'Phil, you've got to stop cuddling me in front of the customers.'

'Not this again. Look, when you said I could work with you, I thought it meant we were bringing our relationship out into the open at last, but instead you're acting like you're ashamed of me.'

'Don't be silly, of course I'm not. It's just that we're running a business and cuddling me in front of the customers isn't . . . well, it doesn't look very professional.'

'Professional my arse. You're ashamed of me, I know you are. Go on, admit it.'

'I'm not ashamed of you.'

'Well, how come you haven't told your brothers about me, or your mother?'

'I will. I'm just waiting for the right time.'

'Yeah, that's what you always say, but that time never comes.'

The bell above the door tinkled, another customer coming into the shop. 'Twenty Woodbines, please,' the young man said.

'Coming up, darlin',' Phil said, smiling coquettishly. 'My, ain't you handsome.'

Chris knew that it was a tactic to make him jealous, but it didn't work. The young man obviously wasn't interested – few would be – his smile nervous as he paid for his cigarettes before almost fleeing the shop.

Chris shook head with exasperation. Since their relationship began, Phil had fiercely fought to keep him, looking after him, spoiling him, seeing to his every wish – except one. In front of the customers, Phil continued to touch him, to make it obvious that they were a couple. Chris knew that he was fighting a losing battle. From now on it would be impossible to hide it. His secret was out.

Two days after Pet promised to care for her cousin, Ivy came home, and at midday, as the ambulance drew up outside, Pet ran to the gate, watching as Ivy was lifted from the back. Steve had been up since the crack of dawn, clearing the path to make it safe before rushing off to work. He hadn't wanted to go in, but the animals still needed tending, the farmer saying kindly that he could finish early.

'Hello, Pet,' Ivy said. 'It's lovely to be home.'

Pet fought tears. She couldn't cry. For Ivy's sake she had to be strong, but oh, it was going to be so hard. Forcing a smile she said, 'It's about time you showed up. I made a pot of tea ages ago and it must be stone cold by now.'

'You'll just have to make another one,' Ivy quipped as Pet ran ahead to open the front door.

'Where do you want her?' one of the men asked as they carried Ivy over the threshold.

'Oi, I ain't an imbecile and I can talk for myself,' Ivy said. 'If you ain't a pair of weaklings, you can carry me up to my boudoir.'

'Oh, your boudoir is it? Right, Your Majesty,' and on that light note, they did indeed carry the chair upstairs.

Pet had hurried ahead, and in Ivy's bedroom she threw back the blankets, watching nervously as her cousin was lifted out of the chair and into the bed. Ivy seemed in good spirits, laughing with the ambulance men, and though she looked haggard, thin, she didn't seem to be in pain.

'Right, Pet, show these pair of clowns out and then you can make me a fresh pot of tea.'

'It sounds like you've got yourself a handful, miss,' said one as Pet led them downstairs.

'I heard that,' Ivy called, 'and the only handful I've got is for my hubby.'

The men laughed, but no sooner had Pet closed the door behind them than she had to open it again, finding the district nurse on the step. The woman was tubby, cheery-looking with round pink cheeks and a kind smile as she stepped inside.

'Hello, ducks,' she said. 'Now where's my patient?'

'This way,' said Pet, leading her upstairs. 'Ivy has only just arrived home.'

'Yes, I know, I passed the ambulance men on the path,' and as they walked into the bedroom Ivy received an equally cheery greeting. 'Hello, ducks. I'm Nurse Alwood, but you can call me Gloria.'

'Watcha,' said Ivy.

'I was just about to make a cup of tea – would you like one, er, Gloria?'

'Yes, please, and biscuits if you've got some. I've not stopped this morning and I could eat a scabby horse.'

Smiling, Pet left the room, her heart a little lighter. She liked Nurse Alwood, and with her help, maybe she really would be able to cope.

'All right, Charlie, I'm going,' Danny said, scowling as he walked out of the pub. He might not be going after Garston, but in his own borough he wanted the Drapers' reputation to remain intact.

When he'd first entered the pub, Danny had

thrown his weight about, but the landlord, Charlie Parkinson, had intervened. As an old friend of his father's, Danny allowed it. However, he'd been unprepared for what Charlie had told him.

He went back to the yard, saying as he went in, 'Bob, can you manage on your own for a bit longer?'

'I suppose so, but what did you find out?'

'From what Charlie told me, I don't think it's just rumours.'

'It can't be true, Danny. You know Chris, and as I've said before, it's got to be rubbish.'

'I'll soon find out. I'm going to see for myself.'

'Maybe you should leave it, Danny. If it's true, which I doubt, and Chris wanted us to know, he'd have told us.'

'You must be joking. Chris must be sick, a pervert, and I'm not standing for it, Bob. We're Drapers, but he's turning us into laughing stocks.'

'Why don't we lock up for an hour and I'll come with you? I can just stick a note on the gates to say that we're closed for lunch.'

'No, we can't afford to turn customers away. I'll be as quick as I can,' Danny said, turning to leave before Bob could argue.

Danny took his car and in ten minutes he was pulling up outside his brother's shop. He had never understood why Chris had wanted to go it alone, buying a poky corner shop that was unlikely to show much of a profit, but if the rumours were true, maybe this explained it. He and Bob had been so busy setting up the yard that they had seen little of Chris, this the first time he'd been to the premises.

He got out of his car, but before entering the shop Danny looked through the window. Chris was behind the counter, but he couldn't see anyone else, so moving to the door, he threw it open, hearing a bell tinkling above his head.

'Hello, Chris.'

'Danny, what are you doing here?'

'I've been hearing rumours, gossip, talk about you being a pervert. Where's this so-called assistant?'

Chris was red-faced, blustering as he said, 'I don't know what you're talking about.'

A curtain was pulled back, and as a woman walked through holding two cups of tea, Danny blanched. She was old, at least sixty, her face lined with wrinkles, and though he had thought himself prepared, Danny found his stomach lurching. Bile rose in his throat. No, no, this couldn't be right – Chris couldn't be sleeping with that!

'Here you are, love,' she said, holding a cup of tea out to Chris, 'and I've made us both a sandwich.'

'For fuck's sake, Chris, tell me it isn't her.'

She turned, looked at him, puzzled. 'Who are you? Chris, what's going on?'

Chris drew in a great gulp of air, then said, 'Danny, this is Phil, my girlfriend. Well, it's Philomena really, but that's a bit of a mouthful. Phil, this is my brother Danny.'

'Oh, hello, ducks. Nice to meet you.'

Danny ignored her greeting, instead spitting out, 'You must be out of your mind, Chris. Get rid of her, and now. I ain't having you turning us into laughing stocks.'

Chris stared at him, their eyes locking, a range of emotions crossing his features, but then his eyes narrowed and, shaking his head, he said, 'No, Danny. I've been seeing Phil for years, hiding her, sneaking around to her place, but not any more.'

'Leave it out. Look at her. She's older than Mum.' Danny paused, frowning. 'I know Mum didn't show us any affection. Is that it? Have you got some sort of mother complex? Is that old hag some sort of replacement?'

'No, of course not and stop insulting her. I love Phil, and whether you like it or not, she's my choice. You can either accept her, or you can get out.'

'Right, if that's the way you want it, you're no brother of mine. I'll make sure that everyone knows it too – that as far as the rest of us are concerned, you are no longer a Draper.'

'That's fine with me.'

Danny spun on his heel, leaving the shop without a backward glance. He still felt sick to his stomach, and knew that Bob would feel the same. With George still missing, Maurice in Devon, and Chris out of the picture, it left just two of them – two of the Draper boys. Chris had made fools of them, but as he'd told his brother, he'd put it about that they were finished with him, and then, if anyone so much as looked at them the wrong way, they'd suffer for it. He and Bob were still Drapers, a name that still meant something, a name to be feared, and a name that he passed proudly on to his son.

Chapter Thirty-nine

Spring turned into early summer, and Ivy was still clinging to life. For most of the time she was barely lucid, the nurse warning Pet that when the medication had to be increased again, Ivy would probably slip into a coma. Pet had seen Ivy's agony and thought it would be a blessing. At least her cousin wouldn't be suffering any more.

Whilst Ivy slept, Pet spent a lot of time thinking, her mind often turning to Garston and that poor little girl in the film. She was still swamped with guilt that she had done nothing to help her, but doubted that she was the only child who had fallen into Garston's hands. As always, fear of the man held her back, but gradually an inkling of an idea began to form, one that grew more and more compelling.

Ivy turned her head, her voice a rasp as she struggled to speak. 'I deserve this, Pet. The guilt caused this. It's been eating me up.'

Pet shook her head. Of course Ivy didn't deserve

this, but she often said strange things, the drug sometimes making her hallucinate. She always made a supreme effort for Harry and Ernie, but even that was beyond her now, and lately, when Steve sat with her, she didn't always recognise him.

Ivy groaned and Pet glanced at the clock, hoping that Gloria would soon arrive. She was a wonderful nurse, offering so much support, and Pet knew she couldn't have coped without her.

'Pet, did you hear me? I said I deserve this.'

'Of course you don't. Rest, love, don't try to speak. Gloria will be here soon, and the doctor to give you your medication.'

'It'll knock me out again, you know it will. I've got to tell you now before it's too late.' Ivy gasped then, unable to help crying out in pain.

'It's all right, Ivy, it's all right.'

'I killed him, Pet.'

'You're dreaming, Ivy. It isn't real.'

'No, it isn't a dream. I . . . I killed George.'

Pet shook her head. Poor Ivy, these hallucinations were nightmarish.

'It was after he attacked your dad,' Ivy said, the pain causing her to clench her teeth in agony before she was able to continue. 'I guessed your dad had money stashed and as George ran off with nothing, I hoped he'd come back to get it. With this in mind I waited until you all came home from the hospital that night and spiked your chocolate drinks to make sure you slept soundly.'

'Stop it, Ivy, please. This can't be real – it can't.'

'It's the truth,' Ivy insisted, groaning before she began to speak again. 'I was right about George too. He did come back and . . . and I killed him. It was in your mother's bathroom and . . . and I took all the money.'

Pet frowned. Ivy was talking about the past, not the present, but it couldn't be true, it just couldn't. 'You're hallucinating, you've got to be.'

'No, no, it's real, it happened. He's in the factory.'

'Who's in the factory?'

'George . . . he . . . he's in one of the big vats and I covered him with coal.'

Pet slumped with relief. The factory had been closed for years. There wouldn't be any vats in there, let alone coal. 'There's nothing in the factory, Ivy. It's empty.'

'Pet, please, listen to me. It was a jam factory and the vats are still there. I found coal too, in a bunker. Oh God,' she cried, 'this pain, I can't stand it . . .'

As Ivy gripped her hand, Pet's mind was reeling. Ivy seemed lucid; her eyes, though filled with pain, were clear. 'No, Ivy, please, tell me it isn't true.'

'Th-this house. I didn't get a council exchange, Pet. I bought it with some of the money I stole from the box. The rest is in—'

There was a knock on the street door, Pet fleeing

the room to answer it. She pulled it open to see Gloria and the doctor. Their faces creased as they looked at her, both brushing past to hurry upstairs. In a daze, Pet walked into the sitting room, shaking her head in anguish at what she now believed was the truth.

'Goodness, Petula, when I saw your face I thought that Ivy had gone,' Gloria said as she bustled into the room. 'The doctor is giving her morphine now, increasing the dose. Oh, my dear, don't cry. I know how hard it is when the end is near, but you've been so brave, so strong.'

Pet's throat was so constricted that she couldn't speak. She'd been looking after Ivy, caring for her, a woman who had killed her brother. Oh God, she couldn't stand it, she had to get away. With a sob she fled the room, running upstairs to thrust a few things into a bag.

As Pet ran from her room and onto the landing she almost collided with Gloria, the woman calling as she thrust past her to run downstairs. 'Wait . . . where are you going?'

Pet didn't answer. She flung open the street door, and only stopped running to draw breath as she headed for the train station. It had been ages since Pet had been to the village post office, but Steve had refused to take anything for her keep, so the money she had drawn out had remained in her purse.

When Pet reached the station she found that there

was more than enough to buy her a ticket to London, but it was over half an hour before the train was due. Desolately she sat in the waiting room, her bag clutched to her chest.

Her mind churned and Pet was surprised to find that she was fighting guilt – guilt that she had abandoned Ivy. What would happen to her cousin now? No, no, she'd be all right. The nurse was there, and the doctor. They'd sort something out, and anyway, it was likely that Ivy was now in a coma so they could have her admitted to hospital.

Pet's eyes filled with tears. *Ivy, Ivy, why did you do it? Why did you kill George?* Money, she had mentioned money, his life snuffed out to buy Ivy a house. Oh, she knew that George was no angel – that he had attacked her father – but despite that he was still her brother and she loved him. *Oh God, he's dead, my brother's dead! Ivy murdered him!*

Pet was barely able to hold herself together, and when the train pulled in she climbed into an empty carriage, sobbing as she slumped onto a seat.

It was some time before Pet stopped crying, but as she drew in juddering breaths, her mind began to clear. Without thought she had purchased a ticket to London, yet how could she go back? She had been with Ivy for over six months, so intent on her cousin's care that she had tried to put the past behind her, to forget her family and what Jack Garston had done to her. Yet during the many hours she had sat by Ivy's side, her mind would wander and she was unable to hold back the memories – the sickening things she had seen and heard replaying again and again in her mind.

She had tried to focus on her future, on what she wanted to do with her life, and a tentative idea formed. Now, sickened by Ivy's confession, her determination strengthened and Pet knew what she wanted to do. It would take her a long time to reach her goal, and in the meantime she would have to find a job, along with somewhere to live.

Her eyes closed, fighting tears again. First there was George – poor George, thrown in a vat and covered with coal. She had to tell the police, had to tell her mother. If nothing else, George deserved a decent burial. Pet's mind churned. God, what would happen to Ivy? But Ivy was dying, might already be in a coma. Did Steve know? Did he have a hand in George's death?

Finally, unable to face the questions that plagued her mind, and mentally exhausted, she slept.

Pet woke with a start as the train pulled into the station, groggily climbing out of the carriage to stand lost, alone, on the platform. People rushed past her, barged against her, and at last her feet moved.

After handing in her ticket, Pet's eyes roamed the station, and though she wasn't yet in Battersea, her stomach clenched with fear. Danny was in London – Danny and his threat. She licked her lips, her throat dry, and seeing a café on the far side of the main concourse she headed towards it.

Pet ordered a Coke and then carried it to an empty table by the window where she sat, bleakly looking out of the window. After the stillness of Kent, Pet found the hustle and bustle of the station, the cacophony of sounds, intimidating. She knew she couldn't sit there for ever, but so great was her problem that her mind refused to function.

A voice spoke in her ear and as Pet spun round her arm shot out, knocking over the Coke, the liquid running across the Formica-topped table before spilling onto the floor. The colour drained from Pet's cheeks.

'Mrs Fuller, what are you doing here?'

'I could ask the same of you,' Betty Fuller said, moving forward with a cloth in her hand to wipe the table. 'I work here, love, have done for years. It's a short hop from Clapham Junction station and the hours ain't bad.' She eyed Pet's bag. 'On your way home, are you?'

Unable to think of an explanation Pet sputtered, 'Er, yes.'

'You'll find some changes,' Betty said, her eyes flicking behind her. 'I'd better get a move on or the boss will be after me.'

'Wait, Mrs Fuller. What do you mean by changes?'

'Well, to start with, your mum's the only one left in Drapers Alley.'

'But why? What happened to my brothers?'

'I ain't privy to how it came about, but from what I've heard, Danny and Bob have set up a builders' yard just off Northcote Road, and Chris, well, the least said about him the better. If you ask me, it's disgusting.'

Pet's stomach lurched. Did Mrs Fuller know about the pornographic films her brother had made? But no, that had involved more than just Chris. The woman's eyes flicked behind her again, but as she went to move away, Pet clutched her arm. 'Please, tell me what Chris has done.'

'He's got the corner shop now and has moved his woman friend in to work with him. She's at least sixty, old enough to be his grandmother, and from what I heard, your other brothers have disowned him. Now look, I've got to go.'

As Betty Fuller bustled off, Pet's head was spinning. They had gone, they had all gone. She could go home.

Nervously, Pet approached Drapers Alley. She had been told the houses, all but one, were empty, yet still her heart thudded with fear.

For a moment she hesitated outside the street door. What if Betty Fuller had lied – what if her mother wasn't alone? Come on, she told herself, show a bit of spunk. You've come this far and nobody would have dared to call it Rapers Alley if they were still around.

Her hand slowly lifted to the small lion's-head knocker, and after rapping three times she involuntarily stepped back a pace.

The door slowly opened. 'Is it really you?'

'Yes, Mum,' she said, and seeing the smile of welcome on her mother's face, her eyes filled with tears as she stepped inside. What she had to tell her mother would break her heart.

'Oh, Petula, I can't believe you've come home. I've been hoping, praying, but when the boys couldn't find you I began to think that, like George, I'd never see you again.'

'Mum, I've got something dreadful to tell you. You . . . you'd better sit down.'

'If it's to do with the stuff that your father and brothers got up to, I already know all about it.'

'Dad! Dad was mixed up in making those films?'

'Yes, and from the start. Now come on, put that bag down and I'll make you a nice cup of tea. Your room is waiting for you and I've done it up a bit. Oh, Petula, I still can't believe that you're here,' she cried, her eyes moist with emotion as she bustled into the kitchen.

Pet was still in shock as she slumped onto a chair. Her dad, her father, mixed up in pornography too. Her last illusion was shattered, her memories of the man she had adored, forever tainted. Pet rubbed both hands over her face, only looking up as her mother came back into the room.

'The kettle's on. Now come on, tell me where you've been and what you've been up to.'

'Oh, Mum, I don't know where to start.'

'Try the beginning.'

'I've been staying with Ivy in Kent. She took me in, but then she became ill – really ill – and when I left, she was dying. That's not all, Mum,' Pet said, dreading this. 'It's George, Mum. He . . . he's dead.'

'What? Oh, no, Pet. No . . .'

Chapter Forty

It had been a fraught seventy two hours. The police had been told, George's body found, the questions endless, but at last Pet and her mother were alone.

'Pet, a long time ago, I found blood on the bathroom floor, and I . . . I thought that Chris had done something to George, that he had hurt him, but I never expected this. For over a year my George was lying in that factory. I should have known. I should have felt something. It proves what a useless mother I am.'

'No, Mum, that isn't true.'

'Yes it is, and not only that, I can't believe that that Ivy has got away with it. Sod's law, that's what it is. The rotten cow went and died just when the police went to question her.'

'I know, Mum, I know,' Pet said, yet in reality hating herself – hating her feelings. When the police told them that Ivy had died, she actually cried, was mourning her cousin and the closeness they had shared. Yet even as she mourned, Pet felt betrayed and knew that she would never be able to forgive Ivy for killing George. How could she feel like this about Ivy? Part sorrow, part anger, part love, part hate?

'Do you think Steve was telling the truth? Do you think he knew nothing about it?'

Pet chewed on her lower lip. She had asked herself the same question, but felt she knew the answer. 'I got to know him well, Mum, and he's a lovely man. I don't think he had a clue and I dread to think how he's taking it. He thought the world of Ivy, and it must be tearing him apart to know that he was married to a . . . a murderess.'

'Will you go back to see him?'

'No, I don't think so.'

'I treated you badly. All I cared about was your father and I didn't show you an ounce of sympathy, but you're all I've got left, Petula. You will stay, won't you?'

'Yes, of course I will.'

'There's something I haven't told you. It's coming down, Petula. Drapers Alley is coming down. Along with the factory it's going to be demolished and a housing estate is going to take its place.'

'When, Mum?'

'I dunno, but soon, I think. I'm just glad that you came home before I had to move out.'

Pet was pleased about the factory, knowing that

every time she looked at it she would remember that her brother's body had been dumped there. She knew that Linda had been informed, could guess her reaction, but it was still awful to know that George had died without ever seeing his daughter. Oh, why was it that when someone died you only remembered the good times, the good things? She could remember laughter, celebrations, every birthday, every Christmas a time when the family came together, but all that had changed when just over a year ago, her illusions had been shattered.

'Do the boys know about the alley?'

'I haven't told them. In fact, other than Chris pestering me, I hadn't seen them until the police told them about George.'

'They weren't too happy that you wouldn't let them in.'

'I told them that I didn't want to see their faces again, and I meant it.'

'What about . . . about the funeral?'

'There's to be a post mortem before George's body can be released. I can't do anything, make any arrangements, until then, and anyway, I don't want them there.'

Pet heard the bitterness in her mother's voice, saw the hardness in her eyes. It had been six months since she had seen her brothers, but the pain remained raw. She knew that she was safe now, that Danny wasn't after her, but like her mother, she still didn't want to see them. They would be at the funeral; there would be nothing her mother could do to keep them away. Her seeing them again was inevitable.

When there was a knock on the street door, Pet had been so deep in thought that she jumped.

'What now?' her mother moaned as she moved across the room to open it. Then she said, 'No, Chris, you can't come in, but you can answer me one question before you bugger off. When George went missing and I found blood on the bathroom floor, why did you lie about it? It must have been George's, I know that now.'

'Blimey, Mum, that was ages ago. Why bring it up now?'

'Because I thought you had hurt George, injured him, and that you were covering it up.'

'Me! You thought it was me? No, Mum, when you found that blood I just assumed that George had been injured in that fight with Dad. You were already upset, in an awful state, so I just said the first thing that came into my head.'

'George wasn't injured, he was already dead.'

'Don't, Mum. I know that now and the thought makes my guts churn. Please, can I come in? I'd like to see Pet.'

'No you can't. Like me, she doesn't want anything to do with you. Now bugger off back to your tart, or should I say your grandmother,' and with that, she slammed the door. 'Honestly, Pet, I never used to swear, but now I even swear in my thoughts. Everyone is talking about Chris and that old woman he's living with. They're laughing at him and because he's my son, at me. Oh, I'll be glad to move, Pet, glad to be away from here.'

'Where will we live?'

'I dunno, love. The council will have to offer us something, and to be honest, I can't wait to go. This place holds nothing but bad memories and the further away we're housed the better.'

An hour passed, Pet helping her mother with the housework that she refused to leave, insisting that even if the house was going to be demolished she had no intention of lowering her standards. As they worked, Pet found that her mother's fussy cleaning, every nook and cranny getting a thorough dusting, kept her mind occupied, and for the first time began to understand her mother. This must be why she always worked like a beaver, all her mind and energies on the housework, her fears and worries at bay as long as she continued to scrub, polish and dust.

Once again there was a knock on the door, her mother's face reddening with anger. 'That'll be Chris again and I'm sick of telling him to bugger off.' With that she marched to the door, flinging it open. 'I told you to— Steve, what are you doing here?'

'I had to come. Can I come in?'

'I suppose so.'

Pet rose to her feet as Steve walked in, horrified by how haggard he looked. She tensed, expecting him to have a go at her, but instead he broke down, sobbing as he said, 'When . . . when the police told me, I couldn't believe it. Oh God, I'm so sorry, Joan. I didn't know, honest I didn't.'

'Yeah, that's what Petula said.' As Steve continued to sob, Joan said, 'Sit down before you fall down.'

It took Steve some time to calm down, but when he finally did, he said, 'Ivy told me about her childhood, about Dan taking her father's money. I knew she was bitter, but why kill George?'

'What are you talking about?' Joan asked. 'What money?'

Steve drew in a gulp of air. 'Ivy said that Dan and her father had money stashed away, money that should have been her mother's.'

'This is news to me, Steve. If you'd told me before I found out what a bastard my husband was, I wouldn't have believed you. Now, though, I feel like I was married to a stranger, that the man I thought I knew didn't exist.'

'Yeah, that's how I feel about Ivy,' Steve said, his voice rising to a strangled cry, 'but she's dead, my Ivy's dead, and I don't know how I'm going to cope with the boys.'

'Oh, Steve,' Pet cried. 'I'm sorry that I ran off like

that, but . . . but when Ivy told me that she . . . that she had killed George, I was in a bit of a state.'

Steve fought to pull himself together, his voice calmer when he answered, 'Of course you were, and no wonder. I don't blame you, Pet, for running off or for telling the police.'

'Where are the boys, Steve? Who's looking after them?'

'They're with a neighbour. I know I shouldn't have left them, but at the moment I'm in no fit state to look after them. Pet, please, will you come back? They're fond of you, they . . . they need you.'

'She'll do no such thing. My daughter is staying with me.'

'It's all right, Mum,' Pet said. She then turned to Steve. 'I'm sorry, really I am, but living with you wouldn't be, well, appropriate, and not only that, I can't leave my mother, not now, and there's still the funeral.'

'I know, and I'm sorry, I shouldn't have asked. I'm not thinking straight and it was daft.'

'What about the rest of the money? Have you found it?' Joan snapped.

'What are you talking about?'

'Ivy killed George for money. She murdered my son to buy the house you live in. Tell him, Petula, tell him what Ivy confessed to you before she died.'

And so Pet did, Steve's eyes, red from crying,

widening. 'I didn't know. I thought we'd got an exchange – that our house is council property.'

'Don't give me that. If it belongs to the council, what about the rent?'

'I can answer that,' Pet said. Her mother was so bitter, so hard, taking her angst out on Steve. 'I lived with Ivy for over six months and I know that she handled all the finances.'

'That's true,' Steve said. 'I always left the running of the house to Ivy. I just stumped up my wages and she paid all the bills, which I assumed included the rent.' Steve then lowered his head, raising both hands to bury his face. For a while he was quiet, but then he looked up, saying, 'If the house was bought on money that Ivy stole from you, there's only one thing I can do. I'll have to sell it to pay you back.'

'No, Steve, no, you can't do that. It's the boys' home. If you sell it, you'll have nowhere to live,' Pet protested.

'Oh yes he can. Ivy stole that money and I want it back.'

It was too much for Pet and she surged to her feet, glaring at her mother. 'Hasn't there been enough pain? Enough death, enough hate and anger. You don't need the money, Mum. From what you've told me, you did well on the sale of the yard and have you forgotten that the money Ivy took was made from porn? I don't want anything to do with it. The thought of it makes me sick. So tell me, do you really want it back? Do you really want to take Harry and Ernie's home? Because if you do, if you're so bitter and twisted that you'd make two innocent children and their father homeless, I'm going, and this time I won't be coming back.'

Her mother was gawking whilst Pet's shoulders heaved with emotion. With a sob she ran from the room, dashing upstairs to fling herself across her bed. Oh God, when would it end?

Pet's door opened and her mother came into the room. She stiffened, expecting a tirade, but instead the bed dipped and she found herself in her mother's arms.

'Petula, I'm so sorry, really I am. I've been so wrapped up in anger, so disgusted at what your father and my sons did to make money, that my mind has become bitter and twisted. When you came home I was so happy to see you, but then you had to tell me about George and, well, it all started up again. I know he was a bad 'un, but he was still my son. She killed him, Pet, Ivy killed him, and I can't stand it that she got away with it.'

Pet clung to her mother. 'No, Mum, it's me who should be sorry. You've been through so much and no wonder it's made you bitter, but Ivy didn't get away with it. She told me that the guilt had eaten at her, sure that it had caused the cancer that took her life. She suffered, Mum, months of dreadful pain before she died.'

'It's no more than she deserved.'

'Mum, please . . .'

'Oh, Pet, take no notice of me. I've been so wrapped up in George that I've forgotten you've been through hell and back too. You didn't deserve it, and it must have been dreadful, but you're all I've got left now. Pet, please don't leave me. As you said, I've got money and I could even buy a little house. We could make a fresh start, just the two of us.'

'Mum, I'm not leaving you. When that . . . that man raped me, it almost destroyed me and, like you, I became bitter. I don't want to go on like this, Mum. I don't want what happened to ruin my life. If I do, he'll have won. Do you really think we can make a fresh start? Do you think we could put the past behind us?'

'I dunno, love, but we could give it a bloody good try. Look, I'll tell you what, after George's funeral we'll make a start. We'll have a look at some property, maybe somewhere out of London. How about the coast? I've always fancied living by the sea.'

'What about Steve? The house?'

'You were right, Pet, and I'm ashamed to say it took you doing your nut to bring me to my senses. I don't want anything to do with it. As you said, it was bought on money from porn and if Steve ever finds the rest of the money, as far as I'm concerned he can keep it. At least it will give the boys a start in life, so something good will come out of it.'

'Oh, Mum,' Pet said impulsively, 'I love you.'

'And I love you too.'

For the first time in her life, her mother had said she loved her, and Pet clung to her waist as tears spurted from her eyes. Yes, they could make a fresh start. They had each other, and as memories returned again of happier times, she wondered if she would ever be able to forgive her bothers – if her mother could ever forgive her sons. Even if they found it impossible, Pet knew that her brothers would be all right. Thanks to their mother they all had businesses. They had their wives, and Chris his woman, albeit in a strange relationship. Pet wondered if she'd ever marry, if she'd ever have children, yet even if she did, now that she knew her mother loved her, needed her, she would always remain central in her life.

Yet before any thoughts of marriage, Pet had an ambition to fulfil. She knew what she wanted to do with her life. She wanted to break the mould – to be a Draper who wasn't involved in crime. When she eventually had children Pet wanted them to be brought up without the stigma she had suffered – to see that they grew up knowing right from wrong, but there was more to it than that. The film that Jack Garston had forced her to watch, the terror she had seen on the little girl's face, would always haunt her. She wanted men like him stopped, but alone Pet knew she could do nothing – that alone she could never make a difference.

During the last few days, for the first time in her life, Pet had had dealings with the police and it had strengthened her ambition. That was what she wanted – to join the force – and as soon as she and her mother were settled she would work towards that goal.

She hugged her mother, feeling a hug in return. 'Come on, Mum, let's go and tell Steve that he can keep the house.'

Her mother smiled at last, nodding in agreement, both leaving the room, both now knowing that when the pain of George's funeral was over, their new life would begin.

Read on for an exclusive extract of Kitty Neale's new book, coming in 2009.

Prologue

The woman was sure her actions were justified, not just for her, but for the others she had managed to harvest into her small circle.

It was 1969 and women had come a long way since the war, gaining independence with the opportunity to take up careers that were once considered outside the norm. Yet to gain promotion they still had to fight every step of the way, to prove themselves as good as men and as capable.

She had been one of these women, her career her life and promotions hard fought. She knew she was considered a feminist by many of her male colleagues, but in truth she wasn't interested in emasculating men, only wanting the same opportunities they all took for granted. She worked equally hard, in truth harder, and by doing so she had increased sales by a far greater percentage than any other sales rep, male or female, that her company employed.

To achieve this she had travelled the country extensively, working long hours and often having to stay overnight in hotels, some grotty, but some comfortable.

She had given her life to her career, sacrificing any chance of marriage, a home, and children, only to be betrayed by a man who professed to love her.

The woman tugged on her small dog's lead as her thoughts raged. The anger consumed her, ate at her, becoming the whole focus of her life. She got up every morning, she went to work, she functioned, but as though on automatic. Since the day it had happened, since he ruined her life, she wanted only one thing. Revenge.

Chapter One

Battersea, South London, 1969

It happened on June 28th – a day that had changed everything. Four years had passed, but for Betty Grayson it was as though it were yesterday. She hadn't moved forward – couldn't move forward, her bitterness a living thing that gnawed away in her brain, the memory of Richard's gut-wrenching words forever fresh in her mind.

Early on Saturday morning there were already signs that it was going to be a hot day, the sunshine drawing Betty out of her poky flat to the park that was on the opposite side of the road. She watched a small, brown dog as it circled a large tree, sniffing the trunk, until finally satisfied, it lifted its leg.

'Treacle, come here,' a woman's voice called.

Betty saw the dog's ears twitch, but intent on fresh pastures the command was ignored. It trotted towards the bench she was sitting on, tail up, and obviously liking what it saw, reared up to place its paws on her lap.

'Oh, I'm so sorry. Get down, Treacle.'

Whilst stroking the dog's head, Betty looked up at his owner. She had seen the elegant, middle-aged woman before, had noticed her dark-brown hair, styled into a French pleat that emphasised her high cheekbones. 'It's all right, I like dogs,' she said.

'Not everyone feels the same and he's a holy terror. I shouldn't have let him off the lead, but I'm trying to get him to obey me,' she chuckled. 'As you can see, it isn't working.'

'He looks so sweet.'

'Don't let that fool you,' the woman said as she sat down. Treacle immediately jumped onto her lap, the woman laughing as he slobbered her face. 'Oh, what am I saying. He's a darling really, but as I said, he won't obey my commands.'

'What breed is he?'

'He's a Bitsa. You know, bits of this and bits of that.'

As Betty smiled, Treacle turned to look at her again, his head cocked and soft brown eyes intent on her face. He then left his owner, moving across to sit on Betty's lap, his tongue soft and wet on her cheek.

'He likes you,' the woman said. 'I'm Val by the way. Valerie Thorn.'

'I'm Betty. Betty Grayson.'

Treacle jumped down, heading for the nearest tree as Val said, 'It's nice to meet you at last. We live in the same block of flats and I've been meaning to introduce myself.'

'Yes, I've seen you. You're on the ground floor.'

'That's right,' Val said, but then seeing that her dog was running off she rose swiftly to her feet. 'Treacle! Treacle,' she called, and saying a quick goodbye she hurried after him.

After this brief interlude, Betty was alone again. Since moving into her flat she had seen Valerie Thorn a few times, but this was the first time they had spoken. It wasn't unusual. Betty had found that living in London was very different from her life in Surrey, the other tenants were usually distant. Ascot Court was a small, purpose-built block of flats and no worse than others she had rented, and at least it faced the park so the outlook was lovely.

Betty had found the pace of life faster in the capital than in the country, all rush, hustle and bustle, with everyone seemingly intent on their own business. She had judged Valerie Thorn on her appearance, her hard veneer, expecting her to be brittle and stand-offish. Instead she had found her warm with a lovely sense of humour and hoped she'd bump into her again.

The park began to fill and Betty surreptitiously eyed two young women as they walked by, guessing

517

them to be around eighteen years old. She frowned, still unable to get used to the way youngsters dressed nowadays. They were both in A-line mini dresses, one blonde, one dark, their hair cut in the geometrical shapes made popular by the hairdresser Vidal Sassoon. Make-up was skilfully applied, and at least they weren't wearing the thick, black, false eyelashes that were at last going out of fashion.

Betty sighed as she stood up. She was fifty-one now, but when a young woman a bit of powder and lipstick were all she'd been allowed to wear, and her clothes had been respectable, in the same style as her mother's. And not only that – what about underwear? These young girls didn't wear vests, or corsets, and worse, sometimes they didn't even wear a brassiere. Betty heaved a sigh. Her daughter, Anne, accused her of being old-fashioned, saying that things were different now. Women were no longer beholden to men, Anne insisted, and were no longer shackled. They had freedom, equality, the means to make their own way in the world.

As Betty walked towards the gate, a young hippy couple came towards her. The girl was wearing a cotton, flowing, maxi dress with long strands of love beads around her neck; her hair was long, fair and with a flower tucked behind her ear. She looked carefree, happy, but when Betty looked at her young man she frowned. He was wearing a colourful kaftan, purple trousers and sandals, his hair almost as long as the girl's. Betty thought he looked disgraceful and if her son dressed like that she would die of shame.

The couple were intent on each other as they passed, their faces wreathed in smiles, and now Betty felt a surge of envy. They were in love. She had felt like that once – just once in her life, but oh, what a fool she had been – a blind, stupid fool.

Betty saw the red mini as soon as she left the park and as she approached it, her daughter climbed out of the car. It never ceased to amaze her that Anne had her own car – that she could drive – something she would never have dreamed of achieving as a young woman and something she still couldn't master. Of course when she was Anne's age few women drove, in fact, unless very well off, a car was a rarity. When she had Richard she'd been eighteen years old and had felt fortunate to have a bicycle, one that she rode to the local village, the basket on the front crammed with local produce when she cycled home. *Home*. Her stomach lurched. No, she couldn't think about it, not when Anne was standing there, a bright smile on her face.

'Hi, Mum. I can't stay long but I thought I'd pop round to see how you're doing.'

'I'd hardly call driving from Farnham, popping round,' Betty said as they walked into the flats where climbing two flights of stairs, she opened her front door.

Anne followed her in, her face dropping as she took in the small living room. 'Oh, Mum, this is almost as bad as your last place.'

'It has a nice outlook and after the pittance I got as a settlement, it's all I can afford.'

'Please, Mum, don't start. Every time I come to see you it's the same old thing.'

Betty clamped her lips together. Her daughter had always been a daddy's girl and despite everything, quick to Richard's defence. Betty knew that if she said any more Anne would leave and as she hadn't seen her since she moved into the flat, it was the last thing she wanted. She forced the parody of a smile, asking, 'What would you like to drink?'

'A bottle of Coke if you've got one.'

'Yes, of course I have,' Betty assured as she went through to her tiny kitchenette. Coca Cola was something Anne always asked for on her rare visits so she always kept a couple of bottles in the fridge for just such an occasion. She found the bottle opener, snapped off the top, and wondered as she returned to the living room if Anne had seen her brother. 'Have you heard from Mark?'

'Not for a while. He's too busy with his latest conquest.'

'Like father like son.'

'Mum,' warned Anne.

As soon as the words left her mouth, Betty had regretted them, but it was hard to stay silent in the face of her daughter's loyalty to Richard. She felt that like her, Anne should hate her father for what he had done – that she should be on *her* side, but instead Anne had refused to cut him out of her life. When it happened, Anne had been twenty-five, living away from home in a flat share with another young woman. Her son, Mark, had been twenty-eight, a surveyor and buying his own mews house, but unlike Anne he'd been sympathetic, severing all ties with his father. For that Betty was thankful, but with a busy career she rarely saw her son these days.

'How's Anthony?' Betty enquired, hoping that asking about Anne's boyfriend would mollify her daughter.

'He's still pushing to get married, but I'm happy to stay as we are. I mean, what's the point? It's only a ring and a piece of paper.'

Betty managed to hold her tongue this time. When she met Anne's boyfriend eighteen months ago they had moved in together. She had been shocked to the core, glad that she no longer lived in Farnham for her neighbours to witness her shame. It had also surprised her that according to Anne, her father didn't object, but as he had lived in sin until their divorce came through, he was hardly an example.

'What about children? You're twenty-nine now.'

'I'm up for promotion and a baby would ruin that. I'm happy to stay as we are.'

'You could still become pregnant. If that happens, surely you'll marry?'

'I'm on the pill so there's no chance of unwanted babies. Anyway, I'm not a hundred per cent sure that I want to spend the rest of my life with Tony. Living together is ideal. It's like a trial marriage and if things don't work out we can both walk away without regrets.'

Despite herself, Betty found that she envied her daughter. There had been no trial marriage for her – no chance to find out that her husband was a womaniser before he put a ring on her finger. Divorce had been frowned on too, so when she married Richard she'd expected it to be for life. Instead at forty-seven years old she'd been cruelly discarded as though Richard had thrown out an old, worn-out coat.

'Mum, I've got to go.'

'But you've only just got here.'

'I know, but Tony and I have booked a holiday to Spain and I need a couple of outfits. I couldn't find anything swish in Farnham, so I'm off to Selfridges.'

'Spain! You're going abroad?'

'Yes, but only for a week. We got a good price on a flight with Laker Airways.'

'You're . . . you're flying?'

'Don't look so shocked, Mum. I know your idea of a holiday is a caravan in Margate, but things are changing nowadays and more and more people are going abroad. I doubt I'll see you before we get back, but I'll send you a postcard.'

Anne then swallowed the last of her drink, picked up her bag, and left in a whirlwind before Betty got the chance to say a proper goodbye. With a small wave her daughter was gone, hurrying down the stairs while Betty managed to gather her wits in time to call, 'Have a good time.'

'Thanks, Mum. See you when I get back.'

With a sigh, Betty closed the door. Never in her wildest dreams had she expected to holiday abroad, but as Anne had a career as a Personnel Officer, and Tony an engineer, no doubt they could afford it. Once again Betty felt a frisson of envy, which was soon followed by bitterness. Unlike her daughter, she'd never had a career, her life spent intent on being the perfect wife and mother. She had married Richard in 1936 and Mark had followed a year later. They hadn't been well off and it was sometimes a struggle to make ends meet, but then war had been declared and Richard eventually got called up. Anne had been conceived when Richard had been on leave and when he returned to the fighting she'd been terrified of losing him.

When the war was over and Richard came home without a scratch, Betty had been overjoyed, but he was different, more assured, and full of ideas to start up his own business. He said cars were going to be the up and coming thing, available not just to the wealthy, but the middle classes too. To start up the business they had to make many sacrifices but she'd been one hundred per cent behind him. Her friends and neighbours were getting modern appliances, vacuum cleaners, the latest electric boilers with mangles, but every penny that Richard made had to be ploughed back into the business. She'd continued to make do with hand washing, brushes and brooms, with any spare time spent knitting or sewing to make clothes for both herself and the children.

Betty smiled grimly. Of course Richard had to make an impression, so he'd worn nice suits, shirts and ties. Her thoughts were interrupted when the telephone rang. She hurried to answer it, thrilled to hear her son's voice. 'Mark, how are you?'

Unaware that she had a huge grin on her face, Betty listened to her son, pleased to hear that he was doing well, though disappointed when he said that he was too busy to pay her a visit. 'But I haven't seen you for ages,' she protested.

Mark made his usual excuses, Betty now saying, 'Anne called round today and she's booked a holiday to Spain.'

Mark didn't sound all that interested and soon said he had to go. Betty replaced the receiver, her face now straight as she wandered over to the window. She looked across to the park, wishing that she still had a garden to fill her time. When married to Richard she had spent hours gardening, growing fruit and vegetables to save money on food bills, and though it had been hard work, she had grown to love it.

The sun was shining in a clear blue sky and now Betty knew that Mark wouldn't be paying her a visit, she was tempted to go out again. She could walk to the pond, feed the ducks and it would be better than sitting here alone. When she threw bread, the ducks would leave the pond to crowd around her – they'd be aware of her existence, and at least for a short time she wouldn't feel as she always did in London – invisible.

Betty made herself a quick snack, then stuffed a few slices of bread into a paper bag, her thoughts returning to her daughter. Unlike Anne, she couldn't remember the last time she'd had a holiday. If she'd been treated fairly, she too could have gone overseas, but thanks to Richard it was impossible. It wasn't fair, it just wasn't, but there was nothing she could do about it – Richard and his solicitor had seen to that.

Chapter Two

Valerie Thorn was standing at her window, her eyes following Betty Grayson as she left the flats. The woman had moved in upstairs about a month ago and since then Val had taken every opportunity to surreptitiously observe her. She had contrived to bump into the woman earlier and at least she now knew her name. Betty was short, stocky, her expression sad and manner browbeaten. Her clothes were old-fashioned, her light brown hair tightly permed, and Val had judged her to be in her mid fifties.

Was Betty a possible candidate? Val wondered. The woman certainly looked unhappy so that was a good start, and she had seen few visitors which boded well. It had already been a long haul to find her first two recruits and if this woman could be the third, her harvest would be complete.

She would have to contrive to bump into Betty again, to open another conversation and perhaps make tentative overtures of friendship. If she could discover a shared interest it would break the ice, give them common ground, and then, when the time was right, she'd make her move.

Softly, softly catchy monkey, Val thought as she turned away from the window. She had been too wound up to eat any breakfast and now went to her tiny kitchenette to make a sandwich, her eyes avoiding the empty mantelshelf. It was her birthday, but she didn't have one single card on show. Her mother had died when Val was forty-one, followed only three years later by her father. As an only child there had been no siblings to share her grief, just two distant aunts and a few cousins that she hardly saw. Heartbroken she had channelled all her energies into her career, rising to the top, hoping that if her parents were looking down on her, they'd be proud of what she had achieved. She'd been so busy, so intent that she'd lost touch with her scant relatives, yet on days like this, when the postman didn't deliver at least one card, she sometimes regretted it.

Val tried to push her unhappiness to one side but found it impossible. It was always the same on birthdays or Christmas, when, unbidden, memories of her happy childhood filled her mind. There had been parties, laughter, love, but she wasn't a child now, she was a mature woman and it was silly to let things like birthday cards upset her.

If her parents *were* watching over her, it upset Val

that they would have seen her promising career destroyed – seen her foolishness and therefore her failure. Val's unhappiness now festered in anger, the sandwich tasting like sawdust in her mouth. It was always harder for women to make it to the top, but through sheer hard work and dedication she had gained promotion, eventually becoming the Sales Manager. Yes, she'd been ambitious, yes she wanted to rise, but then like a fool she had trusted a man – one she had thought herself in love with – and he had betrayed her and ruined her career.

There were times when Val's anger almost consumed her, when impatience overwhelmed her. She wanted to get on with it, and with a grunt she pushed her sandwich to one side. It was no good, she had to get out, to breathe fresh air and as her possible candidate had gone to the park again it would be another opportunity to bump into her. At work during the week, there were only the weekends to carry out her plans so she had to make the most of them. 'Treacle, walkies,' she called, the dog's ears pricking up as he immediately ran to her side.

As Val bent down to clip on the dog's lead, he eagerly pulled her towards the door. Treacle was her one consolation and she had never regretted getting him from Battersea Dogs Home. He might be a bit naughty, but he was loving, loyal, and on that thought Val's lips thinned again. She wanted to get on with her plan, to wreak her revenge, but without another recruit it would be almost impossible. She left the flat, crossed the road to the park, her eyes peeled for Betty Grayson.

It was still a glorious day, the park full of people intent on making the most of the brilliant summer weather. She unclipped Treacle's lead, the dog scampering off in front of her, but so far there was no sign of Betty. She walked the paths, her eyes constantly on the lookout, but it wasn't until Val neared the duck pond that she saw the woman.

Val drew in a deep gulp of air, forcing her shoulders to relax. Take it slowly – just be friendly, she told herself. She called Treacle and knowing that the dog couldn't resist trying to catch the wild fowl, she clipped on his lead.

'Hello, Betty isn't it?' Val said. 'Treacle wanted another walk but I didn't expect to bump into you again.'

'It was too nice to stay indoors,' the woman answered, 'and lovely to have the park so close by.'

'Yes, and with a dog but no garden, it's a Godsend. Do you mind if I sit down?'

'Please do,' Betty said, her smile one of pleasure. With Treacle around, the ducks had waddled quickly away, and after shoving a paper bag into her pocket, Betty bent to stroke the dog's head. 'I'd like a dog too, but as I work full-time it wouldn't be fair to leave it in my flat all day.'

'Oh, do you live alone?' Val asked, yet she already knew the answer.

'Yes, I do. I have two children but they're grown up now and living their own lives.'

'I live alone too, but fortunately my employer is a lovely man and lets me take Treacle to work. He even got him a basket to sit beside my desk.'

'That's nice,' Betty said, then raising a hand to wipe it across her forehead. 'Goodness, it's hot.'

'Yes, and look at poor Treacle, he's panting. If you're going home now I'll walk with you.'

'Yes, that would be lovely.'

They began to stroll along and Betty enthusiastically spoke about the summer planting in the flower beds that lined the path. 'Oh, look at those petunias. Don't they make a lovely display. I used to have a large garden and miss it.'

'I'm afraid I know nothing about gardening, but they're certainly colourful.'

Betty indicated another flower bed, saying, 'They've used geraniums in that one.'

They continued to chat, but when they arrived at the flats, Betty sort of hovered smiling tentatively and Val could sense the woman's loneliness. She spoke as though on impulse, 'Look, I tell you what. I live alone – you live alone, so if you've nothing planned, why don't you join me for tea?'

'Oh, I'd love that,' Betty said.

'I expect you want to freshen up, so give me half

an hour to make some sandwiches and then pop down.'

'Yes, all right,' Betty said and with a small wave she went upstairs.

Val went inside her own flat to make a plate of cucumber sandwiches, and then finding a packet of individual chocolate rolls she arranged them before going to the bathroom to refresh her make-up.

Shortly afterwards the doorbell rang and Val tucked a stray lock of hair back into her French pleat as she answered it, a smile of welcome on her face. 'Come on in.'

Betty stepped inside, her eyes scanning the room. 'Oh, this is lovely and I just love your décor. Youngsters nowadays go for all the modern stuff with bright, garish wallpaper, whereas this is so soothing, so sophisticated.'

'I prefer soft colours and as I can't tackle wall-papering, I just gave it all a coat of paint. Would you like tea or coffee?' she asked.

'Tea please,' Betty said.

'Sit yourself down and I won't be a tick,' Val said, before going back to her small kitchenette.

When the tea was made she carried the tray through. 'I hope you like cucumber sandwiches.'

'Yes, lovely,' Betty said, whilst eyeing the plate of cakes with appreciation.

Val sat opposite Betty, pouring the tea into small, delicate china cups and then offering cubes of sugar from a bowl, complete with little sliver tongs. Betty took two lumps, then said, 'My daughter was waiting for me when I came home from the park this morning. She couldn't stay long as she was off to buy new clothes for a holiday in Spain.'

'I once went to Barcelona and the architecture was stunning.'

'You're lucky. I've never been abroad.'

'Yes, well, nowadays I'm lucky if I can afford a day trip to Brighton.'

'Me too,' said Betty.

So, the woman was hard up, Val thought as she mentally stored this small piece of information before saying, 'There are some lovely places in England and I've always been fond of Dorset. Do help yourself to a sandwich.'

'Thanks,' Betty said.

Val fumbled for common ground. 'I suppose you heard that Judy Garland died on Monday?'

'Yes, I saw it in the newspaper. It said she died from an overdose of sleeping pills.'

'She was one of my favourite actresses and I was so sad to hear of her death. Do you go to the cinema much?'

'Not really, but I did go to see Maggie Smith in *The Prime of Miss Jean Brodie*.'

'Me too and it won a well-deserved Oscar.'

Betty just nodded, munching on her sandwich, and when it was finished, Val held out the cakes.

'Thanks,' Betty said, taking one and biting into it with obvious relish.

Maybe food could be a common interest, Val thought. 'I'm not much of a cook. What about you?'

'I used to be, but now that I just cook for myself I usually make something simple.'

'I love eating out, and I often go to a lovely little French restaurant in Chelsea.'

'I've never tried French food.'

'It's delicious, Betty, and if you aren't doing anything tomorrow, we could go there for lunch.'

Betty's eyes lit up for a moment, but then her face straightened as she said, 'I . . . I don't know. Is . . . is it expensive?'

'Not really, but don't worry, it's a family run business and I know the owner so he usually gives me a discount.'

'Oh, in that case, I'd love to.'

'Wonderful,' Val said as she stood up to move to the mantelshelf where she picked up a packet of cigarettes. She took one out, and then proffered the packet to Betty.

'No thanks, I don't smoke.'

'At six shillings a packet I know I should stop too, but I have managed to cut down.'

'Do you work locally?' Betty asked.

'I'm a receptionist for a solicitor on the Kings Road.'

'It must be nice to work in an office, especially in such an interesting profession.'

'It can be sometimes and Mr Warriner is a lovely man. What do you do, Betty?'

'I'm just a sort of cleaner cum housekeeper in Kensington. I used to live in Surrey, but when I heard about the job I moved to London. My employer is away at the moment so there's little to do, but when he's in town he keeps me busy with his incessant demands.'

'Oh dear, he sounds a bit of an ogre,' Val sympathised.

'He's all right, it's just that he's used to servants seeing to his every wish. His home is just amazing and such a shame that it remains empty for most of the year. He has wonderful antique furniture, paintings and bronzes which he has a passion for. He used to have a large staff, but when his wife died he started to spend most of his time in his country home. I was lucky to be kept on in the London house, but as I said, only as a sort of care-taker cum housekeeper.'

'If you're the only one there, don't you find it lonely?'

'Yes, sometimes, but I keep myself busy. It's a very large house with lots to do to keep it up to scratch. Just polishing the silver can take all day, but I keep dust covers over most of the furniture. I'd love to work in an office like you, but I was a stay at home wife and mother so I'm not trained for anything else.'

'There's nothing wrong with being a housewife and mother,' Val said. She had caught the trace of bitterness in Betty's voice and though tempted to ask questions, she held back. It wouldn't do to show her impatience, so instead she smiled softly, 'Would you like another cup of tea, Betty?'

'Yes, I'd love one.'

'I'll just top up the pot,' Val said, taking it through to the kitchenette. So far she had gleaned a little information, but her experience had found that if you shared a confidence it was likely to be returned. When she knew Betty a little more, she would start to open up, and with any luck Betty would do the same. Val crossed her fingers, hoping she wasn't wasting her time and that Betty would turn out to be a suitable candidate.

SILK
Penny Jordan

Dangerous liaisons . . .
Skeletons in closets . . .
A scandalous web of lies and deceit . . .
The Pickfords are just your average family.

Cheshire, the 1920s, a time of great glamour and decadence, high living and loose morality, a time where anything goes – and does.

Amber Vrontsky is the heiress to the Pickford dynasty, presided over by the formidable Blanche.

Obsessed with social climbing, Blanche wants nothing more for her granddaughter than a titled husband – something which, despite her immense wealth, she failed to secure.

But Amber is a free spirit, intent on forging her own artistic career with the silk she loves so much. Unable to disobey Blanche, however, she moves to society London to become a debutante – and enters a world of illicit affairs, drug-taking, gambling, lavender marriages . . . .

From the lavish decadence of society London to the opium dens of the Far East, the chic boutiques of Paris to the Nazi-controlled streets of Berlin, *Silk* spans the depravity and the glamour of this tumultuous time.

Spoil yourself with this dazzling, decadent treat by international multi-million-copy selling Penny Jordan – the ultimate guilty pleasure for fans of Danielle Steel and Penny Vincenzi.

ISBN: 978-1-84756-073-5

Out now